NICK CROWE

A COLD NIGHT
FOR
ALLIGATORS

A Novel

ALFRED A. KNOPF CANADA

PUBLISHED BY ALFRED A. KNOPF CANADA

www.randomhouse.ca

Grateful acknowledgement is made to the following to reprint lyrics from
"Down South Blues" written by Richard Dale Boggs: © Stormking Music
(BMI) administered by Figs. D Music (BMI), Under license from The Bicycle
Music Company. All Rights Reserved. Used By Permission.

Library and Archives Canada Cataloguing in Publication

Crowe, Nick
A cold night for alligators / Nick Crowe.

Issued also in an electronic format.

ISBN 978-0-307-39969-4
I. Title.
PS8605.R693C65 2011   C813'.6   C2010-904196-8

Text design: CS Richardson

First Edition

Printed and bound in the United States of America

2 4 6 8 9 7 5 3 1

To my Mum and Dad for vacations, stories and everything else.

I'm a going to the station
Going to catch the fastest train that goes;
I'm a going back South
Where the weather suits my clothes

Dock Boggs, "Down South Blues"

1.

IF I'D BEEN PAYING any kind of attention, I might have recognized Ronnie Orsulak as he paced the subway platform that Friday afternoon, late in June. I'd seen Ronnie twice before, once in December, when I saw him mine deep into his left nostril with one skinny finger, and then again in May, when he asked me if I had change for a five. I didn't. But in the daily blur of commuting, Ronnie's face was just another in the grand mosaic of stress, heat and delay. So, his face didn't mean anything to me that day in June as he walked across my line of vision while I stood talking with Phil Bothwell, a colleague from the office.

It had been another riveting day at the office. I spent most of the day aimlessly searching the internet, reading in turn about Scrotum Smasher, a punk rock band from Northern Ontario who released one classic record in 1986 then promptly disbanded, and Creutzfeldt-Jakob disease, an affliction caused by a slow-moving virus that destroys memory. I'd been having difficulty motivating myself to perform small, simple tasks, and I had been wondering if the problem was one of faulty internal wiring. When five o'clock rolled around, I was trying to get my head around the reproductive properties of protein molecules called prions. The sheer effort of it all made me think that CJD (as it's known in short form) was probably not my problem. I went back to

Scrotum Smasher, whom I had seen play in Timmins during a one-summer stint as a camp counsellor after high school. They were back together and doing a tour of Manitoba and Saskatchewan. Maybe there were more horrible ways to try and make a living than working in an office.

Phil came by at one minute to five, as he always did, a fact that had recently begun to annoy me. Phil had been living in the suburbs with his wife of two years, until he came home one night and found her in bed with a city employee who had been working on a storm drain outside the house. That the employee was a woman was small consolation to Phil, who was out on his ear within two weeks and had to move back to the city. He was compensating for his loss through compulsive organization, as if micromanaging his own life could make him impervious to any potentially nasty surprises that might sneak up on him. I could see the potential in this approach—Phil spent so much time planning and making to-do lists that nothing very interesting was ever likely to happen to him again. But the problem was you couldn't be in all places at all times, which left the door open to the random freak occurrences of this world, such as your heretofore straight wife ending up in bed making squeally with a strapping municipal worker named Terri. I didn't want to be the one to make this point, so I did my best to play my part: public transit companion and coffee mate during working hours. It was the least I could do. Smile and nod.

"Well, there's another day put in." While I don't really remember Phil saying this, I'd bet anything he did. He did every night.

A train came in on the opposite platform, and a sweaty, urgent horde flooded out and up the stairs toward the northbound train. There was a cheerful bing-bing-bing, the subway doors closed, and the train disappeared into the blackness. These inevitable interruptions were like godsends on days when I didn't manage to make it to the subway alone.

"She called last night," Phil said. "Says she's not sure she's a dyke. Well, not in those words exactly, but you know what I mean."

"Right."

"Wonders if it's just something she needs to experiment with. At least that's what she's saying now." He squeezed the bridge of his nose between his thumb and index finger. "I don't know, Jasper, what do you think?"

This was the part I dreaded most. "Not sure," I said. "Maybe it's just something she needs to get out of her system. Like jumping out of an airplane or getting a tattoo."

Phil kicked at a scrap of paper on the platform. "Yeah. It's fucked," he said. "Someone had told me when I was sixteen I'd marry a lesbian, I'd have thought it was pretty cool. Goes to show how baffling life can be when you get right down to it."

This was beyond a response, so I shook my head slowly and soulfully and kicked at my own scrap of paper, this one imaginary. People pushed behind me, moving further up the platform. I stepped closer to the track and looked up the line for a light. A sign of reprieve. Mercy.

"I don't know, what do you think?"

Another train roared in on the other side of the platform.

"How many trains are they going to get?" a man behind me said, exasperated.

"What do you think?" Phil repeated.

"I don't know," I started. "Maybe you need to blow off some steam. Go out, see a movie. Something violent. Go check out the strippers. Get drunk. Rent a porno." He'd introduced the sixteen-year-old motif, and I was running with it. I wasn't sure if my suggestions would help him de-stress or trigger a killing spree.

"Yeah," Phil said, as a train rumbled overhead and people began to pour down the escalator. "I'm just thinking too much. I can't let this screw with my head anymore. Good idea, Jasper. You want to come over? We can throw a couple of burgers on the barbecue, grab some beers. Rent a porno, if you want . . ."

"Sorry, Phil. Got plans." It was true. Kim and I had been fighting again and I had promised to take her out to dinner. Given the way things had been travelling, it was a breakable engagement, but the alternative wasn't that attractive. Better to sit and deal with my own problems than Phil's.

"Shit," he said, crestfallen. "I may as well just head to bed early. Drinking isn't going to solve anything."

"Don't be so sure about that," I said. "Booze can be a clarifying force. At least the hangovers are." I'd suffered through enough of them to know this for a straight-up, genuine fact. In the cool distance deep in the tunnel, a light went on. Thank God for that, I thought. Salvation. A couple of mice scattered in the dark, pebbly spaces between the tracks. Run, mouse, run, I thought. Behind me, the crowd surged and pushed, whipped on by the sweltering humidity, hell-bent on getting home. I could wait.

I could wait because there was nothing to look forward to. An argument at home, perhaps, a conversation about why Pam Anderson should make a comeback, or the benefits of the new, cheaper line of makeup she had found at Kmart. Listening, feeling guilty for being judgmental, feeling annoyed for having to sit and listen. In a best-case scenario, an evening of avoidance, escape in the form of a baseball game or a book I'd read before. Then off to bed to rest up for another day of the same thing. I'd been thinking about a change, all the while knowing I didn't have the strength to make it happen. The fear that I'd put too much time into it, time I could never get back, loomed over me.

This was of course cut through with the question of what I'd *rather* be doing with my time. I honestly didn't know.

I needed to make a break, switch things up, get going on a new path, fear and dread be damned. But in the meantime, I could wait to get home.

I needn't have worried about getting home. Because at 6:15, as the train finally barrelled down the line toward the station, Ronnie Orsulak, having recognized me as the man-devil who would not change his five-dollar bill weeks earlier, walked up and pushed me off the platform and onto the tracks. I fell into the swell of approaching lights. There was a scream behind me, then a whole chorus of them, and then blackness.

A change was upon me whether I liked it or not.

2.

INTERSTATE 75 IS AN ARROW in flight; a projectile that wavers in its path southward, as though the wind has blown it off course in places along the way and forced it to meander. If you pick up the highway at the border in Windsor, Ontario, and head due south, beginning in Detroit, it will take you to the very tip of Florida, which to a kid born into a world of hockey and snow blowers was like a lost, magical world.

Growing up, I thought of I-75 as the road that never ended. Every summer, at the beginning of August, we'd pack the car up with suitcases, Styrofoam coolers, books and sun visors and head south. It was a three-day journey that began in the pre-dawn dark of Ontario and took us through the heartland of the United States and into the South. Michigan to Ohio, Kentucky, Tennessee, Georgia and into Florida. States that rolled past in elapsed time, each one progressively longer and hotter like the circles of hell, until the hours seemed as though they were piling up into days, months and years.

My brother and I found various means to pass the time, like playing travel Yahtzee, trading baseball cards (a serious pastime that often led to arguments and once caused my father to pull the car over to break up a fight—I believe I was trying to trade a late '70s St. Louis Cardinals Keith Hernandez card for a Cal Ripken Jr. rookie, a player Coleman woefully underrated from the beginning of his career), and maintaining a log of licence plates from different states. These serious pastimes were often interrupted by my mother, hell-bent on pointing out every beautiful mountain vista, sunset or babbling brook within eyeshot. Picturesque is a foreign concept to a ten-year-old—you just haven't been around long enough to consider that the world is anything but beautiful. Or maybe it's just that, at age ten, you haven't had to deal with enough evil and hardship to realize that watching the sunrise from the back of a station wagon in the hills of Tennessee is a very fine thing indeed.

My brother and I are both named after towns just off I-75 in Florida. After my parents were married in 1969, my mother, the only daughter of German immigrants from Dresden, and my dad, the son of English farmers, went off down I-75 in their first car for a week-long honeymoon in Florida. This trip produced both a lifelong love of the Sunshine State as well as my older brother, Coleman. Coleman is a small town a few hours out of Naples, known in the 1920s as the cabbage capital of the world. These days, it is far better known for a federal prison that houses more inmates than there are people in the town itself. This would be the first of many trips to Sanibel Island, just down the highway from Coleman. While I have often wondered about the circumstances leading to my brother being named Coleman and not Sanibel given the relative proximity of the final destination to my brother's namesake, my curiosity was never great enough to ask. Maybe they stopped up the road, thinking Coleman just had a better ring to it.

Jasper is a little further up the highway. In August 1971, my parents would have known that my mother was pregnant when they stopped for the night. While this spares me from the specific mental image of being conceived in a wood-panelled motel room while my brother slept, I can't help but wonder what happened in Jasper that was special enough to give me my name.

After the first trip to Sanibel, my parents, great creatures of habit, would not go anywhere else but Florida until I was ten years old. The year things changed.

Every August, down I-75 we went, bickering, laughing, reading in silence, bent over maps, eating horrifically greasy roadside food, all dreaming of the patch of heaven where we would sit by the ocean for two weeks. For my father, it was a brief reprieve from the world of toil and worry that he slogged through the rest of the year. I wish I had known then that they were the greatest times of my life, and that after the last trip I would not return to Florida for another sixteen years. Not until I went looking for my brother Coleman.

3.

I WAS AN EAGLE FLOATING far above the highway. Below me, the white tops of transports and red blurs of sports cars hummed past, busy insects jockeying for position. The plains of Ohio rolled by, squares of farmland bearing the striped pattern of recent mowing. I could smell cut grass drying in the afternoon sun.

I floated over Big Sandy River and saw the mountains of Kentucky from on high. I held my wingspan steady and glided, feeling the raw kinetic power beneath feather and tendon, the perfect architecture of flight laid out in the minutiae of bones.

Knoxville and Chattanooga, the sweet smell of Tennessee. I drifted over rivers and roads, cabins and pickups.

Down into Georgia, not another bird in the sky. I wanted to land and put my feet in the red earth, to feel the coolness of the soil, but I found I could not. Up was the only way to go, higher and higher toward the sun, the white light throwing off a heat so intense that I was sure I'd burn up. Macon, Georgia, faded into an abstract grid of greenery and highway below.

I was flying through a white space, the heat dwindling above me, when the ground opened up. On my right was the deep, dark turquoise of the Gulf of Mexico, splashing up on a pure white coastline.

Florida.

As I approached the tip of the continent, my wings began to weaken. I passed over Big Cypress and felt the sky falling out underneath me. Now the white light was below me and as I fell it grew. The ground caught me. I opened my eyes and looked into the deep blue Florida sky and saw a thunderhead. Then the white light was pulled over me like a blanket and I slept.

4.

I WOKE UP IN A BRIGHT, white place. As I struggled to open my eyes, I realized it was the sun on my face. I swallowed and my throat felt like a sunburned fist full of sand and pennies.

I was in a bed, and it felt like I had been tied down. My eyelids still weren't cooperating, and when I tried to rub at them, I was surprised to find that I could not lift my arms. Jesus Christ, I thought, wake up. Wake up. I felt like I'd been sleeping off the world's worst hangover. Somewhere close by there was a whir and a soft, steady beeping sound. As I listened and struggled to make sense of where I was, the beeping picked up. Oh shit, I thought, then footsteps approached across a hard floor and a door opened.

"My God," a voice said. "You're awake."

I tried to speak but the sound was like the dying gasp of a punctured whoopee cushion. My first reaction was to laugh and it sent an agonizing jolt up my leg and into my chest.

"Take it easy," he said. "Just relax." Like I had any choice at this point. "I'm going to get you a glass of water and I'll be back." Still unable to open my eyes, I tried to wave and felt my arm flop like a bag of jellied ham on the bed beside me.

By the time he returned, my eyes were open. The sun on my face made him a silhouette, shrouded in light.

"Am I dead?"

He laughed and took a step forward, out of the glare. "No," he said, rubbing at a pink patch of neck below a bushy red beard. "But you ought to be. I'm surprised you're still in one piece. You had an accident at the subway. Someone pushed you." There was a flash of white teeth, grinning through the beard. "Most people in your shoes end up in more pieces than a bucket of KFC."

The thought of chicken made my stomach growl. "Jesus," I said. "I'm starving."

"Start with this," he said, handing me the glass of water. "But take it slow."

It tasted like cool liquid heaven and when I finished it, he refilled the glass from a pitcher sitting on the small table beside my bed. He pulled the curtain so that the sun was no longer blinding me, and then pulled up a chair beside my bed.

Now his face was drawn and serious. "My name is Dr. Meeks. You were in an accident at the subway. Try and think for a moment, then tell me what you remember," he said.

I exhaled and tried to recall. "I remember leaving work and chatting to Phil. He wanted me to go over to his house for a barbecue. But I had to . . ." It was beginning to feel like grade twelve algebra.

The doctor nodded. "Okay," he said. "Don't strain yourself. It doesn't really matter at this stage. You're awake. That's a good thing." He pulled the chair closer to my bedside.

"You've suffered some pretty serious injuries," he said. "You broke your right arm in the fall from the platform to the tracks, and your left leg was broken as well—what we call a transverse fracture. That's a pretty serious break. The arm wasn't so bad—a Colles fracture. But gosh," he said, "you're lucky. You managed to roll between the rails and the train passed over you." I had a sudden image of large steel wheels rolling toward my head, screeching like a large mechanical animal in the death throes. "You're pretty bruised, scratched and banged up, but in time you will be as good as new. Probably," he added.

Probably. The word made me flinch.

"But things are healing quite nicely." He smiled. "Not bad at all. Better now that you've woken up."

A bad feeling began to unfurl in the back of my listless head and I brought my hand slowly up to my face. I'd been wheeled in ready for casual Friday at the office and had woken up Grizzly Adams.

The doctor spoke up. "Your girlfriend was too scared to shave you." He smiled. I was beginning to draw less comfort from his smiles. "She said you had always wanted to grow a beard." He handed me a small pocket mirror, the kind women carry in their purses. It was adorned with hearts and said "My Little Pony" in cursive, girly writing on the back.

"Sorry, it's my daughter's," he said.

I raised the mirror slowly and looked into it. There was a moment of disconnection; an instant where I wondered who I was looking at. The face that looked back was drawn, pale and sallow. Sunken cheeks, a purple scar burnt from the forehead into the hairline, dark circles, and the kind of beard that was standard issue for Confederate soldiers who'd defected and spent a year wandering the Appalachians.

I turned to the window. Snowflakes fell in a gentle cascade, spread at perfect intervals across the frame.

"Jesus," I said. "How long have I been gone?"

The doctor sighed. It may have been the sound of exertion, the force of trying to summon a smile that would not come. "A while," he said. "Seven months."

We let this hang in the air for a moment, like the snowflakes. I looked out the window and the snow had started to fall a little faster.

"You had the fall in June," he said. "It's January second, 1998. Yesterday was New Year's Day."

I rubbed at my new beard and laughed. "I must be the ugliest New Year's baby in years," I said.

Dr. Meeks grinned.

5.

ONTARIO IS HELL ON EARTH in winter, albeit the frostiest Hades you could ever imagine. Recent years have been the worst of all; mild, autumnal Novembers and Decembers giving way to blasts of ice, sleet and snow in January, with the warm weather staying far away until April at the earliest.

Still, as I wheeled out of the hospital and into the snow, I was glad to see it. The doctor had decided to keep me around for a couple of days to make sure everything was okay. The cast had come off in late summer, while I was still sleeping the deep sleep. Even though months had passed, my leg still looked like something suffering from ill neglect behind a deli counter—a scaly, purple-scarred mess. The leg was thin and had begun to atrophy and felt weak and bandy underneath me. I was thankful when the nurse arrived with a wheelchair.

In the front lobby, orderlies were taking down a large green wreath. Christmas had come and gone without me. For all the years I'd fantasized about this scenario, it didn't feel all that great. Kim was waiting by the front door. She'd rushed in the day before, as soon as she found out that I had come out of my coma, but seven months on the nod had me feeling a little lethargic and by the time she got there, I was asleep.

She started crying as I rolled toward her. One of the orderlies, a ruddy-faced man with a massive, distended stomach, finished packing a Santa suit into a box and shook his head at this public display of emotion. Seven months of floating in space and two days awake to reflect on my own mortality weren't enough to stop me from sympathizing with him.

"Hi, Kim," I managed before she bent and grabbed me in her arms, her face sheened with tears.

"Oh, my God," she said. There was snow on the back of her jacket and I scooped some of it up in my good hand and squeezed. The cold water felt good as it ran across my wrist and down my arm.

She broke the clutch and looked at me. "I can't believe you're okay." She was about to say something else then stopped and let out a long shuddering breath. She hugged me again.

I watched the ruddy-faced man snort down his nose and pick up the box, balancing it on his stomach and still shaking his head.

"Come on, let's go," I said. Kim took the chair from the nurse and wheeled me out into the snow, toward the car.

We rode in silence for a while. It was late afternoon, in the thick of the year's shortest days, and it was already pretty dark. I kept catching myself rubbing at my arm or touching my cheek against the cold window. For someone who had always feared death, I can't say I was too bothered. Being in a coma was like that long void before I'd been born, where I'd been in 1919 or during the Dark Ages. Which is to say, nowhere. I caught a glimpse of my eyes in the window and blinked. When someone tells you that you've been asleep for seven months, you tend to keep making small status checks to make sure you haven't dozed off again.

Kim sighed and fiddled with the heat controls on the dash. A weak breeze of moderately warm air sighed through the vents and then died. "Drat," she said.

"Still not working, eh?" I watched her in the darkness of the car, stray headlights grazing her face at odd intervals, lighting up her pale skin and the flush in her cheeks. I didn't remember her looking so beautiful.

"What?" she said, feeling my eyes on her. "What are you looking at?" She brushed a strand of hair from her forehead. "Do I look funny?"

"That'd be the pot calling the kettle black," I said. "I'm just happy to see you." I put a hand on her leg. She flinched under the cold denim.

"I got home that day," she said, a catch in her voice. "I could hear the phone ringing as I unlocked the door." Her eyes stayed on the road ahead. "I was in a crummy mood and I wondered why you weren't home, why you weren't picking the phone up." Now she looked at me. "We hadn't been getting along."

"No," I said, "I guess we hadn't been."

"It was the police calling. And I can remember the moment, that I could hear a plane outside, that you'd left the milk out that morning, and it was like I wasn't even hearing what the man was saying to me."

I smiled. "Was the milk spoiled?"

Kim didn't smile. "What do you remember?"

"Not much," I said. "I was waiting for the subway with Phil after work, we saw the train coming, and then all I remember is seeing the wheels pass over me."

"They got him, you know."

"Who?"

"The man that pushed you. Ron something. He's crazy. One of those schizoids. They stuck him in the loony bin."

"Psychiatric hospital," I said.

She sighed and fiddled with the heat some more. "Fine," she said, "psychiatric hospital. Anyway, he's crazy as hell, and apparently crazy people don't go to jail. Still feel sorry for him?"

I shrugged.

"They say he doesn't remember doing it at all, but that he had been having dreams about you."

It was all beyond me at this point. I returned to looking out the window. Thankfully, we were getting close to home. I watched the snowbanks pass outside and wondered if the driveway had been shovelled. There had to be some perks to getting run over by a train.

I'd started to doze in my seat, hypnotized by the black breaks of asphalt between snowdrifts, when the next question came: "What about after you saw the wheels?" she said. "What do you remember then?"

"Waking up," I said.

"You don't remember talking to anyone?" We came to a stop sign and she looked at me.

"The doctor," I said, "after I woke up. But that was less than a week ago, so I don't think remembering that is any great shakes."

"That's not what I mean. I mean when you were out. Did you talk to anyone in the spirit world, anyone dead that was important to you? Your father maybe?"

I closed my eyes. "No, Kim, I didn't communicate with the dead."

"Don't be sarcastic," she said. "It's quite common."

"Common?"

"Studies have shown," she said, "that a large proportion of people who suffer near-death experiences and end up in comas travel to a world in between where they can speak to the dead."

I bit down on my bottom lip. "Interesting," I said.

"It all depends on how open you are," she said, "what kind of a conduit you can become." She pronounced *conduit* with two syllables so that it rhymed with *twit*.

"Kim," I said, "I was about as much of a conduit as that milk, going bad on the counter."

"Forget it," she said. I wondered how long this restraint would last.

I put my hand on her leg again. "I'm glad to see you, Kim. Really, I am." I waited for her to start crying again, but she looked straight ahead, holding the middle distance. "It's just such a . . . headfuck."

"I just wondered . . ." she said and then trailed off.

I waited the token moment before taking the bait. "Wondered what, Kim?"

"If you'd talked to your brother."

I was glad to see that we'd turned onto our street. My brother had been gone for a long time, but he wasn't dead. Although she had never come right out and said it, I knew that Kim didn't agree with me. Living together in my parents' old house—the place where I'd grown up—meant that these unspoken tensions were always drifting through our space like old ghosts.

As we approached our driveway, my attention turned to a shiny red pickup truck parked in the driveway.

"Whose truck is that?" I asked.

Now the tears came again. "We need to talk, Jasper," she said. A man's face appeared in the front window.

Apparently Kim hadn't expected me to wake up from my long winter's nap.

I reached out and turned the radio on. "Free Bird" was playing. I shit you not.

6.

ALL IN ALL, DONNY ESFORD was being pretty good-natured about the whole thing. Donny thought he'd died and gone to heaven when he met Kim at Johnny Rye's over Labour Day weekend during an end-of-summer "Beach Slam" promotion complete with faux beach volleyball, summer shots (UV Slammer, Sunburned Nipple) and a conga line. According to Kim, it was the last thing she had been looking for, but in her personal cosmology, that attitude would have given her the receptive aura that allowed Donny Esford to approach her. Not that Donny Esford's confidence needed any propping up; we were the same age and I remembered him as the most feared kid at my high school, a nice enough guy, but not to be crossed. He once knocked a kid's teeth flat onto the roof of his mouth behind Mac's Convenience on an icy day after Christmas break while a crowd (including me) looked on. The kid had been picking on a cousin of Donny's who was a little on the slow side. When the kid opened his mouth to scream, all the roots were sticking straight out. To this day, the thought of it sets my own teeth on edge.

Later, Donny was drafted in a high round as a linebacker by the Saskatchewan Roughriders. He didn't last long in the CFL, and was back home working at the recycling plant within three years of the draft, his career cut short by a knee injury or excessive steroid use, depending on whom you believed and how charitable you were. So, like many popular high school football goons, Donny hadn't found adult life to be all smiles and chuckles, which is why meeting Kim must have been somewhat akin to winning the lottery. She was pretty, well turned out, had a job (part-time in the canteen at the local hospital), a house (being paid for in part by a catatonic boyfriend with disability insurance whose wages kept drifting in while he slept), and she liked snowmobiling.

And then I'd gone and woken up.

I heard Donny come down the stairs early, while it was still dark out. I listened to the stairs creak under his side-of-a-house build, his CFL weight plus fifty pounds. It was odd to think of him waking up in my bed and creeping down the stairs to avoid waking me, but there it was. Odder still was being on the couch, the couch Kim had always wanted to get rid of. I'd wanted to avoid going up and down stairs, but sleeping on it made me realize she was right: the thing had all the give of a cinder block.

Kim and I had worked out a tenuous arrangement. The three of us would live under one roof until they found somewhere else or I decided to move on and sell the place. Kim and I had been paying down the last remnants of my parents' mortgage, but it was my house. Kim would have liked to think that she'd laid down the ground rules—that she was letting me stay until I figured things out. I didn't have the energy to point out that if I wanted to be a dick about it, I could send them packing to the nearest fleabag inn. Truth was, I just didn't care that much. One thing was clear: she and Donny Esford were staying together. My untimely near-exit had been the catalyst for a spiritual awakening in Kim (as she put it), even if it had not effected the same change in me. It had given her time to think, time to look at her life and realize that she wasn't happy and that we weren't happy.

I was thinking about Kim's spiritual awakening, wondering if utter detachment was an early warning sign for such an epiphany, when Donny came into the living room.

"Hey, bud," Donny said. "You awake?"

I rolled over uneasily on the couch and feigned sleep.

"If you need something, I'm in the kitchen." Donny's civility made me want to go back to sleep for another seven months.

I listened to him banging around in the kitchen, putting coffee on and cracking eggs. Bacon called to me from a frying pan with a sizzle. Buck Owens sang about "Kicking Our Hearts Around" from the radio. I could hear Donny Esford humming along. Either he was a man not easily fazed or he was doing a pretty good job of pretending. I decided to meet him halfway and got up.

"Morning," I said, hobbling into the kitchen.

"Morning," he said, draining the grease from the frying pan into a large Mason jar. "If you're hungry, I can put some more on for you."

I held my hand out and almost fell off my crutches. "That's cool," I said. "I'm going to have to ease back into the whole eating solid food thing. Bacon might not be the best place to start."

"Don't count on that," he said, taking his plate to the kitchen table. "Bacon is God's meat." Gnawing on my maker's rashers didn't appeal, so I passed.

"There's coffee, anyway," he said.

"Sure," I said, hopping my way across the kitchen to the coffee maker.

Donny stood up from the kitchen table and knocked his knife and fork from his plate. "Wait," he said. "Let me do that."

"It's cool, Donny." I picked up the half-drained decanter and wobbled with it for a moment before bringing it to a steady halt above my mug. I was concentrating so hard I realized my tongue was hanging out.

"Seriously," Donny said.

I held the pot firm. "I can do it, Donny," I shouted, and poured coffee in a liquid vector onto my bare foot. It quickly made me forget the dull ache in my leg.

"Whoa," Donny said, rushing over to me. "Are you okay? Here," he said, grabbing a wet cloth from the sink under the kitchen window, "let me wipe that up. Otherwise you're going to break your neck."

I did my best to lunge out of his way. "I'm all right," I said. "I was in a goddamn coma, but I've been here before." I regretted saying it immediately, partially because I sounded pissed off, also because it didn't really make sense. Donny Esford was also built like an ox and sleeping with my ex-girlfriend.

Donny looked up at me with big, sad brown eyes and then began wiping at the floor around my foot. "I know this is still your house," he said, "but I'd appreciate it if you wouldn't use the Lord's name in vain."

The awkward moment was broken by the sound of Kim coming downstairs. It was a familiar sound in a strange, new context. My eyes met Donny's and he gave me a smile and a little shrug. The man was doing his best.

I picked up the half-poured cup of coffee and lurched into the living room. Kim was on the couch watching television in a long, plum-coloured robe. My robe.

"Good morning," she said, only glancing at me. "How'd you sleep?"

"Not so hot," I said. "That damn couch is uncomfortable."

Her eyes were fixed on the television where a 1-800 number was scrolling below a montage of third-world misery.

"Yes," I said, "damn uncomfortable, just as I've always said." She didn't look up. "Don't know why we didn't get rid of it a long time ago." I took a few steps closer to the couch. "Just making a joke, Kim."

"Look," she said, pointing at the television. On-screen, a young leper was staring into the camera while a voice-over described her wretched life and the various donation plans available to sympathetic viewers. There was nowhere to go. The tension would not be broken, even with a dumb joke. I tried another tack: I sat down and put a hand on her shoulder.

"It's okay, Kim."

"I know," she said, still staring at the television. "It's God's plan."

I let this hang in the air for a moment with the hope that something else might come on the television, or that I might spy the remote and commandeer it. It was still my place, after all.

"Yes," Kim said. "God has a plan for all of us."

I looked at the television. "Some plan," I said. "I think I'd be a little pissed with God if being a leper was my ultimate destiny." I felt her watching me, but I kept looking at the television. Donny was still banging around in the kitchen, doing the dishes from breakfast. He was well trained, I'll give him that much. "You know, 'Hey thanks, God, my path in life has been illuminated now that my face is falling off.'" I gave a mock game-show-host smile and realized I'd gone too far.

"I would have thought a little suffering would help you out," Kim said. "Help you get in touch with a higher power or make you a little more . . . spiritual. You've always been so negative." I put my head in my hands. "That's why this was destined to fail, why you and I could never work," she said. "I just didn't have the strength before your accident. Coming to grips with it helped me grow as a person."

"Glad I could help out," I said. Kim had gone from party-girl extraordinaire to God-botherer in a span of seven months.

"You know what your problem is?" She paused until I looked at her, and then she put her hand on my shoulder. "You don't take anything seriously. You joke around about everything when really it all just scares you to death. Even now."

A one-liner didn't come to mind.

Donny came into the living room holding a mug of coffee. I could have kissed him. He had a look about him like he'd been listening in and I could tell already that he didn't like conflict, fearsome high school reputation be damned.

"Listen," he said, "my buddy Duane and I are going ice fishing. Wondered if you wanted to come along. I figured you could use the fresh air. No pressure though, what with your leg and all."

Kim finally looked away from the lepers. She gave Donny a beatific smile. "That's a really nice idea," she said. "Very sweet of you."

I found myself agreeing before I'd really thought about it. I had to get out of the house, away from God, leprosy, and Kim. Besides, I was beginning to think Donny was okay.

7.

"I BROKE MY LEG PRETTY BAD in Saskatchewan," he said. "In a pre-season game we were playing in Red Deer against the Stampeders. I got knocked back onto my butt and then Kenny Mobler fell across my left leg." He chopped at his leg with the edge of his hand. "Snapped it in two. Heard the crack. It was like a tree going down. A big one. Kenny Mobler was listed at three hundred pounds but probably weighed three fifty. The leg healed up, but never good enough to play again. So . . ." he said, waving a hand toward the snow-covered fields blurring past alongside the highway, "I came back, and here I am."

"What about Kenny Mobler?"

Donny smiled. "I don't think Kenny ever recovered from it," he said. "He sent me flowers in the hospital." He shook his head. "I think he played another season or two, now he's a wrestler, tours small towns in Alberta. Someone told me he's up over four hundred pounds now, wrestles as 'The Glutton.' His whole thing is hitting people with sides of beef or roast turkeys."

We had been going up a rural route sparsely populated with farms and horse barns. Now we turned down an even more desolate route, where the snowplows hadn't been yet. The fresh snowfall was blinding, twinkling under the morning sun. I closed my eyes and could feel the light shining through the thin membrane of my eyelids. I was beginning to realize that there was a whole world of simple pleasures waiting to be rediscovered.

"Hold on," Donny said, and shifted the truck into four-wheel drive. The vehicle protested under his foot, fishtailed, then corrected itself as we picked up speed. We drove for another ten minutes, through the open space all around us, past men plowing out long driveways with snowplows, past two children fighting over a snowman, down hills crowded by woodland on either side, then up again into the open sky. Just as I was beginning to really enjoy myself, Donny shouted "Hold on," and pulled the handbrake. The entire truck swung on its axis, shifting into a sharp right angle so that we came to rest pointed up a long driveway.

"Jesus," I said, one hand on the door, the other on the seat. Donny was smiling, pulling slowly up the drive.

"You didn't mess your shorts, did you?"

I leaned forward and reached down the back of my pants. "I don't think so," I said, only half joking.

Donny laid on the horn and rolled the window down. "Duaner," he shouted. A face appeared in the window and then a hand wagging a raised middle finger. I noticed a case of beer on the front step, nestled into the snow, and then a slightly built man with jeans hanging low came out the front door, picked the beer up and ran to the truck.

"How are you today?" he said, leaning in the window.

"Duane," Donny said. "This is Jasper."

He extended a bony, nicotine-stained hand in through the window. "You must be Rip Van Winkle," he said. "Pleased to meet you." He threw his beer in the back of the truck and got in. "Shit," he said, looking at me. "You must be pleased to meet anyone."

Duaner was right. I was glad to meet anyone, but would have been pleased to meet him under any circumstance. Lack of conversation was not a concern with Duane around, and as we drove out to the lake, he chattered a rapid-fire blur through a variety of subjects.

"Jesus Christ, I almost didn't make it out. Had today booked off for two weeks, got a call first thing this morning, Blair, you know Blair Bancroft, don't you Donny? Idiot at the bass derby two summers ago whose dog ate all the steaks out of the coolers while we was out on the lake? Blair calls in sick this morning, and no way he's sick. Well, if drunk's sick, he's sick as they come. Terminal. Likely took on a bellyful over at Nat Toomey's last night. Couple of real fucking drunks right there."

I glanced at Donny, wondering how he'd react to his friend cussing a blue streak, given the admonishment I'd been given for a single "goddamn." Donny just looked resigned. He'd obviously given up long ago.

"So Grady calls me this morning, says he needs me in. Vacation or no vacation, he needs me to come in to work. 'Blair's sick,' he says. 'Well, I'm sick too,' I says. Just like that. 'Come on,' he says. 'Okay, well I'm fucking drunk then. How's that suit you?' Duane pulled an open beer from the interior pocket of his voluminous winter jacket that had once been brilliant fluorescent ski-colours of green and gold but was now a murky grey. It hung around his slight frame like a parachute.

"Turn here," he shouted, gesticulating madly at a dirt road that shot away at a 45-degree angle from the rural route we were on.

"I got you," Donny said, making the turn.

Duaner took a large swallow from his beer and winked at me. "Then sure as hell act like you got me, you stunned mule."

I'd never been ice fishing before, and my feeling of being one of the boys dissipated like smoke when Duane and Donny started unloading the truck and dragging their gear out to the ice and I realized I had no idea what any of it was.

"Great idea," Duaner shouted to Donny who was halfway across the ice. "Let's bring Tiny Tim here ice fishing." Donny didn't turn around, but I could see his head shaking. "Don't worry, Jasper," he said, "we won't let you fall in."

Out on the lake, Donny pulled an array of augers and drills from his pack and set to work drilling a hole. The man had hands like ten-pound mallets, but watching him measure and drill with such ease was a thing of beauty. I saw his eyes occasionally move skyward as he worked, as if he was making sure the glorious day hadn't been pulled out from under him. He had the look of a man who counted his blessings often enough to stay thankful.

"Come on, hammer," Duane said, "you making a career out of that?" He pulled his toque off and waved it at me, rolling his eyes. "Hey, Jasper," he said, pulling a label-less green bottle from his jacket, "have a taste of this."

"What is it?"

I shifted on my crutches and he handed me the bottle. A vapour of vaguely Varsolish-smelling fumes hung around it. "Never mind what it is," he said. "Get it in you and get it working."

The term "hard liquor" did not adequately describe the contents of that green bottle. It tasted like a fortified plant food cut with antifreeze and a jigger of Tabasco. It was so strong that it hit my gullet and disappeared into the roof of my mouth. I scooped a handful of snow up and sucked at it desperately.

Duane was in hysterics. "Jesus," he said, "you look like a bullfrog gulping lightning. Ain't that shit a trip?"

I swallowed the snow and exhaled. "What's in it?"

"That," he said, "is homemade cherry brandy. Only the cherries were off when I made it. Didn't think it'd matter, but it tasted like shit, so I dumped half a bottle of hot sauce in to mask it." He scooped the bottle up and took a swallow. "Put hair on your chest," he said. He winked at me. "But if you start seeing black, stop drinking."

I stopped drinking two hours later, around the time Donny caught the first fish of the afternoon, a minuscule sunfish roughly the size of his thumb. And while things had yet to go black, the world was beginning to get rather kaleidoscopic.

"Throw 'er back, you cruel fuck," Duane slurred, swiping at the fish with one sodden glove. Between the two of us, there wasn't much cherry Varsol left. "Jasper," he said. "Drink."

I held up my hand. "Leave him be," Donny said. "He's fine."

Duane stood up on the ice. "Okay," he said, wobbling.

"Sit down, Duaner," Donny said. "All we need is you breaking your dumb skull."

Duane rapped at the side of his head with the bottle. The sound made me feel ill. "Doesn't hurt," he said. "Doesn't hurt at all."

"Cool," Donny said. "Now sit down."

Duane rapped the bottle on his head again. "Check it out," he said. "Don't hurt."

Donny tugged on his line, eyes focused on the hole in the ice. The sun was beginning to set and I was hammered. Duane sat down on the ice.

"I'm drunk and my ass is wet," he said. We sat in silence for a while, me watching the sky change from a swirled blue and white to a deep pink colour, Donny fixated on the hole in the ice.

"You're a lucky guy," Duane said, quietly. When I looked at him, he was staring at the hole as well. "Most people wouldn't survive getting flattened by a subway train."

I noticed a ripple up Donny's jawline.

"It's hard to believe," I said. "I can't believe it. One minute you're heading home for a beer, next thing a train's running over you."

Donny nodded at me, his eyes like a basset hound's.

Duane shook his head and looked at me. "Your family must be happy." His head lolled and he tried to fix his eyes on me. "Happy that you didn't get totally fucking killed," he said. "You know what I mean, anyway."

I nodded.

"Your parents live in this area?"

"Yeah," I said. "Well, they did. My father died years ago, my mum's in a home in the city." The thought of my parents sobered me considerably. The cherry brandy had left a syrupy paste at the back of my tongue and I would have killed for a drink of water.

"We should pack up," Donny said. He stretched his legs and stood up.

"You got any brothers or sisters?" Duane was doing his best to show he was no one-trick pony; he could make serious conversation *and* hit himself over the head with a bottle.

"Come on, Duane," Donny said. "Let's get going. It's cold."

I might have been hypothermic for all I knew. Duane's brandy had me feeling very little below my neckline.

"Jesus, Donny. Relax for a fucking minute. Been sitting out here all day already, fuck's sake." Duane stroked his moustache and looked at me.

"One brother," I said. I saw Donny stiffen.

"Where's he at?" Duane said.

I grabbed the bottle of cherry brandy off the ice and took a swallow. I got shakily to my feet, both crutches tucked under my left arm, the bottle in my right.

"Is he in town?"

"No," I said, feeling unsteady on the ice. "He was abducted by aliens." I handed him the bottle and shrugged. "He's been in space for . . ." I counted on my fingers. "Shit, over ten years. But he's coming back."

Duane's mouth was open. "Careful, man," he said. "You don't look too steady."

"I'm . . ." . . . *fine,* I thought, as the ice went out from under me. A fireball of agony ripped through my leg and I felt my head bounce off the ice, like an errant melon on a grocery store floor. I closed my eyes. There was silence on the lake.

Then Duaner spoke: "Jesus, Jasper. You ain't having any luck at all."

8.

COLEMAN WAS BUILDING a spaceship. Like all truly great and insane things, it started out small.

Throughout our lives together, we had maintained one custom—walks together in the woods behind our house. Don't get me wrong, this wasn't a tradition of genteel, bucolic appreciation and fresh air, as there was always a practical, utilitarian purpose to these walks. When we were kids, it was to scout out fort-building materials. Coleman was always the master of fort building as he was blessed with a mind that could find unforeseeable uses for the common garbage all around us. A length of pool tubing became a whisper-sensitive means of communication when strung between floors of a multi-storey tree house. An old picnic table became the exoskeleton of a winter fort where we smoked our first cigarettes and burned sickly-sweet votive candles while my parents shook their heads behind the living room curtains.

In the summer of the spaceship, my reason for wandering in the woods was to sneak a joint and then spend the afternoon walking it off. Coleman's intentions were less clear. He didn't normally smoke dope. He'd already drifted far enough into the outer fringes of reality by that point without needing pot. Coleman didn't say very much, while I provided rambling discourses on everything from the supremacy of Teutonic heavy-metal merchants The Scorpions to whom I planned to ask to the spring dance (Tara Ladocoeur, who politely declined then went with Bill Oster, the nerdiest kid in grade nine. I was crushed). Coleman had a habit of nodding non-stop while I spoke, all the while scanning the woods for something of interest. He was my older brother, and I didn't really care if he was listening or not. It was enough to be away from school, away from our parents, out in the crisp air, leaves blossoming from buds, squirrels chattering from one branch to another. We were doing what we had always done, together.

On one such afternoon, we found the chair.

"Look at that," Coleman said. "Look at that."

I looked. It was a blue-checked, tattered armchair on a swivel. An errant spring had burst through the arm like a shank. It must have been twenty years old. "So," I said.

"So," he said. "Look at that."

Coleman went over to the thatch of shrubs and ferns that had grown around it. "It's wet," he said.

"No shit it's wet. It's spring. It's been raining all week, and a winter's worth of snow just melted. Why would it be wet, Coleman?"

Coleman continued to spin the chair, now crouching and examining the swivel. "The swivel still works," he said. "Wow." I heard the ting-ting of his fingernail on the rusting metal. "Come here," he said. "Let's see how heavy it is."

"Forget it. Dad'll hit the roof."

Coleman shrugged. "Let's just see how heavy it is. That's all."

"That's all," I said.

The chair wasn't very heavy at all. As it turned out, Coleman could lift it on his own, which he did. I helped him manoeuvre it onto one bony shoulder, and then stood finishing my reefer as he walked off with it. The rotten easy chair had probably been the centrepiece of a living room somewhere nearby. I thought of this and watched my brother disappear into the trees. He made a strange and lonely figure and the rotten easy chair was a fitting prop.

Little did I know that the chair would become a symbol of my own sorrow.

As it turned out, my dad wasn't so bothered. My parents had tried numerous approaches to understand Coleman's increasing eccentricity and detachment from everyone and everything around him. My brother and his peculiarities, as my mother put it. The strangeness that had collected around the border of our lives like a fog, all in the five years following our last family vacation in Florida.

My father was a quiet, practical man. I think he hoped that Coleman had taken after him and was just going through a weird phase. He was, but unfortunately, the next phases would only get weirder. In the end, my folks were happy he was doing something—even if that meant watching a discarded blue-checked armchair being transformed from garbage into something far stranger.

On the day Coleman brought the chair home, my father waited for me to return. He was watching college football in the den, stretched out in a burgundy leather La-Z-Boy with a beer in his hand.

"What's your brother doing?" My father didn't take his eyes off the small television, which flickered violently just as a kicker punted the ball. "Goddamn reception." He sighed, leaned forward and smacked the television.

"Dunno," I said, trying not to look at my father. I was worried my eyes were still red.

"What've you been up to?"

I shrugged. "Went for a walk. Out in the woods."

"Fresh air," my dad said, leaning forward in his chair to watch a pass sail beyond a gaggle of fingertips into the end zone. "Shit," he said. "That's it. That's the game."

I hated football. Maintaining an ignorant obliviousness to it throughout my childhood and teenage years was one of the few small-scale acts of teenage rebellion I carried out against my father. I don't think he ever noticed.

At this point, I began to hear the sound of hammering from the garage. My father closed his eyes for a second then pushed himself up and out of the chair.

"Come on," he said. "Let's see what your brother's up to."

My father sighed when he opened the door into the garage. It was the sigh that I came to characterize him by. If he had been an animal, it would have been his call: a long, expressive blast of air that carried the weight of great irritation without the energy to channel his dismay into any kind of action.

My brother had the chair upside down and was examining the swivel mechanism. I noticed that he'd used steel wool to buff the rust away. He looked at me with a smile and spun the rotary mechanism. The air was thick with the damp stink of mildewed upholstery.

"Check it out, Jasper."

Conscious of my father beside me in the doorway, I nodded. "Cool. It's a chair. Upside down."

"What's up, Coleman?" My father stepped down into the garage. "Man, it's cold in here. You ought to get a jacket."

Coleman shook his head. He crouched into a leap-frog position and flipped the chair back over onto the swivel. It rotated slowly and then came to rest. Coleman grunted and, taking the chair in both hands, began to move it back and forth, his eyes growing brighter, a smile spreading across his face.

"Say, Coleman," my father said. "What're you doing?" He sat down on a stack of empty beer cases. "Going to fix it up and sell it at the garage sale?"

My brother paused briefly. "No," he said.

"I don't know, buddy, but that looks like just the kind of chair your grandmother would like. I could help you get that ratty upholstery off it, we could really . . ."

"No," Coleman said. He turned the chair over again, picked up a screwdriver and began tightening the swivel. The whole scene made me want to go lie down.

"Hey—anybody want a cold beer?" We both looked at my father. "Your mum's not going to be back for another hour."

Coleman kept working.

"I'm okay, Dad," I said. "I have some math to do." Neither one of us had taken our eyes off my brother.

My father stood up and sighed. "All right, guys," he said. "I'll leave you to it." He walked slowly toward the door, one eye on his older son. I waited a moment, until I was sure he was inside.

"Coleman," I said, gesturing at the old chair. "What the fuck are you building?"

Coleman put his screwdriver down and looked at me. There was a brightness in his eyes I had never seen before, as though the whites had been turned up until they swallowed the blue iris.

"A spaceship," he said. He shook his head slowly, his eyes turning back to his work. "I need something I can sit in that spins. This bottom part is going to attach to . . ." He looked up at me and smiled wryly. There was suspicion in his eyes, as plain as the confusion that must have filled my face.

"A spaceship," he said, turning the chair over again and turning the swivel.

From inside, I heard a sigh.

Spring quickly turned to summer. School ended, the days grew hot and humid, and the trees in the woods became so dense that you could not see someone approaching until they were right on top of you.

Meanwhile, the chair in the garage morphed. First the upholstery came off; then a layer of tinfoil was applied. My brother built a mechanism that allowed the swivel to telescope up and down as well as in circles. I didn't see much of Coleman that summer. While the rest of us grew brown and lithe under the sun, playing baseball, riding bikes or swimming in the lake, my brother remained a pale, afflicted figure, working in the garage half the night and then sleeping the day away.

Obsessed.

He no longer talked to my parents or me about the chair or the project he was working on. He didn't talk much at all, even to me. We had always been pals, and I had never considered that this could change. One Christmas when we were little kids, our parents had given us a telephone set, one for each of our rooms. The phones weren't connected to any actual line and couldn't dial out, but instead were a two-way line between our bedrooms. This gave us the luxury of being able to talk without leaving our rooms. It had been our covert means of communication; a way of sharing plans that we didn't want anyone else to know, a channel of co-conspiracy. A sharp knock on the wall meant "pick up the phone." That summer, my knocks echoed off into a room that might as well have been empty. My brother was screening his calls.

Coleman's project was banished to the back yard as it began to accumulate a wide range of discarded and obscure items. One night, from my bedroom window, I watched him going through the trash next door, carefully removing a stack of broken picture frames. They were disassembled and used to create a framework around the bottom of the chair. Other items surfaced: I noticed the same tubing we'd used for our forts coiled like a python in the corner where I kept my skateboard. Panes of cracked glass and copper piping from the dump. A broom handle. A moth-eaten fur coat, which my brother wore home from wherever he found it, appearing from the woods at the end of the street like a 1940s film starlet raised from the dead.

Meanwhile, the strange creation grew in the back corner of the yard. It looked like a gyrocopter that had crash-landed into the city dump. I knew my brother was smarter than me, but even I could tell that his "project" wouldn't get to the corner store, let alone outer space.

But worst of all, for the first time my brother began doing things that scared me. I was used to his peculiarities; accustomed to odd behaviour in public places. One afternoon at the Bay he picked up a phone and started reading a copy of the

Old Testament he'd bought at the dollar store over the public address system. A red-faced man with a moustache and high-waisted pants rushed over and yanked the receiver from his hands. Nobody laughed: not me, and not even Coleman.

One night, I woke up from a deep sleep and heard voices. This wasn't out of the ordinary, as my mother didn't sleep well and was prone to keeping my dad up half the night talking. But, as I lay there, I suddenly realized that the voices weren't coming from my parents' bedroom. It was Coleman.

The conversation was between an East Indian woman and an elderly British gentleman. She had a soft, squeaky voice, his was a pure, dulcet tone. They were discussing a platter of sandwiches. She liked the cucumber and watercress, he the cheese and tomato. My brother was playing both roles. I had no idea where he could even be getting this stuff from. That night I lay awake, watching the ceiling.

Then there were his notes, voluminous stacks of crumpled, water-stained pages, the ink running between scrawls of numbers and lines. Everywhere you looked in Coleman's room there was paper: busting out of manila folders on his desk, scattered across his carpet and under his bed like dead leaves on the sidewalk in October. One of my most vivid pictures of Coleman is him at his desk, tongue darting around his top lip, scratching at a piece of paper, shaking his head and sighing, then pushing the work on his desk onto the floor. My mother had given up bothering him about it. To make life easier for her, I had been going so far as to vacuum my room.

I heard other conversations from my room at night. Ones that were even more troubling because they suggested the horrible impasse ahead.

"It's a phase, Ron."

"Like hell. Long hair is a phase. Punk rock is a phase. Building a goddamn junk pile in the back yard and thinking it's a spacecraft is not a phase."

"He's okay. You'll see. He's just expressing his creativity." My mother had been an art teacher for five years before giving it up to be a full-time housewife, which, with the advent of Coleman's spacecraft, had turned out to be a much more challenging proposition.

My dad sighed. "I don't have the energy for it, Susan. I work all day. I spend half my life sitting in traffic. And then I have to come home and watch my seventeen-year-old preparing for the War of the Worlds. He needs help. We need to find it for him."

"He doesn't need help."

"But what if he does? Is it better to just say it's okay? Pretend that it's a phase?" Another sigh. "Come on, Susan. Don't be so naive. You see where this is leading."

And always, between the lines, the words and the sighs were the sounds of construction.

My brother started talking again around the time my parents sent him to see a shrink. It was a cold, damp fall that year, and Coleman was keeping his project under a ragged tarp in the back corner of the yard. Early one morning I'd gone to the window and watched my father in the yard, putting the tarp back over Coleman's would-be spacecraft, a sad, furrowed look on his face.

"Mum and Dad are sending me to see someone," Coleman said one afternoon. I'd been out for a walk in the woods and I'd found him wandering. Coleman nodded at me and we walked together for a while in silence, before sitting down on a cluster of large rocks off the trail.

"Who?"

Coleman picked up a stick and twirled it in his hand. "You know Carl Pearson? His dad."

I didn't get it.

"He works at the psychiatric hospital. He's a psychiatrist."

I picked up a handful of pebbles and threw one off into the distance. "Why?"

"They're worried about me," he said. "I don't know why. They shouldn't worry."

I didn't want to offer any theories of my own so I threw another pebble.

Coleman turned to me. "Are you worried, Jasper?" The brightness was still in his eyes, but there were dark circles surrounding them.

I shrugged. "I don't know."

A sparrow landed on a rotten log nearby. We watched him peck at the sodden, crumbling wood in hunt of grubs and other insects.

"Want to smoke one?" I asked.

My brother and I stretched out on the large rock covered in bright green moss. We passed the joint back and forth and looked up at the sky through an open space in the canopy of maple and oak leaves.

"Man, look at that cloud," Coleman said. "It looks like a rutabaga."

"What the hell's a rutabaga?"

"It's a fruit. Or a vegetable. I forget."

"That cloud? It doesn't look like a vegetable."

Coleman laughed. "You're right. It looks like Dad's nose." We both laughed. I realized it had been a long time since I'd heard Coleman laugh.

"That one looks like a gator," Coleman said. "A twelve-footer. Ready to chomp down on a garfish."

"I don't see it."

"What's new? You never saw them."

It was true. During our trips to Florida, when we'd driven across the Tamiami Trail to Miami, I had never been able to spot the gators swimming in the murky canal that ran parallel to the road. Coleman never missed one.

"I miss seeing alligators," he said. "What does Canada have?"

"Squirrels," I said.

"Right. Squirrels."

"Forget alligators," I said. "I miss swimming in the ocean. Lakes don't cut it."

"There's nothing like an alligator," Coleman said. "They've hardly changed in millions of years, yet no one understands them. They're like big dogs. Swamp dogs."

"Yeah, except when they bite you, they don't just rip your pants, they take your whole leg off."

Coleman shook his head. "Myth."

"Myth," I said. "What about that guy when we were kids who got attacked and bled to death on the road? He was trying to protect his dog and it grabbed his leg."

"The paper said he'd been feeding it chicken. When he walked past with his dog, the gator thought his white tennis shoe was a piece of chicken and went for it. The old guy shouldn't have got his leg in the way."

"For Christ's sake," I said. "Chicken."

"That ain't chicken, boy," Coleman said in an authoritative Southern drawl. We both laughed.

"I wonder how Aunt Val and Rolly Lee are."

Coleman turned his head and looked at me. "Forget Rolly Lee," he said.

"Yeah, but . . ."

"Wonder about Aunt Val. But just forget Rolly Lee."

We lay there for ten minutes looking up at the sky in silence. The calm was broken by a freight train, slow and heavy and carrying a hundred boxcars, most spray-painted with graffiti. It took so long to lumber past that it became part of the silence, a sound as native as the birds or the wind.

"Do you ever wonder what's out there?" Coleman said after the train had disappeared up the line.

"I guess." I wasn't sure what he meant.

"Up there, Jasper." I turned my head. My brother was pointing a long finger at the sky. "Who might be out there?"

The rock began to feel hard and unyielding under my spine. I shifted uncomfortably.

"I have dreams, Jasper."

"Me too, Coleman. Everybody does. Last night I was making out with Heather Locklear."

Coleman shook his head. I could hear the sound of his brush cut moving back and forth on the rock.

"Not the same," he said. "Mine aren't like a regular dream where you can't quite figure out what's going on. These are more like . . . sounds. Sounds and blurred images. Like I should know what I'm hearing and looking at, but I can't quite make sense of it."

The rock suddenly began to feel very cold under my bare neck.

"It's like . . . I feel like someone is trying to communicate with me but I can't quite get the words." A robin landed on a stump, clacked at us, then flew off.

"Whatever," I said.

He ignored me. "They tell me things, but not in words or anything like that. I wake up with ideas and I wonder where they've come from. I wonder if it's someone out there, putting ideas in my head. I don't know where it's coming from."

I sat up.

"I think they've been telling me what to build and how to build it. I already knew about that chair." Coleman turned to me, his eyes wide. "If I could just get the words."

"Fuck off," I said. "I don't even know what you're talking about."

"The chair. I knew where it was going to be. When we saw it that day, it was like walking into a scene I'd already lived through."

I stood up and threw a pebble toward the railway line. "Whatever. You're just baked."

"Shut up," he said. "Baked has got nothing to do with it."

"Whatever."

Coleman sat up. "Seriously, Jasper. You don't know. Mum and Dad don't know." He looked at me with his bright eyes and placed a palm over his heart. "I know."

I didn't say anything.

Coleman looked off toward the railway line. "I think they're coming to get me," he said.

Another freight came clattering down the line. "Fuck off," I said, the words disappearing into the din of steel wheels moving along iron rails. "Fuck off."

9.

THEY WERE CALLING FOR A wet weekend; thunderstorms, wind and rain. After the past few months, the prospect of a weekend inside with my family was not an appealing one. My parents were verging on exhaustion—I could see it in their eyes, their

voices, even the heavy-shouldered way they walked. My brother
and I had always been easy enough kids. For the most part, we were
uncomplicated and easy to deal with. But that had all changed,
and my parents wore the strain on their faces. Late night conversations drifted around the upstairs of our house like stale smoke.
I wondered if Coleman could hear them. I wondered if he cared.

Saturday morning I awoke to the sound of rain. Shadows of
branches swaying in the wind swept across my blankets. I'd
spent Friday night in my bedroom, reading a book for school—
Day of the Triffids. It was supposed to be scary but it seemed
pretty phony and my mind kept wandering. Although I didn't
realize it, I was tired too.

The wind kicked up and rain pelted the window. I pulled the
covers over my head and tried to get back to sleep. I was drifting
off when there was a quiet knock at my door and my father
stepped into the room.

"You up?"

"No," I said, smiling. "I'm talking in my sleep."

He picked up a dirty sock and threw it at me. "Smartass.
Get your clothes on, let's go get something to eat."

Weekend brunch at Madeline's had been a family tradition
when we were younger. It started one year after our annual trip
down I-75 to Florida. My brother and I got so used to eating at
Howard Johnson's that, once back, we decided we couldn't live
without at least one breakfast of syrup-slathered pancakes and
bacon a week.

On this morning, the trip to Madeline's was business. After
the waitress left the menus with us, my father sat turning his in
his hands, eyes looking through the words into the table, blue-
grey circles around his eyes like smudged ash. In the midst of a
bustling weekend breakfast, kids screaming, men and women

chattering and laughing, a heavy silence enshrouded us. My dad had always been a good father to us; but talking through the rough patches had never been his style. My mother was the one who'd wade in up to her knees and sort things out. My father was the mountain we could lean up against.

That aside, the purpose of this breakfast was plain: he wanted to talk about Coleman. More specifically, Coleman losing his mind.

"Jas . . ." my dad started, and then the waitress appeared holding the coffee pot. We watched her fill the cups with serious intent.

"What's up, Dad?" I wanted to save him the discomfort. His shoulders seemed to sag a little, maybe with relief. He shrugged.

"What's up," he said, and we both looked out the window. It was still raining. "We've got to talk about Coleman, Jas. I need to know what you think."

"I know. I figured, anyway."

He tipped the circular sugar dispenser. The trap came open and the sugar rushed into his coffee. "Shit," he said. "I'll be bouncing off the walls." He laughed nervously and our eyes met across the table.

"Your brother is having some troubles," he said. Then, "Your mother . . ." but he thought better of it and took a swallow from his coffee.

"Coleman's always been different, Dad."

"I know that." He nodded. "I never wanted you guys to be conventional. I want you to do whatever it is that will make you happy. You shouldn't worry about what other people think, what other people do." This had been a mantra from the onset of puberty. My father despised fads, trends, mushy thinking and wishy-washy people. "But this is different. We're really worried about your brother, Jasper."

I didn't know what to say. I knew that my father wanted my opinion, but as he sat looking at me, I could almost feel myself shrinking into the seat. I was on the cusp of being able to drive, getting laid for the first time, a few short years from university—but I still felt like a kid. Luckily, before I had to say anything, he spoke up.

"Your mum and I are going to send Coleman somewhere. We think he needs help. Help that none of us can give him."

Going to send Coleman somewhere. I didn't know what he meant. My first thought was Africa.

"To a hospital, Jas." He rubbed his forehead with the heel of his hand.

"Does . . ."

"No, he doesn't know. It's something your mother and I have been discussing." He laced his hands behind his head and sighed. "I don't know what's going on anymore," he said. "I need to know what you think, Jasper."

I looked out the window. The wind had picked up and was needling in great sheets against the window. *"I think they're coming to get me,"* I remembered him saying.

"I think Coleman's losing his mind," I said.

I would live to regret it.

So that was that. Only of course it wasn't.

The rain didn't relent and my parents decided we should go out for dinner. I somehow doubted the spontaneity of the idea. Coleman and I had been in our bedrooms all afternoon, and at no point did I hear either of my parents visit my brother. All I could hear was his usual low muttering and the occasional crumpling of paper. It was like rooming next to an aged mathematician. I didn't envy what my parents had to do, but I can't say it troubled me all that much—yet. Up until a certain age, you think things will eventually pan out, no matter what. Looking back, I know I wasn't all that concerned. I figured it'd be like a visit to the garage—my parents would drop Coleman off, they'd kick under the tires, look under the hood, fix up whatever was broken, and he'd be back at home, muttering in the room next to me in no time at all.

Still, late that afternoon, I decided to go see him. Maybe it was the guilt of talking about him with Dad over breakfast. I knocked at his door and when there was no answer, I pushed it open. He was at his desk, bent under his fluorescent light, arm poised over a notebook.

"Coleman," I said. "What's going on?"

He sniffed, cleared his throat and kept writing. "I'm just . . . kind of busy," he finally said.

"Well," I said, "I thought you might want to hang out or something."

Now he straightened and stretched his neck. "To do what?" he said.

I shrugged. "I don't know. Listen to some tunes, watch a movie. We never finished *The Road Warrior* last week."

He let out a long sigh and looked back at his paper. "Pretty busy here," he said. "But thanks," he managed to say, as if it pained him to do so.

I was about to duck out the door when I stopped. "You know," I said, "Mum and Dad are pretty worried . . ."

"Yeah, yeah, yeah. I know. But of course nobody gets what I'm doing."

"Well, what are you doing?"

Another sigh, now accompanied by some emphatic head shaking. "Jasper," he said, "you just wouldn't understand."

"I thought maybe if you tried to explain it to me, it'd be better for both of us."

"Better?"

I shrugged. I really didn't know what else to say. "Just forget it," I said.

"Will do," he said.

The waiter was a slightly built, officious-looking man with a large red moustache that he'd taken great care in twisting up at the ends. The moment he appeared, my brother kicked me under the table. I burst out laughing. The waiter and my mother regarded me suspiciously while my father looked from Coleman to me with a smirk. We had inherited his sense of humour.

And this is how it went. After months of white-knuckled, subtext-ridden family dinners, low-voiced disputes drifting through the vents late at night, concern, worry and outright bizarre behaviour on the part of my brother, things went back to normal, if only for one dinner. My parents relaxed and made jokes with us about the waiter (who played his role perfectly, growing more and more austere as the evening stretched on), and my brother was composed and focused on the matter at hand. But I couldn't help but notice the dark circles under his eyes. They were like the ones circling my father's eyes, only deeper. I knew my parents hadn't spoken to Coleman about the hospital. I wondered when they would. By the end of dinner, I couldn't look at my brother. It was like running around the barnyard playing with the turkey a day before Thanksgiving.

The rain had stopped by the time we got home. My father eased the car into the driveway and we got out. The rain had stopped and a warm wind swept across the damp asphalt.

"It's gorgeous," my mother said. "Look at how clear the sky is."

My father shot her a look. Outer space was not a topic we idly bantered about in our house. But Coleman wasn't looking up.

"Do you hear that?" He nodded toward the back yard.

"No," my mother said, still looking up. "Beautiful," she said.

There was a clatter from the back yard. Coleman took off running with my father and me close behind.

Coleman turned the corner just in time to see the last remnants of his spacecraft going into a trailer, bound for the dump. The two men my father hired had started the job a day early. One of them held his hands out and shrugged.

My brother's spaceship would never make its maiden voyage.

Coleman collapsed to his knees, his head in his hands. A thin, desperate wail came from his mouth, growing in volume until it was all around us. Moonlight lay across his face and brightened his eyes. I stood next to my father, mouth agape, watching the scene unfold.

If I think about it, I'm right there again, watching my brother on his knees, sobbing in the mud. If only I had known what the spaceship, crazy as it was, meant to Coleman: escape. If only my parents and I had known what might happen next, now that interplanetary travel had been scratched from the agenda.

If only to forget.

10.

I WOKE UP CHOKING on my beard. A mouth full of cotton wool and a dull, menacing throb deep in my skull.

I opened my eyes and looked at the ceiling, my mind racing through the fog, trying to place where I was. Stucco ceiling, blue curtains, a small room. The realization that I was in my house, sleeping in Coleman's old bedroom, settled over me with a chill. I pulled the blankets back up and a rippling ache shot through my leg and into my lower back. The smell of bacon and coffee drifted under the door. My stomach flipped over like a dying fish and I had to sit up just to stop myself from retching.

How long had I been gone this time?

All at once, a taste came back to me: cherry brandy. Homemade, seasoned to taste with hot sauce. Moonshine, Ontario-style.

I slowly raised myself up to a sitting position. Every movement made the blood pound in my head like a pair of Louisville Sluggers on a bass drum. Mercifully, there was a glass of water beside the bed. I drank greedily from it, the effort straining my dry throat, the lukewarm liquid spilling from the corners of my mouth and down my neck. I was still getting the hang of being conscious.

Waking up in this bedroom was like the final kicker in a bad dream. When I closed my eyes I could still see the room as it had been ten years back, Coleman's books and posters and things re-populating the space in a burst inside my mind. I took a deep breath and slowly opened my eyes, reluctant to lose the picture of how things had been. In its place, old questions stacked up: what might I have done differently? Where had all the time gone?

There was a knock at the door. I lowered myself back down with a groan and pulled the covers over my head. And waited. There was another knock.

"Yes," I said.

"You decent?"

"Depends what you mean."

The door opened and Kim stood looking at me, a mug of steaming coffee in each hand, shaking her head.

"Look at you," she said. "Can I come in?"

I nodded. "Here," she said, handing me the coffee.

"This is worse than waking up from my coma," I said. The coffee was an instant elixir: hot, strong and sweet.

"Oh, Jas," she said. "You look terrible. How's your leg?"

I felt under the covers. "Still there."

"Did you have fun?"

"I did," I said. "I must have, anyway, because I can't remember shit."

Kim scowled. "Language," she said.

"Sorry," I said.

"I'm sorry," she said, sitting down on the end of the bed.

"For what?"

She waved her hand. "For this," she said. "For what happened to you." She rested a hand on my battered leg. "You know, Jas, I thought you were gone," she said.

"I was."

Outside, a snow blower roared to life. It sputtered, stalled, then after a few pulls was reborn. "That snow blower," she said. "It'll outlive all of us if Donny has his way." Her eyes darted away from mine at the mention of his name.

"He's a nice guy," I said. "Don't worry, Kim." Things have a habit of working out, I thought.

She nodded, her eyes filling up with tears. Mine had grown heavy; the hangover, briefly waylaid by coffee, had made a hard right and was heading back my way.

"Jas," she started, "something really weird happened last night."

But as the story goes, I'd fallen asleep.

And that was how the next six weeks went: lots of sleep, beer and downtime in Coleman's old bedroom. I was fine with Donny and Kim. How could I not be? Lots of guys would dream of waking up from a coma to find someone had taken their girlfriend off their hands. Conflict had never been my thing, and besides, I still had somewhere to lay my head at night.

The doctors were amazed at my progress. The physio gave me something to focus on. It felt like the first thing I'd actually worked at in years. My leg healed to the point where I was getting around the house without crutches although I still limped and lurched. Aside from some residual stiffness, my arm felt good as new.

I somewhat begrudgingly shaved off my voluminous, reddish-brown beard. Nobody else seemed to think it suited me. I was almost surprised to find that underneath it was the same non-descript, vaguely expressionless face I'd always had.

Sitting on the bed at night, I traced the path of my scars, livid purple rivers that ran up and down my leg and arm. I tried to picture myself falling from the platform into the path of an oncoming subway train and somehow having the presence of mind to roll underneath it. I'd heard stories of firefighters dispatched to the subway line, stories that never made the papers: body parts being collected in plastic bags, an errant head up the line, a schizophrenic woman jumping onto the tracks with her baby in her arms. In the urban world, the subway had become our river. We didn't drown our babies in the spray of rapids; we threw them onto the subway line. I had no desire to ride public transit ever again. Looking at my scars, I wondered if I'd been touched by the hand of God.

God or a good surgeon? Clearly, a few weeks in the company of the born again was getting to me.

So where did it leave me? I'd made one phone call to the office since emerging from the deep sleep. Told the boss that

I wasn't sure when I'd be back. They had a temp filling my shoes, and truthfully, I knew that they wouldn't have a problem replacing me. Chances were they already had. All I had to do was not go back.

But a nagging sense of "what now" had entered my consciousness, like sighting a train in the middle of the night, way up the line, a distant light getting closer and brighter all the time. I told myself that I was lucky. That it was a chance to start over, a time to appreciate all the things that I'd ignored both willfully and without malice, the people and places I'd taken for granted. But that was only how it looked on paper. I was less than two months out of the hospital and boredom had set in. I was nagged by a profound lack of purpose. Every morning when I woke up thinking of my brother in his old bedroom, ready to spend another day where "inconspicuous" was my governing modus operandi, all I could be sure of was where I was at.

I was in limbo.

Donny and Kim threw a small birthday party for me. I came home from a check-up with the doctor to find about twenty people in the house, sausages sizzling in a frying pan, cold beer in an ice chest on the floor, and a slobbery set of false teeth on the kitchen table.

"Now tell me what I look like," Duane lisped, slobber collecting at the corners of his contorted, toothless mouth.

"A fish," a little girl shouted.

"A dummy," Donny's nephew said.

Duane frowned at the little boy, the scowl bringing his top lip flush with the bottom of his nose. "Not nice," he managed, and then swigged from a beer. Rivulets of ale ran from his mouth, over his chin and across his neck.

"Gross," the boy said.

I'd never been too big on celebrating birthdays. Sure, I played up the "another year older" bit, but the reality was another birthday meant one more year without Coleman. Another year piled on to the likelihood that I would never see my brother again.

Still, I appreciated the gesture. I'd begun to feel like a stale fart drifting around the house, and I knew that my increasingly grim outlook had started to rub off on Donny and Kim. An uneasy mix of Christian duty and guilt and the fact that they were living in my house had kept the three of us on friendly terms. I supposed I had Jesus to thank.

The people crowded into the kitchen and living room were chatting in small groups, telling jokes, complaining about their jobs with a natural ease that felt foreign to me. I'd spent most of the last year in a coma and had no idea where I was headed next. Consequently, small talk didn't come easy. With my old jeans hanging off my ass and a perpetually bewildered look on my face (this is how I imagined it, anyway), I suppose I wasn't the most approachable guy—even at my own party.

"Hey Jasper," said Duane. He rubbed his false teeth on his T-shirt then stuffed them back into his mouth. "Need a brewskie?"

"I'm good," I said.

He pulled a beer from the ice chest and popped the cap. "Here you go," he said. "Have one anyway." Duane grinned and staggered off toward the bathroom.

For a moment, I was alone. I sat down at the kitchen table and looked out the screen door at what had once been my family's back yard. The place where my father had stood at the grill grinning, a spatula in one hand, where Coleman and I had thrown a baseball and caught garter snakes, and where my mother had sat reading a book, a slight, satisfied smile lighting up her face. The place to which Coleman's spaceship had been banished before it had ever had a chance to leave the ground.

I could tell that Donny and Kim's friends couldn't quite figure out the arrangement: the ex-boyfriend emerges from a coma and then comes home to live with the happy couple. People I'd met a handful of times through Kim smiled grimly at me and nodded as they went for another sausage or beer. That's it, I thought. Time to grab reinforcements and head for the television. I was struggling to my feet when I felt a hand on my shoulder.

"Need some help?" It was a woman I'd noticed earlier. She'd arrived on her own. I guessed she was in her early thirties. Red hair, freckled nose, long legs.

"I'm cool," I said, wincing from the pain in my leg. I sat back down at the table.

"Mind if I join you?"

I minded. Reruns were waiting. "Sure," I said. "But could you grab me a beer?" If she couldn't take a hint, then maybe rudeness would drive her off. She glanced at my bad leg and smiled sweetly. For fuck's sake, I thought.

While she went for the beer, I struggled to my feet, bracing myself on the table. Sweat beaded on my forehead with the exertion.

She handed me the beer with a smile. "Carol," she said.

"Jasper," I said. I noticed Duane leaning against a wall in the living room a little unsteadily. He threw me a wobbly thumbs up. "How do you know Donny and Kim?"

"I do Donny's hair," she said. I watched Duane slump down the wall to the floor.

I nodded toward the living room. "You do Duane's too?"

She laughed. "He told me he cuts it with nail scissors."

"Quite a guy," I said, taking a large swallow from my beer. There was silence. We were hedging toward chatting about the weather or, failing that, the relative merits of sausages versus burgers.

"Donny set me up with him about a year back," she said. "He took me to the farm expo in Kaladar. First thing he did was point out a bull with an erection."

Beer sprayed from both my nostrils. She patted my back. "Easy," she said, laughing. When I managed to swallow my beer, I was laughing too.

"I take it there wasn't a second date."

"Oh, but there could have been," she said. "I mean, there's no greater aphrodisiac than seeing a pig slaughtered. I think it's the smell of blood mixed with dung."

"So he asked," I said.

"Yep. Wanted me to come over for dinner."

"Give him credit," I said.

"I don't eat giblets," she said. As if on cue, Duane smiled toothlessly at us from the other room.

From the corner of my eye, I watched her cross her butterscotch legs. Maybe I wasn't as out of step as I'd imagined. But the next step in the dance wouldn't come to me. Instead I sat turning my hands over in my lap, waiting for Carol to say something else. I felt her eyes looking at my legs and realized that she felt sorry for me.

When the phone rang, I almost leapt up to get it.

"I can get it," Carol said. "You sit down."

"No," I said, getting to my feet. "This is good practice."

I felt a flush of pride when I picked up on the second ring.

"Hello," I said.

No one spoke at the other end. I pressed my ear into the phone. "Hello?" I said again. There was no reply, but there wasn't exactly silence on the other end. I heard the sounds of a car rush past. Other, stranger sounds called from the long distance. Then there was some fumbling with the phone and someone cleared their throat.

The party noise around me seemed to drop away until I could hear my heart, hammering away inside my chest. This is crazy, I thought. Hang up. But I couldn't. Not this year. My grip tightened around the phone, sweat beginning to form in my palms and along my hairline, and I listened. Another car went past. I imagined I could hear the hum of insects and the sound of water running through a ditch. There was an odd grunting somewhere off away from the phone. I pictured who might be at the other end of all the miles of wire, listening to me, a stranger at my own birthday party. I listened for a second more and then I cleared my own throat.

"Coleman," I said.

11.

AFTER FINDING HIS SPACECRAFT in ruins, Coleman had walked slowly into the house and then up the stairs. The light in his room went off. Then, for half an hour, my parents and I sat at the picnic table in the dark under the star-filled sky. My father tossed pebbles into the darkness. Nobody dared break the silence.

I awoke in the middle of the night covered in a sheen of cold sweat. I'd been dozing in fits and starts, wondering about my brother and the secret world he'd taken up full-time residence in. I was losing my conviction that things were going to turn out okay, that one day we'd all wake up with things back to normal. Instead my brother was travelling further and further into a dark place wholly beyond my comprehension. I looked around my bedroom in the dark, at my posters of base-ball players and rock bands, my models of cars and airplanes perched high above shelves filled with all the books I'd ever owned. My world was populated with familiar things: an old toy box, a stuffed bear, my baseball card collection, my parents, my house, and the streets I'd played on since I could walk. In my brother's world, these familiar, comforting landmarks were being pushed to the periphery to make room for something cold and shadowy.

From the kitchen, I heard the soft clatter of spoon meeting bowl. Coleman. I'd always slept like a log while my brother tended to be restless. It was a running family joke that you might find my brother alone in the kitchen eating cereal at any hour of the night. I guessed he had some things on his mind.

I knew my parents still hadn't spoken to him about the hos-pital and I wondered if their plans had changed at all.

In the distance, a train whistle sounded up the line. I heard Coleman place the bowl in the sink. I wondered what the hospi-tal would be like. A kid at school, Kent Palmer, had a stepfather with schizophrenia. Kent claimed that the hospital only made him crazier. I imagined Coleman in the hospital, a blank look on his face, shuffling around the halls with the other patients. For the first time, I felt truly scared. The train passed outside, send-ing shadows careening across my bedroom walls, and I began to cry. I got out of bed, rubbed my eyes on my pyjama top and went to the window to watch the train. The darkness was beginning to lift, the sky changing from bell black to indigo.

When it had gone past, I heard the back door slam. I figured that Coleman had been out in the back yard, searching for any last traces of his project. Knowing my brother, by first light he'd be starting from scratch, whether he found anything or not. I'd always admired his practicality, his ability to put aside the small complications and focus on the task at hand. I waited for him to appear, hammer at the ready, his head full of ways to move forward. After a moment, Coleman did appear. To my surprise, he wasn't holding anything. He walked across the back yard, unlatched the gate, and then, with the sun beginning to glow above the horizon, disappeared into the woods. I caught a flash of his pale grey windbreaker through the trees, and then he was gone. I stood at the window, my elbows on the frame, staring into the woods until the sky had gone blue and the sun burned overhead. Later I would imagine the light illuminating his every step, and me running from my bedroom to follow the trail into the forest.

12.

CAROL WAS SNORING GENTLY in bed beside me. She'd gone to sleep minutes after we finished, and I was grateful for it. I was out of shape and out of practice. My bum leg made even getting into bed a minor triumph. Rolling around with another person required careful consideration, lest I kill the entire mood with a cry of agony or a locked-up knee. Mickey Rooney was probably a better lay. Still, Carol was attractive and her attention was wholly surprising. I guessed that I came out looking pretty good amongst the Duanes of this world.

But as I lay there, eyes fixed on the ceiling, my thoughts

were elsewhere. I couldn't stop thinking about the phone call I'd taken earlier in the evening.

In the days and weeks after Coleman left, the search for him widened steadily. The police wouldn't consider it anything other than a standard runaway case—particularly given the circumstances—for the first forty-eight hours. We combed the woods over those two days, our friends and extended family by our side. I knew from the start we wouldn't find him. I think my parents did too. Coleman hadn't been abducted. I had watched him leave the back yard and then latch the gate behind him.

We never found any trace in the woods. And as the days became weeks and months and finally years, no sign that Coleman was alive and well ever came.

With one small, flimsy exception.

Over the last five years, I'd received phone calls on my birthday with no one at the other end. If the first year I'd never considered that it might be Coleman, hope grew in small increments over the next four. Deep down, my bullshit detector told me I was projecting. Coleman leaving had been the defining moment of my life and I had long gotten used to seeing the small mysteries of the world through this lens.

But this year, the call had disarmed me. It might have been my recent tussle with the rush hour train, but something felt different. I could almost see the person at the other end.

No one had spoken. But the line wasn't dead. There was a sound that could only be cars passing at high speed. A highway. In the dead space, there was a low drone that suggested cicadas.

"Coleman," I'd said. It sounded as ridiculous as "Jesus," or "Santa." I could hear breathing at the other end. Then, when no reply came: "I'm going to hang up now." I felt ridiculous.

Just as I was about to put the phone down, I heard something. One word: "Wait." It emanated from a dry throat, a pack-a-day smoker, someone in rough shape. I could hear a car go past on the other end of the line, and then the engine sound got closer. A car door slammed and there was an odd grunting noise, almost piglike. I heard someone shout and then the line went dead in my hands.

I'd stepped outside. It was warm for February and the snow glistened with the moisture brought on by the early melt. I leaned back until I felt the coolness of the aluminum siding against my head and watched the sky, black as the ocean. I thought of my brother walking into the forest. I wondered where every night in the interim had gone.

Then the door opened. Carol took my hand and led me into the house.

"I remember when your brother disappeared," Carol said, her hand on my shoulder. "I remember the search party. We lived down by the lake. There were divers . . ." I had told her about the phone call. Now, post-sex, I regretted the disclosure. I rolled over in bed so that my back was to her. "Hey," she said, shaking me slightly. "Are you just going to sleep now?"

I rolled over again. "Sorry," I said. "It's just been a weird night."

The whites of her eyes glowed at me across the pillow. "What did he say?"

"Nothing. It was a wrong number."

Carol looked at me. "But you don't think that."

I sat up in bed and drank from the lukewarm beer at my bedside. "Forget it," I said. "I always get a little weird on my birthday."

"Okay," she said, rolling over. "Consider it forgotten. But . . ."

"But what?"

"Forget it," she said. "I should stay out of this."

I drained the beer and turned out the light on the bedside table. I thought Carol had gone to sleep when she spoke again.

"You could do star 69 if you're really curious."

I'd had about all the sex my battered body could handle for one night. "I don't know," I said. "Please don't take any offence, but I'm really tired."

She laughed. "No, dummy. Last call return."

An hour later, I was still awake, watching the ceiling, trying to put the call out of my mind. Forget about it. It was the only rational thing to do. But another part of me kept thinking about the call. I was sure the number would be local. Probably kids having a laugh.

I was readying myself to get up, go downstairs and try last call return when exhaustion finally overcame me and I drifted off.

And into the thick of an old dream.

I was in the back seat of a large car. My bare arms and legs stuck to the sweaty, torn vinyl of the seat. My father was driving and I could see the sweat on his scalp through his thin hair. In the passenger seat was a scrawny man with long blond hair and a mesh baseball cap. His arm dominated the real estate of the armrest between him and my father. The tattoo of a Dixie flag on his bicep gave him away: Ronnie "Rolly" Lee was in the passenger seat.

We were on a dusty, unpaved trail, only a car-width wide with water on both sides. The road fell away quickly at the edges, just a pebble's tumble from the swamp. I could smell the thick, brackish water, feel the weight of humidity. Mosquitoes and tiny no-see-ums banged against the windows, a few getting in. I watched Rolly crush a mosquito with the palm of his hand against the front windshield. It left a smear of blood and I saw his cheeks swell with a smile. But my mind was elsewhere. In the water with the alligators.

The water was full of them. Every branch in the water, every air bubble rising to the surface—be it from fish, bug or turtle—every ripple was an alligator to me. I reached for the door lock and pushed it down. Terror began to creep into my heart the way a maggot infiltrates an apple.

Now we were walking along a footbridge, away from the narrow road. Off in the distance, thunder rumbled.

Now I realized I was alone. As the sky grew darker still, the thunder drew closer like a slow-moving train. I caught movement in my periphery. Rows of spines drifted to and fro, just under the syrupy water. Eyes glowed at me from points across the swamp. Lightning flashed and the water itself seemed to twist. The swamp was boiling with alligators.

The footbridge fell away and I was left standing on a small platform in the middle of the swamp. Then, from across the water, something caught my attention. A flash of white. Movement.

I realized it was a man.

He approached slowly, gliding across the surface of the water. I could see now that he was only wearing a small pair of white shorts. He was a white man but his skin had turned a deep, dark copper from the sun. His hair sprouted from his head in thick, twisted coils. Even at a distance, I recognized his eyes. It was my brother.

Think of pure joy. An unexpected gift on a bad day. Waking up on a Friday morning to find three feet of snow on the ground and school closed for the day. Meeting a beautiful woman who loves you and looks after you. Getting the promotion you wanted. Getting laid. A cold beer in the summer. Roll it all into a ball and stuff it into your heart and you would not even approach the joy I felt at seeing my brother. "Coleman," I shouted into the storm. "Coleman." Tears rolled down my face.

Coleman had stopped and was ten or fifteen feet away, staring back at me.

"Where the fuck have you been?" I called out.

Coleman smiled and shrugged. Then the platform was crumpling under me as though it were wet cardboard. An alligator grunted and drifted past as I fell.

The water was thick and hot. I sank into it, thrashing my arms and legs against a swamp full of alligators, trying my hardest to keep my eyes on my brother as I disappeared into the murk.

I woke up to blackness, cold from lying in a swamp of my own sweat.

I stood up and went to the window. A few empty beer cans littered the snow in the back yard. The back gate hung open and I looked through it and out toward the trees, hoping that time itself had frozen and that I might catch a glimpse of Coleman disappearing into the woods.

A napkin drifted up from the picnic table, a small ghost pinned against the night sky. I watched as it climbed and then seemed to hang suspended. I thought of my dream and I thought about the phone call. It was a bad time to be chasing ghosts. Chances were that my brother was dead. I realized I'd never truly considered that my brother was gone, that he wasn't out exploring the galaxies or pumping gas in Topeka, Kansas, or Red Deer, Alberta.

The dream was one I'd had before, now and then with less frequency over the years, the main details always the same. I guessed it was one I'd have to live with.

The napkin was stuck in the branches of a poplar, fluttering in the cool night air. I imagined an alligator sauntering across the back yard, looking for the swamp, leaving tracks in the snow as it looked for somewhere warm. It was a cold night for alligators.

Then it hit me like a brick to the temple: the grunting noise I'd heard over the phone.

As kids down on Sanibel, Coleman and I had loved to walk to the store for ice cream at dusk. We'd sit in the parking lot, listening to the drone of cicadas, the asphalt finally cool enough to go barefoot, struggling to finish the ice cream before it melted down our wrists. When we finished, we'd walk back along West Gulf Drive to the cottage. Coleman would tell me that the alligators were waiting in the deep dark ditches that lay on either side of the road. They would wait for the return trip to get us, he said, because then we'd be fattened up with ice cream. Coleman's story would always be punctuated with grunts like those a pig makes. The grunts always made me jump, because they were made by alligators.

The sound I'd heard was the sound of an alligator, grunting in the blackness down thousands of miles of wire.

The wind stirred again and the napkin came loose from the poplar. I stood at the window and watched it float to the ground. Then I went downstairs to the phone.

I dialed *69. In the dark of the kitchen with no sound but my own breathing, the numbers sounded like blasts off a bullhorn. I scribbled the number on a pizza box next to the phone. When I hung up, I stood staring at the number, my bad leg feeling weak underneath me. I didn't need the phonebook to identify the area code.

It was a number from Fort Myers, Florida.

13.

A FEMALE ALLIGATOR GRUNTS to call her young. Out in the swamps at night, the small gators swim off in search of bugs, small frogs and lizards, straying progressively further as they get more confident in their surroundings. But a small alligator is also good eating for any number of other animals—birds, snakes, snapping turtles. The piglike grunt emitted by mama gator is a sort of "get your asses home." It's not the sound you'd expect from an alligator. The bellows and hisses that are also part of their communicative repertoire are far more fitting, fierce, dinosaur-like emittances that nearly always stand as a warning of some kind. A serious one.

Rolly Lee knew all about alligators. Born and raised in Fort Myers, he was pure Florida Cracker through and through. He'd spent most of his youth barefoot in the Everglades, chasing down alligators, catching snakes and searching for the ever-elusive Florida panther. You know, the stuff that nightmares are made of for anyone born on the cold side of the Mason-Dixon Line. Rolly Lee had never been further north than North Carolina, a fact he delighted in telling us every year when we arrived in Fort Myers on our way through to Sanibel. It was Rolly's way of saying "if you were really smart you'd cut this vacation shit and settle down here in God's country." Never mind that for the rest of the world God's country was on the other coast, in California. If a world existed outside the South, Rolly wasn't interested in it.

What Rolly was interested in was my Aunt Val. Val was ten years younger than my mother. She went to the University of Guelph for a year, met a guy, dropped out of school, and before she realized it she was married and living in North Bay, three hours up the King's Highway from Toronto. For all its natural

beauty, North Bay is a small town and can get boring. And cold.
I'd spent a weekend there on my way back from my summer in
Timmins working as a camp counsellor and struggled to imagine
my Aunt Val living there. I guessed that devotion could lead
people to any number of strange places.

Apart from the cold weather, avid bear hunting, and lack of
almost anything interesting to an attractive woman in her twenties, the major pitfall for Val in North Bay was that her new
husband was a manic-depressive alcoholic. Val had caught him on
the upswing; by the time they arrived in North Bay, he'd hit the
downward slope and was tumbling. He was arrested one night in
what passed for downtown North Bay, sitting in the middle of
the strip with a claw hammer, banging away at the asphalt. The
police picked him up and he spent a week in the psychiatric hospital. Then, one night in July when Coleman and I were about
nine and seven, Aunt Val appeared at the front door with a black
eye and a suitcase held together with white carpet tape. She'd
been determined to stand by her man, but this was the final straw.
We happened to be heading to Florida the next morning. My
mother bought Val a bathing suit and away we all went.

Coleman and I loved Aunt Val. She told us jokes that our
parents would deem inappropriate, she listened to the same kind
of music as teenagers did, and most of all, she was pretty. Florida
suited her. I can recall waking up one of the first mornings that
trip and seeing her come up from the beach, a paperback in one
hand and a beer in the other, whips of coal-black hair blowing
about her back and neck. She had on a white cotton shirt that
she'd tied in the front just like Daisy Duke. Aunt Val could have
passed for a native daughter. It was no wonder that she never left.

As the story goes, one night my mother and Aunt Val went
into Fort Myers to a place called the Warehouse. I vividly

remember staying behind with my father and brother, eating pizza then watching a movie. A "girls' night out" was how my father put it.

This was the late 1970s and the whole Southern rock thing was in full swing. Lynyrd Skynyrd and the Allman Brothers had done well enough to inspire a whole legion of second-rate bands that grew beards, flew the flag for old Dixie, and played endless, spiralling guitar jams for scraggly, swaying crowds up on pills, Jack Daniel's, dirt weed and Bud. Second-tier acts like Blackfoot or Molly Hatchet never would have set foot in a place like the Warehouse. It was strictly for the third- and fourth-rate bands, like Fort Myers's own General Gator, fronted by one Ronnie "Rolly" Lee.

Everyone called him Rolly. In the sixth grade, there were three Ronald Lees. One night after school, they took their sling-shots behind the corner store and set up a row of beer bottles. The first Ronald Lee to hit a bottle picked "Ronnie," the second "Ron," the third became "Rolly." The way he told it, he would have picked Rolly even if he'd hit the bottle first. That was Rolly Lee, always able to see the fertilizer in a shit heap.

Rolly Lee wasn't much of a singer. But to hear my Aunt Val tell it, this had little or no relevance, despite Rolly being the front man and vocalist for General Gator. What Rolly did have was charisma and good looks. Back in those days, he had long, straight blond hair that he wore under a leather cowboy hat with the crossed rifles of the Southern infantry on the front. Rolly was over six feet tall and built like a broomstick. Somewhere early on, Rolly had deemed shirts as attire for special occasions only, and his skin was the colour of burnished wood from the Florida sun. He added weight to his narrow face with a thick brown beard that hung off his jawline in a frizzy fringe. When I first met Rolly Lee that summer, he let me tug on his beard and I was an instant fan.

To call General Gator fourth-rate was probably a compliment. The band self-released one record, a six-song affair titled *Keep On Keepin' On (Takin' Er Ezy)*. After Lynyrd Skynyrd, deliberate misspelling was the name of the game. One song, "Crawfish and Gar," got some play on the local Fort Myers station, but then again, Rolly fished with the DJ. But, much like their front man, General Gator had an appeal all their own apart from the music. Rolly set fireworks off onstage. He called members of the audience up to drink Jack Daniel's through a funnel while the band jammed away. And, for their final song of the night, Rolly brought out a live gator and wrestled it onstage while the crowd went berserk. I later found out that the gator was normally out of his mind on Budweiser and Quaaludes. He lived in a pit out behind the Warehouse and, as Rolly told it, looked forward to gigs, possibly because his reptile brain spent the interim cooking in the infernal Florida heat, craving nothing more than an ice-cold Budweiser.

My mother ran serious interference for Aunt Val that night. Every biker, would-be rocker and bearded weirdo in the Warehouse had his eyes on my Aunt Val. My mother was an attractive woman, but Aunt Val was a knockout. And she knew it. She let guys buy her beers and shots, danced up a storm, and most of all, kept her eyes on the stage and the man singing. As my mother later told the story, it was as though she could see Aunt Val shaking off the not-so-happy recent past that night at the Warehouse, dancing her way out of the chill of North Bay and into a new start somewhere warmer. By the end of the set, Rolly Lee had his eyes on her too. That night, after he'd put his alcoholic alligator to bed, Rolly drove my mother and aunt back out to Sanibel to our cottage, along the quiet of dark streets, the Gulf of Mexico slipping up onto the white sand shores with barely a sound. Aunt Val stayed in the truck and went home with Rolly Lee. I can remember building a sandcastle on the beach the next afternoon and looking up to see my aunt with a strange, long-haired guy in blue jeans. They'd come to pick her stuff up. Aunt Val never did bother to send for her things from North Bay. They were all for cold weather anyway.

14.

THE MORNING AFTER the phone call, I had an appointment in court.

I was surprised at how familiar Ronnie Orsulak looked to me. It was almost as though we'd hung out in high school or worked together at a dead-end job, washing dishes in the back of some restaurant together, horsing around just to kill the time.

"Just a formality," the lawyer had told me. "I know it must be fresh and terribly . . . difficult," he said. "But trust me on this—no big deal."

The lawyer had contacted me in the first week after I'd woken up. He struggled to tactfully explain that I'd woken up just in time: Orsulak's court date had finally come and I would probably need to identify him. They'd been holding him at a psychiatric facility and treating him with the hope that he'd be able to stand trial. Fact was I didn't feel much of anything at all. There had even been moments where I could have thanked Ronnie Orsulak. Normally in the mornings when I woke up, the press of getting to work was still heavy in my mind, feet hitting the floor before I realized that the life of managing a small team of data entry drones at the insurance company was over. My boss had stopped calling me and I hadn't been checking in to begin with. I'd never been a model employee; just one among many who clocked in, clocked out and did enough in the interim to stay under the radar. The last I'd heard was that they had hired someone to replace me on a year's contract until I got myself sorted out. I realized that the governing assumption was that if I took more than a year to get my shit together, I'd probably be dead weight anyway.

Carol drove me into the city. A knock on the door woke us up at eight—Donny reminding me that I had to get up and be in court. His manners were impeccable: he knocked with the light touch of a bellhop in an expensive downtown hotel. Carol rolled over and put her hand on my chest. "Can't we stay for another ten minutes?" she said. We closed our eyes and what seemed like moments later there was another knock. Donny again. "Uh, Jasper," he said. "I'm worried you're going to be late." God bless him.

Carol, like most of Kim and Donny's friends, drove a pick-up truck and we rode into the city with the windows down, the cool morning air and sunshine being just what I needed. I had always hated the commute into Toronto, as it involved driving to the train station, then catching a subway full of the disgruntled, the irritable and, worst of all, the hygienically challenged. But with Carol beside me and endless rectangles of snow-covered farmland passing outside the window, it was as close to good as I'd felt in a while. It was almost enough to make me forget the phone call from the previous evening.

Ten years back I'd given up hope for my brother because there was no other choice. I waited through a series of long days and sleepless nights. Weeks became months. Seasons changed. The stands of poplars, oaks and maples at the edge of the forest were laid bare to shudder in the wind. Then one day, I woke up with a thought that made the blood throb in my temples: there was no reason to believe that Coleman was alive. Teenagers disappeared every day for any number of unfathomable, unforeseeable reasons: abductions, runaways, drugs, abuse at home. Coleman had taken off because his life had gained momentum toward an end he could not accept—an eccentricity that my parents were convinced had blossomed into mental illness. In the years since his disappearance, I had grown to accept it through small, invisible increments: Coleman was not coming back.

While I still firmly believed this, I realized that, since the accident, something sour and insidious had crept into my head and my heart: hope. I supposed it was normal enough. My brush with the great equalizer had made me realize that no matter what you think, anything can happen. All I had to do to remind myself of this was to look at the scars on my arms and legs. Another inch or two in the wrong direction and I'd have been fodder for the glue factory.

We arrived at the courthouse and had to wait to turn left into the parking lot for a stream of commuters filing past in a thick, steady stream. Carol looked at me. "We hooking up tonight?" Her hand moved into my lap and rubbed furtively.

"I don't know," I said, nodding toward the courthouse. "I can call you after I see how this goes."

She frowned. "Why do you have to wait until after the hearing? Can't you tell me now?"

I shrugged. "It could be a long day."

"Well, all the more reason to hook up," she said with a smile. "I can help you relax."

"I can call you," I said, inching toward the door. I was beginning to feel slightly claustrophobic. "I guess."

"Fine," she said. "At least you got a lay and a ride into town out of it, eh?"

I felt like I'd been slapped. "Sure," I said, slowly.

"Sure," she repeated. Then, "So that's it? That's all you have to say?" She looked straight ahead out the windshield and for a second I worried she might gun the engine and drive over the commuters passing on the sidewalk. "Another instant sweetheart," she said. "Just add beer."

I put my hands up. "Listen, Carol," I said. "I've kind of had all the craziness I can deal with at the moment. I didn't mean to offend you."

"Craziness?" she said, starting the car. "You'd know about craziness. You and your brother."

15.

"ORSULAK'S CHANGED HIS PLEA," the lawyer said. He was a thickly built, ginger-haired man in his fifties with black-rimmed glasses and a nicotine-stained moustache that hung over his top lip like a thatch of tattered shag rug. The early word on the case was that Orsulak was going to plead not criminally responsible due to mental illness.

"Guilty."

I leaned away. We were standing outside the courthouse where Carol had dropped me. I'd been watching the traffic and pedestrian commuters, prolonging the inevitable, trying to get my head around all that had happened in the last day—Carol, the phone call, the dream—when Larry Brickheimer walked up, a battered leather attaché case under his arm.

"Really?"

"I don't get it," he said. "Not at all what I expected." Brickheimer was a close talker and I backed off a step. His breath was a mixture of multiple coffees and even more cigarettes and could probably cut glass. He took a step forward to compensate for the one I'd taken back and leaned in. "If there was ever a more picture-perfect NCR case than Orsulak, I'd like to see it. Crazier than a shithouse rat," he said. "But I guess he's responded well to treatment up at the bughouse and there's fuck all his lawyers can do about it. See you in there. Appreciate you coming down, but I don't think I'm going to need you."

"Glad to hear it," I said.

"You don't sound so thrilled." A symphony of bleating horns took up at the stoplight across the street. An old Honda had stalled and was blocking traffic.

I shrugged. "What's his story?"

Brickheimer pulled out a cigarette and lit it. "In and out of trouble since the time he could walk," he said, exhaling a blast of foul vapour across my face. "Setting fires. Shoplifting. The usual shit. Spent some time in the loony bin. He gets out, does okay, then he goes off his meds. The classic story. This time, he heads to the subway station, and that's where you come in. After you end up on the tracks"—Brickheimer held one arm floppy and bent for illustration—"old Orsulak takes off up the stairs. Meanwhile, people are shrieking and crying, the train's being evacuated, the whole nine yards. Two guys standing on the eastbound platform tried to catch up with him. He kicked one of them right in the nuts, and the poor son of a bitch falls down the stairs. Guy happens to be a neighbour of someone I work with. Well, he's off work for a week with a badly sprained ankle and nuts the size of a cantaloupe." He shook his head and sucked a final drag off his cigarette. I watched the soggy filter collapse in his twitching fingers. They were stained the same shade of dull orange as his hair. "Real nut," he said, eyes half closed. "Fucking whack job. Guy needs a couple of electrodes strapped to his head and another one shoved up his ass." He ground the cigarette under the heel of his shoe. "Anyway, thanks for being here," he said. "Chances are I won't need you."

"Don't think of it," I said, then took a step back from Brickheimer and turned toward the courthouse. "By the way," I said, "your breath stinks." Then I went in.

They brought Orsulak into the half-empty courtroom after an interminable amount of talking between Brickheimer, the defence and the judge, during which time I felt myself nodding off. It had been a long time since I'd been up half the night with a woman, longer still since I'd had my old nightmare. The fatigue made my eyes burn and left a sour, metallic taste on the back of my tongue.

Orsulak could hardly stagger in under the weight of whatever medication they had him on. They'd been keeping him up north at Penetang, a maximum-security psychiatric facility that I'd been told made most prisons seem like Disneyland. His hands were cuffed behind his back, and two police officers held him upright and walked him to the front of the court, where he was pushed into a chair beside his lawyer. I watched his head bob and swivel as though his neck was too weak to support the chaos erupting inside his skull.

As I sat and stared at the back of Ronnie Orsulak's head, a funny thing happened. The man who pushed me onto the subway line turned around and looked at me. It was as though he knew I was there and could read my thoughts. While I hadn't remembered his face, it now seemed perfectly familiar to me. What unsettled me most were his sad eyes. They could have belonged to a ten-year-old boy, if it hadn't been for the deep, indigo-blue smudges underneath them. Orsulak and I held the stare for what seemed like minutes, then his lawyer nudged him and he turned around.

When the lawyer entered his plea of guilty, Ronnie Orsulak started to cry. Small, barely audible sobs at first, then his sides shook with gasping, grief-stricken cries. "Sorry," he managed to say, then, "Somebody fucking kill me."

The judge banged his gavel half-heartedly. "Counsellor," he said, "get a hold of your client. Please. I will not tolerate that kind of language in my courtroom. Do your best to compose yourself, Mr. Orsulak." I could see that his heart wasn't in it. Orsulak continued to wail and the judge called for a recess until the next day.

The lawyer patted Orsulak's shoulder then motioned to the uniformed cops. They got Orsulak to his feet, turned him around and led him up the aisle toward the back of the courtroom.

I tried to catch Ronnie Orsulak's eye on his way out. I'm not sure why. Watching the sagging, broken man about my age being walked out of the courtroom, his head nodding and twisting as he went, made me inexplicably sad. This was the man who tried to kill me, the man who had nearly taken my legs from me and sent me home to live with my ex-girlfriend like some kind of charity case. Yet what I felt was grief. It was only when Larry Brickheimer turned around and nodded at me with a smirk that I realized why: Ronnie Orsulak, with his sad, confused eyes and head full of strange impulses, reminded me of someone I knew. Coleman. I watched him being led from the courtroom through the heavy oaken door to the outside world and then the door swung shut and Ronnie Orsulak was gone.

16.

MOTHER HADN'T SPOKEN a word in five years. One quiet morning at the grocery store, she reached for a can of tomato soup on a top shelf and had a massive stroke. She wasn't even fifty years old. It was either more bad luck or the inevitable end to all the raw-nerved years she'd spent wondering when Coleman might come home.

The stroke should have killed her, but some small measure of luck was on her side that morning. When my mother hit the ground, she took half a shelf's worth of soup cans with her. The cashiers at the front heard the din right away, found her and called for an ambulance. Even still, she was speechless, paralyzed up one side, blessed with the capacity to move around, and cursed with the complete lack of motivation or reason to do so.

The halls of the home were cool and quiet. Someone coughed at the other end of the floor.

My family had been cursed by silence. My brother had disappeared into a netherworld that held neither the living nor the dead, only the missing. After Coleman's disappearance, I would find myself standing in his room at odd times of the day: sometimes after school, my book bag heavy in my hands, often early in the morning on the weekends, the time when he might have left his bed for a bowl of cereal. It was difficult to comprehend that someone had once lived in the room and now there was only silence. I stood and listened for the ghosts of conversations, the signs that someone had once been there, living, breathing, struggling to understand whatever menace plagued his inner thoughts.

Hope left my father first. Within a year of Coleman's disappearance, my father had withdrawn. He seemed to shrink inside himself. Gone was the easiness, the jokes, the levity. He spent most of his non-working hours in his chair, his shoulders sagging, asleep. A paperback dropped beside his chair, one hand hanging down, the book just out of reach. Many times I stood in that doorway and watched his heavy shape in the chair, his chest rising and falling with every breath. I wanted to talk to him, to tell him that somehow, everything would be okay. That I loved him. But I could never bring myself to walk across the carpet to where he slept, immobile as a mountain. He would be dead from a heart attack before I ever got the chance. This was the official explanation. My mother maintained that he'd given up.

Giving up was one thing she would never do.

"Mum." She hadn't heard me come in. I spoke softly. Her roommate, an English woman in her sixties who was quickly losing her sight to a progressive ocular disease, was asleep, the covers drawn up tightly under her chin and a pained expression on her face.

My mother had her back to the door. During the afternoon, she liked to sit at her window and look out over the grounds. Often there would be men working: cutting the lawn, pruning trees or washing windows. It never failed to remind me of the many times Coleman and I would be toiling away at our chores and I would look up, feeling someone's eyes on me, and see my mother, grinning in the window, a look of "keep at it" on her face. Now, watching her turn from the window, I wondered where the years had gone.

I put my hand on her shoulder and she blinked at me. How much she took in, processed and understood was a mystery. After my accident, Kim had gone in and explained to her that I'd been hurt but the doctors were hopeful that I would recover. She didn't seem to think that it had registered, but when I arrived six months later, I swear that her eyes misted with a mix of joy and relief.

"You okay?" I ran my hand over her hair, the same shade of chestnut brown it had always been. She rocked in her chair.

We sat together for a while, listening to her roommate snore, my mother holding my hand, occasionally squeezing it in odd, insistent rhythms. Once a week, barring falls from the subway platform, this was how things went.

On my way out, I turned my mother's chair slightly so that she was looking out over her windowsill full of pictures toward the grounds. When I said goodbye, she motioned with her good arm toward one picture: an old shot of my brother and me standing on the back lawn in our baseball uniforms.

I paused, wondering if I should mention the phone call. I'd never mentioned the others and I decided this one should be no different. It was just false hope, my mind imposing its deepest desire—finding Coleman—on the flimsiest of evidence. "No, Mother," I finally said. "Still nothing."

As I closed the door, I could have sworn that I saw her kick at the radiator with her one good leg.

Standing on the subway platform, my mouth went dry and I took another step back. My heart seemed to have moved into my throat and my clenched fists held a swamp of anxiety. I looked around and stifled a nervous laugh. If I moved any further away from the line, I'd be waiting for the train coming in the opposite direction.

The subway was nearly empty. A small mercy. It reminded me of going home from work sick (or not) in the middle of the morning, the crowds having dispersed into office buildings like vermin into cracked baseboards. It had always been my favourite time to travel. When the first car came roaring up the line, I took a tentative step forward. I wondered what I'd looked like, falling from the platform. It must have been a picture.

When the train pulled up, I got on and was pleased to find that I was the only person in the car. Crowds had always bothered me and the commute to and from work had guaranteed that I'd be part of one twice a day for the rest of my life. No more. I closed my eyes and leaned up against the window, my heart slowing from a sprint to a healthy trot. Reflections of cables and cobwebs in the dark tunnels outside the car drifted across my face and a few stops later I dozed off into a dreamless sleep.

I woke up three stops from my transfer, still alone. I noticed a newspaper on the seat across the aisle from me. It was the travel section of the *Toronto Star*, with a cover feature on the Florida Everglades. When I got to my stop, I rolled the paper up and stuck it in my back pocket.

I pulled it out after getting on the northbound train. The picture of the swamps could have been taken from my dream: Spanish moss hanging from mangrove trees, an alligator grinning on a muddy riverbank.

If I never returned to Florida, my feelings wouldn't be hurt.

I thought about the last twenty-four hours: the phone call, my dream, Ronnie Orsulak, my brother. And in doing so, a strong notion swept across my mind like the beam from a lighthouse. Let go. Let go of it all. The hope. The image that had become seared into my mind through revisiting it day after day, year after year: Coleman disappearing into the woods behind my parents' house. My life had become an act of deferral—filling my time and space with disposable things and people that would distract me until my brother came back and real life began anew. It was time for facts. Coleman was gone. Coleman was not coming back. The phone call was a wrong number or a crank. My father was dead, my mother in a nursing home. It was down to me, and I'd have to start again. Strangely, the thought of it made me feel better. I tossed the paper onto the seat beside me and closed my eyes.

When I stood up to get off the train, the paper caught my eye. It had landed back page up to the end of the article and a small sidebar that read: *Man in the Swamps?*

It was an old Florida legend. I remembered Rolly telling the tale, on one of those nights where we gorged on barbecued chicken then headed down to the beach to watch the sun fall into the ocean.

The Everglades, vast, dense and mysterious, had gathered innumerable myths over the years. In the 1960s, a man walking his dogs near Big Cypress spotted what he believed to be a UFO in the sky, hovering above the trees. Seeing the light slowly descending, he went for a closer look. The object emitted a strange whirring sound and bathed the swamp in an orange light.

A group of neighbours found him the next day, wandering blindly through the sawgrass, soaked with sweat and delirious from mosquitoes and unnamed panic. The man was blind and his dogs were nowhere to be seen. "An alligator ate them," I remember saying, always the skeptical one. Coleman shook his head and looked at Rolly. "These things *eat* alligators," he said.

"What things?" I'd asked.

"Aliens, dummy."

I arrived at my stop, got off the train and went up the steep flight of terrazzo stairs.

Man in the swamps. The Tamiami Trail had always inspired nightmares in me, especially at night. I'd driven that stretch of Highway 41 many times, followed the southward shift from Naples to the eastern swath across the swamps toward Fort Lauderdale and Miami. It was the most desolate highway I'd ever been on—nary a gas station, fast food joint, corner store or rest area for miles. If you happened to break down on Highway 41, you were on your own. God forbid that it happen at night. But I remembered something my father had pointed out on one of our countless drives across the swamp: "That's why they have those phone boxes every mile or so. If you break down, then you can call someone to come get you."

I thought of the phone call. And then the lonely sound of a line ringing over and over, echoing off into the dark corners of a hot black night.

I decided it was time to take a vacation. Facing the facts could wait.

17.

AN OLD FRIEND OF MINE always said that drunkenness was opportunity. Then again, he was painfully shy until he'd had a beer or seven, after which point the whole world was his oyster and he was able to do any number of admirable things: piss in a phone booth, start fights with bigger, meaner guys, and once, break his ankle trying to catch a squirrel in his back yard on a five-dollar bet.

He might have been smiling over me as I woke up in the cramped back seat of a pickup truck, shivering amidst empty Styrofoam coffee cups at my feet and a cooler digging into my side. The air was choked with fresh cigarette smoke.

I realized I was in motion.

The light through the windshield woke me up. It played across my forehead as though it were being filtered through a magnifying glass. A headache gathered steam behind my eyes, throbbing like two damaged pistons. I wiped at my eyes and made out two men in the front seat. Baseball caps and scraggly hair.

"We're at the border." It was Duane. I struggled to sit up in the back seat, which was packed with fishing tackle, rods, back-packs, a cooler and two pairs of thick green rubber boots. "Come on, Tiny Tim," Duane said, his bony hand grabbing at my leg. "Get the fucking dope put away, don't think because you're on crutches that they'll be sparing you the fickle finger of fate." He held up his hand, a cigarette squashed and burning between two fingers, and pretended to pull a rubber glove on. In the passenger seat, Donny laughed and shook his head.

"Bad enough we just about had to carry you out to the truck to begin with," Duane said.

Donny smiled and glanced back at me. "You were tired."

Oh shit, I thought, and then it began to come back to me.

The day I went ice fishing with Duane and Donny, Kim had a peculiar phone call. She'd been surprised that anyone was call-ing during the day; most of her friends worked and it was strange to hear the phone ring before five in the afternoon, particularly a long-distance ring. The phone call was from a police officer in Florida, a member of the highway patrol. It was a routine phone call, the man said, nothing to worry about at all. Probably a mix-up. The man was calling from Immokalee, Florida. A week or so prior, he'd been out on I-75 first thing in the morning, feeling the temperature rise, watching for fresh roadkill (it was part of his job to report deer, gators, armadillos and raccoons that had been knocked down during the previous night), basically easing himself into his day the way you would if you worked highway patrol in Florida.

On the stretch of 75 leading into Fort Myers, he spotted a man by the side of the road, tottering along. The officer took him for a drunk and pulled the car to the soft, sandy shoulder.

The man had no identification. He'd obviously been sleeping outside and was cooked to a deep brown. He was tall, slim, and had long, unkempt hair and a beard. The man was shirtless; in fact he was naked save for a pair of ratty, yellowed jean shorts and flip-flops that had seen better days. This was nothing out of the ordinary for the officer. As he explained to Kim, there were plenty of homeless men and women in Florida, only thing was you didn't usually find them wandering the highway in between cities where there was nowhere to sleep or find food, water or shelter. The cop said the stranger was pleasant, forthcoming, and definitely not drunk. When the cop asked if he could take down his information, the man merely shrugged and smiled. He gave the cop a name, a last known address and a forwarding number. My number.

The cop never got a chance to ask whom the number belonged to or where the man was headed. Twenty miles up the road toward Sarasota, a fuel truck making a lane change hit a minivan that had been sitting in its blind spot. There was a fire and possible casualties. The cop had to wheel around and head north, leaving the tall, bearded man on the shoulder staring at the cruiser through the dust.

Kim had started to tell me the morning after my ice fishing excursion and I had dozed off.

I could have strangled her. "You didn't need this," she kept saying. "It was a wrong number. It had to be. I just figured with everything else you're going through . . . what *we're* going through. Besides, the name he gave wasn't . . ."

She couldn't even say his name. There was obviously only one reason that I'd be interested in homeless men in Florida or anywhere else, for that matter. Kim was merely following the protocol we'd lived by before my accident: Coleman was gone and not to be talked about. I'd been living like this for as long as I could remember, first with my parents, who learned that it was too painful to go on hoping that someday Coleman would come home.

In ten years, there'd been nothing, other than the strange calls on my birthday. Not a single postcard from some obscure town in the Midwest with an obscure note scrawled on the back, not a single news story to make us prick up our ears, nothing to rekindle the embers of hope for a call from a hospital in some far-flung town. The knock on the door never came.

Now I found myself thinking my way through it more and more.

The cop had never called back, but he had a name: Manuel Sherrill, Florida Highway Patrol. "I tried to tell you," she said, "but you fell asleep."

"Kim," I said, when I finally managed to unclench my jaw. "I don't think I want to go out with you anymore."

Her head bobbed back with stunned confusion and then she reached out and touched my arm. Seconds ticked past and her eyes filled with warmth and understanding and then the glaze of tears. "This is good," she said. "I think we only really get closure when we work through things. So I'm glad you've opened the dialogue."

I might have wept with frustration. Instead I went to my room to commune with my old ghosts and nurse a warm beer.

After a while, I went out to the back yard. Duane and Donny were out there, drinking beers of their own and picking through a tangled heap of fishing equipment stacked on top of the picnic table. They were about to make their annual fishing trip, and this year they were going further afield: a derby in Bedford County, Virginia, and then another one outside Fort Myers. Sometime between the beer I'd nursed while sulking in my bedroom and the beer that had me playing air guitar on my crutches four hours later, I'd secured a spot on the annual Duaner/ Donny fishing trip. Which, as Duaner put it, "was nothing to fucking sneeze at."

We pulled up behind a late-model sedan dragging a low-riding tent trailer and waited.

"Wouldn't you like to have one of them there," Duaner said. He looked over his shoulder at me. "You're nobody's bitch when you got one of those. You could set it up in your driveway, Jasper, rent it out to Kim and Donny."

Donny shot him a look.

I leaned back into the seat. "Maybe I'll set up in yours," I said. "All that fresh country air might do me some good." I was pleased to see Duane's head twitch at this response. The border guard emerged from the small booth and waved the sedan toward a parking spot adjacent to the customs building.

"Holy shit, boys, we got a bad one. Likely just started his shift. That's when they're at their meanest." Duane put the truck in gear and lurched ahead.

"Hey," I said, noticing a stop sign fifteen feet before the booth. "Stop, Duane."

"No one's in front of us," he said. "Fuck it."

"I wouldn't," Donny said.

"Of course you wouldn't," he said. "You're a goddamn pussy." Donny exhaled.

We pulled up and the heavy-set border guard didn't even look at us. He stared out ruefully through the small Plexiglas window at the sun, which burned off in the distance, unable to even bring the temperature to zero. He ran a thick, T-bone-steak-sized hand over his brush cut, which was so short that I could see beads of sweat glistening on his scalp.

Oh shit, I thought.

"Morning," Duane said. Double oh shit. My father's border crossing procedure had been to never speak first. In his reasoning, a pre-emptive "good morning" worked about as well as "eat shit and die" or "fuck yourself sideways, jarhead."

Another guard emerged from the main building holding a coffee decanter and waved at our man. His lip curled and he nodded back. I supposed they were well used to one another's squint-eyed macho histrionics. "Black two sugars!" he barked through the window. The sound of it made me bang my head off the ceiling in the back seat. The other guard went back into the building.

In the front seat, Duane shrugged his shoulders, kicked the seat back and lit a cigarette. He was one of those guys who got through life with a jovial kind of antagonism toward one and all. Problem was this approach didn't work for everyone. Border guards being somewhere near the top of that list.

The guard pushed off his wooden stool and materialized at Duane's window. "Where are you from?" Then to Donny: "Where are you from? Driver's licences! Get them out!" He cast a yellow eye toward me. "You? Where are you from?"

"One at a time," Duane said. "You're confusing us."

"You looked confused to begin with," the guard said, "back when you missed that stop sign."

Duane shook his head and exhaled a blast of smoke. I watched it hang blue-grey in the sunlight, hoping that it would be the last thing to come out of Duane's mouth. We gave the guard our passports. "Optional stop," Duane said, "not to be heeded unless another car is up front. Army bases, parking lots, et cetera," he said, "border crossings. Check your rulebook."

"Shut up," I hissed from the back seat.

The border guard stretched his neck out, bringing each ear in turn toward a shoulder. There was a pop and a crack that seemed to satisfy him, and he turned back to Duane. Then, a reprieve: the man emerged from the building holding a Styrofoam cup. Our guard received it shaking his head, as if to say "get a load of these morons." I looked out the window at Detroit, crouched in smog across the river.

What he said next surprised me: "Do you have more than an ounce of marijuana in this vehicle?" Maybe they were taught to avoid a logical flow to their questioning in order to mix up possible smugglers. Duane was so mixed up to begin with that this line of reasoning might cause him to actually make sense.

"No," Duane said.

I noticed Donny's shoulders stiffen.

"Okay," the guard said. "You have less than an ounce of marijuana then." Earlier in the year, laws for possession had been relaxed in Canada and the American government, with their on-going war on drugs, was not pleased.

"Yes," Duane said. "I have zero marijuana."

The guard nodded with a smirk. "Where you all going?"

"Fishing."

"Where?"

"At a derby down Bedford County way. Know of it?"

I thought I saw the faintest inkling of a smile on the guard's face. Across the river, Detroit had disappeared into the smog.

The guard leaned on the windowsill. "Humour me," he said. "We have fifty states in this fair country. Within each state, there must be sixty-odd counties. That's three thousand counties laid out behind me. If I happened to know which godforsaken patch of water you ninnies would be fishing on, I might not be standing here. I'd be bending spoons on television for a million dollars a day."

Donny leaned over. "Sorry, sir. It's outside Roanoke, Virginia. Staying there two days, then heading down to Fort Myers, Florida, for a week. More fishing."

"All Canadians?"

I leaned in from the back seat and we answered in unison. "All Canadians."

"Go ahead," he said, then leaned in one more time. "Next time, you ought to drive," he said to Donny. He handed our passports back to Duane. "You let this dill weed do the talking for you and you're liable to end up in trouble."

I half-expected Duane to squeal his tires, but when we pulled away, it was as slow and cautious as if he were doing a driving exam.

"Your mama," he said, under his breath.

An hour later, Detroit towered in the rear-view, all exhaust-stained factories and abandoned office buildings with smashed-out windows and vacant interiors blinking like a hockey player's half-toothless grill.

"The motor city," Duane shouted over the din of open windows. He turned the radio on in time to catch the opening strains of Ted Nugent's "Stranglehold."

"Holy fuck!" Duane looked over his shoulder at me and I felt the truck swerve. "You like this one, junior?" Duane had maybe ten years on me, and to look at him you'd think he'd served them in canine years.

"Not bad," I said.

"Not bad," he said. "Give your fucking head a shake." He began to howl along with the Nuge. A minivan passed us, three boys of about ten pressed up against the back window laughing at Duane.

Donny looked back over the seat at me. "All right back there, Jasper?" he said.

"Doing fine," I said with a laugh as Duane caterwauled along with the guitar solo. "Glad to be here."

"Glad to be here, are you?" Duane said. "Then get this across your chops." He passed his open cigarette pack to me. It was full of immaculately rolled joints all about the size of my baby finger.

"I knew it," Donny said. "I knew it." He turned to Duane. "You promised after last year, never again. Numbskull." He rubbed his forehead with the heels of his hands. "No," he said. "I'm the numbskull. For believing you."

Duane ignored him, although his ever-present smirk seemed suffused with even more self-satisfaction than usual. "Start at the left-hand deck," he said. I took one out. "Tell me what it says." I turned it over in the palm of my hand. There was a word scribbled in blue ink.

"Ohio."

"Take the one to the left of it then. There should be a few for Michigan."

"Duane," Donny said. "Next year, we won't be fishing in any derbies. We'll be making some new friends in a holding tank. A big, strong guy like you will probably do really well, too."

"Never mind, never mind," he said, "you'll all be queuing up to lick my rod when we're through, so get 'em in you and get 'em working and save me the grief. And to answer the man's question, less than an ounce."

I shrugged. "All's well that ends well," I said.

Duane shrieked with delight. "Tiny Tim back there's got more cojones than I thought. Go easy on Michigan," he said, "it's laced with speed." We swerved and a transport rolled past us blowing its horn. "Don't want to be going to sleep at the wheel."

On the radio, Nugent was wrapping things up. I put a flame to the joint and sucked furtively at it. Testify, Ted, I thought, then started to cough.

Twenty minutes and a driver change later, I was staring slack-jawed out the window when a sudden electronic keening made me sit bolt upright in my seat.

"Jesus," Duane said, throwing his head back with a laugh only slightly less jarring, "the old Thai stick's got your nerves a little frayed, eh?"

"What the hell is that sound?" I said.

Duane patted a black object roughly the size of two shoe boxes, wedged between the front seats. "Meet innovation," he said, with a smirk. "This is a state-of-the-art car phone, young Jasper."

"State-of-the-art?" Donny said. "For when? 1990? Where'd you get that damn thing anyway?"

"You remember Cougar McKeon?"

Donny shook his head. "That the guy with the nose whistle?"

"That's a medical condition," Duane said. "Sleep apnea or something."

"He seemed to be awake when we met him at Red Lobster."

The phone kept ringing.

"Someone going to answer that?" I said.

"Probably just Cougar," Duane said. "He's not going to be too happy when he gets into the wine I traded for this bad boy. Ran out of the hot sauce, had to cut it with Thousand Island dressing. Didn't come off so well."

"It might not be," Donny said. "Pick it up."

Duane looked at him warily. "What do you mean 'might not be'?"

"I gave Kim the number."

There was a slap as Duane's palm met his forehead. "You gave Kim the number."

"In case of emergencies."

"Hey," I said, "how about someone picks it up. That ring really is something."

Duane looked back at me, bobbing his head squint-eyed, as if rocking out to some righteous jam. "Ain't it?" he said, then turned back to Donny. "What kind of emergency might that be? A 'needing to throw a wrench in our good time' emergency?"

Donny reached for the phone. Duane slapped his hand away and then picked the receiver up. "Cougar," he said. "Talk to me." I watched him shrink in the front seat. "Oh hi, Kim," he said, "you must be looking for Donny. I'll put him on. It's actually dangerous to speak on a car phone while driving, but I'm assuming this must be some kind of emergency so here he is."

A brief conversation followed, drowned out by the low rumble of four wheels on blacktop, and then Donny handed Duane the receiver.

"She was just checking in. She was asleep when we left so she wanted to wish us luck and to tell us to have a good time."

Duane fiddled with the receiver until it was back in place on the black box. "You know, I guess when your last boyfriend ends up this close to the old dirt nap, you'd want to check in." Duane took his hat off and rubbed at his head. "All this time, the lone wolf, now I'm wondering if I ain't missing out." We drove on. "Shake it off," I heard Duane say, "just shake it off, Duaner."

—

Michigan passed in a blur, flat and unremarkable, small ponds off the side of the highway here and there, patches of forest and the usual slew of fast food restaurants and gas stations. I leaned up against the window and watched the highway run past. The joint had brought my head up and I felt pretty good, although the speed had me licking the roof of my mouth non-stop. Around Toledo, when we crossed over into Ohio, Donny and Duane had a fight about directions. Donny couldn't understand why we'd driven all the way to Detroit to go east again; Duane insisted it was a shortcut. I was just happy to be along for the ride.

We got to Sandusky, Ohio, about an hour away from the junction with I-77 South, and decided to stop for gas and lunch. We'd been going since seven in the morning and the pot had inflated whatever appetite we'd had to begin with. Ohio made Michigan look like a theme park ride and I'd found myself staring out the window, my mind completely blank, mouth agape and fogging on the glass.

"Pull off," Donny said. "Up here. There's a service area."

Duane shook his head and snorted under his breath. I felt the truck pick up speed.

"Whoa," Donny said, "up here."

"No," Duane said, "not 'up here,' actually."

I noticed the tops of Donny's ears reddening. He rubbed at his thick neck and turned to Duane. "Why not, Duane? Tell me: why not up here?"

"Highway inflation, young grasshopper," he said. "We'll pull into Cleveland and get something."

Donny nodded. "Pull into Cleveland. Sounds good."

"They've got you by the short and curlies out here on the road," said Duane. "Gas is more expensive, fuck, even the lousy food they sell is more dear. It's for housewives and vacuum sales-men. I always head into the city."

"Well, that makes much more sense."

Duane looked at him from the corner of his eye.

"Sure," Donny said. "Just pull into the biggest city within two hundred miles and get what you need. Never mind the pain of getting in and out, the rough area you might end up in, or whatever . . . But you got it, Duane." Donny, forever the pro athlete, didn't smoke pot and was still pissed off about Duane bringing it over the border.

"Sweet Donny," he said. "Always with the tried and true." He tapped at the side of his head and looked back at me. "Eh, Jasper? You know what I'm getting at, don't you, man? We're taking old poopy pants here on a paradigm shift. Yet again." To punctuate this, Duane veered the truck onto an off ramp at the last minute. I steadied myself with both palms on the seat.

"I see," Donny said, "and you always want to take the first exit into the city, right, because normally the best neighbour-hoods are built right off the interstate. That much I know. Do you know how I know it?" Donny didn't wait for an answer. "Because we find out first-hand every single year."

"Dear, sweet Donny," Duane said. "You've got to get your ass out of Ontario more often."

"You mean other than our trips, which is the only time either one of us goes anywhere?"

Duane turned the radio on.

It was like we'd driven through a rip in the space-time con-tinuum. I couldn't spot a car built after 1980. A Cadillac rolled past, thumping on hydraulics, the driver glaring at us. The area looked like a thriving place to do business, if your business was buying drugs or getting shot. Grey warehouses with steel garage doors butted up against graffiti-covered low-rises. Abandoned fast food restaurants with windows boarded up stood next to the few establishments still open for business: Ace's Liquor, Bail Bonds, and a 7-Eleven. A red-haired kid who somehow managed to look menacing at the age of thirteen rolled past us on a bike with a low-riding banana seat. He looked like he had the run of the place.

Duane braked suddenly. Two impossibly tall teenagers walked right out in front of the truck, baggy pants hanging somewhere around their ankles. I watched Duane's hand creep toward the horn then move away when the two kids, one black, one white, but both wearing the same "I dare you" expressions, slowed their pace and peered out from under their baseball caps at us.

"Leave it," Donny said.

"Goddamn kids," Duane said through clenched teeth. "I'll beat you like a red-headed stepchild."

"I think the red-headed stepchild went past on his bike a few minutes ago," I said.

Duane pulled away slowly. A beaten-up Cordoba streaked past on the inside blaring its horn at us. "Asshole," someone shouted from the front window.

Duane's jaw muscles clenched like knots in wet rope and we pulled into the 7-Eleven.

I wanted to call Aunt Val, let her know that I was on my way down to Florida. After the phone call on my birthday, I'd resisted the temptation to call and ask if they'd happened to see Coleman, wandering around on the side of some sun-bleached highway. We hadn't kept in close contact with Aunt Val and Rolly Lee. Aunt Val still wrote to my mother, and some years I would get a note at Christmas or a birthday card. The last summer vacation in

Florida had not been a good one. When we crossed the causeway from Sanibel Island to Fort Myers on our way home, I looked back through the window at the white sand, the pelicans diving for fish, the men with their sons sitting on coolers off the road, rods dangling into the warm salt water, and I knew. This was it. Of course, after the events of that summer, it didn't take Nostradamus to see that more vacations in Florida might not be in our future.

While Duane and Donny stocked up on cold drinks and snacks for the truck, I went to the phone booth outside the 7-Eleven. It stood on its own at the end of the sidewalk outside the store, next to a tall garbage can that spewed Slurpee cups and chocolate bar wrappers onto the hot pavement. I might have used Duane's car phone, but I didn't want the guys to hear my conversation. When I stepped into the phone booth, I might have changed my mind. Someone had been smoking inside it, and the mouthpiece stank of cigarettes, bleach and the kind of breath that could bring large men to their knees.

The phone crackled then rang at the other end. It rang again and I watched the red-headed kid appear in the parking lot, circling around on his customized bike. He pulled his front wheel off the pavement and cat-walked toward the phone booth, sneering at me as he went past. It rang again and I was about to hang up when someone picked up.

There was an unintelligible grunting sound.

"Hello?"

"I said yeah." The accent was pure Florida: a laconic burr that might mean laid back, or maybe just aggression dulled by humidity and Budweiser. "Who am I talkin' to?"

"Uh, Jasper—"

"Jasper?" There was a cough. "Never met no Jasper."

"Who's this?" I tried to sound polite and friendly. Possibly the worst approach I could have taken.

"What you mean 'who's this'? Who the fuck is *this*? You selling something?"

"No, no," I said, watching the red-headed kid make another pass. "I'm looking for Val or Rolly. Val's my aunt."

"Like hell." The line got muffled and I imagined a grease-stained hand covering it at the other end. I picked up some dull, low-voiced talking through the line. Then it got clear again.

"All right, Jazzman." The voice had lightened some. "This is Hoyt Lee. Val's my momma. That'd make you my cousin."

I laughed. "No kidding. It'd be cool to meet face to face sometime."

Hoyt Lee was Rolly's son by a previous romantic entanglement, if you wanted to call it that. He'd gone to live with Aunt Val and Rolly shortly after our last trip to Florida, after his birth mother died of a drug overdose.

"Sure would," Hoyt Lee said. "But you still ain't told me what you want."

Aunt Val was out grocery shopping. I decided to save the news of my trip to Florida until I got her on the line. Hoyt said he'd tell her that I would call back.

When I got out of the phone booth, the red-headed kid was sitting next to the garbage can smiling at me.

"I saw someone take a shit in that phone booth last weekend," he said. He smiled, revealing small, yellow teeth. I hoped for his sake that they were baby teeth.

"Sure smells like it," I said.

He flicked a bottle cap out into the parking lot. "Whole place smells like shit," he said. "There's a garbage strike going on. My dad's a garbage man and he's been doing nothing but drinking beer and listening to Indians games on the radio. But I guess you ain't from around here."

"Nope."

"There's a park two blocks up people been dumping their garbage in. Me and my friend Randy been playing King of the Castle up there, until he cut himself on a tin can."

"Stupid place to play," I said. "You guys should be careful."

"Eat shit and die," he said. Duane and Donny emerged from the 7-Eleven, holding Slurpees and plastic bags.

"Come on, hammer," Duane said. "Let's go. You want to be seen chatting up strange kids in a 7-Eleven parking lot? You'll end up in lockup learning the fine points of man love from a dusky gentleman."

"Suck a Doberman's fat dick," the red-headed kid said.

Duane's jaw dropped open. "You little shit," he said. "Someone ought to wash your fucking mouth out with turpentine."

"Yeah, and how about yours, you ugly monkey? At least I'm only twelve, so I'm still going to grow. What's your excuse?"

Donny and I looked at each other. His face had gone a deep shade of crimson, his eyes squinting with the effort of holding back laughter. Duane had his hat off and was shaking his head while he rubbed at his thinning hair. We burst out laughing.

The red-headed kid beamed at us. "Hey, buy me a Slurpee? Would you?"

I gave him two wrinkled dollar bills and we headed across the parking lot to the truck.

18.

MY BROTHER LOOKED UP to Rolly Lee right from the start and his admiration only grew over the next few annual trips to Sanibel. Even in the dead of winter, back in Ontario, Coleman would talk about Rolly Lee like he'd just seen him that day. Coleman had energy to burn and needed adventure. My father worked in marketing for a mid-sized textiles company and he put in long hours. A real company man. Oftentimes, he arrived home after we'd all eaten dessert and were playing in the yard. His plate always seemed to be waiting in the oven, covered with tinfoil. My father worked hard, gave us all the things we needed and a good chunk of those things we simply wanted. But by the time we got to Florida every year, his routine was clear: take his watch off, put it in a drawer, take a stack of paperbacks out to the beach with a beer or two, and wind down. With a return to the rat race two short weeks away, my father's relaxation required a deliberate, focused attack. Our role in this, as my mother often reminded us, was to give him some peace and quiet.

Enter Rolly Lee.

Rolly Lee had a motorboat, a canoe, two bows and arrows, pellet guns and snorkelling gear. Anything that you might imagine appealing to a twelve-year-old boy was littered in or around his and Aunt Val's trailer home. Nobody knew what Rolly Lee did for a living (a fact my father was always fond of pointing out), beyond the odd bit of casual labour he picked up in Fort Myers, helping friends build docks or decks. But Coleman and I could have cared less: he had all the right stuff in stock and therefore might have been the richest man in Florida, if not the world.

My mum and Aunt Val used to go shopping in Fort Myers a couple of times a week. Besides the Shell Factory, a warehouse-like monstrosity filled with every piece of Florida-related kitsch you could imagine, there was a modern shopping centre with air conditioning and a decent restaurant that served half-price beer at lunch. On these days, my mum would leave my father on the beach with his spy novels and bring us into Fort Myers to hang around with Rolly Lee. Who, no matter how long we knew him, never became Uncle Rolly. He was always just Rolly Lee.

Somewhere near the beginning of Aunt Val's third summer in Florida, she and Rolly Lee moved into the Duck Lake Trailer Park, a ten-minute trip off the Tamiami Trail into the less populated fringes of Fort Myers. Forty trailers were spread out over a yellowing sprawl of land that was bordered on one side by a forest and on the other by a swamp. In the hot days of July and August, the smell coming off the swamp was enough to knock you over. Rolly Lee took me aside one day and told me that a dinosaur had died out there. He said he had gotten up one morning to go to work (in hindsight a sure sign the story was pure bunkum) and seen the ridged top of a great beast sinking into the mud. A brontosaurus, Rolly figured. He said that by the time he got home from work it had disappeared into the murk but it would still take years to decompose. Sometimes when we'd walk around the swamp, he'd pick up a shell or a piece of rock and claim it was a bone fragment, clearly amused by my excitement while he and Coleman exchanged conspiratorial glances. I bought the story wholesale and even got into a schoolyard scrap back in Ontario defending the veracity of this tale. But Rolly needn't have told tales: the swamp was full of dinosaurs that were all too real to a ten-year-old like me.

My brother was fascinated by reptiles. I was scared shitless. In the woods behind my parents' house there was the odd garter snake, difficult to find and, from Coleman's perspective, even harder to get excited over. "Glorified worms," is what he called them. In a way, they represented where we lived: a cooler, gentler version of Florida, a place where snakes stayed small and venomless.

Rolly Lee had a knack with reptiles. He'd grown up in the swamps. His father had been an avid outdoorsman and raised Rolly in the ways of the swamp: catching fish, hunting wild boar, knowing which snakes to avoid and how to spot a gator in a mile of water that on the surface was as placid as glass.

One of the first days we got to spend at Rolly's trailer, he took us on a walk around the property. My brother's obsession in those days was with exploring and finding reptiles. We'd already exhausted the area around our cottage on Sanibel: my brother poking through shrubs with a long stick while I observed from a comfortable distance. He had yet to find anything worthwhile, other than the half-shed skin of a small black snake. He kept this treasure on the table beside the pull-out couch where we slept until my mother complained that it smelled like rotten fish and he was forced to hide it in his knapsack.

Rolly Lee's trailer park was full of largish people sitting on lawn chairs, red faces smiling out from under greasy, bent baseball caps. Because we were in Florida on vacation, I think I assumed that everyone else was on vacation too. It would have been difficult to argue this notion within the confines of the park: everywhere we went there was someone offering a beer and a joke, someone interested in us being from Canada, always wanting to know if it was really *that* cold up there and how we liked the Florida heat. There was one older man named Gordon who'd lost a leg during World War II. He spent his days circling the property on his crutches, a cheerful but determined look on his face, sweat welling in dark circles under his arms. When he spotted my brother and me, he would lurch back to his trailer to fetch a couple of cold sodas for us.

On this day, Gordon had some news: "They found a nest of cottonmouths down by the swamp," he said, shifting on his crutches. "Gladys Wilkeson wants us to burn the nest out before some kid gets bit." Rolly Lee pulled at his beer and then licked the stray suds from his thick moustache. "Come on, boys," he said. "What do you say we go take us a look?" Coleman took off running for the swamp.

A portion of the bank had given way and Coleman was standing over it when we caught up with him. "Careful there," Rolly said. "Don't go falling in."

The muddy bank had hollowed out underneath an overhanging brow. "Looks like some kids hacked away at this with a rake or something," Rolly said. In the mud directly below Coleman, there was a nest of writhing snakes the colour of well-water, lighter markings sparkling on their undersides. "Cottonmouth moccasins," Rolly said. "Kill you graveyard dead."

A couple of guys in their early twenties, both with straw-like hair stuffed under soiled mesh ball caps, sauntered over. Both had beers of their own, and one held an oily, large red can in his other hand. Gasoline.

"What's up, Rolly Lee?"

Rolly Lee scuffed some dirt onto the cottonmouths and we watched them writhe, some of the snakes falling into the water, others opening their mouths wide, revealing the silky white inner surface. One snake set out across the water, wriggling like a muscle through the brackish water.

"Cool," Coleman said, "cottonmouths."

"Don't know about cool," one of the men said. "Gene Boggess sure as shit didn't think so."

The other man snorted and spat toward the snakes.

Rolly Lee pulled out a cigarette and lit it. "Where's Gene at now?"

"Living with his dad up in Waycross," the first man said.

The second man looked at us then smiled. His teeth were brown and intermittent. "Gene Boggess got snakebit," he said, looking at us, then spat again. "Lost his hand."

"Is that true, Rolly?" Coleman looked away from the man.

Rolly nodded. "You don't want to get bit by a cottonmouth," he said. "The poison gets into your blood. Gene's hand swelled all up, but he didn't go into the hospital right away."

"Fetchin' a goddamn Frisbee of all things," the first man said.

"Too drunk," the brown-toothed man laughed.

"Too drunk," Rolly Lee said. "Next morning, his hand was the size of a rump roast, blacker than Toby's ass."

"And he shit hisself."

Rolly looked at the brown-toothed man. It wasn't an altogether friendly look. "You can lose control of your bowels," he said to us, stroking his moustache. "Also, fever, chills, and a general notion to jump out of your skin. Gene'd waited another hour, his brains would have been rice pudding." I took a step back from the swamp. Coleman took one toward it and peered over.

The first man set the can down on the grass. "Take a good look," he said. "Not going to be much left when we get done."

"They're amazing," Coleman said, ignoring him. "There must be forty of them down there."

"All right, guys," Rolly said. "What do you say we go back to the trailer for a Coke."

Coleman didn't move from the bank. He sat down on the edge and looked over, his legs dangling off to the right of the cottonmouths.

"Careful, son," Rolly said. I noticed the brown-toothed man shaking his head. "Let's get going."

Coleman looked at him. "What are they going to do?"

"Going to burn them out," the brown-toothed man said. He kicked at the gasoline can. "Pour this down there, drop a match, fix their wagon."

Coleman shook his head.

"Come on, Coleman," I said. "Let's go."

"No," he said. "There's fish in here, alligators too. Isn't the gas bad for them?"

"I don't know about that, son," Rolly said. "Most of it's going to burn off." He looked at the two men. "Canadians," he said, and they all laughed.

"Come on, kid," the first man said, "move up out the way. You don't want to get snakebit, do you? Lose a couple of fingers? Your foot maybe?"

"Bite you on the head, they take it off at the neck." The brown-toothed man leered at Coleman then swigged from his beer.

Coleman shook his head and, keeping his eyes on us, leaned forward and reached over the bank. His hand came up holding a writhing cottonmouth, the swamp water glistening all along it.

"Jesus Christ," the brown-toothed man said. Rolly and the two men backed up.

"Coleman," Rolly Lee said, "that's stupid. Drop the snake back into the water. Carefully."

The first man picked up the can of gas and stepped toward Coleman. "You want to die on your uncle's watch, you little shit? Put the goddamn snake down and get the fuck out of here." I watched for Rolly Lee's reaction, but there was none.

Coleman held the snake out in front of him and walked toward the man. "Don't be scared," he said. "He's just a little one."

The brown-toothed man spit in the grass. "Let's go," he said. "We can come back."

His friend looked at Rolly Lee. "Jesus Christ, Rolly," he said.

We watched the men make their way back across the grass, stopping to talk with a man cooking at a hibachi. I saw them motioning back toward us, shaking their heads, the gas fumes from the barbecue distorting their faces. When I looked back at Rolly Lee, he was grinning at my brother, silent laughter rippling up his sides. "Come on, Coleman," he said. "Put that goddamn snake down and let's get us a drink."

19.

WE ARRIVED IN ROANOKE, Virginia, at sunset. Mountains lay off in the darkness to the east like sleeping giants. We checked into a motel that looked like a row of converted storage lockers and crashed. It had been a long day—the Ohio joints giving way to the West Virginia specials until finally I gave out and went to sleep curled up in the back seat, surrounded by fishing tackle and the standard detritus of any road trip: empty coffee cups, cigarette packages and plastic bags that crackled in the breeze. Add this to the hangover I'd woken up with and my aching leg, and I felt like five pounds of shit in a four-pound bag.

Duane and Donny found plenty to argue about. At home, I'd never seen Donny's patience pushed. But Duane knew how to push his buttons. The man enjoyed debating the relative merits of any particular approach to any particular thing, be it ever so misguided or backward. In Duane's eyes, it made more sense to take a series of arcane county roads out of Charleston because they essentially drew a straight line across the state to Roanoke.

Of course, when we got onto the first one, the speed limit was half that of the interstate and there was a red light every quarter mile. "They must have just changed it," Duane rationalized.

Similarly, in the United States, you could turn left on a red light.

"How's that make any sense?" Donny said. "You'd run into oncoming traffic."

When Duane didn't have a good response he just kept nodding the affirmative, eyes on the road.

"All right," Donny said. "Then how come we've been driving all day and you've never turned left on a red light?"

Duane continued with the nodding, more insistently now. "I'm Canadian," he said after a moment.

On the last stretch of highway before our stop in Roanoke, Duane was clearly trying to get Donny's attention, checking the inputs and buttons on the car phone with a stagy set of sighs, all the while watching the big man out of the corner of his eye.

"All right, Duane," Donny finally said. "Just because I know you want me to ask: What are you doing?"

"Well," Duane sniffed, "just making sure everything's on the up and up with the phone here."

"And why's that?"

"Well, Kim hasn't checked in yet. Want to make sure the phone isn't broken."

"Who said she was going to check in? She just called yesterday to wish us luck."

"Luck, sure. Checking in by any other name."

Donny took a deep breath and stretched his neck.

"You know," Duane said, "not checking in could be worse than checking in."

"Bored, Duane?"

"Just looking out for a friend," Duane said, "you know, when the cat's away and all that. Look at what happened when Jasper here ended up in the hospital, along comes big, brawny Donny with his kind eyes and big hands. I mean I don't know . . ."

Donny pulled out into the overtaking lane and put his foot down. Deliberately or not, Duane's head bounced back against the seat.

"What you don't know would fill a book," Donny said.

The phone rang and the very sound of it, a trebly bleat akin to an aural cattle prod, made Duane sit straight up and clap his hands, a grin spread across his face. "Well, well," he said. "Don't say I don't know women."

"Just pick the phone up," Donny said.

"Yes," Duane said into the black receiver. "We are standing by to respond to any emergency, be it ever so small." His eyes scanned the road as he listened and I saw his cheeks deflate as the grin disappeared. "Cougar," he finally said. "I told you to let the wine sit for a few months. That taste will age right out of it."

When I woke up, Duane and Donny had left for the fishing derby. I didn't have a rod or a fishing licence, or even a remote interest in the sport—if you wanted to call it that. My head was thick with all the hours on the road and Duane's state-specific joints. I was still wearing my clothes from the day before and had sweated through my T-shirt into the mattress. The air conditioner clattered away, sounding like it was choking on thick, tepid water. I got out of bed, limped to the window and turned it up. Then I picked up the phone.

This time, a woman picked up. Though three years of Texas tea and Virginia Slims had passed since we had last spoken, I knew it was Aunt Val.

"Sweet Jesus," she said when she realized who it was. "Rolly Lee, I got your nephew on the phone." There was some mumbling and then, off in the background, a door slammed. "He thinks it's his nephew from Mobile," she said. "Wanting money again."

"I'm good for money," I said, "at least for the time being. I'll give Rolly a call if that changes."

"You do that," she said, with a laugh. "See what good it gets you." There was an uneasy pause. "It's good to hear from you, Jasper. It's been a long time."

"I'm sorry, Val."

"Hey," she said. "It goes both ways."

More awkward silence. I broke it. "How are you? How's Rolly Lee?"

"Rolly Lee hasn't changed one bit," she said. "Still running around like a twelve-year-old with his buddies, you know, doing their thing." *Their thing* suggested any number of activities that might involve drunkenness and/or illegalities.

"Good for Rolly Lee," I said. "Did he ever get a haircut?"

"What do you think? Rolly's the last of the old-time Southern rockers. The whole scraggly bunch will fall off his head before he gets a chance to cut it," she said. "But never mind Rolly Lee and his golden locks. How's your mother?"

"She's good," I said, then caught myself. "As good as she can be, anyway. I see her once a week. She looks forward to your letters."

I heard Val take a drag off her cigarette. "I got to get writing," she said. "I haven't been good with it."

"It's hard," I said. "Writing letters and not ever getting any back. But I read them to her. They make her smile. I think she's got a better idea of what's going on than the doctors give her credit for."

She inhaled, and then what sounded like a sob caught in her throat. "I'd like to make it up there sometime," she said. "I need to make it up there. We're just so damn busy all the time. There's never a moment."

"It's okay, Val." My mother hadn't seen her sister since the last trip to Florida, over fifteen years back. After what happened on that vacation, it had taken over a year for the lines of communication to open again. Even when they did, things had soured in a quietly irreparable manner.

"Listen," I said. "I'm in Roanoke."

There was silence. The air conditioner seemed to get louder, rattling against the radiator.

"Roanoke," she said. "Where's that now? Still in Ontario?"

"Roanoke, Virginia," I said. "I'm on my way down to Florida."

A fly drifted past my line of vision and landed on the mildew-stained pillow next to me, the perfect visual accompaniment for a long moment of dead air.

"Florida," she finally said. "That's great, Jasper."

"I'm travelling with some friends."

"Y'all going to come see us? You on vacation? You're a little late for spring break."

Here goes, I thought. Aunt Val was the closest family member that I could confide in. "I'm looking for Coleman."

When she spoke, her voice was low and pinched. "Coleman?"

"Coleman. My brother."

"Jasper," she said. "You okay, hon?"

"I'm fine. There's a story, but I'll save it. This is just something I need to do."

I could hear her searching for something to say. I swatted the fly off the pillow and watched it circle and then buzz back toward my ear.

"I'll give you a call when I get down there," I said. Then: "If that's okay."

"Of course it's okay," she said, the vague hint of tension beginning to uncoil from her voice. "You just let us know when you get here," she said.

Aunt Val thought I'd lost my marbles.

There was a red, white and blue wreath on the front of Donny's truck, draped over the hood ornament and hanging down across the bug-spattered headlights. After talking to Val I'd lain down on the bed, tracing water stains in the ceiling with my eyes and wondering if maybe I had lost my marbles. When I woke up three hours later, I felt as though years had been tacked onto my life. Since the moment I'd woken up from the coma, I'd been losing sleep.

The truck was parked in the lot across the street, backed immaculately into place as was Donny's habit. The parking lot belonged to the Traveler's Inn, a small blue motel attached to what was billed as "Shaker's Lounge." The letters were faded across a pockmarked blue sign that looked like it had been shot at on more than one occasion. I got my clothes on, splashed cold water across my face and headed across the street to Shaker's, where, as the sign put it, "The Stars Come Out to Shine." I hoped that Duane and Donny were having a cold beer and leaving the local constellations alone. The wreath didn't bode well.

I heard Duane before I saw him, in the moment my palm touched the front door of Shaker's Lounge. I stepped away from it and looked back across the street. The motel room, turn-of-the-century air climate control and all, beckoned to me. I could always use another three hours of sleep.

Shaker's Lounge hadn't seen natural light since sometime around the Battle of Appomattox. I stood inside the door and waited for my eyes to adjust. Outside it was a picture-perfect spring day with the sun blazing overhead and not a cloud in the sky. The only light inside Shaker's was created by the fluorescent beer signs illuminating thick, drifting clouds of cigarette smoke.

"Look who the fuck it is," I heard someone shout. I squinted through the haze. "Come on over here to the winner's circle." Duaner.

Duane and Donny were at a round table in the back corner with two other men and a woman. The woman was blonde, thin and wearing a grin that suggested dizziness brought on by prolonged exposure to heavy sunlight and many tins of Bud Light. She turned her head to look at me and the effort nearly knocked her off the chair.

"Leshondra," she managed.

"Leshondra," Duane said. "You don't look like a Leshondra."

"You already said that," she slurred. "You dingbat."

"Settle down," Duane said, "you're talking to the champ here."

"Jasper," Donny said, "this is Billy, JD, and that's Leshondra."

Duane stood up suddenly. He'd been sitting on his cooler, the white top of which seemed to glow in the dim bar. "And we won the fucking derby!" he shouted.

"Sit down," Donny said. Duane tilted on his feet and then sat down. I noticed Billy and JD looking at each other from the corners of their eyes.

"Your buddy here brought in a pretty good-sized blue catfish," Billy said. He lifted his baseball cap up and rubbed at his thinning scalp. Billy and JD might have been brothers. They were both heavy, balding and red, with matching goatees and filthy baseball caps.

Duane stumbled off the cooler again and looked at Donny. "Never mind, you big pussy, we got to show Jasper here." He lifted the lid of the cooler and I peered in. A cold, fishy breeze seemed to blow out of it.

The fish was so big that it had been bent into a U shape just to fit the cooler. A bright, jewelled eye stared up at me, as if to say, "What now?"

"Thirty-five fucking pounds," Duane said. "Took me an hour to bring it in." He turned to the bar. "Another round," he said, "on the champ." A plain-faced man who resembled JD and Billy only bigger, balder and redder nodded solemnly.

"Smaller fish this year," Billy said. I looked at Duane. His bottom lip hung open and glistening.

"How long have you guys been here?"

Donny looked across the table, his eyes crystal clear in the darkness. "Too long," he said. "Two hours."

"Long enough to finish up the Virginia doobies," Duane said. "Not bad dope, eh?"

Leshondra wobbled in her seat. "When y'all say 'eh,'" she said, "do you mean it like a question or more like a 'fuck yeah'?"

"Shut up, Leshondra." It was the first thing I'd heard JD say, and there was a palpable change in the atmosphere. "A Canadian won the derby." He looked at Billy. "A foreigner ever win the derby before?"

"Nope," Billy said. "Two years ago was the first year they let 'em in."

JD glowered at the table until the next round arrived. I decided to drain my beer quickly, make my excuses and head back to the motel. I grabbed a slice of pepperoni pizza on the way, making doe eyes at an attractive black girl with light blue eyes working behind the counter. Back at the motel, I stretched out and turned the television on. Within five minutes I'd eaten the pizza and drifted back to sleep. Roanoke was all right with me.

I woke up two hours later, the pizza burning like a hot coal in my stomach, radiating dizzying waves of acid up my esophagus. I was alone. I went to the window and pulled the heavy vinyl curtain across. The sun had set and there were now twice as many cars outside Shaker's. When I'd left, hours back, I wasn't sure if Duane was on his way to making lifelong friends or losing the rest of his teeth. I rubbed at my eyes, groaned, and got my pants back on.

Like a bad dream, the first thing I heard was Duane's voice.

"You're not taking this fucking fish, no goddamned way you are."

I pushed through the door and went in. They were at the same table, only the crowd of locals around them had tripled. Donny looked up as I walked in. He pushed his chair back from the table and came over, looking more unsteady than he had a few hours back.

"This is getting stupid," he said, shaking his head. "Stupid." One of the men I'd met earlier, either Billy or JD, had leaned across the table and was banging the tip of his index finger into the table while his face got redder.

"Shit," I said. "I don't think I'm up for much, Donny." I held out my bad leg for emphasis.

"No, no," he said. "That's the thing. These guys claim they're non-violent."

"Pacifists?"

"Well, that's not how they put it, but I guess that's the overall gist of it," he said.

I looked back over at the table. Leshondra was curled up in

the corner behind Duane, a flannel hunting shirt laid across her.

"Well, at least no one's going to be fighting over the woman," I said.

"The way she was headed, she was going to knock one of these good ol' boys on their ass," he said. He raised his beer. "Anyway, cheers, Jas. Glad you came with us." He nodded toward Duane. "It makes for some sensible conversation beyond what wing nut over there can offer."

I watched Duane balance a full shot glass on top of his head. "He won?"

"He won," Donny said, "as hard as that may be to believe."

"What's the problem then?"

"He's done nothing but gloat about winning since we got here," Donny said. "Billy and JD were in the next boat over, so he invited them out for a beer. One became fifteen and now half the derby's drinking in here."

Duane leapt off the cooler and opened the lid again. He danced around it like a carnival barker, flailing his arms and kicking his twig-like legs. His blue jeans were soaked with sweat and beer and looked like two lengths of electrical cord.

"Fucking fish'll turn to rot if you keep opening that god-damned cooler," said a tall, thin man with orange-tinted sun-glasses and a cigarette wagging from his bottom lip.

It was bound to end badly. I told Donny as much.

"I don't know," he said, swallowing his beer. "The derby gets mostly the same guys every year. These guys love nothing more than their fishing, drinking and fighting. Local sheriff in town, his brother's the guy who runs the derby. Things got so bad last summer that they promised to cancel the derby if one single en-trant had been charged with drunk and disorderly or fighting in the last year."

"Progressive," I said, nodding.

"They're trying to decide on a challenge," Donny said. "A way to get a little back."

I didn't get it.

"Thankfully, they're not going to beat the tar out of him," Donny said. "Because I'm so sick of listening to him I'd head back to the motel for a nap before I got involved. But old Duaner's claiming he'll take on any challenge."

I noticed the attention had turned toward where we were sitting. "Shit," I said.

"Don't worry," Donny said, laying a cinderblock-like fist on my shoulder. "I got you covered."

But they weren't looking at us. The attention of every sun-burned, drunken fisherman was trained on a spot just down the bar from me, where in and amongst pint glasses and empty Budweiser bottles sat a murky gallon jar of pickled eggs. Billy got up from the table and sauntered over.

"How y'all doing," he said to us.

I nodded, waiting for it.

"Your buddy there's got a bet with us," he said. He pulled a pack of Marlboro Reds from the pocket of his salt-stained golf shirt and lit a cigarette. "He reckons he can eat this whole jar of pickled eggs," he said, exhaling smoke over the jar like a redneck warlock, "in one sitting."

"Sounds like something he'd say," Donny said, as the bar-tender rushed out of the kitchen carrying a basket of chicken wings.

"He reckons he can do 'er," Billy said, raising his eyebrows. "Whole reason it came up was we had a guy in here a few years back made the same claim. Blew his fucking guts clear out. Right back where we're sitting." I looked over and the tall, thin man with the wagging cigarette pointed at the floor with a solemn nod. I wondered if they'd bothered to mop up afterward.

Back at the table, I noticed Duane and JD, head to head, deep in discussion. Waylon Jennings came on the jukebox singing "Are You Ready for the Country."

"What's he get out of it," I said, "if he does it?"

The bartender poured Billy a shot of Jack Daniel's and he tossed it back with a smirk. "We took up a collection." He nodded at the table. "We'll double his prize money. If he can't fucking do it, and you better believe he *cannot*, we get the money and the fish." He stood up, nodded seriously at us and went back to the table.

"And we're all winners," I said, "because this is so patently retarded."

The first few seemed to go down easy. A crowd had gathered and the bartender had, by request, turned down the jukebox. He did so with a scowl.

There must have been fifteen people clustered around Duane's table. I had the feeling that most of them were fishermen. I surmised this from the predominance of Wellington boots and the overall stench of fetid lake water and rotting fish that seemed to hang over the crowd.

Until Billy opened the jar of pickled eggs, that is.

"Sweet Jesus," one of the men said, fanning at his nose.

"Last time that jar was opened, Hank still had hair," someone else said. Everyone laughed but the surly bartender. He put the glass down that he was wiping and held up a sausage-like middle finger.

"That is rank," Donny said to me. In the corner behind the table, Leshondra moaned and turned over.

Like a prizefighter ignoring the obvious, sneering in the face of seemingly insurmountable odds, Duane sniffed once, cocked his head, and popped two of the eggs in his mouth. The removal of the eggs stirred the brine and I caught a flash of iridescent oiliness through the bar light. There was some cheering and a lot of laughing. I peered through the crowd at the jar of eggs. I had the feeling that it held years of jokes within its murky confines. The overall feeling in the crowd was one of disbelief. Not that someone would try and eat all the pickled eggs, but that someone would even eat one.

"Come on, Cold Hand Luke," Billy said, "we're going to be here all night at this speed."

Duane sipped lightly at his beer. "Not too much," a short man with an enormous red handlebar moustache said. "Carbonation'll kill you."

"Thanks, Red." The man patted Duane on the shoulder and nodded toward the jar. Red must have had money on the challenger.

Egg five and egg six were launched into the hopper. Duane's face contorted. "There's a fucking hair on one of these," he managed.

"You'll be thankful for the fibre tomorrow," someone shouted. By this point, the crowd had filled in behind Donny and me. It seemed that every person in Shaker's had come to watch Duane disgrace himself. He took down eggs seven through ten in a flurry, like a welterweight absorbing rabbit punches. A small belch escaped his mouth. The stink of brine, beer and chicken wings wafted through the crowd. A few people stepped away and went to the bar. Others cheered. Hank pushed the fader back up on the jukebox. Steve Miller's "The Joker" was playing.

By egg number eleven, Red had crouched on one knee next to Duane's seat and was rubbing at his stomach.

"While you're down there," someone said. Duane laughed then groaned.

"The task at hand," Red said. "Focus on the task at hand." He produced a plain silver tube of something from his back pocket and smeared what looked like lard into the palm of his hand and then onto Duane's stomach. When he lifted Duane's T-shirt, a few people gasped. His small, pale stomach looked like it was ready to bust, stretched to the point of near translucency.

"She's going to give," someone shouted. Red glowered in their direction and things quieted down.

"Another," Red said. Duane squinted and then his eyes widened.

"He's done," Billy shouted. "Finished."

For a moment, I was sure he would vomit. Then a massive belch racked his slight frame, rippling his spine from top to bottom. There were groans of protest. The smell reached Donny and me at the bar.

"That man is my best friend," Donny said, then rubbed at his eyes wearily. "How did my life turn out this way?"

I put my hand on his shoulder. "There are a lot of boring people in the world," I said. "Be thankful that your best friend isn't among them."

Red was thrilled with the belch. He patted Duane's stomach and pulled the T-shirt down over it. The brightness had returned to Duane's eyes and he quickly devoured eggs twelve through fifteen. "Holy shit," I heard someone whisper. The remaining eggs lay in the bottom of the jar like stones on the ocean floor, the sea above a cloudy swirl of vinegar, dust and egg detritus.

The last egg might as well have been a stone. It even looked like one. Duane's face was a pale shade of green. The sausage-fingered bartender had shut the jukebox off. Billy, JD, the thin man with the wagging cigarette, Donny, Red and I, everyone in Shaker's Lounge, waited and watched. Duane had eaten twenty-one pickled eggs. Looking at Billy's face, I knew he believed that twenty-two might not be possible, that he might reclaim his money and the fish. He was wrong.

Duane lifted a heavy arm and dropped his hand into the jar. Brine splashed onto the table and the laps of those around him, scattering spectators away from the table. I noticed Leshondra stirring and then saw her sit up on the floor. Duane withdrew his hand from the jar and held the egg up in the light. There he held it, every eye in Shaker's upon it, as though it were a diamond, the last beer in the world or the second coming of Jesus Christ, until it fell from Duane's hand and landed flush in his gaping maw.

The bar erupted. There were cries of protest, cheers from fishermen who enjoyed a good underdog story and had changed sides, and most of all, laughter. Red danced around slapping hands, shaking his head and talking a mile a minute. I saw him lift his shirt up to reveal a thick, waxlike scar across his stomach and realized that Red had been the last challenger to take on the pickled eggs. Leshondra threw her arms around Duane and kissed him, only to have him emit another world-ending belch. Donny looked at me and we broke up laughing. We ordered another beer and a shot of bourbon apiece.

"To Duaner," we said, and tossed them back.

Duaner, for his part, looked like he needed a nurse. He swayed on his chair, cheeks bloated, eyes puffed out and red, an aura of egg and brine wrapped around him like a camping blanket. I thought he might fall from the chair to the scarred, muddy floor, but there he sat, proud as a king. That is until I saw Billy rear up behind him and level Duaner across the head with a thirty-five-pound blue catfish. The fish vaporized into a pinkish blur of scale and gut, and down the pickled-egg-eating champ went.

Back in the room, I sank onto the bed and dreamed my dream of the swamps. This time, Ronnie Orsulak appeared from the swamp fog next to my brother, beckoning me closer and closer until I fell into the thick, boiling water.

20.

AT 10:00 THE NEXT MORNING, we rolled away from Roanoke. It wasn't quite the early start Donny wanted, but more pressing matters intervened. Like Duane's head and stomach. Sometime in the middle of the night, Duane had sequestered himself in the bathroom, an ice pack on his head, his other hand holding his overstuffed gut. Around nine the next morning, he finally emerged, his eyes surrounded by deep, dark circles, cheeks gaunt, the paunch round his middle diminished only slightly.

"I did it," he said.

"Smells like it," I said.

"Come on," said Donny, "let's go before they charge us for another day. Or for specialized cleaning services on that bathroom."

By the time we hit the highway out of Roanoke, Duane had collapsed in the back seat, snoring softly. It was the quietest I'd ever heard him. A beautiful morning had emerged through the thick, dark clouds we'd woken up to. The sun beamed in through the windshield and we rolled down the windows and cranked up some Motown from a local radio station. The syrup-voiced DJ threw to "I Second That Emotion," a warm breeze blew in through the window, and I realized I was happier than I'd been in a while. Since the fall.

Donny wasn't much of a talker. For the first hour of the drive, we rode in silence, listening to the radio and Duane's heavy breathing. There were moments when he seemed on the verge of starting a conversation, but didn't.

"You think he's okay back there?" I said, breaking the silence.

"Sure," Donny said. "Duane's like a cockroach. Nothing can harm the man. Anyone who lives on beer, cheese doodles and cigarettes like he does ought to have died three times by now."

I looked over my shoulder at Duane, his slight frame curled in the back seat. He might have been a ten-year-old boy. "Well, I think he's got his protein for the next year," I said.

"And you," Donny said, looking at me. "You okay?"

I laughed. "I'm fine, Donny."

"What's funny?"

"I don't know," I said. "Don't take this the wrong way, but I can't believe how cool you've been to me. Given that I'm the ex-boyfriend."

Donny checked the side mirror and made a lane change. "You never know how things might turn out," he said. "It's better to help people than hate them," he said. "When I played football, it was all anger. Getting up every day to knock people over. When my career ended, that was it. You let go of that baggage, life gets easier." If this had come from anyone else, my cynical side might have called it bullshit, but Donny didn't waste words. "Besides," he said, "I've been living in your house, sleeping in your bed."

He looked over at me. "Surprised you didn't take a swing at me."
We both laughed at that.

"How long since you've been to Florida?" Donny asked.

"A long time," I said. "I was ten the last time."

Donny nodded. "You excited? Or . . ." There was a catch in
his voice.

"I guess," I said, then told him about my call to my aunt the
day before.

"Damn."

We rode through two miles of silence.

"Listen," he said. "Tell me to shut up if you like . . ."

I knew where this was headed. "Donny," I said. "It's cool.
You're not going to offend me."

"All right." He nodded. "You really think that was your
brother on the phone?"

"No," I said quickly. In the vast blue sky overhead, a pair of
vultures circled languidly.

Donny ran his hand through his hair. "Okay, let me ask you
this then. Why are you on your way to Florida?"

"I don't know," I said. I shifted in my seat and a twinge shot
up through my bad leg. I winced. "You ever lose someone?"

Donny nodded. "Sure."

"Okay."

"But not like this," he said. "I've had people die. Family,
friends."

"I know," I said, "this seems different. A disappearance. But
my brother's been dead to me for over ten years. It sounds harsh"—
I held up my hands—"but it was all we could do. You can't spend
your whole life waiting for something that will probably never
happen. So this was a death. It's just that there was never a fu-
neral. And now something like this . . . Imagine finding out

someone you buried might not be dead." I caught myself. "'Might' being the operative word, of course. It turns things on their head."

"I guess it would," Donny said. "Listen, Jasper . . . I don't mean to dredge all this up if you don't want to talk about it . . ."

"No, no," I said. "I'm just not used to it is all. Put it this way: maybe growing up means going through a series of harsh revelations . . . that things aren't real. There's no Santa Claus, the Easter Bunny is a joke, the girl with the blonde hair in your algebra class will never go out with you, and when you grow up, you will not drive a fucking Ferrari just like Magnum PI." Donny laughed. "So," I continued, "if it seems too good to be true, guess what? It probably is."

Donny nodded. "All right, but look at it another way. Maybe sometimes things work out." We passed a minivan full of kids, suitcases battened to the roof, back wheels sagging, and hit a stretch of open road. "Have faith, Jasper." He caught me looking at him sideways. "Listen, I'm not going to try and convert you." There was a long, ripping fart from the back seat. "I've never even bothered with numbnuts back there." I laughed. "But one thing I know," he said. "Things need an ending. That's what you can hope for."

An eggy waft drifted into the front, strong enough to make us wince. We rolled the windows down and fanned desperately.

"We in Florida yet?" Duane sat up and rubbed at his hair. It stood up in greasy, intermittent spikes like a toilet brush. He lifted up one leg and let out a long, lugubrious trump. "Shit," he said. "Florida or not, we got to stop."

Back on the road, Duane had drifted back into his egg-induced coma when the phone rang.

"You mind picking that up?" Donny said. "Don't want to run us off the road."

I caught a glimpse of Duane stretched out in the back as I reached for the phone. A sliver of a smile had split his sleeping face.

"Hello," I said.

"Oh," a voice said. "Jasper."

"Kim."

There was a barely audible chuckle from the back.

"Where are you guys?" Kim said. "Virginia?"

The specificity of the question ought to have troubled me. "How'd you know?"

"Amazing," she said. "I have a favour to ask." She paused, seemed to consider that. "Actually, it's more of a mission, really."

"A mission?"

"A small detour."

Totally absent was any uncertainty in Kim's voice about our ability to carry out said mission. Now I was troubled.

"You guys stayed in Roanoke last night? So you're near a place called . . . Rattner?" It sounded like she was reading off a piece of paper. Either way, Kim's familiarity with small-town Virginia only intensified the swirl of dread deep in my gut.

"We passed it," I said, "about an hour back. Sorry."

"Just an hour then," she said. "Won't be too bad to backtrack."

"Listen," I said, "maybe I should put Donny on."

"Not if he's driving. But listen, Jasper, I need you guys to do this. I just finished watching a show about a woman in Rattner who makes her own beauty products. An incredible woman. I couldn't believe the coincidence."

"Great," I said.

"It's like fate, really," Kim said. "Because she doesn't ship to Canada."

"Kim . . ."

"Just tell Donny," she said.

"We're past Rattner."

"Rattner's not going anywhere," she said. "And I know you have time. You guys take off on your little field trip, it's the least you can do. It's not going to kill you."

"Kim . . ."

"Jasper, I don't need you to understand because I know Donny will." There was a pause and then Kim issued a set of vague directions. "And I'm sorry for not telling you about the phone call. Sooner, that is."

As I hung up the phone, the laughter began in the back seat.

Vera Vukovich's place wasn't easy to find. Not surprising considering we didn't really have directions, just Kim's description that it was in Rattner, somewhere off the beaten path, near some woods. That described most of the town, save for the ramshackle dwellings on what passed for Main Street. They weren't near any trees, so that narrowed things down.

We pulled over and Donny ran into a hardware store to see what he could find out.

"Just look at him," Duane said. He'd been fairly quiet since Donny had told him we were turning around to pick something up for Kim. "You saw that facing you down in a fight you'd be shaking in your shorts. But that Kim's got him by the nads. Beauty products," he said, voice quiet but venomous. "Imagine."

I shrugged. "We'll be back on the road in no time."

"We've already had to drive an hour in the wrong direction. Tell me, Jasper, would you be making this detour?"

I thought on that. "I suppose not," I said.

"Well," Duane said, and by this time Donny was coming out of the store, the grin on his face transmitting success on the locating Vera Vukovich front. "I guess that's why you and I are still on the market."

Vera Vukovich's was a sprawling ranch-style house at the end of a long drive.

"Old boy in the store asked if we had an appointment," Donny said. "I got the feeling that Ms. Vukovich might be a little particular."

"Well," Duane said, "that settles it. No need to ruffle any feathers. Let's wheel it around and get back on the road."

Donny shook his head and killed the ignition. "Nope," he said. "No can do." He looked at us. "You guys coming?"

We stood on the porch and composed ourselves. A smell of pine and damp, rich soil drifted on the breeze. A bird chattered high up in a tree. "This place gives me the creeps," Duane said, running a hand over the immaculately varnished wood railing. "Just knock on the damn door already," he said.

Donny knocked. There was silence. We could see that behind the swinging screen the door was open. Donny cupped his hands to the glass and looked in. "I can see some stuff on shelves in there," he said.

"All right, Sherlock," Duane said, "you found a house. What can we deduce now?"

Donny shot a glare over his shoulder. "I mean products. Like she's selling stuff."

"Well," Duane said, pushing Donny away from the door. "It's a damn store then. Let's go in."

The house was morgue-quiet but Donny was right—there were things on display on shelves around the room. The natural pine scent had given way to a thick confrontation that took me back to the family functions of my childhood, of being in uncomfortably close quarters with the over-perfumed blue hair set.

"Man," Duane said, running his hand over a shelf. "What is all this stuff?" He picked up a round canister and examined the label. "Vera's Essence," he read. "Is that a fart in a jar?"

"Quiet," Donny said, flashing wide eyes toward the open door that led off down a corridor. "Hello," he called. We listened but there was no answer.

Duane pulled his baseball cap off and scratched furiously at his head. "Donny," he said, "what is it we need to get here?" He peered at the shelf. "Vera's Vavoom? Vera's Vitality?"

Donny ignored him. "I know what I'm looking for, Duaner. Go wait outside if you want."

"Vera's Vivify? Vera's Vicuña Soft?" Duane let out a long, shuddering sigh, then held the label of the last jar up to the light. "A rapturous tincture to render your skin soft as the lustrous coat of the alpaca-like mammals that wander the Andes." Duane looked from the label wide-eyed. "Am I on acid? Where the hell are we, Donny? Because I'm not holding a fishing pole or a beer and I'm sure as hell not sleeping." In the small spaces of Duane's rant, I became aware of another noise: footsteps. "How about Vera's Vienna Sausage?" He looked down at another shelf. "She got that in stock? Because I'm starving. I'd eat the arsehole out of a dead skunk, that is if I wasn't poking around the Avon Lady's parlour . . ."

"You."

It was but a single word but it stopped Duane's rant cold. We turned to the doorway where a diminutive older woman stood, red hair piled high on her head like flames reaching upward. She had cold, fierce blue eyes. The kind of eyes you only found on wolves and Nordic hit men. And they were fixed on Duane.

"You," she repeated, taking a slow step toward him.

I saw the muscles flex along his jawline, watched his Adam's apple bob nervously in his throat.

"Ms. Vukovich," Donny said. "I'm terribly sorry to disturb you but . . ."

"You." She'd kept moving—gliding, almost—toward Duane and now she pushed a small, thin finger into his chest. "You, little man," she said. "Who do you think you are?"

Duane's bottom lip wagged as he struggled to get a word out.

"You walk in here," Vera Vukovich said, sweeping one hand around the room, "in your filthy dungarees, smelling like a fish cannery." She looked him up and down. "With that ridiculous haircut and moustache," she said, "slam the door and that pathetic thing would fall right off your lip. Designed, no doubt, to disguise the fact that you're the same size you were at age thirteen when you started smoking and stopped growing. You rude little man," she said. "I heard you mention you were hungry."

"Yes," Duane managed, his voice sounding distant and dried out.

"What was it you said you'd eat?"

"Vienna sausage," Donny offered, looking at Duane with kinder eyes than I'd seen all trip.

"Quiet," Vera Vukovich said, not even glancing at Donny. "I've no truck with the two of you. What is it you said you'd eat?"

Duane winced. "Was it something about a skunk?"

Her mouth twisted upward with a cold, grim smile. The small blue eyes only seemed to intensify, like tiny bodies of water turning to ice. "Why yes," she said, "it was something about a skunk. But I'm not sure I could replicate your delicate turn of phrase. So repeat it."

Duane shrugged, pawed at the hardwood with the toe of his sneaker.

"Repeat it," she said.

"I'd . . . eat the bum from a dead skunk," he managed.

"The 'arsehole,' I believe it was," she said.

"Yes," he said. "The arsehole. I'd eat the arsehole from a dead skunk."

"Now then," she said, turning to us. Duane looked like he'd had a bucket of cold water thrown over him. "How may I help you gentlemen?"

"Vera's Vein Glory," Donny said, reading from the ubiquitous scrap of paper.

"An excellent choice," she said. "My top seller. Kills varicose veins in a single swipe."

Vera Vukovich lifted a small, square set of reading glasses to her face and peered along a row of her products, murmuring as she went. "Now then," she said, "just a single jar today?"

"Well," Donny said, looking at the paper again, "she didn't say. I better pick up two just in case." He sighed and looked out the window. "Call it three."

The small woman bounced on her feet, wagged her eyebrows and began to smile. She went to Donny and in an instant had his cheek between her fingers. "Now this," she said, looking in Duane's direction, "is a man. He knows that where one might do, three's sure to be better. My kind of man."

Donny reddened. "What do I owe you for that, Ms. Vukovich?"

"For you, let's drop the odd dollars and cents and call it a hundred and fifty even," she said, still rolling Donny's cheek between her fingers.

Duane gave a derisive snort.

"Got something to say, small fry?" She relinquished Donny's cheek and once more stepped toward Duane. I believe I saw him flinch.

Duane held his hands up. "I'm terribly sorry," he said, long-faced. "I consumed a large quantity of eggs last night and am not feeling my best today." He glanced around the room. "This is not my usual . . ." He looked at Vera Vukovich, nearly wincing as he searched for the right word. "Habitat?"

Vera Vukovich took a deep breath and then once again looked at Duaner from heels to hair. "Let me tell you something," she said. "What I'm selling here is possibility. The notion of better times and happier places within reach. The same things I'm sure you reach for in a case of beer. But it's no accident that it's your friend buying my product and not you. You," she said again, the word rolling off her tongue like a curse, "I've spent but five minutes with you and you think you know it all. Truth is you're probably dumber than a sack of wet oatmeal."

"Thanks," Duane said, "that's about what my dad used to say. With more swearing, of course."

The faintest trace of a smile fought against her pursed lips. "You've got a sense of humour though," she said. "That counts." She pulled her glasses off and took another step toward him. Duane shrank back against one of the shelves. "Like I said, potential. It's all about potential." Her eyes narrowed as if gauging exactly how much or little of it Duaner might hold.

"You got a line in palm reading too?" Duane said with a defensive smile.

"Some watch the weather," she said. "I watch people. Enough to know you're a foul-mouthed weasel but maybe not all bad, and enough to know that there's some lucky woman waiting at home for your friend Goliath."

"How about Tiny Tim over there?" Duane said, jutting his chin toward me.

For the first time since we'd entered her house, Vera Vukovich turned my way. I glanced down at the floor but felt her eyes on me all the same. When I looked up again, her face seemed blank. Gone was the look of sharp-edged mirth.

"This one," she said with a nod, "is carrying loss." She pulled a small white tube off the shelf. "Vera's Volitive," she said. "For thwarted wishes. Buckhorn essence, horsemint and jimson weed." She looked me square in the face. "Guaranteed to kill the thwart in one application. That's my treat, son."

"Ms. Vukovich," I said, taking the tube from her hand. "Thank you."

A silent moment passed and then Donny reached for his wallet. "Well then," he said. He settled up for the jars of Vera's Vein Glory and we said our goodbyes.

"You," she said to Duane one more time. "If you've got an hour to spare I could do wonders with those eyebrows and that cookie duster you're trying to pass off for a moustache. You'd clean up okay."

We pulled out of the driveway with the door still swinging behind us.

"I got feelings too, you know," Duane was saying when, once again, the phone began to ring. We'd put no more than ten minutes between us and Vera Vukovich. "A foul-mouthed weasel?" I looked in the side mirror and could see Duane in the back seat, trying to gauge his reflection in the window. The phone kept ringing. "I know you guys look up to me, see me as the Fonz of this crew, but shit, you don't think that hurts?" He turned to the phone. "Good goddamn," he said, "am I ever getting sorry I ever laid eyes on this piece of . . ." He picked up the phone.

"Yes." I heard Duane's breathing get shallow and irregular as he listened. "You've been trying to get a hold of us? It's too late," he finally said. "No, he's not here. Goodbye." He set the receiver down. "Good news," he said, his voice quavering. "Kim says we don't need to make a detour after all. She realized she could have the stuff sent to her friend in Buffalo. Because she thought on it and realized it's just a little *out of our way.*" I looked over my shoulder and caught Duane, teeth bared, trying to rip his baseball cap in half. "I hadn't realized that, myself," he said. "You know, feeling so energetic and full of can-do after eating every pickled egg in the state of Virginia last night. I was thrilled to go on some split-tail reconnaissance mission where I got my ass handed to me by some raisin-faced psychopath. But rejoice, fellows! We don't have to go! Maybe you could call Kim back, Donny, and tell her to send that information to a fucking hour ago when it might have done us some semblance of use." Duane sank into the back seat, his entire body trembling like a divining rod.

"That was Kim?" Donny said.

"No," Duane said. "Whatever made you think that?" I looked back at him, wondering if he might start to weep.

"Well, why didn't you put me on?"

"Doing you a favour, Donny. Whether you know it or not."

From the receiver there came a long, agonized squall. Duane closed his eyes and when he spoke again, it was with a preternatural calm. "Fiddle-dee-dee," he said. "I didn't hang that phone up properly."

Donny reached for the phone. "Hey Kim," he said. "Sorry about that. You know how Duane gets. I got the stuff though." He paused. "Yep. You would have loved Ms. Vera Vukovich. Duane did, anyway. No problem at all. Anyway, I'm driving so I better sign off. Love you." Donny hung up the phone and looked at the road ahead. "Duane," Donny said, "Kim says you sound stressed out. Maybe you ought to ask Jasper for some of that cream he got."

21.

COLEMAN LOVED FLORIDA. In another life, he might have been a wizened swamp rat, an original Florida cracker helping to settle the last true wilderness on the North American continent. My parents always wondered if this stemmed from his being conceived in the Sunshine State, but then again, the same could not be said for me.

Shortly after the incident with the cottonmouths at the trailer park, we spent another afternoon with Rolly Lee. This time, he had a field trip in mind.

When my mother dropped us off that morning, Rolly Lee was loading a heavy steel cooler into the back of his truck. Aunt Val was at work. She'd taken a part-time job waiting tables at a diner on the strip in Fort Myers. It gave Rolly Lee more freedom to "do his thang" as he put it. He waved wearily at us, watching as we climbed out of the station wagon.

"Looks like someone had a late night," my mother shouted, "out at the Warehouse, no doubt." Rolly Lee laughed and feigned collapse. "You look after my boys now," my mum said. Then, to us, more quietly: "You boys be careful." But Coleman had already run across the grass to Rolly Lee. "Sure, Mum," I said. She smiled and laid a tanned hand on my arm. "Keep an eye on your brother," she said, "he thinks he can fly."

Rolly Lee's truck stank of his unfiltered cigarettes and rotten fish. Even with the windows down, the combination of heat and stink was dizzying.

"Bait," he said when I complained. "I got a line on some raw squid." He stuck his cigarette in his mouth, reached down under the seat and pulled out a dirty white plastic container. "Here, Coleman," he said, "take a look."

Coleman sat the container on his lap and opened it. The smell hit us like a ten-pound sledge. "Gross," I said.

"It's not gross," Coleman said, reaching in. He withdrew a slimy tendril of squid and held it out to me.

"Screw off," I said. "Rolly!"

"Now, now, young Jasper," Rolly Lee said, "no one likes a whiner." He winked at my brother and Coleman beamed. "Now put that bait away, Coleman, before you get squid shit on my fine upholstery."

Lake Okeechobee was about an hour east along a clattering, sun-bleached highway that had potholes like teenage boys have acne. Before we got to the water, Rolly Lee had to make a stop.

"An old boy I know's going to lend us his airboat for the afternoon," he said. "Got to stop in Clewiston, pick up the keys."

Main Street, Clewiston, Florida, was like any other central drag in the South. Gas stations, motels battered from years of sun and wind, dingy liquor stores, pancake houses, used car lots and Dixie flags. The only full parking lot on the street belonged to the tavern. Rolly Lee nodded at it as we went past. "Had a hell of a fuss there one night," he said, almost wistfully.

The good old boy Rolly Lee knew lived in a small, single-storey house ten minutes off the strip. He was sitting on his stoop when we pulled up. If he saw us or recognized Rolly Lee, he betrayed no sign of it.

"Rook," Rolly said as we pulled up. "Rook Bannister?" He laughed as he said it, but the man did not. He nodded in our direction and ejected a thick stream of rust-coloured juice into a Chock Full O' Nuts coffee can next to his frayed, sagging lawn chair. Coleman's eyes widened. "Cool," he said.

"Come to get the keys for the airboat, Rook," Rolly said.

Rook Bannister didn't answer until we were within earshot. When he did, I couldn't understand a word he said. His mouth dribbled the rusty water down onto his unshaven chin and I noticed his teeth shifting uneasily. The effect was like seeing someone speak with a mouthful of ball bearings on spin cycle.

Whatever Rook Bannister said, it wasn't what Rolly Lee wanted to hear.

"Jesus Christ, Rook," he said. "We talked about this."

The older man emitted a mushy, inquisitive yelp.

"Two weeks ago," Rolly said. "Over at Jim's." I recognized the name from the tavern on the way into Clewiston.

Rook shook his head and punctuated the thought with an emphatic expectoration into the can. More garbled words stumbled from the swamp of his mouth.

Rolly Lee took his cap off and ran his fingers through his hair. Back behind the trailer, I noticed a peanut-butter-coloured dog straining and salivating against a chain. I swatted a mosquito off my leg.

"For fuck's sake," Rolly Lee said. "Clear your mouth so I can hear what you're saying."

Rook Bannister kicked at the sand in front of his chair and reached into his mouth. Coleman and I watched wide-eyed as he pulled a yellowed, oversized set of false teeth out of his mouth and dropped them into the coffee tin, where they floated in the sepia water amidst ragged strands of tobacco and downed mosquitoes.

When he spoke again, it was with new clarity, although now his mouth distorted and shifted almost magically. "You're not going anywhere near my goddamned airboat, Rolly Lee." He shook his head. "Already told you that." His lips touched the tip of his nose for emphasis.

"Fuck's sake, Rook." Rolly Lee's eyes narrowed. A grey-haired, shirtless man went past the end of the driveway on a ride-on mower. Rook waved at him. Rolly's eyes never moved.

"Rook," he said. "Go on and get me the keys."

"Nope," Rook said, shaking his head emphatically. He reached down to the coffee can, shook the excess juice off his teeth and then popped them back into his mouth. His face shifted as they found their rightful place in his mouth. Case closed.

A pair of large black birds, their wings shining iridescent in the afternoon light, touched down in the back yard, sending the peanut-butter-coloured dog into a frenzy. Rolly Lee rubbed at his temples. "Christ on a crutch, Rook. Do something about that goddamned hound."

Rook glared at him, then turned his head toward the back yard. A jarring, unintelligible sound came out of his mouth. The birds took off with a cackle and I watched the dog lie down under a pine tree, the weight of remorse heavy in his soulful eyes.

"Boys," Rolly said, "go on and wait for me in the car."

The truck stank even worse. Watching Rolly Lee and Rook discuss the airboat from inside, I swear my ears started to ring with it. "What do you think he's saying?" I asked Coleman.

"Shh," he said, "I'm trying to listen."

"You think they're going to scrap?"

Coleman shook his head and swatted a bug off the back of his neck. I shifted uncomfortably on the bench seat and the scalding buckle of the seat belt touched the small of my back. I howled in protest.

"Shut up, you goddamn baby," Coleman said. He sounded like Rolly Lee.

We could see Rook Bannister shaking his head as if it were run on a motor.

"Guess we're not going," I said.

"Look," Coleman said.

Rook Bannister had stopped shaking his head. Something in Rolly Lee's hand glinted in the sunlight, down by his side. When he motioned toward Rook with it, I realized it was a knife. We saw Rook get up and go into the small trailer, slamming the door behind him.

Two minutes later, Rolly Lee jumped back in the truck grinning, the keys to the airboat in one hand. "All right, boys, let's go," was all he said.

Lake Okeechobee was a massive expanse of brackish water shot through with sawgrass and peppered with small islands that Rolly Lee called hammocks. We picked up the airboat not fifteen minutes from Rook Bannister's place and set out across the lake, kicking up a storm of mosquitoes, weeds and water as we went. Other men in airboats and motorboats gave Rolly a nod or a wave as we went past. One man, in an official-looking brown shirt and hat, paid us a little more notice, watching us until we'd gone past. I waved at him and he gave a short nod. Rolly noticed this and shook his head at me. "Game warden," he shouted over the din of the engine.

The fan from the airboat was nearly deafening. I noticed others wearing the orange headphones I'd seen on construction workers back home in Ontario. Rolly Lee didn't bother with such trivialities. All he'd packed was the squid, a case of beer filled with ice, and a couple of bags of chips. Lunch for us, I guessed.

Once every other boat on the lake was out of sight, we stopped to fish. Or at least Rolly Lee and Coleman did. I was too fascinated by the bugs that glided over the water, the large bullfrog I'd noticed darting under a lily pad, and what looked like an endless prairie off in the distance, floating under thick white clouds. We were a long way from Ontario.

The fish didn't seem to be biting. "Go on and grab your rod, Jasper," Rolly Lee said. His long blond hair hung out from under his dirty red cap and stuck to his cheeks. The incident with Rook Bannister seemed to have soured his mood. "Got to let these goddamn fish know we mean business." He punched my brother in the shoulder and I saw Coleman wince. "Right, Coleman?"

"Right, Rolly." Coleman bit his lip and cast out again.

An hour later, the sun had risen higher and burned even hotter. I wouldn't have thought it possible. I'd given up swatting the mosquitoes from my legs, arms and neck. The stink from the open container of squid was making me dizzy. Rolly Lee must have seen it in my face.

"Goddamn, Jasper, you're greener than a bullfrog." He spat in the water and sighed. "Reel in, Coleman," he said. "Let's pull up on that island over there and give your little brother a break." He put the emphasis on "little." As he fired the engine up, a serious-faced white bird landed on the water in front of us. Rolly Lee gunned the boat right at him. I watched the bird take to the sky, his long orange-brown legs tucked straight back underneath him. The sight of him looking back at us made me want to cry. Instead, I vomited over the side of the boat. When I'd finished, I turned around and looked at Rolly Lee. His lank hair was whipping back over his shoulders, his eyes impenetrable behind dark glasses, but I could tell he was looking at me, a sneer on his face, words I could not hear muttering across his lips.

Once on land, Rolly Lee chugged the first can of beer then went for another. This time he grabbed three cans and threw two of them at Coleman and me. They landed in the water just off the hammock. "Nice catch," he said. Coleman waded out through the sawgrass and picked them up. "Watch them gators," Rolly shouted. My brother ignored him and handed one to me.

"Let me show you how to drink a beer, boys," Rolly Lee said. He pulled the tab, turned the beer upside down and tilted his head back. I watched his legs move unsteadily in the muck of the hammock as though he were balancing something on his nose. He drained the can, and then squashed it easily in his hand. "Bet me," he said, taking aim at a palm tree on the hammock. Rolly Lee went into a wind-up and threw the can. It plonked unsatisfactorily off the tree trunk. Rolly Lee gave a whoop and went for another beer.

"You better pick that up, eh Rolly," Coleman said.

Rolly Lee swigged from his beer, crocodile eyes peering over the rim of the can. Finally, when he'd swallowed, he wiped his mouth and said, "Eh, Rolly, better clean up, eh Rolly." Coleman's back stiffened. "Sound like your soft little bro there, Coleman," Rolly said. "Toughen up."

I felt the nausea hit me again and I threw up into the sawgrass. Coleman took my hand. "Stand up," he said. "Now." He led me back away from the water and sat me down under the tree.

"There aren't snakes here, are there?"

Coleman exhaled and closed his eyes, waiting for it.

"Y'all afraid of snakes, afraid of the water, afraid of every good goddamn thing," Rolly said. "You're lucky you got an uncle who can toughen you up." He leaned back unsteadily, unzipped his fly and peed into the water. "This water's cold," he said, then in the absence of any of his drinking sycophants added his own punchline: "And deep too." It was lost on us. He zipped his fly and pulled a bent cigarette from his pocket. "You fraidy cats sit tight," he said, "your uncle's got business on the other side of this here hammock." He wobbled out of sight. A match was struck and a sweet, foreign smell crossed my nose. Coleman shook his head. Then I saw his eyes alight on the water.

Something that looked like a log, only with symmetrical bumps and ridges, was floating in the water just off the hammock. "Wow," Coleman said. The log appeared to rise out of the water a couple of inches and I realized what it was. "Wow," Coleman repeated. He stepped closer to the water. On the other side of the hammock, I could hear Rolly Lee singing, his low voice cracking and bending notes like the country singers he played in the truck. Coleman stepped closer still, and as he did, the alligator suddenly thrashed in the water. I caught a glimpse of teeth and the soft, pink inside of his mouth and he disappeared under the water. "He got a turtle," Coleman said.

I believe I whimpered.

"Fraidy cat, fraidy cat," I heard Rolly Lee sing.

I noticed more logs in the water. It seemed to get hotter and I took a furtive sip at the beer, which was now warm. Small red ants crawled over my feet and bugs I couldn't see pinched at my arms and legs. Waves of humidity seemed to roll off the surface of Lake Okeechobee. I felt like I was seeing through gasoline fumes. It was like I'd died and gone to hell.

"One, two, three, FOUR!" Coleman counted the logs. "There's more," he said, "there has to be more." He waded out into the water until it was somewhere between his ankles and his knees. "Five," he said. "Look, Jas, out toward the horizon, near where that pelican is. Six."

"Come back," I said. "Please."

Coleman laughed. I could still hear Rolly Lee singing. "Don't worry," my brother said. And he waded out a little deeper. I watched the logs react to this new, foreign presence in their water. They seemed to scatter and then realign with a near-magnetic grace. The water was up to my brother's waist. I watched it lapping against the bottom of his T-shirt, turning the baby-blue to navy. I vomited under the palm tree, my stomach attempting to turn itself inside out. "Fraidy cat, afraid of the dark," I heard Rolly sing. I watched my brother and tried to call him back, but the words would not come. The beer was on its side, the foamy contents sucked into the loam of the hammock, my throat a dry gulch.

Only Coleman's head was above the water. The logs were all around him now. My brother's eyes were wide and bright, a combination of joy and disbelief on his face. "I can feel them against my legs," he said. "Hey," he said, then put his hand under the water. "One just bumped my leg. Bad gator," he said, as though he was scolding a poodle or a hamster. "Check this out, Jas," he said, then disappeared under the water.

A crumpled can landed by my side. "Look out, boy." Rolly Lee peered from around the palm tree, eyes like a Cheshire Cat. He laughed, then looked around. His face immediately sobered. "Where's your brother?" I managed to point toward the water where Coleman had just surfaced.

"I can see them under the water," he said. "Smiling at me. They want to play."

Rolly Lee's mouth dropped open. "Shit," he managed. An alligator swam around my brother and then rolled, his soft, pale belly reflecting light before it disappeared under the water. Another did the same. More logs floated around my brother. "They feel softer than you'd think," he said, "like frogs."

"Get out of the water," Rolly Lee said softly. The aggression seemed to have gone. "Get out of the water and let's go on home," he said. I dry heaved under the tree again. Rolly Lee took his hat off and ran his hand back across his forehead, his eyes widening. He looked out at my brother again, laughing and swimming with the alligators. A thought seemed to occur to him and he spoke again: "Please," was all he said.

We packed up and rode across the lake in silence. The sun had fallen in the sky and the bugs were out in earnest. Rolly Lee could barely muster the energy to swat them from his neck and arms. A plastic bag of crumpled beer cans sat at his feet. My brother rode all the way back with a smile on his face, his eyes closed and the wind in his hair.

When my mother picked us up, her jaw dropped. We were both sunburned and it was all I could do to summon the energy to get into the car. "Thanks, Rolly," she shouted out the window. "Should have lathered you guys up a little better with sunscreen," she said. "That man's head is in the clouds." We let it rest at that. It had always been my nature to be open with my parents, to tell them everything that happened to me. This time, I kept the details of the day to myself. I would later wish that I had opened my mouth.

The next time, Rolly Lee left me with my aunt while he and Coleman ventured out into the swamps. If Lake Okeechobee had been the warm-up for the real deal, the swamps, I'd failed the test.

Unlike Coleman, the boy who swam with the alligators.

22.

WE DIDN'T STOP DRIVING after we left Vera Vukovich's. The
wheels rolled beneath us endlessly, to the point of disorientation,
so that when we stopped for a pee break, I felt like I was stepping
off a fishing boat. The next derby was on Lake Okeechobee and
Donny aimed to get there with time to spare. "This one better
not be a goddamned circus," he said, then caught himself. "*Gosh
darned*, I mean. Kim would kill me if she heard that." He smiled.

The way he drove said a lot about his personality. Five miles
above the speed limit all the way, he kept the captain's chair for
the entire day, his thick fingers flexing around the steering wheel.
Donny was a classic case of slow but sure. As gentle as he seemed,
I knew that anyone who'd made a living as a linebacker likely
wouldn't acquiesce once the bit was between his teeth. For his
part, Duane passed the drive supine in the back seat, the occasional, residual emissions of eggy gas reminding us that he was
still alive, while I sat rubbing at my ever-stiffening leg in the
passenger seat.

"Must have hurt," Donny said, as we passed signs marking
the turnoff to Sweetwater, Tennessee. My family had once spent
a night in Sweetwater after our station wagon threw a rod. I remembered nothing about it other than our hotel room smelling
like an ashtray and my father being biblically mad.

"Your leg," Donny said, interrupting my reverie.

"Like hell," I said, and then caught myself. Donny looked at
me askance and we both laughed. "Still does," I said.

"I remember when I broke my leg," he said, "it made a sound
like if you backed a truck up over a walnut." I grimaced. "I knew,
too," he said, "as soon as it happened."

"Knew what?"

140

"That it was over." He shook his head and tapped at the dash. "That it was going to be time to head home and forget about football. Once you hit 275 pounds, your knees are on borrowed time anyway."

I nodded. "The doctor says I should be happy I can walk on it at all."

"Well, you've been working hard on your physio. But you've been blessed, too. Life is full of things to be happy about," Donny said.

I nodded, my bullshit detector quaking in my chest. "I guess it's all relative," I said. Far up above the highway, I noticed a vulture circling. I searched the blue for his partner and realized I was watching an eagle.

"Spare me," came a voice from the back seat. "We going to stop soon? That'd make me happy. I'm crippled up back here like a dog trying to fuck a football."

Donny looked over his shoulder. "And you wonder why strange Americans would be inclined to hit you over the head with a catfish," he said.

I ran my finger up and down the raised, purple scar on my leg and watched Tennessee blur into Georgia. If there'd been an on-ramp to this strange, unpredictable journey south, it started with the scar.

Somewhere south of Atlanta, on a desolate stretch where, in the darkness, the pines loomed up from red soil like Confederate ghosts standing sentry, the phone rang once again.

Duane, like Pavlov's dog, began to twitch. "No," he said, "no more." He picked it up. "Yes, Kim," he said, "what can we do you for?" He scratched furiously at a patch on his neck that had begun to redden with the first sound of the ring. "Cougar," he said, "I told you to let it sit." Duane paused and I could hear Cougar yelling down the line. "Not my fault, Coug. Not my fault you're all sick as dogs. No, no, goodbye, Cougar. Goodbye . . ."

He'd no sooner hung up than the phone started to ring again. "Let me find the ringer," he said. "I'll fix this rotten dog-faced phone."

"Dog-faced phone?" Donny looked at me and we stifled laughter.

"No ringer switch," Duane said, turning the big black box over in his hands. It was still ringing. "No ringer switch. No problem." He set the phone back on the floor and began to pile our bags on it. The phone stopped ringing.

Inevitably, a short time later the stack of bags slid off the black box and just as inevitably, the phone began to ring again. "Pull over," Duane said. He pushed the door open with his foot and a glorious wash of thick, damp air rushed into the truck. I watched him walk to the shoulder, phone in hand, headlights illuminating an aura of gnats around him.

Duane stood at the shoulder's edge and raised the phone over his head. As the black box hit the ditch water, it began to ring once more, until the electronic bleat began to fade, like the final death throes of a bullet-struck animal.

A few hours later, Donny nudged me awake. "Jasper," he said, "wake up." I came to and realized it was dark out and we'd slowed to a near crawl. The last few months had taught me to expect the worst. We'd been in an accident. Or perhaps Duane had had an accident. I sniffed at the air like a hound and came back with the usual road-trip scents: stale coffee, staler breath and the hot Southern air drifting in from the night sky through my open window.

Off the highway, I could hear the drone of insects: cicadas, crickets and the buzzing hordes of mosquitoes. They carried the smell of the swamps from the trees, through ditches filled with thick brown water and out to the highway with the flutter of a million pairs of wings. The smell was akin to finding a long-forgotten, yellowed Polaroid. It was sulphur and thick vegetation, boggy water and humidity, dead things sinking into the primordial ooze and returning from whence they came. It was Florida, the land of my memories and my nightmares.

"We just passed the welcome sign," Donny said. "I thought you'd want to know."

I closed my eyes and drank in the smell. I knew full well that sleep was out of the question.

23.

THE NEXT AFTERNOON, surreal as it seemed, we were on our way to Rolly Lee's. We'd arrived in Fort Myers somewhere between two and three in the morning and checked into a motel room. Duane was just waking up. Having spent the whole day recuperating from the physical and mental stresses associated with eating two dozen pickled eggs, he was full of energy. Donny and I weren't. Fifteen hours of driving had left dark, greasy circles around Donny's eyes, and my bad leg was feeling like something slow and heavy had made a return pass over it.

I woke up before Donny or Duane and let myself quietly out of the room. Even though it was early morning, the asphalt was oven-hot under my bare feet and I had to hop from leg to leg until I got used to it.

I might have been anywhere; such were the landmarks outside the motel: a McDonald's, a pancake house, a couple of gas stations with trucks pulled up at the pumps, a used car lot, and further off in the distance, an overpass for the major highway that stretched like a black ribbon along the periphery of Fort Myers. But I wasn't just anywhere, and all the little details reminded me of that. The smell in the air, an equal mix of sand and swamp and gasoline, the sole palm tree growing on a lean just outside our room, the sun-baked, slender men on the street, cigarette packs rolled into the sleeves of their sweat-stained T-shirts, their heavy-set, waddling wives, the black family laughing as they went past in their burgundy van, the sound of country music catching on the damp, heavy breeze—this was Florida. More than anything, it was the ineffable feeling that I was within the invisible borders of my most vivid memories—the happy times that stood like highway markers and the darkness that moved out of sight like animals darting across I-75 in the black of night.

I watched a skinny, slouching man in torn jeans wander across the street to the gas station. He disappeared behind the store into the greenery beyond a garbage Dumpster overstuffed with soggy, misshapen cardboard boxes. I tried to imagine Coleman down here, living out some strange, solitary life, eating out of garbage Dumpsters or living in a psychiatric hospital, and found I couldn't. I closed my eyes and pictured him disappearing into the forest. When I opened them, the skinny man reappeared from behind the Dumpster, buttoning the fly on his ratty jeans.

I never would have remembered the way to Rolly Lee's, and as Aunt Val told me on the phone, "Oh, we moved, honey. Long time ago. Just a stone's throw up 41 though."

If she'd sounded a little strained when I'd first talked to her, this time she was as sweet as a slice of key lime pie. "Get on over here, Jasper," she said, "and bring your friends, we're having a cookout."

I decided to avoid any further discussion of Coleman with Aunt Val and Rolly Lee. For now.

It wouldn't be any stretch. I'd been avoiding the subject for as long as I could remember.

Being back in Fort Myers—and behind the wheel no less—was a strange sensation. Since I'd been here last, every major event of my life had taken place: first cigarette, losing my virginity, first fist fight, first paying job, learning how to drive, the loss of my father and my brother. I had a sudden flashing memory of myself at ten, trying to get my head around the fact that one day I'd be able to drive. The thought of it was like being told you'd turn into a girl at age twenty-five. Only having sex could have seemed more abstract.

"Goddamn," Duane said, "you used to come down here on vacation?"

We were stopped at a traffic light. In the car next to us, two unshaven, shirtless men, tanned to a deep brown, stared at us, the passenger holding a beer. On one corner was a gun shop, on the other, a bail bondsman. I wondered where they were headed.

"Not here," I said, "close to here. Sanibel Island. About a ten-minute drive to the causeway, then another ten to the island. It's paradise." It was true. Crossing the causeway to Sanibel was like cresting heaven.

"So is this where they send the people who've been bad?"

"Think of it this way," Donny said. "These people never have to shovel snow."

"They can't have been that bad then," Duane said.

We drove north through Fort Myers until gradually the low-rise cityscape began to fade into a backdrop of scattered Australian pines, ditches filled with tea-coloured water and open fields with thick, ankle-length grass. Donny read the directions as we went.

We got off Summerlin and headed for the Tamiami Trail, which would take us over the Caloosahatchee River and to Rolly Lee's. I had a knot in my stomach the size of a Georgia peach.

Donny sensed that I was feeling a little tightly wound. "You all right?"

"Yeah." I nodded. "Just been a long time, that's all."

"They never come up to see you?" Duane said.

"I don't think Rolly Lee'd make it across the border," I said.

Donny shot Duane a sharp glance. "Yeah, well," he said, "some might say the border's not as airtight as everyone thinks."

"Whoopee shit," Duane said. "Rolly Lee's a criminal, I'm a criminal. We all ought to get along famously."

I laughed softly, the wheel in a white-knuckled clutch.

"Shake it off," Donny said to me. "It'll be fine."

As we crossed the river, Duane asked me, "You think there are gators in there?"

I laughed. "Does a bear shit in the woods?"

"Man," he said, "I got to check one out, I've never seen one."

"That's because you're lily-livered," Donny said.

Duane looked at me and shook his head. "I don't think he realizes who he's talking to," he said. "You know, the champion of the Roanoke, Virginia, fishing derby."

"And unofficial egg-eating competition," I added.

We made a right turn near a trailer park onto a quiet gravel road, flanked on either side by deep ditches. The previous November, a hurricane had made landfall near Cape Coral and the outer fringes of it had ruffled North Fort Myers. The cleanup was still in progress. In the corner of the trailer park closest to the road, there was a pile of scrap metal and broken glass. Two shirtless men and a young girl in pigtails were dropping splintered sections of wood into a fire. They stopped what they were doing as we went past, as if they could smell just how far from home we really were. It made me think of an afternoon years before, during a brilliant Ontario autumn, my brother and I carrying armloads of brush from the front yard to a fire in the back. I remember Coleman grabbing me by the shoulder and looking closely at my face, then collapsing with laughter when he saw that I'd singed my eyebrows and eyelashes to a dull, frizzled nothing.

We rolled slowly along the road for a while, the gravel crunching under our wheels and the sky darkening overhead.

The rain started quickly. Nickel-sized drops spattered against the windshield, at first torrentially, then in a way that might only be described as blinding. I pulled the truck over to the shoulder when, even with the wipers on high, I felt like there was a waterfall on the roof of the truck, cascading over the windshield.

"Holy shit," Duane said. "That's rain." I nodded, watching the drops seethe against the hot gravel, causing a fine mist of dust to hover up off the road. Five minutes later it felt like it was letting up, so I turned the truck back on. As I did, I heard a rumble somewhere behind me. The rear-view revealed nothing but rain and road.

"Hey," Donny said. "Check this out."

The roar had come up behind us. Two men, soaked to the skin, driving an all-terrain vehicle. They sped past in the grass on the other side of the ditch, cut hard, soared across the open space of water, hit the gravel road two feet in front of our truck and quickly disappeared ahead, wagging their fingers at us.

"Morons," Duane said as I pulled away. The rain had stopped and the sky was already beginning to brighten.

"Morons," Donny said, looking over his shoulder into the back seat. "You don't think that'd be you if you lived here?"

I was convinced we'd gotten ourselves lost until I saw the two-by-four nailed to a post with "Lee" written on it. I turned down another road, this one a narrow strip of dirt gone to mud in the rain. The truck bumped over thick roots and scattered storm debris—branches and an odd array of garbage. There were tin cans, sodden and torn beer cases, a bike wheel, and a magazine that flapped open as we went past.

"Slow down," Duane said.

But I already had. As the bush closed around us, shutting out the bright, open space around and above, so had the debris. Now the garbage took on a more organized, utilitarian bent. Propped up against a thick pine were the central parts of a motorcycle, wheel, frame and handlebars. I wondered if the smaller bits were in one of the wheelbarrows lined up like a battered, one-wheeled infantry behind the tree. To the right I saw three rusty boat engines collecting water under a shrub. A rowboat rested uneasily ten feet off the ground in the thick branches of a gumbo limbo tree. Bicycles. Tricycles. Car doors, roofs and hoods. A shopping cart full of windshield wipers. A kiddie pool full of beer bottles. It was as though an automotive supply warehouse had been lifted by the hurricane in Cape Coral and dropped onto Rolly Lee's property, without the niceties of aisles or walls. Fifty years back.

"This makes your place look like the Playboy mansion," Donny said over his shoulder.

Duane's mouth hung open. "No kidding," he said.

"What's all that shit in the trees?" I'd noticed what looked like wires and bulbs, with the occasional box strapped to a branch.

"Christmas lights," Donny said.

"It'd be a bitch to get out of here in the dark," Duane said. "Awful nice of your uncle."

"He's not really my uncle," I said.

The array of mechanical debris continued. It seemed that every tree had something metal leaning up against it, every fern, shrub and bush had an engine or a wheel beneath it. Rolly Lee's property was like the world's largest flea market. We continued deeper into the woods, the three of us silently taking in the sights as they slowly went past. A loud squawking sound from outside the truck made me jump. I heard Duane's head hit the roof of the cab.

"Goddamnit," he said, "bumped my bean."

"Shhh," Donny said, "roll down the window."

We pulled up alongside one of the trees with a box strapped to it. When it crackled, I realized it was a speaker.

"Hello there," a honeyed Southern voice said. "Please note trespassers will be prosecuted. This is your last warning. All of y'all turn around and head back from whence y'all came. We will shoot first and ask questions later." A drip of water landed on the speaker with a crackle and I heard laughter through the box. "Unless y'all are the foreign diplomats we been expecting. The party of Snow Mexicans."

We sat there with the engine idling, listening to the speaker crackle. I heard a woman's voice somewhere in the landscape of static and hiss. When the voice spoke again, it did so with a laugh. "Come on up, Jasper, come on up and see your uncle."

"What the fuck's a Snow Mexican?" Duane said.

"We are," Donny said.

A little further on, the road ended and the trees opened up, revealing Rolly Lee's house and front yard. We drove into a sort of circular parking lot area, roughly half the size of a football field. There were mud-covered trucks and four-wheel-drive vehicles parked on the gravel and the grass. I noticed the vehicle that had passed us, the engine still tick-ticking as it cooled down and muddy water leaking from its undercarriage. Closer to the house, there was a barn-sized garage. Men milled around in front of it, a few standing over large steel drums, welding without goggles with a beer in one hand. And, much like the drive in, everywhere I looked there were spare auto or boat parts stacked and leaning, many out in the open area, rusted to a deep orange.

The house was a smallish bungalow, white with one set of shutters hanging off it. I could see a thick spire of smoke rising up from behind it, and more people milling about, some with paper plates filled with hot dogs, burgers and potato chips, all with a drink or a can of beer in one hand. There was a large blue tarp stretched across a span of trees in the back for people to stand under if it rained.

When we pulled in at the edge of the open area and parked the truck, I noticed a group of men behind the barn. An overweight man with a massively distended bare stomach and matchstick legs was throwing up beer bottles while a rough, smoke-smeared artillery of men were taking aim and firing with slingshots and pellet guns. As we got out of the truck, I heard one pop and shatter. There was a chorus of whoops and cheers. I made a mental note that if I had to go looking for an extra truck part, not to do it barefoot.

"Jesus Christ," Duane said, "your uncle in a fucking militia or something? This is like Waco."

Donny nodded, his mouth agape. "He really knows how to throw a cookout. There must be sixty people here." Another ATV blazed into sight from the mud road and did a donut. Two men got off, beers already uncapped.

"Go man go," Duane shouted. They nodded in our direction and spat as they went past.

"Well," I said, "shall we check this out, or are we going to stand here looking like we just got off the first bus into town?"

"Which I guess we just did," Donny said.

"Snow Mexicans." Duane smiled.

There was a deep, somewhat rhythmic rumbling emanating from the barn. I could feel the ground wobbling underneath my feet as we got closer to the source. Past the welders, the barn door was wide open and a group of people were standing around inside, a couple of youngish-looking men shirtless and passing around a bottle of Wild Turkey. Once we'd joined the crowd in front of the barn, the sound was deafening. A band was playing inside, wedged between the burned-out wreck of a dune buggy and a tan muscle car shot through with rust and wheelless on blocks. I noticed something else: two bang sticks leaning against the wall in the back corner. The air was rife with the smell of weed smoke, gasoline, gunpowder, swamp water and hamburgers. Waco, indeed.

The band was flailing away on the most torpid, sinister-sounding din I'd ever heard. It made the punk rock of my youth like Scrotum Smasher sound like the Carpenters. Two guitarists, one a heavy-set, younger version of the man I'd seen throwing bottles, the other a rail-thin waif staggering and nodding under a thick head of black dreadlocks, the rest of his face obscured by a ragged black beard, raged away through a procession of down-tuned riffs. The drummer thumped away slowly, as though he'd had a breakfast of cough syrup and downers, eyes wide and staring at the bass player, another dreadlocked and bearded rake swaying in front of the bass drum. The music throbbed and stopped then lurched to life again, every empty space shot through with jagged bursts of feedback.

The singer was the only member of the band who might pass for handsome: shirtless and brown, covered in tattoos, long blond hair hanging around his face and down his back. I recognized his face. As he began to screech and gesticulate over the music like a Baptist preacher passing a kidney stone, I realized who he was: Rolly Lee's son Hoyt.

When I turned around, Donny was squinting, his hands over his ears. "Awful," he mouthed. I shrugged. Truth was, the band had a certain primitive appeal. Or maybe it was the fans they'd attracted. One in particular, a blonde in her early twenties wearing faded cut-off jean shorts and a white shirt tied in a knot at the front. I watched her clap her hands in time with the music, an anachronistically cheerful kind of participation in the bleak sonic onslaught. Three days on the road had left me with dulled social graces and I guess I stared too long. She noticed me watching and smiled. I felt my face redden and then a large hand clapped on my shoulder. Thinking it was Donny, I turned around and came face to face with Rolly Lee. Grinning ear to ear.

"You believe this shit?" he shouted, shaking his head at the music, warm spittle spraying my cheek. I held my hand out and he grabbed me in a rough bear hug, a familiar smell of beer, gasoline and tobacco on his skin. The band kicked into a slow, metal version of "Mars: The Bringer of War." I looked at Donny over Rolly Lee's shoulder and raised my eyebrows. Things had gone from surreal to flat-out tripped.

Rolly Lee motioned us away from the barn. "Come on," he said when we'd got round the side of the barn, "let's get the hell away from that racket."

"That your son?" I asked.

Rolly Lee nodded. "Hoyt. He's the sensitive artistic type." We had walked along the side of the barn and come out at the makeshift rifle range around back. The pop of rifles and the curses of those missing the mark provided a different kind of din altogether. Rolly Lee put his hand around one of the shooters' necks, a sullen-faced kid with an overgrown Abe Lincoln beard. The kid shook the hand from his neck, took aim and shattered a long-neck Budweiser bottle twenty paces out. "Goddamn right," he shouted, and drank from the beer wedged in the back pocket of his jeans.

There was some chit-chat, and then a shout interrupted us. "Raccoon!" A set of ringed black eyes peered through the long grass at the periphery of the yard. All rifles turned on it and there was a disorienting blaze of gunfire. I noticed the hind end of the raccoon disappearing into the thick grove. Donny and I put our hands over our ears, the gun smoke limiting visibility to two feet in front of our noses.

Rolly Lee shook his head. "Not that time, boys," he said. "Aim harder or drink less. Let me show you guys around," he said.

I noticed Duane's mouth hanging open. He turned to the heavy-set man with the matchstick legs and grinned. "Mind if I take a shot?" We left him with the shooters and went to the front of the house. In the barn, the band had launched into an impossibly slow number. You could count the seconds between drum hits. Hoyt Lee shrieked away over the glacial noise like a man having bamboo shoots jammed under his toenails.

The house displayed the same sense of order as Rolly Lee's trailer once had. Donny, Rolly and I made a quick pass through the front room, where magazines, empty beer bottles and Coke cans, chip bags and odd shoes were piled on every available surface. A muddy bucket sat in the middle of the aging, water-stained beige shag carpet, minnows skimming the surface of oily-sheened water. The kitchen was even worse. The light caught a layer of grease caked on the cupboard doors, near the stove the linoleum had been burned away, and there were even more empty beer bottles than in the front room. A badly stuffed owl perched uneasily on top of the fridge, jewelled eyes staring off into the long distance, feathers moulting away in the swelter.

Rolly Lee shrugged. "Parties make mess," he said, "and we've sure as hell had our share of both this year." Something seemed to occur to him. "Hold up a second." He went rooting behind the empties and came up holding a long-barrelled revolver. I knew nothing about guns, but this one was old enough to have looked at home in Custer's hands during his last stand. Rolly Lee futzed with the trigger, and then put the barrel to his mouth. I felt my bowels weaken. He pulled a lighter from his pocket, lit it and held it to the trigger. The smell of dirt weed filled the air.

"Jesus," I said.

Rolly Lee exhaled a thick fog of dope smoke then gave a whoop. "Welcome to Florida, boys!" I watched him take another hit off the makeshift bong. I hadn't seen him in more than fifteen years, yet he'd aged much more. His hair was making the slow and steady shift from blond to grey, and the crow's feet around his eyes were deep enough to stall raindrops in their tracks. His skin was the dark, leathery kind that only lifelong smokers who live in Florida have. Rolly Lee had always been a skinny man, but now he gave off a sense of fragility. He exhaled another blast of smoke and handed the gun to me.

"Never mind staring at me, thinking how goddamned old I got," he said, "get your own head up and relax." He watched me fumbling with the gun, a big grin spreading across his face. "Jesus Christ," he said, "you haven't changed a bit. Still that kid I remember, maybe not too sure of himself but sure enough." His eyes narrowed with his ever-expanding grin. I wasn't sure what he meant, and probably didn't want to know.

"What about you, Rolly, what's been going on?" I offered the gun to Donny who waved it off and disappeared into the back yard. A minute later, I caught sight of him with a hamburger in each hand.

"Shit," Rolly Lee said, "not too much. Getting by, you know."

There was silence in the kitchen, the smoking gun between us.

"The band might play a few reunion shows," he said. "Other than that, working here and there, living off the land, playing it cool." He swatted at his neck. "Goddamn mosquitoes everyplace," he said. "Got to fix them screens soon." His response had been of the vague, evasive kind that teenage sons give their fathers. "How about you, Jasper," he said, "what the hell you doing in Florida? You didn't come down here just to see us, did you?"

I told Rolly Lee about my accident on the subway platform. "Holy shit," he said, "you ought to be ground chuck. No wonder you need to get out of the Great White North." There was more silence. Rolly Lee swatted at another mosquito and then added: "Y'all haven't had much luck."

"You all" is a tricky thing in the South. "Y'all" can mean a group of people, or, in the corners of the hot country where things move even slower with the sun, beer and dope smoke, "you all" can just mean you. I knew which one Rolly Lee meant. The whole unlucky lot of us. Coleman, my parents and me. I stared back at him in the dim light of the kitchen, and for a moment the noise around us in the back yard and from the barn seemed to drift away. We held the stare for a full five seconds before we were interrupted by Rolly Lee's son and his band, who had drifted in the front door of the house. They arranged themselves around the kitchen, beers and cigarettes in their hands, vacant, vaguely amused looks on their faces.

"Here's the boys in the band," Rolly Lee said. He held the gun, barrel first, out to Hoyt. "Hoyt," he said, "this is your cousin."

Hoyt shrugged and took a hit off the gun. "Yeah," he said, "from the phone." I noticed the blonde girl with the jean shorts and white shirt come in the front door, the outside light casting a glow down her long brown legs.

"Jasper and his folks used to come down here every year on vacation. Never after you came back from Alabama though." Rolly Lee's eyes darted my way and then back again.

"Right," Hoyt said. He nodded in my direction but didn't offer his hand. "Hey." The blonde girl poked her head into the kitchen and looked at Hoyt expectantly. "Anyway, see you all later," he said, then went out the front door with her.

"That Melissa," Rolly Lee said, shaking his head, eyes stuck in her wake. The gun made the rounds of the kitchen from one dread-locked and bearded dude to another while we stood in silence.

"Rolly Lee," the bass player said. "You ever catch that mother-fucker set fire to your barn?"

Rolly Lee glanced at me. "Not yet," he said. "If I do I'll feed the sumbitch to them gators out back."

"You've got gators out back?" I asked.

There was laughter around the kitchen. The heavy-set guitar player choked on the smoke in his lungs. "Shit, Jasper," Rolly said, "where'd you think you are, Terronto?"

The room broke up. The bass player looked at me across the scarred linoleum and smiled. "If you're Canadian," he said, "do you like to eat beaver?" There was more laughter. More beers were passed around. I noticed the chunky guitarist examining a wilted burrito that he'd found behind a stack of empties.

"What happened with the barn?" I asked, trying to change the subject.

Rolly Lee shook his head and scuffed at the floor. "Some crackpot set fire to it a couple of Saturdays back when we were in Everglades City. Got back and could see the smoke from 41. It must have started pouring shortly after he set the fire. Hardly done no damage at all."

The bass player shook his head. "Think it's the same sumbitch been following you around?"

"Ain't nobody following me," Rolly Lee said.

"But . . ."

Rolly Lee stared at him, eyes narrowing. "You live out here long enough, out in the pines with just you and your thoughts, you get a strange notion or two."

The bass player drew a breath like he might keep along this path of conversation. "Shut the fuck up," Rolly Lee said, and grinned. "That's if you were going to say something else."

Out in the back yard, the festivities were still in full swing. Duane stumbled through my line of vision, a beer in each hand and a huge grin on his face. Luckily, I was saved by a familiar face at the back door: Aunt Val.

Unlike Rolly Lee, Aunt Val seemed to have no reservations about seeing me. She took my hand and led me out into the back yard. "Jasper," she said, her hand ruffling the back of my hair, "I can't believe it's you." Unlike Rolly Lee, Aunt Val was my blood. She wanted to know more about my mother.

"And you, Aunt Val," I said, "you still look great." It was true. Her midnight hair was now shot through with wisps of grey, and the sun and years had settled into her face with a relaxed elegance.

"I don't feel so great sometimes," she said. Then, "Come on, let's go sit down someplace." She led me by the hand across the back yard. Unlike the junk-strewn expanse of front yard, the area behind the house was positively bucolic: thick sawgrass spread out under our feet and stretched to the edge of a wooded area where willows and pines towered over a pond. This was clearly Aunt Val's domain.

Out near the pond, there was a small bench. "Seems like I've been spending a lot of time out here lately," she said, and lit a cigarette. "Want one?"

"No thanks," I said. I swatted a mosquito off my arm.

"Swamp angels," she said. "Thick enough to carry us off."

"Still great to be here," I said.

Aunt Val nodded noncommittally. "The heat and bugs and everything else . . ."—she waved toward the house—"makes me want for Ontario again sometimes. I haven't been back since I left. Almost nineteen years, Jasper," she said, as if she'd been counting the days. "You believe that? But I'm sure if I ever went back, they'd look at me like some old daughter of the Confederacy. And down here, I'm still the Canadian girl."

When I asked what she had been doing with herself, she sighed and rubbed her temples. "Working," she said. "Got a job at the veterinary clinic, doing odds and ends, learning quite a bit. Hoping to make a go of that, maybe go back to school for it and get a diploma so I can actually get an assistant's wage. Also some janitor work over at the high school. Some evenings."

I nodded. "Sounds like you're busy."

She raised her eyebrows. "Someone's got to be." She flicked the small remnant of her Marlboro into the pond. "Rolly Lee keeps himself busy gathering up and trying to sell all this junk, but," she said, "as you can imagine, that doesn't amount to a steady paycheque or anything like that."

"No benefits?" I smiled.

"Not even dental."

"I think I may have just walked away from that myself," I said.

She laughed softly into the darkness. "Kind of surprised me, Jasper," she said, "you working in an office and all. But hell," she said, "last time I saw you, you were burying your GI Joes in the sand and waiting for the tide to come in. It's been a long time. But working in an office," she said, closing her eyes as if trying to picture herself doing such a thing. "Well, I guess that's what most people do. That's what your daddy did."

At the mention of my father, my back stiffened reflexively. Val must have noticed because she touched my knee. "Now, I don't mean anything by that," she said. "Your mom and dad couldn't have lived down here like this. Just like I couldn't deal with that straight world," she said. The hint of a smile settled into her eyes and she took a long drag off the cigarette. "Nope, I don't think I was ever destined to marry an accountant or a dentist." There were whoops from up at the house. "Look around you," Aunt Val said. "This ain't all Rolly Lee's making. When I got down here I was trying to get as far away as I could from North Bay. Now here I am. I guess I've always liked some adventure. Maybe a little bit like your brother."

There was some rustling off in the trees and I jumped. "Just raccoons, Jasper." She put her hand on my leg. "You were always a nervous boy. Still are, I guess."

I laughed. "I guess so." As if to prove myself wrong, I got up and wandered down to the edge of the pond. "Hey, gators," I said, "anyone out tonight?"

Aunt Val laughed. "You can spot a Canadian a mile off down here. But don't talk to me about alligators." I went back to the bench and sat down. "I'm sorry, Jasper," she said, and then tipped her can of Budweiser back. "I just get a little tired sometimes. It hasn't all been some swamp utopia down here, us kicking back and doing our own thing like the last flower children left in Florida." She smiled and I noticed the deep creases around the edges of her eyes. "There's been some rough patches these last couple of years."

"Well," I said, "Rolly Lee still seems to have his Southern charm intact."

She grinned, looked up at the house. "It's funny," she said, "not a whole lot's changed except old Rolly and I getting older." She ruffled her hair and rolled her eyes. "Greyer. Fifteen years ago, we'd still have had a house full of drunken musicians on a rip. They just would have been closer to our age." Val touched her forehead, smiled. "If your grandmother could see me now," she said. "Yikes. I hate to think about it. But I shouldn't complain. I've got my son and my little patch of God's green floor to tend to. I mean, look at this," she said, sweeping her hand in front of her. I looked ahead, out into the clusters of tall, gnarled trees, Spanish moss hanging from branches like the remnants of old ghosts. And all I could see was more darkness.

"Hoyt seems . . ." I searched carefully for the words. "A lot like his dad."

Aunt Val nodded and lit another cigarette. "Kids do grow up a little rough around here, Jasper," she said. "There's just too much trouble to get into. Too much fun is how he'd—they'd—put it. But he's a sweet boy. Loves his mama. When we brought him back from Alabama, he was just a little scrap. A towheaded blond kid so shy he wouldn't say boo. It was no wonder," she said, "the life he'd had. His momma wasn't bad at heart but she was a slave to the needle. Hoyt told me all he can remember is her sitting real still on the couch, staring off into space, mouth hung open. Hoyt was just left to wander around and do his own thing. Nobody made him go to school or change his clothes or made sure he was getting enough to eat or brushing his teeth or anything. Hard to believe he's pretty much a grown man now." She grinned. "Even acts like one some of the time. So yeah," she laughed, "a lot like his dad."

"How old was he when he came to live with you guys?"

She squinted into the darkness. "Six," she said. "It was the year after—" I felt her eyes flit toward me in the dark. "The year after that last summer." She paused, then added, "When you all were down here," although we both knew exactly which summer she meant. A mosquito hovered over the contour of her neck and around her face and then landed on her cheek. Aunt Val swatted it off. "The day Hoyt came here to live," she said, "was the day I knew I'd never leave."

We were catching up, but I couldn't help notice the connection she'd made between that last summer and the thought of leaving Florida.

I tilted my can of beer back and drained the last warm drops from it.

Aunt Val produced two more cans of Budweiser from under the bench.

"Magic," I said.

"Magic." She sipped from the beer. "Now, Jasper," she said softly. "What's all this about your brother?"

I shrugged. "I'm not sure."

She put a hand on my shoulder. "You're okay though?"

"I'm okay," I said. "I just had a couple of strange phone calls."

The hand came off my shoulder and I felt her stiffen. "Phone calls?"

"Nothing all that concrete," I said, and then sighed. "I don't know if it's the accident, but it's just that . . . well, I never knew for sure."

"I know," she said, "it was so . . . hard."

"It still is."

Up at the house, I noticed Rolly Lee dancing shirtless in the back yard, a bottle of Jack Daniel's in one hand. There was some whooping from the remaining partygoers. I recognized Duane's voice among the sozzled masses. Skynyrd's "Tuesday's Gone" floated down to us on the warm night breeze.

"You didn't mention it to anyone else, did you?"

"No," she said. "Rolly Lee's got his good qualities, but he sees the world as black and white. I don't know that he'd understand. Look at him," she said. "Just look at him. You think he's changed one iota since you last saw him? And you, you've lived your whole life since then." She looked into my eyes, her own welling with tears, and stroked the side of my face. "Jasper, I don't know where time goes."

"Things don't turn out how we expect, do they?" I could feel her eyes, jewelled in the darkness, on me. Off in the pond, there was a grunt.

"Frog," she said, "not a gator."

"How do you know?"

"There probably isn't a gator left in that goddamned pond," she said, "with all the ones they've skinned and sold."

Up in the yard, Rolly Lee hit the chorus of "Tuesday's Gone" and pointed in our direction, like he could hear what we were saying.

I spent the rest of the party with Aunt Val back by the pond, listening to the frogs, the swamp and humidity thick in my nostrils. Later on in the evening, after most of the guests had gone, Hoyt Lee wandered down clutching three cold beers in one hand.

"Hi, baby," Val said. "Coming to sit for a while?"

"Uh-huh." Hoyt nodded at me. "Cousin Jasper," he said, handing me a beer.

"Cheers," I said.

Hoyt Lee didn't say much beyond that, but I appreciated the gesture. I was struck by the strangeness of the picture—me back in Florida after all these years, sitting by the swamp with Aunt Val and the cousin I'd never met. This was most of the family I had left.

Hoyt Lee lay back in the sawgrass, propped up on his palms, his bare feet stretched out over the drop where the yard ended and the swamp began. I watched as Aunt Val began to braid his hair, humming softly to herself.

My eyes were beginning to glaze over from the long drive and the steady stream of Budweisers I'd been sipping on when I heard the sound of a guitar approaching. I looked over my shoulder and saw Rolly Lee holding a guitar and wandering in a loose zig-zag across the grass, his eyes on his fingers.

"Look out," Aunt Val said, looking up from Hoyt Lee's hair. "Here comes trouble." Hoyt Lee looked like he'd gone to sleep.

She stopped braiding when Rolly Lee arrived, letting her fingers rest on top of Hoyt's head. Rolly Lee just grinned and kept picking. There was nothing terribly artful or intricate about his playing, but as his fingers moved haltingly across the neck a yearning melody filled the air around us as if it were dripping from the branches of the mangroves overhead. Rolly Lee kept his eyes on Aunt Val, and I noticed the vaguely sardonic look on her face give way to a shy smile, as if they were sharing a secret. When he played the final chord, we sat and listened as it rang out and then faded into the darkness. I realized that I'd been listening so intently that I could hear his fingertips moving along the strings.

I clapped lightly, not wanting to spoil the mood. "Beautiful," I said.

Rolly Lee kept his eyes on Aunt Val. "Almost as beautiful as the woman who inspired it."

Hoyt Lee's eyes opened and he mock-retched toward the swamp. "Please," he said.

"You're embarrassing your son," Aunt Val said.

"You never mind," Rolly Lee said. "Jasper," he said. "Your aunt never aged a day since the last time y'all were down here. Still the prettiest girl in Fort Myers."

"Prettiest girl in Fort Myers," Aunt Val said. "Well, Fort Myers isn't that big a place, Rolly Lee."

"The Princess of Lee County," he said. "Queen of the South."

Aunt Val grinned at me. "You believe this bullshit?"

I shrugged. "Why not?"

"All true," Rolly Lee said, putting one hand over his heart. "The gospel truth."

"All right," she said. "That being the case, I'm going to let you clean that house tomorrow. It looks like a bomb hit it." She fluttered her eyelashes. "I'll be resting," she said, "like a Queen would."

"Well, shit," Rolly Lee said, and he set the guitar down on the grass with a thud. "You could be one of them people's Queens. Pitch in, lend a hand and all that."

Aunt Val just shook her head. "That does sound like something I'd do," she said, "but what with Hoyt helping you, and your buddy down the road who has that fancy carpet steamer, well, I'd imagine the house is going to be plenty full."

"Yes, mama," Rolly Lee said. He looked at me, his eyes swimming, as if struggling to hold focus. "A guy can't get away with jack shit around here," he said. "No matter what she tells you."

Aunt Val's eyes narrowed. "And what would anyone try and get away with in the first place?"

Rolly Lee looked at me, eyes wide. "You see?" he said. He stood up uneasily and then leaned down to grab the guitar. The effort nearly sent him staggering off the edge of the yard into the water.

"Well," he said. "I'm going to get started on that damn house. Must be a couple thousand empty beer cans up there."

"A fine idea," Aunt Val said. "I'll be up in a minute, Rolly Lee."

Rolly Lee started slowly back toward the house, picking the same sweet chords and laughing softly to himself as he went.

24.

I DECIDED TO START with the highway patrol officer.

I'd declined a room chez Rolly Lee and headed back into Fort Myers with Duane and Donny sometime after the last shots had been fired and the heavy-set guitar player had projectile-vomited out the back door of the house. It must have been the burrito. They had enjoyed themselves at the party, particularly Duane, who had been promised a trip out into the swamps with Rolly Lee and his buddies. I was beginning to realize that Donny was that rare sort who was reasonably at home wherever he went. He seemed happy to sit quietly and observe the scenery if that's what a situation called for. It was no wonder that he and Duane were so close.

With Duane and Donny off checking out the local fishing supply stores, I had the room to myself. It was a little nicer than the room in Roanoke, but not by much. I surfed around on the television and then decided to wander down to the Denny's I'd noticed the day before.

A heavily made-up waitress of about eighteen took my order.

"I'll have the 'Moons over My-Hammy,'" I said with a smirk. It was all I could come up with in the absence of anything as straightforward as "bacon and eggs."

"Uh-huh," she said. "Coffee or orange juice?"

"Both," I said.

She frowned. "'Moons' only comes with one or the other."

"Can I pay extra for one then?"

She sighed and scribbled at her pad. "I suppose that's okay," she said.

While I waited for the inevitable mess of grease and yolk deep-fried to a crunchy mortar, I went to the pay phone in the front entrance and called Kim to see if I had any messages. I was pleased to find out that no one had been looking for me, particularly the three horsemen of my apocalypse—the office, the doctor or my lawyer. I was officially off the radar, and with a few months' pay still sitting in the bank, I planned to remain that way.

"Oh hey," Kim said before we hung up. "I almost forgot. You guys ought to bring that car phone into the hotel room. Nobody's been picking it up so I figure you'd left it outside. Wouldn't want to see Duane's new toy get stolen."

"Good call," I said. "I'll pass that on."

When I got back to the booth, Moons over My-Hammy had materialized on the table, a sure sign that it had been biding its time under a heat lamp all morning. I also realized that, against all odds, I recognized the couple sitting across the aisle. It was Hoyt Lee's girl and the overweight guitar player. I said my good-byes to Kim and went back to the booth.

If I'd hoped to sit down, eat breakfast undetected and head out, I was dreaming. Melissa noticed me as soon as I hung up the phone and made my way across the nearly empty restaurant.

"Hey," she said. "I know you."

"Right." I nodded. The guitar player looked up from his eggs and scowled. Yolk had already dried in the corners of his mouth.

"My name's Melissa," she said, "and this is Skeeter." Skeeter nodded quickly and then returned to his plate of eggs and sausage like a recently rescued shipwreck survivor. "You're from Canada, right?"

I was surprised that she knew this, and a little flattered that she even cared.

"Yeah," I said, "from Ontario."

Skeeter looked at me, his open mouth churning through a slightly burnt sausage. "That up in Toronto?"

"Other way around," I said. "I live just north of Toronto. Barsby, Ontario." He shook his head and went back to the eggs and sausage.

Melissa smiled at me. "I want to visit sometime," she said. "Canadians are so cool."

Skeeter exhaled heavily, the air blowing through his lips like a torn inner tube. A fleck of sausage shot out and stuck to the booth next to Melissa. "Bunch of hippies and gaylords up there," he said, and then looked at me. "No offence," he said.

"None taken," I said.

"Skeeter's never been further north than Valdosta," she said. "You'll have to excuse his shitty manners."

I laughed. "I better get to my breakfast before it crusts over," I said.

Melissa laughed. "Ain't that the truth," she said. "It's cheap and it gets the job done, but that's about all you can say for it." She patted the vaguest suggestion of a belly through her white tank top. She was all beautiful contrasts—blonde hair, sun-darkened skin, perfectly straight pearly whites and, elevating her to the point of unfairness, a laugh that suggested glory on earth. From what little I knew about Hoyt Lee, it was hard to imagine them as a couple.

"Why don't you bring your breakfast over here," she said.

I noticed Skeeter shoot her a quick, dark look across the table. "I'm a go out for a smoke," he said, then manoeuvred his ample girth out of the booth.

Melissa looked at me shyly when I sat down with my breakfast. "You know," she said, "I don't think I've ever met anyone from Canada before."

I forked a load of home fries into my mouth. When I bit into them, they had the consistency of a juicy red apple. "Here I am," I said. "Captain Canuck. I'm sorry I left my Mountie uniform back at the hotel."

Melissa laughed. "Actually, that's not true," she said. "I used to help my mom out when she was doing laundry over on Sanibel. Plenty of Canadians there. Y'all are so pale when you show up, spot you a mile off."

"Sanibel's my home away from home," I said. "I stayed there every summer from the time I was knee high to a grasshopper until I was ten."

"Knee high to a grasshopper." She smiled. "You're cute."

I felt my face bloom a bright red. For a moment I was at a loss for words. "That's how we met Rolly Lee. My Aunt Val came down here with us one year."

"Rolly Lee," Melissa said. A muscle rippled up her jawline as if she was biting down on a smile and for the first time since I'd sat down, there was quiet. "Anyway," she said, "what you doing today?"

"Not much," I said. "I have to go see a few people."

Melissa crinkled her nose and slapped my hand. "Listen to you," she said, "off to see some people." She grinned. "You in town on business or something?"

"No," I said, "just some people I haven't seen in a long time."

"Well, listen," she said, "we're going to Sanibel tomorrow, going to lay out on the beach all day, if you want to come."

"I don't know." I shrugged. I was thinking of Hoyt Lee and whether he'd want his long-lost cousin along for the ride.

"I insist," she said. "You being Canadian and all, it's my civic duty to show you around."

"Well, I guess I can't argue with that," I said.

On the way out, I passed Skeeter. He was leaning up against a mud-caked truck on massive elevated wheels, talking to a slightly built man with a moustache and a Dale Earnhardt shirt.

"Later, Skeeter," I said with a nod.

"'S up," he said. Then, as I crossed the parking lot, I heard him say, "There goes Canada." Their laughter was as thick as the Florida heat, pushing up from the cracked asphalt and drifting across my pounding heart.

Manuel Sherrill's office was roughly the size of a broom closet and half as well decorated. A crumbling cork bulletin board hung lopsided on the wall above his computer, overloaded with papers yellowed to varying degrees from the sun that poured in through a murky, bug-spattered window. His desk was a mosaic of torn envelopes, half-empty coffee cups and fast food wrappers.

Set up next to his computer were a couple of pictures: one of two smiling, dark-haired boys, the other of Dan Marino and a lanky police officer who resembled the boys. Manuel Sherrill, I guessed.

"Best quarterback we ever had," a voice behind me said.

The officer at the front desk had told me to go in and sit down. "Manny's just finishing up in the privy," he said. "Spends half his time in there."

"Wouldn't know," I said. "I like baseball."

"Aren't you Canadian? Shouldn't you be a hockey fan?" Sherrill touched my shoulder on his way past then collapsed into a brown upholstered office chair that groaned in protest under him. "They put me in the darkest, dustiest hole they can find and then wonder why I'm losing it."

"How'd you know I was from Canada?"

Sherrill smiled. "I heard somebody say 'eh' when I was in the bathroom."

I must have looked impressed. Sherrill leaned over his desk and grinned at me. "Grant out there told me. You're the number I got from the fella out on the highway a few weeks back?"

"You talked to my ex-girlfriend," I said.

"Ex," he said, then with another, more expansive grin, "eh."

"That's right," I said, "someone gave you my number. A man you picked up out on the highway." I recounted the details as I remembered them, my faintest hopes of finding out something—anything—dwindling as Sherrill gazed at me blankly from across the desk, scraping idly at a patch of dried food on his desk with his thumbnail.

Sherrill raised his eyebrows. "You came all the way down here about this?"

"Not really," I said. "I was on my way as it was."

He flopped back in his chair, which gave the requisite groan.

"Shit," he said. "I don't remember much," he said. "Fort Myers," he said, "we got some homeless. People come here looking for the beach and sun," he said, "don't realize it's mostly swamp and mosquito. A lot of them living under bridges, underpasses, that kind of thing. Trust me, this isn't the place to be homeless. Wander around out here"—he bumped his knuckles up against the mottled glass over his shoulder—"in this heat, your brain's going to boil. Boil right inside your skull cavity." He knocked at his head with a brown knuckle. "Especially," he grinned, "if you're not used to it, like you Canadians. This man, you think he's a Canadian?" I was beginning to realize that Sherrill's MO largely involved disarming you with goofiness.

"I have no idea," I said. "You called me."

"You have no idea."

I shook my head.

"Okay," he said, and raised his eyebrows.

He spun the chair around so that his back was to me and pulled the drawer open on a filing cabinet behind him. "Should be a picture then," he said. "Often just pick these guys up, make sure they're okay, not too messed up on one thing or another, and then send them along. Not much else we can do. The pictures help us keep track. People like this"—he snapped his fingers—"they're here one day, the next day . . ."

"A picture," I said.

He spun back around. "Yeah," he said, "a picture."

"The message I had was you had another call and had to leave the man."

Manuel Sherrill pulled his hands from the filing cabinet and turned the chair around so he was facing me again. He drummed his fingers against his temples, still holding me with the blank stare. "Had to leave the man," he muttered, "had to leave."

Sherrill stretched his arms over his head then shot to his feet. "Right!" he shouted. "The man out on 75. I got you.

"What'd you say your name was?" he asked me.

"Jasper."

Again with the raised eyebrows. Manuel Sherrill transmitted his feelings with all the subtlety of a drunken silent film star. "Come on, Jasper, let's me and you go for a little drive."

"Sherrill," Grant, the cop at the front desk, shouted from behind the sports section as we went past, "bring back burritos."

Sherrill shook his head at me. "Cracker thinks anyone from south of the States is a Mexican. I'm from Cuba, *cabrón.*"

Grant lowered his paper. "So what," he said. "Cubans can't fetch burritos?"

Sherrill drove like his balls were on fire and we were a hundred miles from water. My father had told my brother and me that at a certain age, a man loses his nerve; you realize that bones break, skulls crack and just because you jump doesn't mean you'll land on your feet. I thought of my father as Manuel Sherrill swung the bulky Crown Victoria onto Cleveland Avenue, narrowly missing an older woman with legs like bicycle spokes passing by on the sidewalk. She paused to shake her fist in our direction. I grabbed hold of the door and planted my feet flat on the floor.

"Nervous passenger," he said, peering over his sunglasses at me. "Eh."

"Eh," I said.

We pulled up at a stoplight. "I remembered that there is no file," Sherrill said, tapping at his temple. "I had another call that day. An emergency. Minivan and a propane truck. There's a match made in heaven. Damn thing went up like a Roman candle. That's why I had to leave your guy."

"I told you that."

"You did," he said. "Thank you." He gunned the motor and when the light changed, he punched the shift from park to drive. "No brake," he said. "You feel that?" I glanced in the side mirror and noticed the spattering of cars behind us keeping a safe distance. We hung a hard left on Daniels and the tires squealed in protest beneath us.

We had been on I-75 for about five minutes when Sherrill slowed the Crown Vic and eased us over to the shoulder. "Was up here a ways," he said.

"Wow," I said. "How can you tell?" Other than the occasional bridge over a canal or dried-out swamp full of tinder-dead trees, it all looked the same to me.

"If you lived here, you'd know," he said, unlatching his seat belt. "Come on." We got out of the car and stood on the shoulder. It was midday, and the heat was verging on apocalyptic.

"You're hot," he said, gesturing at the circles of sweat around the neck and pits of my grey T-shirt. I nodded. He wiped sweat from his own brow. "Me too," he said, then started walking up the shoulder, looking off into the woods bordering the highway. "Something dead off in here," he shouted. I limped through his dust after him.

When I caught up, he was looking down into the shallow ditch. "Look at that," he said. I smelled it before I saw it: a raccoon with a whirling halo of flies, smashed in the ditch. "Fucking roadkill," he said. "Breaks your heart."

A thick, wet waft hit me and I felt Moons over My-Hammy lurch in my stomach. "Great," I said. "We've got our share of it in Canada too."

"Reason I stopped that day was because I saw a man poking in the ditch," he said. "Guy was wobbling along, then stopped to look in the ditch, which is where I found him." He shook his head. "Looked like your typical transient, early thirties maybe, hard to tell. Tanned to leather, beard, matted hair, smelled so bad he was paying dog shit royalties."

"You're all compassion," I said.

Sherrill nodded. "Maybe," he said. "This guy was odd though. He wasn't tweaked on booze or drugs, I could tell that. He had clear, smart eyes. Too bad, really," he said, "but it's a wonder more of us don't end up out here wandering around. It's a hard gig to know what to do in this world."

I tried to steer him back on topic. "What was he doing? In the ditch, I mean."

"Even weirder," he said, then lowered himself to the sandy shoulder so that he was crouched down peering into the shallow ditch. He plucked a pebble up and shifted it from palm to palm like a hot coal. "The man had a dead alligator on the shoulder and was trying to get it into the ditch. I'm surprised I even smelled the dude. You want stank, try a gator that's been dead and baking out here for a day or so. Those things would singe your nose hairs in their living state, never mind once they've had all the air let out of them. He wouldn't tell me what he was doing."

"Why not?"

Sherrill smiled and lowered himself to a sitting position. "Man was fairly upset by this. There wasn't much I could do. Part of my detail is keeping an eye out for roadkill. Got someone from the state who comes along in the mornings, but if we see something big out here that might cause a pile-up, got to deal with it. Guy was doing my job, really. But he was upset. I had to tell him to leave the gator alone so I could talk to him."

I could feel the blood throbbing in my temples. High

overhead, two turkey vultures hung suspended in the sky. Waiting. I heard a car approaching from up the highway toward Fort Myers. When it came into view, I noticed it was a battered pickup on oversized wheels, going like shit off a shovel. The truck seemed to slow down when it spotted the black-and-white patrol car, and when it went past, I met the eyes of the driver: Skeeter. A safe distance up the road, I heard the engine roar and the truck picked up speed.

Sherrill stood up and dusted himself off. "Let's go get us some burritos," he said. The wind picked up, and behind me, the footsteps along the shoulder disappeared into sand.

Riding back into Fort Myers, along I-75, a terrible certainty came over me. Things were about to change. As we squealed back onto Daniels, I had an awful compulsion to throw the door open and roll out onto the street, followed by a less dramatic move such as a long walk to the Greyhound station.

"Get the chicken," Sherrill said, "and get it spicy."

I smiled at the guy behind the counter. "When in Rome," I said.

"That means he's getting the chicken too," Sherrill said.

The diminutive burrito guy smiled. "Fucking comedian," he said. "I think Manny eats burritos every day of the week so he can try his 'material' out every damn day."

"It's a ray of sunshine in your dreary world of salsa and torn tortillas and you know it," Sherrill said, then to me, "Let's go sit down. Ricky here can bring us our lunch when we're ready."

Ricky grinned and bit into the side of his tattooed hand. "Extra rat turd on that one," he called out into the kitchen.

Rat turd or not, the burrito was something to behold. It was the closest I'd come to home cooking since leaving Ontario, and it was glorious. Sherrill put his burrito down after I'd moaned my way through three incredible bites. "You need to be alone with that thing?" he said.

I laughed. "Sorry. It's good though."

"Isn't it?"

We ate in silence, focusing on the combination of peppers, cheese, onions and mesquite chicken coming apart in our hands. Willie Nelson was singing about the most unoriginal sin on the stereo, accompanied by Ricky rhythmically chopping ingredients on a heavy wooden block at the counter.

"Listen," Sherrill said, wiping salsa from his bottom lip with his wrist. "Who do you think this guy could be?"

I bit into the burrito and shrugged. "Don't know," I said. "That's what I was hoping to figure out."

Sherrill licked the salsa off his wrist and slouched back in the booth. "Here's the thing, Jasper. I don't believe you. That's my job: listening to people and picking up the bullshit through the regular lines of conversation."

"I thought your job was making speeding ticket quotas."

"I'll ignore that," he said. "It makes no sense to me. You live two thousand miles away, yet here you are, following up on what could be anything—a wrong number, or more likely a random number. You don't know anyone who could be walking around I-75 looking like the missing link, then"—he paused to bite —"you forget all about this. Why wouldn't you?"

I kept chewing. Finally, when I'd swallowed the last of the burrito, wiped my mouth with a napkin, taken a large drink of Dr. Pepper, I looked back across the table at him. "I don't believe in random numbers," I said. "You could make up an area code or a phone number, but try and make up all ten numbers and see what you get. Besides, you called me."

"Okay," Sherrill said, "so? You're that curious?" He leaned across the table until a thin margin of dead air separated us. "This man, whoever he is, he matters to you," he said.

I sighed and sank down in the booth and looked at Manuel Sherrill. He struck me as a good man. Odd, but dependable. Besides, he'd bought me a burrito.

I nodded. "You're right," I said. I pulled out a battered photograph of Coleman at seventeen and began to tell him the story.

"Shit," he said when I'd finished. He pushed the last bite of his burrito toward the centre of the table and picked up the picture. There was no sign of recognition, but I hadn't expected that. "Ten years."

"Ten years." I nodded. "Without a trace."

"Why, though? Forgive me," he said, "but let me play devil's advocate. Why no contact? If he has your number, why wouldn't he just call you? If it is your brother, he's taking a pretty circuitous route at getting in touch."

"I know," I said. "But you have to remember that the last time I saw my brother he was working on a spaceship in the back yard. Coleman never approached anything like the rest of us."

"Sure," Sherrill sighed. "This world, it's easy to get lost," he said. Out in the parking lot, a couple was engaged in a screaming match, lobbing epithets at one another across the roof of their car. "Let me ask you this," he said. "If your brother was down here, where would you look for him?"

I shrugged. "It's hard to say," I said. "I haven't allowed myself the luxury of speculation for years."

"Trust me," Sherrill said, "you're speculating. It's the whole reason you're here."

"All right," I said. "The swamps. The one place my brother was always at home was out in the woods."

Sherrill's eyes widened. "I don't know, Jasper," he said. He crumpled his salsa-and-sour-cream-soaked napkin into a ball and dropped it onto the table. "You think he could survive out there? In the swamps?"

"Yes," I said.

I knew he could because he already had.

25.

ON THE LAST WEEKEND of our final family vacation on Sanibel Island, Rolly Lee was left in charge of us again. On the Friday morning, the manager of the cottage complex came to the pool and leaned over the fence. "Where's your papa?" she asked. "He's got a phone call." Within the hour, my dad had pulled his watch from the dresser drawer and was on his way to the airport. Important business called that couldn't wait. I could almost see the relaxation falling away from him as he packed his bag: the suntan fading away to a pale pink, the dark circles forming around his eyes, his posture slouched. Standing there in my bathing suit, dripping on the coarse cottage carpet, I vowed to never become a "businessman."

My mother was undeterred by the sunburns of the previous outing with Rolly Lee. In her mind, these were the bumps in the road that built character.

Besides, in the interim, Coleman had been out with Rolly Lee a number of times. This thrilled my Aunt Val; that my mother would send her son off with Rolly Lee was a sign that he was becoming part of the family.

I remember it as an odd vacation; a holiday in the sun cut through with a vague unease that, as a kid, I could feel but was unable to describe. Part of it was my brother. I'd grown up realizing that Coleman was unpredictable and prone to saying and doing odd things, but he had always been happy. But not since our day out on Lake Okeechobee, and the further outings with Rolly Lee that he barely spoke of. I looked up to my brother and loved his company. We had always shared secrets. Not now. I'd put aside my feelings of being slighted and asked Coleman a thousand questions about his trips out with Rolly Lee. It was like getting blood from a stone. He'd shrug and say, "We just went fishing. It was boring."

My mother had a simple explanation: "Your brother's starting to hit puberty."

Puberty or not, I wasn't happy at being left out. One night Rolly Lee took Coleman fishing out in Fort Myers and then afterward they went for hamburgers. My brother and I shared a pullout double bed in the living room of the cottage, and when Rolly Lee brought Coleman home, I was already in my pyjamas, stretched out under the covers. While my mother talked with Rolly Lee in the entranceway, mosquitoes dancing around the outside light, I pretended to sleep soundly.

And so it went on that trip. Me, sullen and resentful at being left behind, terrified that Coleman was being initiated to an older, more interesting world that I would not get to glimpse for years, and my brother walking around with dark circles under his eyes, his forehead creased.

One night after lights out, Coleman rolled over and looked at me in the dark.

"I don't want to go out fishing anymore," he said. "It sucks."

The small dishwasher in the kitchen clattered onto the rinse cycle. "So," I said, "don't go."

Coleman rolled onto his back and looked up at the overhead fan. "You think this thing would ever come down on us?"

I turned onto my back so that we were side by side. "I doubt it," I said.

"I wish it would," he said. "It'd be cool."

"Whatever." I rolled back over onto my side and focused on the worn kitchen tiles. When I couldn't sleep, I looked for faces in the small cracks and scratches. I'd already found one that looked like George Brett.

Crickets called from the thick green bushes outside the cottage. I could hear waves folding up onto the white sands in an easy rhythm. For once I wasn't filled with a longing for it to be morning so I could go swimming, a longing tied to a terrible compulsion to walk out the door in my pyjamas to see what skulked around in the nighttime world of Sanibel Island when the couch had been pulled out and the lights turned off.

Coleman kicked at where the sheets tucked into the bottom of the couch until the hospital corner came out. "There," he said, stretching his bare feet through the breach.

"Now you'll get all the sheets," I said.

"No, I won't," he said. Again, there was the unfamiliar snap in his voice.

"Okay, Coleman," I said, "you won't." I rolled over onto my side so that I faced the door, the chain hanging in the latch like an umbilical cord. "But you will," I said, under my breath.

Somewhere far off, out over the Gulf of Mexico, thunder called. I imagined the sea as it looked during the day when a storm was coming, thick blurs of purple-black clouds hanging off in the distance over the water, sea spray drifting across the sand.

Wind rustled the towering pines on the grounds between us and the ocean.

"Jasper," my brother said, the edge gone from his voice. "I don't like Rolly Lee very much."

The dishwasher finished its cycle and clicked off. The cottage was so silent that I could hear the bathroom tap dripping. I didn't want to know about Rolly Lee or why Coleman didn't like him. All I knew was that while they were off fishing and having adventures in Fort Myers, I was at home with my parents, in my pyjamas before the sun had even set.

But this was a moment I'd been waiting for, the equalizer for being left behind: "Go to sleep, Coleman," I said. I closed my eyes and slowly drifted off listening to his short, agitated breathing and the chorus of crickets outside.

I woke once in the night, after I'd dreamed of drifting in the ocean, flat on my back, the sun hanging heavily over me in a cloudless sky. I'd taken all the covers and had sweated through my pyjamas. Coleman was curled up on his side, legs tucked under his chin. I pulled the pilly yellow blanket across the bed and over him. Then I went back to sleep.

Late the next afternoon, we were on our way back to Fort Myers. "Your Aunt Val and I are going out tonight. Rolly Lee's going to take you to a movie," my mother said.

Rolly Lee didn't appear to be in a good mood when my mother dropped us off. He was bringing fishing supplies from his trailer and putting them into the back of his truck. He barely acknowledged us when we pulled up, giving a quick wave in our direction then disappearing back into the trailer. When he re-emerged holding a case of beer, my mother and aunt had already driven off. We stood at the edge of his short drive watching him shift things around in the bed of his truck, grumbling under his breath. A nervous feeling had crept into my stomach like some strange flower and now I could feel it blossoming inside me. "I don't think we're going to a movie," I said.

Rolly Lee loaded the beer into the truck with an exasperated sigh and turned to us. "Jesus, boys," Rolly Lee said, "y'all in shock? Come on and give me a hand."

Coleman made no sign of moving. "Come on, Coleman," I said, grabbing his arm. He pulled away from me and followed slowly behind.

A man came across the lawn toward us, a pole slung over his shoulder and a dirt-caked cooler in his other hand. I recognized him as one of the men who had been determined to burn the cotton-mouths out of the riverbank. He grinned at us through brown teeth then ejected a splash of twiggy tobacco juice onto the lawn.

"Evenin', boys," he said. "Y'all still down here? That's some vacation. Your daddy must be a rich fella. When you going back to Canada?"

"Next week," my brother said, not looking at him.

"Snake boy and his brother, going back to Canada." The man grinned. He looked at Coleman. "I hear you're pretty good with gators too. You ought to come down to live here for good with a skill like yours." He leaned up against Rolly's truck and tipped his oil-stained Atlanta Braves cap back on his head. "Looks like everyone's out fishin' tonight," he said. "I just got to get away from the old lady. Going to find a quiet spot down by the creek and drink a few cold ones. This what they call a prop." He grinned, holding up the rod. I could hear Rolly Lee banging around inside the trailer, cursing to himself. The brown-toothed man peered over the tailgate into the back of Rolly's truck.

"Got lots of beer," he said. "Y'all ain't going to go thirsty, that's for sure." He put his own cooler down and stepped up onto the bumper. I wanted Rolly Lee to come out of the trailer and see the brown-toothed man. I thought if they had a fight then Coleman and I might get to go back to Sanibel.

"Lookee here," the man said, holding up a long, round stick that got thicker at one end and had some kind of cord wrapped around it. He hefted it up in one hand like he was determining the weight of it. Coleman looked away and kicked at the driveway.

"What's that?" I said.

"A bang stick," the man said. He pointed it toward the ground and closed one eye, aiming intently. "He must have just got it. I've seen these things stop a twelve-foot bull gator dead in his tracks." He made a spittly, vaguely explosive sound through the crinkled awning of his mouth. "Trick is to get 'em square between the eyes," he said. "Gators got a brain 'bout the size of a walnut, and you got to hit that. Otherwise you just goin' to piss them off."

"Put it down," a voice said behind us. The banging and clattering inside the trailer had stopped and I could see the vague outline of Rolly Lee's face peering out through the screen window.

The brown-toothed man stepped toward the trailer, the bang stick still in his hand. "Rolly Lee," he said. "You going out tonight? You know, *out*?"

Rolly Lee came around from the window and threw the trailer door open. "I told you to put that thing down," he said. "Now stick it back in the truck and go on with you. I'm busy."

"Well, jumpin' Jesus, Rolly," the man said, "no need to be so goddamned miserable about it."

Rolly Lee nodded toward the truck.

"Later, boys," the man said on his way past, the bang stick back where it had come from. "You take care with them gators tonight."

26.

Bad things spread wings.

I have vivid memories of that night. Rolly Lee, Coleman and I on the bench seat in his pickup, daylight dying, headlights drifting across our faces as we rode out through Fort Myers, the smell of overheated, sludgy coffee emanating from the cup holder. A Burger King with the "g" burnt out. Crossing canals in the dark, the water below like a cool, still slick of oil, reflecting the trees along the banks, our tires going clack clack clack as we went over. A scimitar moon lighting on the bugs that bounced up against the windshield and off into the night. Heavy clouds rolling in and blotting out the sky. Pulling up at Rook Bannister's house and seeing the shadow of the old man on his porch, quiet and still.

Rolly Lee cut the lights as we pulled up but left the truck running. "Wait here, boys," he said. He reached behind the bench seat and withdrew a large bottle of whiskey, then walked up the short drive to Rook Bannister's porch.

Coleman and I watched him disappear by degrees into the night. I could feel the blood pounding in my temples, my heart fluttering like a tethered falcon.

"I'm scared, Coleman." Out over the Gulf, there was a growl of thunder.

I heard my brother draw a deep breath. "Don't be," he said. "He won't take you."

"Take me where?"

"Out," he said. Thunder sounded off in the distance and a breeze picked up. I watched the aerial on Rolly's truck wag in the wind.

"Out where?"

A series of coughs came from the front porch. I turned to Coleman. "Out where?" I repeated. His eyes were fixed on the dark line of trees beyond the reaches of Rook Bannister's back yard, where I'd seen the peanut-butter dog chained rasping to a tree. Off beyond the looming pines hung with Spanish moss and the thick scrub brush were the swamps, the place of my nightmares, the boogeyman rendered physical in a black, crawling landscape filled with spiders and snakes, razor-sharp plants and quicksand. And alligators.

"Out there," Coleman said.

"I'm not going," I said. "I'm not going anywhere." I wormed my fingers into a tear in the seat down by my right side and found a grip. "I'm staying here."

Coleman nodded, his eyes wide and fixed.

There was a knock on the window and I shrieked. Rolly Lee had reappeared, the whiskey nowhere in sight. I could smell traces of it on his breath, his eyes a pale yellow in the moonlight. "Hey, Jasper," he said, "what you think about hanging around with your Uncle Rook for a couple of hours," he said.

I released my grip on the seat and stepped out of the car. Rolly Lee laid a hand on my shoulder. "You be good," he said.

I brushed his hand away and began the slow walk up the driveway and into the darkness where Rook Bannister sat sucking at his teeth, the dog snoring by his side. When Rolly Lee's truck roared to life and spun out of the driveway, I didn't turn around. Then the rain started, sudden and overwhelming as it always is in Florida.

27.

IT WAS MID-AFTERNOON by the time Sherrill and I parted ways and the sky was beginning to darken, purple smudges materializing in the amount of time it took me to finish my burrito and wash my hands. I had promised to check in with Sherrill again, whether I found anything or not. As I headed back up the Tamiami Trail toward North Fort Myers, I had a feeling that I would have no cause to contact Manuel Sherrill again. If this was the case, I'd remember him for the burrito.

When I hit the traffic light at Edison Avenue, the rain started. Dime-sized drops clattered against the roof of the truck like errant currency dropped from above. I noticed a black man, no bigger than I'd been at the age of ten, leaning into the window of the car ahead of me, his head bobbing and weaving like a sandpiper's. When the light changed and the car pulled off with a squeal, he went back to his spot on the concrete median and sat down on an overturned bucket, rain dancing along the brim of his baseball cap. A horn blared behind me. I pulled through the green light and made a right into a Walgreen's parking lot.

By the time I'd walked back to the stoplight, the rain had stopped and the panhandler was wringing his red cap out between his knees, mumbling to himself, oblivious to the warm, dirty water being sprayed up onto his frayed blue jeans by the cars hurtling through the intersection.

The light changed and I crossed the road to the median. The man was three cars down the line, doing a jig on skinny legs for two fat, older women in an Oldsmobile with the hope of a dollar or two. I watched the driver fumbling around inside the car, her face reddening. When the light changed again, she thrust a thick, wobbling arm out and dropped a quarter onto the pavement.

I was sitting on his bucket when he noticed me. "Hey," he said, "what the fuck do you think you're doing? That's my bucket."

I held a dollar out. "Here," I said.

"That bought you the space to stand on my median," he said. "The bucket's extra."

I laughed. "You drive a hard bargain."

"I don't drive shit," he said, "why I'm standing here in the first place."

He sat down on the bucket, closed his eyes and stretched his legs out. He wore no socks and his once-white shoes looked as though they'd been recently dredged from the bottom of a swamp. The fresh rain had awakened the ripeness all over the small man, the smell so strong that I could feel my ears begin to ring.

"Wondered if I could talk to you," I said.

He opened his eyes. "You still here?"

"Still here," I said. I motioned toward the Walgreen's parking lot. The drugstore was flanked by a liquor store and a Popeye's Chicken. "I'm parked over there. Wondered if I could talk to you."

"You a cop?"

"No," I said.

"Not with that goofy limp anyway," he said, "unless you a mark."

"Not a cop," I said.

"Well, it's going to cost you, and I got to bring this fucking bucket," he said.

I laughed. "I'll carry it," I said. He jumped back with his hands raised in a combative stance. "The fuck you will, bitch," he said. "I carry the bucket." I must have looked scared, because now he laughed. "Name's Devron Jacobs," he said, looking across the street toward the parking lot. "And I like my chicken spicy with a little Thunderbird."

Devron Jacobs was a painter. He claimed to have been one of the Highwaymen—a group of African-American landscape painters that produced paintings of sometimes glorious beauty at lightning speed while travelling across Florida. They went door to door, showing their work to anyone who answered, with the hope of five dollars or ten in exchange for a canvas.

Devron claimed to have been a Highwayman until booze got the better of him. Then, one afternoon, tired of lugging his canvases through the stultifying heat, he threw them into the Caloosahatchee River, walked into a diner and asked them to empty the register, a comb pressed stiffly against the inside of his jacket, "the flimsiest excuse for a gun there ever was."

I learned all this as I watched Devron devour a spicy chicken sandwich and french fries in the cab of Donny's truck, alternating between bites of sandwich and pulls on the Thunderbird. When he'd shoved the last, mayonnaise-slathered bite into his mouth, I said, "Let me ask you something, Devron."

He stopped chewing and looked at me with suspicious red eyes. "You not going to ask to blow me are you? I met some German tourist two weeks back wanted to suck a black dick. So he said. Ain't enough Thunderbird on God's green earth for me to go along with that," he said.

"Those crazy Germans," I said. "I'm looking for someone. Homeless guy."

"Shit," he said. He rolled the window down all the way and spat onto the asphalt. "Plenty of them around here. Pick up a rock, throw it, you liable to hit one. Twenty-five years ago, I was a novelty. Nowadays hardly find a spot in the mission at night," he said.

I nodded. "This guy would be about my height, a little older than me, skinny, suntanned, wearing a beard. Cops stopped him out on 75 a few weeks back."

"75?" Devron frowned. "Stupid place to be. Nothing but swamp and tarmac. Highway patrol rolling up and down there all day long, nothing better to do than bust your balls. Most of us want a drink and a place to kill a quiet afternoon," he said. "Doesn't seem much worse than building your dream home where a swamp used to be, driving to and from your job in your big fucking ride, burning gas, complaining when a gator ends up in your swimming pool." He waved his hand dismissively. "But what do I know?"

"What does anyone know?" I said. Thankfully, Donny's gas-guzzling Ford hadn't been idling during the conversation.

He tipped the bottle back and grimaced. "People are stupid," he said, "people are cruel, that's what I know." Back went the bottle. "Fella you're looking for," he said. "White guy?"

I nodded. "My brother."

"Your brother." Devron grinned at me. "I'm no help then, y'all look the same to me." He laughed and then let out a greasy, crackling belch. The stench of spiced chicken, cheap wine and a lifetime of gastronomical abuse filled the cab. "You want to give me a lift somewhere," he said, "maybe some of my friends can help you out."

I reached for the ignition and he stopped me. His gnarled brown hand felt like a warm bag of jumbled pigeon bones. "Hey," he said. "Talk ain't cheap." He nodded toward the liquor store. "But lucky for you, you know how it can be bought." Devron held the empty bottle of Thunderbird up and wiggled it.

"All right," I said, and got out. "More of the same, or would you like to try something in a white?"

"Bottle of Thunderbird and hold the sass," he said, then added as I was walking off, but still loud enough for me to hear, "and maybe I won't run off with your pretty truck."

Centennial Park was a sprawling expanse of piers, walking paths and bandstands on the Caloosahatchee River. A row of benches lined the waterfront, perfect spots to stop and soak in the sights and sounds of Jet Skis, motorboats and joggers. It struck me that had I been here a year ago, I'd have been running along the path or paddling in a boat out on the water, perhaps even with Kim. Now I was limping hard, sweating through my shirt, trying to keep up with a drunk homeless man I'd spent the afternoon enabling, all for information he probably didn't have. I couldn't help but think that all the tiny steps I was making were leading me toward a dead end. Still, if I wasn't moving up in the world, I was at the very least making life more interesting for myself. It sure beat sitting at a desk all day.

"Been trying to run us out of here the last couple of years," Devron said as we made our way across the lawn. There were few people around the park, probably because of the rain and it being a workday. "They was giving out food here once a week to the homeless, cops made them stop it. Don't want to encourage un-desirables," he said. A small, elderly man dressed entirely in white from his bowler hat to pristine leather shoes was feeding crumbs of stale bread to a flock of gulls. They congregated, cackling and two-stepping, vying for the breadcrumbs.

"We're like those gulls," Devron said, nodding toward the man. He smiled at me. "Just as tough to get rid of, too."

We crossed an open area with a fountain and benches. Two elderly women chatting about the unpredictability of Florida weather stared at us as we went past. I guessed we made an odd couple. "Afternoon," Devron said, tipping his baseball cap at them. They frowned in unison.

The group was congregated behind a massive oak tree a stone's pitch from the fountain.

"Here we are," Devron said. There were just three of them, backs up against the stout, roughly barked base of the oak, looking more relaxed than anyone else I'd seen in Centennial Park.

There was a woman about my age, long, frizzled blonde hair plastered against a face which had bloated into a pale doughiness from days of drinking cheap wine. She nodded at me and drew a plug of tobacco from a tin at her side, dropping a few shreds onto her once-white T-shirt that bore the image of a gleefully grinning Minnie Mouse, now a tableaux of varying shades of dirt. I noticed that she was holding hands with the man next to her, a sallow-looking waif who might have been eighteen or eighty. He was asleep. When I said hello, his dull eyes flickered as though he was struggling to come to, then they closed again.

A grinning black man sat slightly apart from them, his back erect and away from the tree, hands folded in his lap. "How do you do," he said. His eyes were hidden behind dark black glasses.

"This is Rodney," Devron said. "Rodney's blind."

Rodney laughed. "Always with the obvious, Devron," he said. "But you know I love you all the same." He held his hand out and I shook it. "Pleased to meet you," he said.

"Jasper," I said.

"Jasper." He nodded. His voice was deep and honeyed.

Devron rolled his eyes at me, scratching under the band of his baseball cap with a long, curled fingernail. "Man here got something for you." He raised his eyebrow at me expectantly.

I put the paper bag filled with bottles of malt liquor and red wine on the grass and sat down next to it. "I was wondering if you might be able to help me with something."

The woman chortled sharply and shook her head. "Help you," she said, nodding at my clean clothes and bright eyes. "Help yourself."

I nudged the paper bag so that the bottles jangled together. It was a low move, but it was the only one I had. The supine man stirred slightly and moaned. "You going to puke, puke somewhere else," the woman said, her mouth a few short inches from his ear. She looked at Devron. "Gravol and malt," she said, "three days of it." I could feel the blind man's ruined eyes on me, his face halved by a grin that went from wide to wider.

I told them whom I was looking for.

"Yeah," the woman said, "I know that guy." She pulled the paper bag across the grass toward her and peered inside. "Nice," she said. "I'm thirsty." Devron pulled it away from her.

"Listen," he said, "he's okay, and he's going to give you the booze anyway, so don't fuck around." She stared daggers at him and let go of the bag. "Man's looking for his brother. Do you know him?"

"Sure I know him," she said. "I know about a dozen guys that fit that description: tanned, hairy and skinny. How else you going to look living down here without a roof over your head and nothing to eat?"

I pulled the picture from my pocket. "This is old," I said, "over ten years ago." Coleman's eyes stared up at me as I passed the picture across the bag of booze to the woman. Seeing it again made me think what I always thought when I looked at it: if only we knew what life had in store for us.

She looked at it briefly then turned it over. "Here," she said,

wagging it under the nose of her sleeping companion. "Jerry!"
she shouted. "You know this guy?" Jerry's eyelids wrinkled and
opened briefly, his eyes rolling backward like greased bearings.
She handed the picture back to me and shook her head. "Listen,"
she said. "If he's out here, this was another life." She raised her
eyebrows and nodded toward the booze. "May I?"

"Sure," I said. It had been a ridiculous notion to begin with,
an idea shot through with the blind hopefulness of a child. I ripped
the paper bag down one side. "Open bar," I said. I held up the
bottle of Thunderbird. "This one's for you, eh?" I said to Devron.

"Sure enough." He took it in his long-fingered hand and
slowly unscrewed the cap. He shot me a sympathetic look. "Sorry
this was no help."

"It's cool," I said. "Here," I said, offering a bottle toward the
blind man. "Want a drink?"

He grinned back at me. In the wake of another disappointment, another omen that this was nothing but a wild-goose
chase, his grinning was beginning to piss me off. "No thanks,"
he said. "I don't drink." I gritted my teeth and picked up one of
the remaining bottles of Old English Malt Liquor. The beer was
warm and bitter. Just like I felt.

"Let me ask you something, Rodney," I said. "How do you
stay so happy?"

If the small measure of frustration in my voice was transpar-
ent, he chose to ignore it. Rodney turned his hands over in his
lap and gestured out toward the river. "There is nothing to be
unhappy about," he said. "I can smell the river, can hear the children playing down by the bandstand, this tree over my head . . ."

"Jesus Christ," Devron said.

Rodney laughed. "Jesus Christ is a long way away. The
Caloosahatchee's right here."

"I can't take this one-hand-clapping shit," the woman said, standing up. She walked off grumbling toward the pier, the bottle hanging limp by her side.

"I better get her," Devron said. "Cops leave us alone until we start staggering around with a bottle in one hand, stinking of rocket fuel." He took off after her, leaving me alone with Rodney and the sleeping man.

"This man you're looking for," Rodney said, breaking the silence, "is from the same part of the world as you. He's been away from home for a while, hasn't he?" He was still grinning, as though he were working his way slowly and deliberately toward an inevitable punch line.

I nodded. "Yeah."

"I know him," Rodney said. "Because he talks just like you."

28.

ROOK BANNISTER WASN'T accustomed to babysitting. But I'll give him this: he had remembered to put his teeth in.

"No snacks," he said. "Green peanuts down the road, but that stand going to be closed now." I sat at Rook's wobbly, fold-out kitchen table ringed with stains from the motion of a million beer bottles and watched him poking through the empty cupboards in the small kitchen. The wind blew sheets of water against the window. "Only a fool'd be out tonight," Rook said, shaking his head.

The terror of being left behind by Rolly Lee had begun to dissipate, partially because I was fixated on Rook Bannister, who seemed more nervous than I was. Now I wondered where they were. "Maybe they called off the fishing," I said, looking out the window. "Went to a movie instead. I can't get into the PG ones." Lightning crackled and the kitchen lit up. The rain seemed to come down even harder. "Hopefully they'll come back," I said, raising my voice over the rain and drawing my knees up on the chair.

Rook ignored me. "Reynolds," he shouted toward the back room of the house, just off the kitchen. The peanut-butter dog wandered in, a stupid grin on his dog face, feet clicking and clacking on the filthy, scarred linoleum.

"Dog's named after Burt," he said. "Florida boy." Rook smiled back at the dog. "Watch this," he said to me. He pulled his teeth out and set them on the table. A string of spit hung in the void between jawline and card table for a moment and then snapped. Rook looked at the dog and started making faces at him, the absence of anything solid in his mouth making his face as malleable as warmed rubber. The dog stood up and yelped, wagging his tail furiously. Rook drew his lips up until they were touching the tip of his nose and held this position. He moved closer to the dog until Reynolds could no longer look him in the eye. Finally the dog moved off into the other room, looking sideways, his tail between his legs. By this point, my cheeks hurt from laughing and I'd forgotten about Rolly Lee and Coleman.

Rook shook his head and grinned, his smile spreading ear to ear. He gathered his teeth up from the table and we joined Reynolds in the other room. Rook Bannister lived simply: a brightly coloured pirate's head, fashioned from ceramic and mounted proudly on the wall above the small black-and-white set, was the only nod toward decor, and even it had been chipped and battered as though he'd brought it home loose in the back of his truck. A soiled stretch of shag rug was spread wall to wall, curling up at the edges. But Rook had what he needed: a small bar fridge within reach of his tattered chair, and the ever-present spittoon on the table beside him. Rook gave me a beer, turned the television on to a Braves game, and within ten minutes I was asleep on the shag rug, Reynolds curled up against me, his feet twitching in his doggy dreams.

Outside, the storm continued.

I didn't wake up until Rook heard Rolly's truck in the driveway and nudged me with his foot. He squeaked and mumbled something I couldn't make out—he'd obviously been into the beer or taken his teeth out. Or, quite likely, both.

I made my way to the front door, rubbing sleep from my eyes as I went. I noticed on the clock above the small stove that it was after four in the morning. There was a honk from the driveway. "Thanks, Mr. Bannister," I shouted toward the living room. There was some mumbling and Reynolds padded into the kitchen, tail a-wag. "See you, Reynolds," I said, patting his head.

Rolly Lee's headlights cast thick parallel lines up the driveway, illuminating the mosquitoes that were in a fluttering rapture following the storm. The sand and shell driveway was pitted with the rain, and as I crossed the beams of light I noticed a raccoon nosing around in the ditch at the edge of Rook's yard. I looked down as I approached the truck. Rolly Lee shouldn't have left me and taken Coleman and I was still angry. Not as angry as I had been, but I didn't plan to let him know that.

As I got to the passenger side and looked up, I noticed something else. Rolly Lee was alone. He was leaned up against the driver's side window, hair wet and matted, eyes fixed ahead, the bench seat between us as vast and empty a void as the night sky.

29.

I HAD A LEAD.

I'd left Ontario on the slimmest of hopes—the latest birthday phone call, the call from Manuel Sherrill, and ten years of wishing and wondering. I knew that the events of the last few months had changed me. There aren't many people who leave work one day and instead of getting on the subway, end up underneath it. Whether it was the accident or the free time it afforded me, Coleman's disappearance had elbowed its way out from the back of my mind and wouldn't be returned to the shadows until I'd answered the question once and for all: dead or alive?

But now I had a lead. A solid one at that.

Devron's friend Rodney had met a man a few years back in Tampa, under the Lee Roy Selmon Expressway. "Back when I was drinking," he told me, "my whole life spinning and spinning like water going down a drain." The man was one among many, just another person without a place to lay his head at night that had four walls and a roof. Under the Expressway, there was a cool, dry spot where you could sit way up and listen to the transports roaring overhead, on their way to Georgia or the few remaining points south. According to Rodney, it was one of a number of places favoured by the homeless, somewhere they could return to after a long day looking for change, food, tobacco and liquor. Some slept outside, others flopped in abandoned, mildewy houses, but sooner or later everyone shared a bottle or a cigarette under the Expressway.

Amongst the hucksters, martyrs and self-proclaimed saints of the overpass, the man Rodney met stood out for how little he said. "He liked to hum," he told me. "The rest of them going on about who they fought or slept with, who'd turfed them out or ripped them off, but this man, he likes to hum." Rodney's face split with a white smile and he shook his head. "So, you tell me: you got a head pounding to beat the band from a bottle of wine you could strip paint with, you rather sit next to the man cussin' and complainin' or the man quietly humming?" We both laughed.

"I know accents," Rodney told me. He pulled his dark glasses from his face, his eyes closed and scarred over, the skin around the lids and eyebrows paler and thicker. "Stepmomma threw lye in my face when I was six years old," he said. "Jealous of the way me and my father got on." He shrugged in a way that suggested he'd gotten over it a long time ago. "Voices to me are like faces and names to everyone else. Walk around with your eyes shut for fifty years and they get to be like fingerprints. And this man, when he did talk, he talked just like you. Voice was the same, and he was from Canada. Must be more Canadians in Florida than there are in Canada."

Rodney didn't know much about the man, only that he found work with a carnival and didn't reappear under the expressway. "If I hadn't been such a damn stumblebum," he said, "there'd probably be a lot more I could tell you. Some days I could hardly remember my name. I been two years sober and that was around the last time I saw him, just before I headed down here from Tampa. Had to get away from the old crew."

This might have been another red herring, another example of finding anything if you looked and wished hard enough for it, until Rodney gave me the one other piece of information he had on the man: "He said he was good with alligators," he said, "which is how he got hired on with the carnival." Rodney shook his head and grinned his flash-white smile again. "Man loved his alligators. Not many people you can say that about."

By the time I left the blind man, a brilliant sunset was exploding out over the Caloosahatchee and the mosquitoes had come out to feast on those still sitting in the park in the dim light of day's end. As I walked back to the truck, I thought about my brother: where he'd been and where he would lay his head when it got too dark to see.

The next morning, we were on our way back to Rolly Lee's compound. Rolly Lee and his buddies were going to take Duane and Donny out fishing for the day, while I was headed to Sanibel for an afternoon at the beach. Before leaving the motel, I'd left a message with Manuel Sherrill, thanking him for his time the previous day and letting him know that I would be in touch.

"Slow up," Duane said, as we got within the confines of the property, the mechanical scrap appearing all along the sides of the crude dirt road like some futuristic flora. "I need a new axle for the Swinger. Your uncle must have at least two or three out here."

As we broke through the line of trees into the open, we could hear the rumble of slow, down-tuned music. "These kids get started early," Donny said. "Guess the neighbours are too far off to hear that garbage."

"I figured people'd be playing country down here," Duane said.

"Yeah, and they think we came from the land where ice was born," I said.

There was a scattering of pickups and late-model muscle cars parked out front of the barn, men leaned up against their rides, most with a coffee in one hand and a cigarette burning in the other. We parked and made our way toward the din. One of the men, a short, skinny man with a ball cap ratcheted onto the lowest possible setting to accommodate his tiny head, nodded toward the barn and cupped his hands. "Rolly Lee," he shouted.

Sure enough, Rolly Lee was fronting the band, his son Hoyt among the men leaning up against various trucks, a Miller Lite in his hand, the scowl of the usurped writ large on his face. The twin stink of burning wood and oil rode the humidity into a thick fog. I noticed that a torn swath of bedsheet had been pulled tight above the drum riser. It read "GRAVEL WORM" in big block letters. With a name like that, Hoyt Lee and his band were destined for the Top 40.

The band shambled into a mid-paced boogie and Rolly Lee started kicking and rooster-stepping across the cement without so much as slopping his beer. There were a few feeble hoots and a raised Styrofoam cup or two. I had to give Rolly Lee this: he had presence.

Aunt Val appeared at the front door and wandered out, a mug of coffee in one hand and a cigarette dangling from her lower lip. As Rolly Lee started to sing, she appeared next to me and took my arm. I kissed her cheek and she smiled at me, and then motioned toward the barn with a tired look. "Kids," she shouted into my ear, rolling her eyes.

The song reached a discordant, unresolved end and Rolly Lee drop-kicked the microphone toward the drummer. An ear-rupturing "pop" echoed through the PA and into the woods. "Fuckin' amateur hour," he shouted. I noticed Hoyt Lee scuff at the dirt with his flip-flop and shake his head. They were just another happy family spending a little quality time together.

"Hey you, what'd you get up to yesterday?" Aunt Val said, squeezing my arm, turning her back to the scene in the barn. She raised an eyebrow, hinting at the question behind the question. Had I been looking for my brother?

"Not a lot," I said, hoping to keep my afternoon of meeting the local police and homeless to myself. Seeing Skeeter drive past on 75 was heavy on my mind. "Relaxed."

"Relaxed." She smiled. In the barn, Rolly Lee was leaning over the drum kit, explaining the turnarounds in "Gimmie Back My Bullets," punctuating the salient points toward the drummer's chest with his skinny finger. The drummer looked back at him vacantly. "What's that like?" Aunt Val said. "People around here think relaxation comes in a six-pack."

"On the four!" Rolly Lee shouted.

Aunt Val sighed and looked at her watch. "Eleven in the morning, drunk already." Then she caught herself: "Sorry, Jasper, I don't mean to gripe. You on vacation and all, probably the last thing you want to listen to." She turned toward the barn, where Rolly Lee was reaching into the cooler for another beer. Hoyt Lee was off behind the drum riser, looking for his microphone, I guessed. "He's just a good old boy," Aunt Val said, "and now I got a son of the South too. You think Ontario would take me back after all?"

I did my best to smile impartially.

A car pulled into the yard, a late '80s model Daytona in red with one grey door. Behind the wheel was Melissa Wheeler. I may have been imagining things, but I could have sworn that she was looking at me, smiling, as she parked the car. "And just to cap off the beginning of a perfect day, here comes Melissa Wheeler," Aunt Val said, a pinched tone to her voice.

I watched Melissa step out of her car wearing a pair of frayed jean shorts and a green and red bikini top along with a posture that suggested she knew that every male set of eyes in the yard was on her.

"Jasper," Aunt Val said, breaking the reverie. "Don't."

"What," I said vaguely, still looking at Melissa. I'd never been an ogler, but I couldn't help myself. She was enough to wake the dead.

"Trust me," she said, grabbing my arm. I looked at Aunt Val, into her tired eyes, the heavy circles smudged blue-black underneath them, and for a moment an uncharitable notion came over me: she was jealous. Back when we'd first come down to Florida together, Aunt Val had been beautiful enough to draw whistles and turn every man's head when we went out. Now she was Rolly Lee's old lady, and it had been a tiring job. I shook my arm free from her grasp.

"Don't worry," I said, smiling. I looked over her shoulder and noticed a couple of Rolly's friends staring under the hood of a muscle car that looked like a replica of the General Lee, another man behind the wheel, gunning the motor in neutral.

"It's not you I'm worried about."

There were some furtive strums from the barn. Rolly Lee had strapped on Skeeter's guitar and was explaining something to Hoyt, Skeeter and the vacant-eyed drummer. He'd taken his shirt off and was strumming at the guitar with the ubiquitous Miller Lite in his right hand. Hoyt Lee didn't look happy. He hadn't even noticed his girlfriend show up.

Duane and Donny had been chatting with the small-headed man and now they wandered over. "Morning," Donny said to Val. Duane tipped his ball cap at her.

"You Canadians," she smiled, "so polite."

"What do you mean, 'you Canadians,'" I said. "More like 'us Canadians.'"

I noticed Aunt Val's smile disappear and there was a voice behind me. "Ready for the beach?" I spun around. Melissa.

"Hey," I said, "how are you?" Off in the background, the

motor gunned and revved again and there were some whoops.

"Good." She smiled. "You? Moons over My-Hammy didn't do you in?"

I laughed. "Nope. Still walking and talking, anyway."

"That's good." She smiled at Donny and Duane. "I'm Melissa," she said, holding her hand out.

"Donny."

Duane wiped his hand on the ass of his jeans. "Brad Pitt," he said, beaming.

As Melissa laughed and took Duane's hand, there was a scream from the barn.

Hoyt Lee was flat on his back. The entire yard went quiet. Even the woodsmoke curling up from behind the house began to drift in the opposite direction.

Hoyt Lee propped himself up on his elbows and looked up at his father, standing over him, his right hand still balled into a fist, an empty can of Miller Lite squashed in his left. They held the stare for a moment, a frozen scene that might have been a postmodern take on Norman Rockwell. Finally, I heard Rolly Lee say, "Your goddamn microphone's fine." Then, turning to the rest of us, "Go on."

As I turned from the barn, I noticed Aunt Val disappearing into the house. I couldn't help but wonder if Rolly Lee had cleaned up inside after all.

30.

ROLLY LEE'S HAND WAS torn and bleeding. I watched it twitch and flex on the blue vinyl of the steering wheel. The blood crawled silver-black across his hand in the dark of the truck. When a rare set of headlights swept across us from an oncoming car, I noticed that the blood had partially dried and cracked.

I was filled with a shapeless, nameless terror. A dread so thick and unthinkable that, despite the early August humidity, my legs were shaking and I could feel my teeth beginning to rattle in my mouth. I was too young and terrified to give voice to the obvious:

Where was Coleman?

Rolly Lee was silent. My eyes kept returning to the rear-view to watch his face. His breath came in shallow, wheezing bursts, and when he punched the dashboard lighter in and withdrew it to light a cigarette, his hands shook so much that there might have been a firefly in the truck with us.

Someone's taken Coleman away, I remember thinking. Someone has taken him into the swamps forever. My brother had been thrust into *my* nightmare: that one night someone would gather me up from my bed, drive out into the swampland and drop me into the brackish waters where the alligators would come and then bury me at the bottom with the bones of all the other little boys. All the things Coleman had never been scared of, that never existed in his world.

It was a validation for me: proof that being scared of something would forever keep it at bay.

Across 80 we went, away from Clewiston and Rook Bannister. As we got into Fort Myers and headed toward the causeway that would take me to Sanibel, to my mother, to the questions that I knew someone else would have to ask, the sky began to lighten. It was approaching dawn.

It was the longest ride of my life.

—

As we pulled into the small parking spot behind our cottage, I could see that the lights were on. With my father having gone home early, she was all alone.

Rolly Lee looked at me, nodded once and then got out of the truck. He slowly made his way around the side of the cottage, eyes on the ground, feet crunching across the pathway made from broken shells toward the screen door.

I didn't get out of the truck. From the passenger seat, I had a clear view of the Gulf, obstructed only in patches by the few palm trees planted on the grounds between the water and the cottages. The sea was a deep army green until further out, where in the half-light of dawn it looked nearly black. The sky was a swirl of deep pinks and greys, the kind of sky that could change easily into a dark morning full of rain. I watched the waves roll in from a point out at sea, pelicans and seagulls gliding above the froth, watching for breakfast in the surf.

Life continuing without interruption.

I noticed the man who was staying in the next cottage coming up the drive, a plastic bucket in one hand. This was a common sight early in the morning. He was a retired baseball scout in Sanibel on a fishing vacation and believed the only time to catch the good ones was at the crack of dawn. We'd made fast friends one afternoon as I was throwing rocks at a palm tree, using a full windup and providing my own colour commentary. "Quite an arm, young feller," he'd said, on his way up from the beach, a small Styrofoam cooler in one hand. Since then, I'd always kept an eye out for him, hoping that he might be able to give me the inside tips that might someday take me to the Big Leagues.

Not today. I could hear him whistling as he got closer and I sank down in the seat, my knees knocking together with the tremor in my legs. He passed the truck on my side and cut between the cottages, heading for the beach.

As he reached the sea oats that separated beach from grass, I heard a scream from our cottage. It was my mother.

"My son," she said. "Rolly Lee, what have you done with my son?"

The baseball scout turned his head slightly, and then kept on walking toward the ocean. In my head, I could still hear him whistling, a high careless sound that grew and grew until my ears started to ring.

31.

DRIVING WEST OUT OF Fort Myers, you pass shopping malls and massive grocery complexes that slowly give way to a scattering of pancake houses and outlet malls, then gas stations and housing complexes separated from the sun-bleached highway by tall palms and deep ditches filled with rainwater, bordered on both sides by thick sawgrass. Finally, with Fort Myers at your back, the continent begins to crumble away at the edges like a damp cookie and you can smell the sea. You come to a series of small toll booths, quaint-looking wooden structures manned by actual people. Just beyond the tolls, the sun glints off the ocean that has swallowed everything but a two-lane causeway that stretches over four miles and will take you from Fort Myers to Sanibel Island.

It was a picture I had dreamed of. An image I had returned to while sitting on the subway after particularly bad days at work, when winter was closing in and the days were damp and miserable. I hadn't travelled much, never further than Florida in fact, but this was my Mecca. Some people went for mountains or the Taj Mahal or the Louvre; but deep at the centre of my being, where I stashed everything I hoped and longed for, was this bridge.

It was more than that. For my family, it was the separation between the before and the after.

Just past the toll booths was a small lot for the fishermen who lined the small patches of beach and grass that quickly receded under the causeway. Then you were out over open water, Fort Myers spreading out to the south, a relative metropolis, Pine Island somewhere off to the north where Sanibel twists out like a snake in digestive repose, and beyond that its sister island Captiva and then Cayo Costa. It was a blue-jewelled paradise, so beautiful that you envied the pelicans that circled overhead, the entire picture spread out below them.

"Say they're going to raise the toll again soon," Skeeter said. "An extra dollar. More goddamn repairs."

"Why's that?" Hoyt Lee said. "Just to make sure a bunch of fucking idiots can get out to their vacation spot?"

I was in the back seat with Hoyt Lee. His eyes squinted at the sound of Skeeter's voice and he pressed the side of his blackening cheek into the window. Despite the altercation with his father, Hoyt had insisted we go to the beach. It was a troubling sign that this was business as usual for the Lee family. From the driver's seat, a mess of blonde hair blew back at me in the breeze coming up off the ocean.

"I love this view," Melissa said. "But it reminds me of working."

Hoyt Lee pulled his face away from the window. "Working," he said with a sneer. "When'd you ever work over here?"

Melissa frowned into the rear-view. "Until I was about sixteen, Hoyt," she said. "Way before I met you." I thought I saw her eyes dance my way in the mirror. "My momma got me a job helping her at Blue Dolphin."

Hoyt Lee snorted through his nose. "About the only reason you'd have for coming over here," he said, "clean up after rich people."

"Jasper's not rich," she said, "and he used to come here. Some people just save their pennies is all." Hoyt turned and regarded me with one raised eyebrow. For a moment, I saw his father's face looking at me.

"Who knows, Jasper," she said, smiling over her shoulder, "maybe we passed on the beach way back when."

"Or maybe you had to wash his dirty sheets," Skeeter said, his thick neck craning toward Hoyt in the back. They both laughed. I let out a token chuckle just to keep my options open. I felt the car pick up speed and then we were off the causeway and onto the island.

"You still playin' ball? My old man says you used to play," Hoyt Lee said. The question came as he was digging a hole in the sand to bury the cooler in. I guessed that actual eye contact would have to wait.

"No," I said. I watched Skeeter pull three cans of beer from a Styrofoam cooler. "It's been a while. High school."

Skeeter handed me a beer. "Good money playin' ball," he said. "You any good?"

I nodded. "I guess I used to be pretty good."

"For a Canadian," Hoyt said. He pressed the cold can of High Life against his cheek. "Motherfucker," he said. "Hurts like shit." He shook his head and reclined on the towel.

"Hoyt," Melissa said, and then crawled from her towel to examine his face. "You be nice."

"He's right," I said. "You grow up down here, you're at an advantage." I looked out at the turquoise waves languidly moving toward the white sand that was as soft as corn starch between my toes. "When you've got four months of snow a year, you're not going to produce a lot of ballplayers. There's a reason everyone plays hockey."

"Ain't no advantage down here," Hoyt said, and then drained his beer. I leaned back on my towel to show I was relaxed. I wasn't. An elderly couple tanned to a leathery brown walked into our line of view holding hands and stooped to look at some shells. "Idiots," Hoyt Lee said under his breath. "Grab me a beer, Melissa." I watched her crawl back across the towel, white sand stuck to the backs of her legs. I caught myself and looked back at the ocean.

Two hours later, the cooler was filled with empties and swirls of wet sand. The sun throbbed overhead in a cloudless blue sky and the sea air hung in a thick mass around us. It was as hot as it was going to get.

"I'm going in," Melissa said, nodding at the ocean. "Anyone coming?" She leaned forward on her towel, a few strands of blonde hair stuck to the back of her brown neck, and pushed her sunglasses up onto her head.

Hoyt Lee smirked at her. "What about the sharks?" He tipped the remnants of his final beer up and laughed when it spilled onto his chin.

"Stingrays," Skeeter added, still wearing a black Molly Hatchet T-shirt that stretched thinly over his robust stomach.

"Manta rays," Hoyt said. "Jellyfish."

"Piranhas."

"Barracudas."

Skeeter scratched at his sideburn and squinted. "Pussy fish."

Hoyt Lee sat up on his towel laughing, rough tattoos shape-shifting across his skinny frame. "Fuck's a pussy fish?"

Skeeter shrugged and finished his beer. "Piss warm," he grunted, and squirted a jet of foam through his front teeth. "A pussy fish?" He lit a Kool and threw the pack to Hoyt. "Well, a pussy fish'll sting your pussy," he said, looking at Melissa and baring his teeth. "So swim at your own risk."

We left them rolling around in the sand laughing, like piglets on angel dust.

"I'm sorry," I said, the water like pea soup around my ankles. Melissa's face was a grimace set in stone.

"Forget it," she said. She looked at me and her face softened. "Last one in gets bit by a pussy fish."

"My momma and I used to come out here and watch the sky," she said, "after we finished working. My mother used to tell me that one day we'd live out here." We were floating a few feet from one another on our backs, looking up into a brilliant cornflower blue sky. "Once she found a rich man and they got married."

I splashed some water across my stomach, which was so hot that I could almost hear it sizzling. I wondered about the boys on the beach. How did Hoyt feel about his cousin lazing around in the ocean with his beautiful girlfriend? I had a feeling that, for the moment, resentment was taking a back seat to beer-swilling with Skeeter. He couldn't possibly be as guileless as he seemed. "Did she ever meet him?"

"No." She giggled. "She lost her job out here. Stealing towels. So she went to work at Walmart and fell in love with her manager." She turned her head in the water so that she was looking at me. "Bucky Benson."

"Bucky Benson?"

We both laughed. "He looks exactly how you'd expect, too," she said.

"Big teeth?"

"Well," she said. "Big tooth, anyway. He's not the most handsome man. But," she said, "Bucky Benson is a perfect gentleman. He holds doors open, he pulls your chair out for you at the Denny's, and I've never even heard him curse. Kind of creepy, actually."

"So," I said. "Did your mum get a house on Sanibel out of the deal?"

"No," she said. "But close. She's in Lawrence, Kansas. Bucky got promoted and manages a Walmart out there. Momma stays home and paints her nails."

I turned over in the water and reached for the bottom with my toes. We'd drifted quite a way out from the beach. I could see Skeeter and Hoyt sitting on their towels. I wondered what they were talking about. Maybe Hoyt was telling his friend how happy he was that his Canadian cousin had come for a visit and hit it off with his knockout girlfriend. I doubted it.

"What are the two dummies up to?" she said.

A wave slapped up against my cheek. "By the looks of it, not a lot."

"Sounds about right."

I noticed Hoyt Lee waving his arms back on the beach. "I think he wants you," I said.

"Doesn't everyone?" She turned off her back and grinned at me. "Just kidding."

Hoyt and Skeeter had walked down to the water. "Beer," I heard Skeeter shout across the water, an empty can in his hand.

"They're like goddamned cavemen," she said. "NEED BEER! NEED BEER!" She waved at them. "Okay!" she shouted.

I heard Hoyt Lee shout something from the shoreline. Skeeter walked back to our spot on the beach and pulled the cooler up from the ground. I realized that Hoyt was waiting for us to come with him. "We should go," I said.

"Forget it," she said. "You didn't come down here to visit the 7-Eleven. We're going to stay out in the ocean. They drank all the beer, let them get some more if they're so goddamned thirsty." Hoyt Lee shouted something else from the shore then went up to meet Skeeter. I watched them disappear up the beach and beyond the clumps of sea oats waving in the slight breeze.

"God, I'm so sick of that boy," Melissa said, after she'd returned to floating on her back.

I felt a twitch in the front of my trunks and decided I'd better hold off on floating on my back.

Far off on the horizon, a few dark clouds congregated.

A way up the beach from where we had been swimming, toward Blind Pass and Captiva, was an old gazebo. I remembered it from walks with my mother. Back then, it had been an anachronistic piece of construction along the beach—an Oriental-themed structure painted in deep reds and browns and dropped at the top of the beach where a cluster of towering pines huddled over it. Coleman, my mum and I had an ongoing game where we speculated who might have built it. Coleman guessed David Carradine. Whoever it was had since passed on and not left instructions for the upkeep. The paint had peeled off, leaving the raw wood beneath exposed to sun, sand and sea. One corner of the roof sagged, as if one of the pines had split and blown down onto it during a hurricane. Now it looked like a gentle morning breeze could probably turn it into driftwood.

With a cold, late afternoon rain starting to spatter the beach, it looked positively palatial.

After waiting an hour for Hoyt and Skeeter, we realized they weren't coming back. A knot tightened in my stomach. I wondered if I had crossed a line by swimming with Melissa Wheeler. In my mind there was a line I'd been crossing over and over all afternoon, like a game of jump rope. But I also knew that what went on in your head didn't count.

"They took my car," Melissa said. She'd been up to the small public parking lot to get a change of clothes. "Of course they took my car. Neither one of those lazy asses'd think to walk anywhere. Even though they've been drinking beer all goddamn day. No consideration. None." Her bottom lip jutted out and the stormy eyes returned. I could see that she was not a fun girl to be around when she was unhappy, particularly if you happened to be anywhere close to the cause of that discontentment.

"My purse was in the car," she said. "But that's convenient, because I mean, how else is Hoyt going to buy beer?" The rain was now beginning to fall in earnest. In Florida, you can close your eyes on a bright blue sky then open them a minute later to the beginnings of a thunderstorm. It was that kind of day. "Now what?" she said. "We don't even have anything to eat. Or drink." I noticed a woman with two small children leaving the beach, carrying a sun umbrella and a beach bag, bent into the wind, heading toward the parking lot. All of a sudden, it seemed like we were the only people left.

I nodded toward the gazebo. "Shall we at least stay dry?" I was leery about giving her the wrong impression, but I was also beginning to get cold. I hadn't thought such a thing possible in Florida, but my towel, damp with the ocean, felt cold and grainy around my neck.

Melissa smiled at me and shrugged. "Dry would be good."
The dark clouds we'd seen off toward the horizon an hour before
were moving steadily above us, like freight trains arriving in a
rail yard.

The gazebo smelled damp and musty. Someone had lined up
a row of surf-battered conch shells along the planks at the entranceway. We stepped over them and were inside. The rain had
picked up and the drops on the roof sounded like hail. Water was
leaking in through the side of the roof that sagged, but lucky for
us, the gazebo had walls and screened windows that for the most
part were intact, save for a tear here and a knothole there. Looking
out through the screen at the ocean crashing in on the shore,
white froth skidding across the sand, I thought of Coleman and
my mother: in all the years that we had admired this gazebo, not
one of us had ever dared to set foot in it. Now I was looking out
from the inside.

"What're you thinking about?" Melissa's voice startled me.
It had gone dark outside, darker still under the gazebo. She'd sat
down on my towel and wrapped her own around her shoulders.
Her hair had taken on a dull gold glow in the half-light.

"Nothing," I said. "You?"

She rubbed at her hair with the towel. "Just Hoyt and what
a jerk he is. Leaving us out here in the rain."

I nodded and looked back out at the ocean. A pelican hung in
the gust, trying like hell to glide and instead taking on a ruffled
and dismayed appearance out over the water. He landed along the
water's edge and picked his way down the beach, eyes on the sand.

"You two been together awhile?"

"Ten months," she said. "Long enough. You know, all the
girls like Hoyt. He's cute and he sings in a band. Most of the
time, he's even nice. More than you can say for a lot of the guys

around here. But I'm not thinking too far ahead or anything like that." She looked out the screen window. The rain was falling harder now, pitting the surface of the pea-green ocean. "Especially after this." A big black ant appeared on the wall beside her, moving frantically for the ceiling. Melissa put her thumb over it and pushed. "Yuck," she said, rubbing her thumb on the towel. "Sometimes you do things just because they're fun enough at the time, you know?" She inspected her thumb and then looked up, smiling. "Hoyt, that is. Not the ant."

If our conversation out on the water had been easy and light, the day had taken a turn, gathering subtext as it went. It left me searching for things to talk about.

"It's been great to see my aunt again," I said. It seemed banal and obvious enough.

I saw her blink in the gathering darkness. "She's a strong lady. Looks out for her family." I wondered if she'd meant it to sound like a backhanded compliment. Then she tapped my knee lightly with one finger and the thought vanished. She looked at me. "Your mother must be something too."

I told her about my mother, how she had been in a home for a few years but had never lost the fighting spirit. "If it wasn't for my mother, Aunt Val would have never come down here," I said. I gave her the quick version. She knew nothing about it. Hoyt Lee obviously didn't go in for family history.

"And I guess we wouldn't be sitting here." She smiled. I laughed uneasily. Outside, thunder rumbled.

"How do you like Rolly Lee?" I asked after a moment. "You think he's good father-in-law material?" I grinned to take the edge off the question.

She scrunched up her nose and shook her head. "First off, I'm not getting married, and if I was it wouldn't be with your cousin."

She looked up at me. "Rolly Lee's okay," she said, then turned her
eyes back to the floor. A moment passed. The water dripping from
the damaged roof was beginning to pool in the corner. "Rolly Lee
told me that you had a brother." I turned from the window and
sat down on the floor across the gazebo from her. "And that he
disappeared." Melissa was looking straight at me now.

"I do have a brother," I said. "I haven't seen him in more
than ten years." The thought of Rolly Lee having this conversation with her threw a chill over me.

She pulled the towel from around her neck and tossed it at
me. "Your hair's wet," she said.

"Thanks," I said, and rubbed at the back of my neck.

"What happened to him?"

I had been asked the question hundreds of times in a decade,
by relatives and old friends, girlfriends and new friends, col-
leagues and teachers. I never wanted to answer and grew more
and more reticent until I simply avoided people who had asked
and, when that couldn't be done, avoided any topic of conversation that might lead to such questions.

"He disappeared," I said. "Coleman was troubled. He had
problems, but nothing that seemed too big. Then one morning
I woke up and watched him leaving out the back gate. We never
saw him again."

"Wow," she said. Her tone was one of fascination and not
pity. "He never called you or wrote you?"

I shook my head. "Nothing."

She looked up at the ceiling. "Can you imagine just waking
up one day and leaving your own life?"

I shrugged. "I suppose. Some days I wouldn't mind it."

"I'm sorry," she said, her tone changing, "you don't really
want to talk about this." She slid over on the towel so that she

was closer to me. "I'm being nosy. But it's so amazing in a way. Sometimes I wish I could just go. Leave everything behind. Florida, Hoyt, my friends, all the stores and the restaurants and the people around here, and just go somewhere new."

"I think things are the same everywhere," I said. "The window dressing is just different."

She considered this for a moment. "Maybe, but it's also you that could change."

"I guess so."

It was beginning to get dark outside. When Melissa spoke again it was like having a Maglite flashed in my eyes. "You think he's still alive, don't you?"

My legs were aching with the cold and the dampness inside the gazebo. I stretched them out and rubbed at my shins, happy that the ugly scars would be invisible in the near dark. "I do," I said. "I don't know why, but I do."

She moved across the diminishing distance in the gazebo until we were sitting next to one another. She took the towel from my fist and wrapped it around our shoulders. When she spoke again, it was a near whisper. "It's why you're here, in Florida, isn't it?"

I looked at her and nodded, tears filling my eyes. She ran the tip of her finger across my eyelids. "You're right to believe," she said. I could smell the traces of her perfume lingering close to her body after a day of sun and sand. She ran her hands through my hair and pulled me closer to her. Our lips met in the dark and I could taste salt from the Gulf on her mouth.

As we stretched out together on the sodden towel in the dark, water dripping from the roof onto the ruined planks below us, I realized that it had stopped raining.

32.

FOR TWENTY-FOUR HOURS, people came and went from the small cottage, always received by my mother, who, to her credit, never wept in front of any of the visitors. She offered them coffee and cookies and answered the same questions over and over with patience and grace. The couple who ran the cottage complex came by with homemade key lime pie and a big bottle of pink wine. There were two police officers and a heavy-set, grey-haired man from the National Park Service. And of course, Aunt Val and Rolly Lee. The phone rang constantly. Most often it was my father, who was unable to get back to Florida and needed constant updates. With every knock at the door, every ring of the phone, the circles under her eyes seemed to deepen. Outside the picture window, the tide came in, and then it went out again.

My mother saved her grief for the evening when she left me in front of the television set and disappeared into the bedroom, closing the door quietly behind her. I listened to her muffled sobs as Magnum PI argued with Higgins in sunny Hawaii and then the A-Team solved another case with a war's worth of bullets and not a casualty in sight.

The only casualty was my brother Coleman, twelve years old, last seen falling from a boat in Everglades National Park during a severe thunderstorm, when his mother thought he was safe in a movie theatre in Fort Myers. In my ten-year-old head, a denial of the kind that keeps kids believing in Santa Claus past the age where they ought to be shaving was in full effect. But I knew that when I lay down that night on the hide-a-bed, the ceiling fan turning monotonously over me, there would be no Coleman to steal the covers, to kick me in the night while he dreamed his crazy dreams. It was no consolation.

It was a tale that had to be told again and again. Rolly Lee was the last person to see my brother alive. At the age of ten, it's hard to believe that the grown-ups close to you could possibly do bad things, but now I see how bad it looked for Rolly Lee that day, driving back to Sanibel with an empty seat in the front of his truck.

The story went like this:

Coleman had been bothering Rolly Lee for another chance to go alligator watching. With the last week of our vacation winding down, it didn't look like there was going to be time. Rolly Lee worked for a living (or so he said), and with Aunt Val in his life, his time was scarce. It would have to wait until next year.

That is, until Rolly Lee was recruited for one last babysitting job before his in-laws headed back to Canada. This time, Aunt Val and my mother were going out on the town—back to the Warehouse in Fort Myers. The plan was that we'd stay with Rolly Lee overnight and get picked up in the morning when my mother dropped Aunt Val off.

Rolly Lee implied that the trip into the swamps was Coleman's idea. We all knew how fascinated he was by the Everglades. For Coleman, such an excursion was a natural progression: he had started off scouring the grounds of our cottage, looking for black snakes in the branches of the tall gumbo limbo, poking around in the small swampland behind the garbage Dumpsters for alligators. The trip we had taken with Rolly Lee to Okeechobee had been the next step. But for a boy fascinated with alligators, the Everglades were Ground Zero, and everything else only served to deepen his desire to explore the fabled swamp. Every summer my father promised to take us there. The only problem was that he always seemed to forget his promise by the time we got to Florida. He worked hard all year round and, for two weeks, he would avoid getting into a car and going anywhere if he could help it. As it was, my father paddling a canoe through the mangrove swamps was a tough thing to picture.

So that night, instead of going to see *E.T.*, my brother talked Rolly Lee into a trip to the Everglades. The distances were daunting: almost an hour from Rolly Lee's trailer in Fort Myers to Rook Bannister's place in Clewiston to drop me off, then a good hour and a half driving like hell down 27 until they met up with 41 and could double back westward toward the swamp. Along 41, a desolate stretch of highway that cuts east and west from Everglades City to Miami, were multiple places to park and head off into the swamp. At one such spot, Rolly Lee had a skiff stashed.

By Rolly Lee's account, when they dropped me off at Rook Bannister's, it was a fine evening. A typical Florida night, thick with humidity and mosquitoes. The drive down to 41 was uneventful, and at sundown that evening they parked the truck, grabbed Rolly Lee's skiff and set off into the swamp, with nothing but something to drink (beer for Rolly, Coke for my brother), a set of fishing poles in case they got bored with looking for gators, and a pair of heavy-duty flashlights. If you shine a light across a pond or a lake in Florida at night, it illuminates the eyes of any alligators that might be in the water. Some gladesmen swear that a male's eyes shine a deep, ruby red while the smaller females shine bright yellow. It was one of many fine points that Coleman had explained to me. In hindsight, I should have been troubled by his knowledge of the finer points of gator hunting.

It was a strange night: quiet and still. It was forty minutes before they spotted their first gator, and as Rolly Lee told it, by

the time Coleman looked in the right direction, it had disappeared under the tea-coloured water, leaving only a string of
pearl-like air bubbles in its wake. That night, there was not a
bird to be seen in the swamp. This was a bad sign, normally an
indication that bad weather was on the way. Rolly Lee picked up
on it, explained to Coleman that birds sensed things first, well
before humans cottoned on, and that they took cover in the mangrove swamps, waiting out storms under the tangles of roots and
thick undergrowth. He thought it would be a good idea to come
back another day, but Coleman knew that day would be a year
later and he was determined to press on. He wanted to go home
having seen a really big one.

He would get his wish.

They'd gone off to explore a cramped area of the swamp, one
of many twists and nooks where the slash pines and dry land
encroach on the shallow water, and you have to navigate through
cypress roots back toward the deeper, more abundant water of a
slough. This is what they were doing when they spotted him.
Rolly Lee heard something behind the boat in the water, and
when he turned to investigate, he saw the gator, floating languidly in the skiff's wake. This time, Coleman saw him. I could
imagine how excited he would have been, could picture him
shining the light across the back of the skiff, the beam dancing
onto Rolly Lee's face and into his eyes as he stood poling them
along, before lighting on the drifting thirteen-foot gator, his
eyes blood-red in the artificial light. I could see how happy
Coleman would be, but also how this wouldn't be enough for
him, that when the gator disappeared under the thick, hot
swamp water, mosquitoes flecking around the spot where he'd
submerged, they would have to find him. One more look. Just
one more.

Now it had started to rain, the warm wind blowing in off the Gulf and through the dense swamplands, and no sign of the big gator. With the heavy rain came swarms of mosquitoes and no-see-ums, their intent so pure and focused that when you stopped to swat them off your right arm, a dozen would be on your left by the time you'd finished. Rolly Lee had bug spray in middling supplies. This was his only concession to his role of babysitter for the night. Bug spray was just one thing among many that Rolly Lee deemed "for pussies and wussies."

Out into the deeper water they went. They caught a glimpse of what they thought was the same gator, the spiny ridges and nostrils cresting above the water. Rolly Lee had started slowly back toward the direction of 41 and the car, hoping he could get them another look at the big gator and back to the car. Two birds, one stone.

They spotted him again. He'd come out of the water and was on the muddy bank, gleaming grey-black in the night, jaw poised slightly ajar. Coleman stood up in the boat to get a better look, and Rolly Lee grabbed him by the back of his waistband and told him to sit down. The wind had picked up and only the intermittent canopy of branches and leaves was saving them from a full soaking. I imagined myself around the same time, dozing off to sleep in front of Rook Bannister's television, Reynolds the peanut-butter-coloured dog beside me, paws atwitch.

Coleman needed one more look. This we could all believe. In a way, this could be the metaphor for his whole life and a summation of the differences between two brothers. He stood up in the front of the skiff unsteadily, craning his neck to get a look at the bank where they'd last seen the alligator. I could see him in the boat, brave beyond his years, the wind howling in his face and the rain drumming on the thick, damp wood of the craft.

A platoon of mosquitoes landed on the back of his neck. He swatted at them, looking downward for a moment in an effort to stretch his neck out and then get them all. When he turned back to the water, the gator was there, rising from the blackness in a rage of swampy froth and hot rain, thick, heavy jaws desperate to clamp down on the front of the skiff. An ancient stink poisoning the air. Rolly Lee grabbed for Coleman, tried to pull him back down into the boat, but the gator rose again, water blowing in a thick, steaming mist from his nostrils, the white of his soft underbelly glinting in the night. This time his front end caught the bow and breasthook and threw Coleman onto one foot.

He flailed for balance then disappeared over the side of the boat into the swamp, his flashlight still in his right hand.

The errant light of that flashlight, its gleam diminishing as it disappeared under the water, was the last sign of my brother that Rolly Lee was able to find. Even the alligator had disappeared. When Rolly Lee got the skiff back to his hiding spot off 41, he was unable to even find teeth marks on the crude swamp craft.

Rolly Lee spent long hours in the swamp, calling out to my brother, tracing and retracing the path of the boat from where they'd first seen the big bull gator to where Coleman had met the water. He was convinced that what had happened was impossible. The swamps were dense, but Coleman had to be somewhere close, sitting on a bank, waiting for Rolly Lee to come fetch him, scared out of his wits but safe.

But he wasn't.

My mother wouldn't look Rolly Lee in the eye. There had been no screaming since that first morning, but when Rolly and Aunt Val came over to check on my mother the next day, the tension was thick enough that even I could feel it. When my mother and

I were alone, she pulled the telephone from the kitchen into the bathroom and closed the door. Snatches of conversations drifted out to me where I sat on the sofa, my hands in my lap, watching the ocean through the window. A thick, pounding dread began to creep into me as I sat there, listening to the alternately hushed and then hysterical dialogue from the bathroom. I had nothing to compare this to, no way of knowing if it would end or if everything would be okay. If a childhood is blessed then it is a childhood without uncertainty; one with solid things to count on and easy points of reference. Now it was as though my family had gone to sleep on Sanibel Island and woken up drifting through a cold, black cosmos, into the uncertainty and menace of a vast universe.

But one thing began to crystallize in my ten-year-old head, a clear notion from listening to my mother, watching her react to Rolly and Aunt Val, seeing the raised eyebrows and solemn nods of the police and the park authority and everyone else who wanted to know *exactly* what happened:

Nobody really believed that Rolly Lee's story was the full story.

It *was* hard to believe, unless you were ten years old, I suppose. An experienced swamper heads off into the Everglades with a twelve-year-old boy for an evening of alligator watching. A storm drifts in, as they often do in Southern Florida. The big bull gator they've been watching turns menace and tries to eat the skiff like it's some oversized steak. The boy goes overboard into the swamp that is barely deep enough to cover him at its darkest fathoms. He disappears into the water, a deep copper from the roots of the mangroves that line the swamplands, as though he's been dropped from a plane thirty thousand feet up in the sky. He disappears and never reappears.

But Coleman wasn't the only person to disappear in the swamps that night. The day Rolly Lee brought me home alone there was a story on the Fort Myers afternoon news about an Everglades ranger who hadn't returned from his shift. It gave some credibility to Rolly Lee's story: the Everglades could be a dangerous place. My mother shook her head and laughed sharply when I told her about it. "He's probably run off with a woman," she said.

It's difficult to know what kind of scrutiny Rolly Lee was about to face. My father was on his way back from Ontario, the police had spent hours interviewing Rolly Lee, both with my mother present then alone in Fort Myers. As the hours passed, a terrible certainty began to mount. Once, from her makeshift office in the cottage bathroom, where the horrifying nature of what had to be discussed could be kept from her remaining son, I heard my mother say this: "Rolly Lee, Rolly Lee." There was a pause and I heard her voice catch. "I trusted you." Bad times had come and worse ones were on the way.

I remember wondering if maybe it was I who had died and was only dreaming a vivid nightmare for the rest of my family. I lay awake on the pull-out couch at night, watching the fan spin around and around, hearing the surf on the shore, waiting for the gentle snore from my mother's room that would let me know that things were changing, that she'd gone to sleep and that everything would be okay. I thought about Coleman, about the hours he spent sunning on his back like an otter, as comfortable in the deep waters of the Gulf of Mexico as he was asleep on the couch. Coleman was a strong swimmer and fearless to boot. A series of grim possibilities played out in my head in lieu of sleep: Coleman falling from the boat and smacking his head on the thick plywood, knocking himself out before he hit the water. The alligator clutching Coleman and going into the death roll, threading its way down to the bottom of the swamp like an auger.

But none of it would matter. Sometime after I finally got to sleep late that night, the second without Coleman, there was a sharp knock on the glass slats of the cottage door. I heard no movement from my mother's room, so I got up from the couch, the tiled floor air-conditioned to a sharp coolness under my bare feet, and went to the door. Standing outside, in the same light of dawn that Rolly Lee and I had driven in two mornings before, was a Florida State Trooper.

Standing behind him was my brother Coleman.

33.

I WOKE UP TO THE SUN playing across my face. I blinked then shielded my eyes against the brightness filling the gazebo window. My back felt like I'd been sleeping on an anchor and I could feel the raw itch of no-see-um bites all around my ankles and on my arms. Waking up in strange places was becoming a recurring theme in my life. I thought things had hit the pinnacle of strangeness when I'd awakened in a hospital bed sporting a Civil War deserter's beard and a leg like a battered rump roast. Little did I know, that was just the beginning.

On the floor beside me, her head nestled on her hands, legs tucked up into her tummy, was Melissa Wheeler. There was a soft smile on her face, eyelids stretched placidly over her baby blues. I watched her sleep and thought back to the evening before, her hot breath on my neck, the wind coming in off the surf, seeing her toned, tanned body lit by shards of moonlight creeping in through the holes in the gazebo. I'd never been a lady-killer.

There had always been someone in my life, but women didn't stop to look at me when I walked past. Melissa Wheeler, on the other hand, turned every head everywhere she went. While I watched her sleep, she stirred long enough to sweep a cascade of blonde hair away from her mouth with an impatient sigh.

I knew I'd fucked up. Walked into an already complicated situation with my own baggage and questions and further muddied the water by sleeping with my cousin's girl. Sure, he was a jackass. Ten minutes in his company was enough to know that. But blood was thicker than water and this was sure to be trouble. It was time to get on with looking for Coleman, even if it meant realizing the futility of the search and going home. I was beginning to feel like Florida was a snare opening wide over me, ready to snap the next time I poked my nose somewhere it shouldn't be. I sat up on the dirty wood floor. A boat passed way out on the water. I waited to hear the ripples from its wake crawl up on the shore.

Instead, I was roused by the sound of approaching voices. An arm was thrust into the gazebo and a bucket dropped onto the floor, the stink of bait filling the air. I looked up and there were two grey-haired men, shirtless and tanned, carrying fishing poles.

"Morning, sunshine," one of them said. Melissa stirred on the floor and sat up, rubbing her eyes.

The other man grinned at me and looked at his watch. "Check-out time is in five minutes, unless you want to pay for another night."

They were still laughing when I looked out the window and saw them jogging into the surf, a glorious day breaking above them, as gleeful as though they'd found the fountain of youth.

We hadn't got very far up Tarpon Bay Road when I noticed an approaching pickup pull off into the entrance of the Bailey Tract.

"Shit, that's Val," Melissa said. She let go of my hand and we crossed the road.

Aunt Val stood with her arms crossed up against the truck watching us silently behind dark glasses. She opened the door for us without a word then went around to the driver's seat. By the time we'd crossed the first half of the causeway back toward Fort Myers, she still hadn't spoken.

"Hoyt ditched us," Melissa said. I was monkey in the middle and she pinched at the underside of my leg where Aunt Val couldn't see it.

Val nodded. "So I heard."

"Him and Skeeter took my car for beer and left us at the beach."

Aunt Val peered over the edge of her glasses at us. "Uh-huh," she said. We crossed the remainder of the causeway and I counted the thick wooden posts that separated the road from the beach as we went past. A big white pelican sat on the last one before the tolls, a stern look on his face. "They got a pay phone up at Bailey's. You know that," Val said. "Boy, even my Canadian nephew here would remember that."

"They had my purse. We didn't have two nickels to rub together." Melissa was beginning to sound frustrated. "Besides, it was raining."

"Sure it was, hon. Ain't it always raining?"

Melissa sighed and pushed her face up against the window. She reminded me of a petulant six-year-old.

"I'm sorry, Aunt Val," I said.

"Sorry's about the size of it," she said.

We dropped Melissa off at the Rolly Lee ranch where Hoyt Lee had parked her car. She squeezed my leg briefly, flashed her sad eyes and went across the yard toward the house. The thought of seeing Hoyt sent a tremble up my bad leg. I gripped it for support.

"Go on," Aunt Val said quietly, watching her through narrow, red-rimmed eyes, "go see your friend Rolly Lee." Then she turned to me. "Stupid," Aunt Val said.

"Seems like there's no love lost between the two of you," I said.

"No, you," she said, looking at me with her tired eyes. "Stupid, Jasper. Stupid, stupid, stupid." She emphasized each one with a tap on my leg. "Not my problem though," she said, "and Lord knows I got enough of them." I was beginning to get tired of her pity trip. "I'll take you back to your motel."

"Thanks."

We backed up and I noticed Rolly Lee emerge from the barn, shirtless and listing slightly to one side as he took slow, deliberate steps. He held something long and metallic in one hand that glinted in the morning sunshine. He shouted something unintelligible in our direction then started toward Melissa. For a second I wondered if he'd been hit over the head with something blunt and heavy. "Aunt Val," I said, "I think Rolly Lee wants you." She glanced in the rear-view mirror.

"Nope," she said.

As we pulled away, I watched him in the side mirror and realized what he was holding: a bang stick. Just like the one Coleman and I had seen in the back of his truck sixteen years ago.

"Jesus," I said. "Is he okay?"

"Tweaking. He hasn't been to bed since he took your friends out yesterday," she said as the car disappeared from the open space and down the dirt road, a bucket of hood ornaments marking the entrance to Rolly's property. "All this shit," she said.

"I don't think he's made one flat dime from any of it. Anyone gets interested in any of it, he's usually so drunk or fucked up that he just gives it away."

"Where's it come from?"

She shook her head and sped up. "I don't know," she said. "Here, there, everywhere. Driving around on trash night, flea markets, dumps. You know, everything that everyone else decided was worthless. Just like Rolly Lee himself. Give him something to do when he's tweaking. Comes out here and arranges it."

"Tweaking?"

Aunt Val lit a cigarette. "Oh, Jasper," she said, "you ain't seen much of this world, have you? Rolly's a meth smoker from way back." She waved her arm out the window. "All this, everything you see, it's all to feed the beast."

"Shit," I said. The mysterious barn fire Rolly Lee had alluded to suddenly made sense. Cooking meth was a dangerous hobby.

"Shit's right," she said. We were getting toward the edges of their property. "If Rolly Lee's daddy hadn't died and left him this land, we'd still be living in a goddamn trailer or under a bridge." I thought of Rodney.

"Shit," I said. This was a far cry from the "nobody's perfect but we're still together, getting by" picture Aunt Val had painted the night we'd arrived. I wondered if things always swung this wide between Aunt Val and Rolly, or if my visit had anything at all to do with it.

"So you said," she said. "And you don't know the half of it. Rolly Lee's never done an honest day's work in his whole life. Any shady business you could ever get your head around, he's been there, done that."

"I'm sorry, Val," I said, and put a hand on her shoulder. She shook my hand off. "Uh-uh, Jasper," she said, "you're just one more fly in the ointment." She was driving faster now and not looking at me. I could see the muscles in her jawline tighten. We hit North Fort Myers, a few cars slow-poking it in either direction, typical mid-morning traffic in the hottest state. There was silence.

"I don't know why you're here, Jasper, or what foolhardy idea brought you this way," she said. I started to respond and she cut me off. "And I don't want to know," she said. We stopped at a light. "Sometimes you got to learn to let things go. No matter what you think, gone's gone." A pickup truck towering on massive, oversized tires pulled up next to us and revved its engine. It seemed like there was one at every stoplight. A man grinned down at us behind sunglasses.

"I'm so sick of Florida," she said, finally looking at me.

I nodded, not sure of what to say.

We pulled away from the lights and I saw her bottom lip tremble and she cleared her throat. "Oh, Jasper," she said, reaching for my hand, "your mother would be so ashamed of me if she could see me now."

"I don't think that's true."

"Yeah," she said, "it is, Jasper. Your mother, in her own quiet way, told me what she thought about Rolly Lee." Aunt Val sighed her way into an exhausted smile. "Said her and your daddy were concerned Rolly Lee might not be the best provider. And this was before"—she looked over at me, all traces of the smile long gone from her face—"this was before the way that vacation ended. After that, your mother didn't bother telling me much of anything she was thinking anymore." Aunt Val ran one trembling hand through her hair. "Rolly Lee was going to smarten up. He was so scared, so shaken up by what happened with your brother. I saw that side of him, that side nobody else ever saw." I felt her look over at me but I kept my eyes on the road ahead. "Rolly had an uncle with a landscaping business up on the Panhandle and we were going to move up there. For years we always seemed to be a week away from moving, starting something new. But you know, it can take years to realize that there just ain't no changing some people."

She rubbed at her eyes, smearing her mascara. Two teenagers in low-slung shorts walked across the road in front of us and she blasted the horn. "Move!" she shouted, slamming her fist into the steering wheel. "Move, goddamnit!" I caught a look of genuine surprise on their faces as we roared past.

We pulled up outside the motel. I could see Donny's truck parked below the room, mud spattered across the tires and wheel wells and Donny himself leaning over the balcony above.

"I'm sorry, Aunt Val, really I am."

She shook her head and smiled. "I'm sorry," she said. "I just get so dog-tired sometimes. I just want to see your mother again."

"You will," I said. I kissed her on the cheek. "You're okay to get back?"

She nodded.

"I'll see you soon," I said. I got out of the car and stood on the hot tarmac. She looked at me through the open door.

"You tell me when you're going," she said, "and maybe you could save a seat for me."

I nodded and slammed the door.

"Hey," Donny said, "starting to worry about you."

I shook my head. "Don't worry," I said, grinning. I told him where I'd been the previous night.

"Ah, I see," he said, looking off toward the interstate. "No kidding?" He laughed softly. "Wow," he said. "You and your cousin must be making fast friends."

The door to the motel room was cracked slightly and there was a whoop and a crash from inside. I looked at Donny quizzically.

"Duaner," he said. "And his new best friend. Your uncle's buddy Woody. Came out with us yesterday." I noticed heavy, dark circles under his eyes. "These fools haven't been to bed."

"Where'd you sleep?"

Donny nodded toward his truck and I noticed the front seat was fully reclined. "I'll give him one night," he said, "he's on vacation."

"You're a better friend than I'd be," I said. "How was the day out?"

Donny's eyes flashed at me and he looked out toward the highway again, at the big rigs crawling across the overpass. "Well," he said, "we didn't do much fishing, I can tell you that much." He stopped himself.

"What happened?"

He squeezed the railing and sighed. "I don't know, Jasper," he said. "I don't feel right getting involved in all this."

"All what?" He shrugged and kicked a frayed cigarette butt over the edge of the balcony with his flip-flop. "Donny," I said, "where'd you guys go?"

"We went to Lake Trafford, near Immokalee," he said.

A face appeared at the window. "Look who's here!" There was some garbled, shouty conversation in the room and then Duane appeared in the doorway, swaying lightly, eyes poppy-red. "Jasper," he said, "ain't seen you in a coon's age!"

"Shut up," Donny said. "You trying to sound like a redneck?"

Duane's new friend pushed his way into the doorway. "Someone say redneck?" he slurred. I recognized him as the impossibly small-headed man from Rolly's driveway. He'd looked a lot fresher then. I could smell his breath from five feet away and it suggested that he had been drinking paint thinner. I caught a glimpse of the room behind him. It was as though an abstract artist had completed an installation involving empty beer cans and flat surfaces.

"Jeez," I said, "you guys having a good time?"

"We're havin' a go at it anyhows," Woody said. "You're Rolly Lee's nephew," he said. It was a flat statement. I nodded. "Lucky for you," he said, and disappeared back into the room. I looked at Duane, still wobbling in the doorway, his eyes closed.

"Feel like a drive?" I said to Donny.

He grinned. "Love to," he said. He took Duane by the shoulders and gently led him back into the motel room then shut the door behind him.

"Let's go," he said.

We didn't get very far. Two blocks up the road from the motel was a small bar nestled at the periphery of a mid-sized shopping centre that boasted a JC Penney *and* a Kmart. The Painted Frog's marquee advertised a special on steak sandwiches and draft so we decided to stop for a bite to eat before heading out for our drive. As we got out of the truck, rain began to spatter the pavement and we had to make a run for the front door of the Frog.

"Hope the weather's better the day after tomorrow," Donny said, rubbing at his pate with a napkin off the table. Other than two baseball-capped men slumped at the bar nursing mugs of draft beer, we were the only customers in the entire place.

"Better hope your partner's recovered," I said. "That's going to be some hangover, even without the eggs."

Donny grinned. "He's a laugh a minute. God love him, but I'll be happy to see the tail end of him when we get home."

Home. The word held only a vague meaning to me. I was unemployed, my father was gone, my mother in care, and I was sitting in a dive two thousand miles away with my ex-girlfriend's boyfriend.

"Sorry," Donny said. "You're probably not looking forward to heading back."

I shrugged. "It's looking like a dead end," I said.

Donny waved at the waitress who was leaning up against the end of the bar. "Let's eat," he said, "then we'll go for a drive. Don't call it a dead end yet. You're probably just tired."

I could have leaned across the table and hugged him. "You'd be tired too if you'd slept in a gazebo with your American cousin's girl."

Donny's eyes widened and he looked out the window. I'd seen less of his devout side since leaving Ontario, but I knew that I'd probably crossed a line or three in his books with Melissa Wheeler. He turned from the window, a grin slowly spreading across his face. "I'll give you this," he said, "you're obviously not worried about keeping life simple."

We ate lunch in silence, jaws straining against thick, stale bread and rubbery steak. It was sub-par all the way, but I was hungry. A man can't live on beer alone. Donny watched me mop up the ketchup from my French fries with the tail end of the bun and smiled.

"Terrible, eh," he said.

"Wretched," I said, jaws still working through the bread.

He waited until I'd finished chewing. "Jasper," he said. "I'm not sure about your uncle. Rolly Lee."

I raised my eyebrows and dabbed at the corner of my mouth with a napkin. "Makes two of us," I said. "I wasn't sure about him when I was ten years old."

Donny nodded heavily. "Yesterday afternoon," he said. "Six of us went out in two boats. As I said, we barely got our rods in the water, him and his friends were so drunk. Of course Duane doesn't need any encouragement, so I'm out there sober as a judge with a bunch of drunken maniacs."

"I guess you had yourself a real Florida experience."

"No. Florida's filled with serious fishermen . . . With the fish you find out here you have to be. You'd find the same idiots back home." He smiled. "Face it, we're staying with one."

"In the best possible sense of the word, of course."

"Of course." Donny shook his head and looked out the window. In true Florida fashion, it was a sunny afternoon again. "I'm a hunter," he said. "Always have been. My father and uncle took me out from the time I was thirteen years old. Deer and duck. A lot of people don't like it. They think it's cruel." I was one of them but wasn't going to interrupt. "It took me a while to get used to it. They talk about men losing their nerve when they sight a buck. You get looking at their faces, at their eyes, and you can't hold the gun straight. But what my dad taught me is that if you take an animal's life, you best honour it as well. You kill an animal, you ought to be looking to eat that animal." He stopped and sighed. "Your uncle, Rolly Lee . . ." He stopped again.

"Go on," I said.

Donny looked at me, his brown eyes wide and intent. "That bang stick he's got." He held his hands out as though he were holding one. "He brought it with him yesterday. Didn't bring no fishing pole, but he brought this bang stick."

"I've seen it," I said.

"We stopped for a beer and a bite along the shoreline partway through the day," he said. "Sure enough, we've been there about half an hour and a gator appears at the edge of the water. Not out of the water, but just laying there checking us out. We're in his house, you ask me." He shrugged. "Your uncle," he said, "crept over, making I guess an alligator call. Like a distressed baby. 'Watch this,' he said. When he got within spitting distance of the alligator, he shot it in the head with that bang stick. Let it bleed out in the water and left it there. When we finished up and got back in the boats, it was floating on its back. It had a pale white stomach that almost looked soft. I don't know much about gators, but the sight of its stomach surprised me. There was blood in the water. One of Rolly Lee's buddies said another gator would come for him. And your uncle thought it was funny. He sat back in the boat and laughed as we went out, away from the shore."

A hollow ache spread through the pit of my stomach.

Donny looked across the table at me. I could see that there was something else, something that he wasn't sure he wanted to tell me.

"Spill it," I said.

Donny nodded, his eyes flitting away to the floor. "This Melissa," he said. "For your cousin's girl, Rolly Lee sure brings her up a lot."

34.

GARY TOMLINSON WORKED at the Shell Factory, a Fort Myers landmark that I remembered visiting on rainy days with my mother and aunt. Sanibel and Captiva islands were a mecca for shell collectors; barrier islands that stretched out into the Gulf of Mexico as part of a large plateau and acted like a scoop for drifting seashells. The Shell Factory was part of an older Florida, a pre-Disney tourist attraction from the days where every roadside gas station had a gator pit to entertain the children while Daddy got the sedan fuelled up. You could buy shells freshly plucked from the Gulf: clams, augers, whelks, tulips and coquinas that were gently stacked into cloth-lined baskets around the massive, barn-like store. Or, if your tastes ran to kitsch, there were clam ashtrays and conch toothbrush holders, rubber pelicans and shark's tooth earrings.

The events of the past day—the trip out to Sanibel and the night with Melissa—had waylaid me from my search for Coleman. Now I was going to make up for lost time. I'd got Manuel Sherrill on the phone after lunch at the Painted Frog. I told him about meeting Devron Jacobs and Rodney at Centennial Park and the one lead I'd managed to dredge up.

"Devron Jacobs," he said. "He tell you he was one of the Highwaymen?"

Sherrill gave me Gary Tomlinson's name when I mentioned the carnival. "Gary's not the friendliest boy on the block," he said, "but he was one of the assistant general managers up in Gibsonton, near Tampa, at the carnival. Until he got picked up in his car outside the pancake house a couple of summers back. Had his pants around his ankles and a seventeen-year-old boy that worked for him at the carnival. Fellow was so goddamned embarrassed I let him go. Not much I could do. It got back to his boss up in Tampa though. Last I heard he's working out at the Shell Factory in the warehouse, sorting through conch shells." I could hear him grinning down the line. "Anyhow . . . stay in touch, Jasper," he said, and there was a pause. "That's me subtly keeping tabs on the shady Canadian element that's arrived on my doorstep." I promised I'd be good as long as he took me for another burrito before I left town.

Donny and I found Gary Tomlinson behind the Shell Factory,

sorting through a cardboard box lined with plastic and filled with shells. We'd parked the truck around the side, away from the tourists filing in and out of the front doors. Another employee, a heavily made-up Southern belle with a thick stomach and scratchy tattoos, told us where to find Tomlinson.

He stopped working when he saw us approaching, looking toward the loading dock and into the open, warehouse section of the Shell Factory where new shells were processed before being sold inside the store.

"Got nothing to say," he said. "Talk to Barry, he already knows when he's getting the money."

It occurred to me that travelling with Donny was already paying off —muscle made people uncomfortable, muscle made people talk.

"Are you Gary Tomlinson?" I held out my hand.

He wiped his hands on the back of his overalls and extended one hand tentatively. "What's this about?"

"I wanted to ask you about someone you might have worked with."

"This ain't about the car?" He drew a Kool from the front pocket of his overalls and tapped it on his arm. "Figured this was about the car."

I shook my head. "Nothing to do with money," I said.

Tomlinson grinned. "Well, fuck me," he said, "I thought it was always about money."

"You worked at the carnival, correct?"

He yanked the cigarette from his mouth and blew a fog of menthol smoke toward us. Donny shifted his feet and looked off toward the Tamiami Trail, where a slow snake of cars headed toward the Caloosahatchee. "Fuck yourself," he said, and went back to work picking through the shells.

"Whatever you think this is about," I said, "it isn't."

Gary Tomlinson ignored me.

"I'm looking for someone you might have worked with. A guy who went missing a long time back, might have worked for you. Alligator guy."

He glanced up only briefly. "Missing a long time usually means dead," he said. "Now go on, I got work to do."

I noticed Donny's eyes drifting slowly from the horizon to the skinny man sorting the shells in front of us. It was as though he was following a bird in flight that had landed. He took a step toward Tomlinson. "We're hoping that this man isn't dead," he said, "so we were wondering if you might remember anything about him."

"Don't remember shit," Gary Tomlinson said, "makes life a whole lot easier that way." He put his right hand palm down on the tarmac to steady himself as he worked. Donny's size twelve sneaker was on it before Tomlinson saw it coming. He yelped and tried to yank it out from under the heavy rubber sole. "Fucker," he said. "Get it off." There seemed to be a lot more white to his eyes now and they darted off toward the loading bay. A lanky black man with a red ball cap who'd been working there grinned at us then disappeared into the warehouse. Gary Tomlinson was obviously popular with his fellow employees.

"This isn't about your young boyfriend," I said. "I'm looking for a guy, maybe homeless, good with reptiles, especially alligators."

Tomlinson's eyes flitted about as though he was searching the dusty reaches of his memory. "I don't know," he said. "Get off my fuckin' hand. Let me think." Donny smiled at me and moved his sneaker. Tomlinson shook his hand and cringed. "Fucking ape," he said, not looking at Donny. "You're lucky you didn't break it."

"Did you have alligators at the carnival?"

He pulled another cigarette out, this time with less aplomb. "Ancient history," he said. "I ain't worked there in two years. You know how many people I had working for me?" I repeated the question. "Yeah," he said, "we had a couple of gators from a farm in Everglades City. Charged kids ten bucks to pose with them. Fuckers were doped out of their heads and had their jaws taped shut. Cruel, you ask me."

"Sure," I said. "You're all heart. The guy I'm looking for was Canadian. About my size."

He shook his head. A grin slowly began to spread across his leathery face, his lips stretching thinly over two front teeth that had been broken off halfway down. It was a face that had seen a dispute or three. "Well," he said, "good news is I do remember. Bad news for you is that you're shit out of luck. Unless this boy you're looking for is a big black fucker with one hand. That was our gator expert." He held his hand up and flexed it. "Had some mechanical job, could even hold a cigarette with it. Rest of those boys came up from Everglades City with the gators. Didn't work for me."

Gary Tomlinson went back to his work. "Fuckers are all cracked up," he said as we walked away, then, "A fucking Canadian gator handler," he said, "ain't that a trip."

It was a dead end. I'd returned to the Sunshine State on the thinnest of premises and now I was realizing just how futile it'd been to begin with. Throw a stone in Florida these days and you're more likely to hit a sunburned Canadian than you are a native. My other piece of information did little to narrow down the sheer size of the sample I was working with: Coleman was good with alligators. Florida had built an entire tourism industry on

the back of the not-so-distant cousin to the dinosaur and was one
of a handful of Southern states where the alligator was even
found. I suppose things could have been worse. I could have been
looking in Lincoln, Nebraska, or Washougal, Washington.

"Hey," Donny said as we merged back onto 41, heading
south, the first drops of afternoon rain beginning to fall, "it could
be worse."

I thumped my head theatrically off the dash. "Tell me," I said.
"I'm all ears."

A transport cut in front of us, trying to make an approaching
exit off the highway. Donny's eyes narrowed and he eased up on
the gas. "You don't know that your brother isn't here," he said.

"Thanks, Donny," I said, "really. You've been a rock through
all this. But . . ." I waved out the window at a sign with approaching cities and their mileage. "It's a huge fucking world out
here. Coleman could be anywhere. Florida's just one of those
places." I laughed in spite of myself.

"You're frustrated," he said. "But think things through.
Look at the leads you've got down here. Rearrange them. Go out,
have a beer, think things through. Don't throw the towel in yet."

"Sure." I nodded. I planned on drinking a beer or two. That
much I was sure of.

We pulled off at our exit. "Seriously, Jasper," he said, looking
at me out of the corner of his eye as he wheeled around the circular exit. "You ever going to come down here again? You think
you'll be taking up the hunt again after this?" Donny was a soft-
spoken man, but his zeal on this subject was approaching evan-
gelical. "Ask yourself this," he said. "Why are you here in the
first place? I know you like to come off like it doesn't matter, that
it's all a bit of a joke, but look at you, Jasper. You're here. And,"
he said, grinning, "I have a feeling it isn't for the fine company."

I nodded.

"So," he said. "Why?"

I realized I'd been clenching my jaw. If there'd been a walnut between my back teeth, it would have exploded. "You're a religious man," I said. Donny nodded softly. "My brother was touched. I always felt—we, my parents and I, always felt—that whatever scrape Coleman ended up in, he'd find a way out. He disappeared in the Everglades. I was ten years old, but I knew he was dead. Twelve-year-old kids don't disappear into the swamps in the middle of summer then emerge two days later grinning like they'd just come back from Disney World. Coleman did."

"There you go," Donny said.

"Can I ask you something?"

"Shoot," he said.

"Why do you think this is so important? I've waited ten years as it is."

We pulled into the motel parking lot. The door to the room was closed, the shade drawn. The party was over. "This is your brother," Donny said. He put a hand to his heart. "Blood," he said. "Nothing's more important."

"If I find him," I said, "you mention that to him. He's never even sent a postcard."

Donny smiled, but only slightly. "The derby's the day after tomorrow," he said. "Day after that, we've got to be on the road." He looked me dead in the eyes and then shrugged.

Two days left in Florida. I aimed to soak up some sun, drink a beer or two, and relax. Then it was time to head home and begin life anew. Find a job, a girl, and a quiet place to live.

Once I left Florida, I planned to never come back.

35.

HIS SHOES WERE GONE. Somebody, probably the police officer, had given him a pair of white athletic socks to wear. They
were pulled up to his knees. I noticed spots of blood soaking
through the white cotton around his feet and ankles. The brightness of the fabric was a sharp contrast with the mud that began
at the exact point the socks ended. It had caked and dried on his
legs, shorts, shirt and arms. Mosquito bites had given his face a
mumpish look. His forehead and cheeks were scratched and
scabbed, presumably from walking through briars and branches.

It was a miracle.

This was the first thing out of my mother's mouth when she
emerged from the bathroom, where she'd been talking to my
father in hushed, sobbing tones about "arrangements" and saw
Coleman at the door, standing behind a police officer.

"It's a miracle," she said, then her eyes flashed white and she
crumpled to the tiled floor.

36.

A SLIGHT, SINEWY MAN with a rawboned face and white
T-shirt was picking away on a steel guitar. I went to the bar and
got a beer and a shot of Jack Daniel's, found a table near the
stage, and sat down. The man played alone, accompanying
himself on a stomp board that his microphone picked up and
echoed through the Painted Frog like the sound of time itself
draining away. Melissa Wheeler hadn't arrived yet. I had two
days left in Florida and if I couldn't find my brother, the least I
could do was clean up the mess I'd made. I tossed the shot back.

It hit my gullet like rusty nails soaking in warm water. Whiskey had never been my thing except during episodes of blinding drunkenness—the times I was least likely to need it. Jack Daniel's had always reminded me of Florida vacations, of the first time we'd brought Aunt Val with us and she'd met Rolly Lee. After one of their first dates together, Aunt Val showed up at the cottage wearing a sleeveless black Jack Daniel's Old Time Tennessee Whiskey shirt, a present from Rolly Lee. Some guys used flowers to woo women, but good ol' boys from Fort Myers used whiskey.

The singer introduced a song called "Raiford Prison" and went into a mumbled monologue about his time as a prison guard and how he'd met Ted Bundy shortly before his execution. Chatter picked up around the tavern. Some regulars seated at the bar were in a spirited discussion about the Buccaneers' chances in the upcoming season. A howl came from the back of the room followed by laughter. The singer's large brown eyes made a quick dart around the room and, feeling he was losing his tenuous grip on a clientele that would have been equally satisfied with Charlie Daniels on the jukebox, he thumped a four count with his foot and hit the first chords of "Raiford Prison." The song was far more interesting than his introduction—Delta blues that had been disassembled and recaptured in dusty angles and jagged, thumping rhythms. A new take on an old feeling. Loss.

Halfway through the song, I noticed heads turning near the front door. The singer's plaintive narrative about last meals and hundred-degree cell blocks had captured the Painted Frog, but when Melissa Wheeler walked in the front door, the singer was back at square one. Shallow as it was, I had to admit my chest puffed with pride when she saw me, smiled, and made her way over, every set of eyes in the Frog trailing after her.

She sat down near the end of the song, and I nodded toward the stage. I wanted to hear the end of it.

"What is this crap?" she said, after the last chord had dissipated. She scrunched her nose toward the stage.

"Good stuff," I said, as the singer started singing without accompaniment, moaning softly about "stones in his passway" while he fitted a metal slide over his pinky. "Take a listen," I said.

She was wearing jeans and a white cotton blouse that emphasized her tan, and she'd pulled her hair back into a loose ponytail. Looking at her across the table, my mind couldn't help but drift into thoughts of the night before in the gazebo. "This is like what my mom listens to," she said, and went to the bar to get a drink.

Things were off to a good start. The day before, we'd gone from an innocuous trip to the beach to sex in a rotten gazebo. Now I couldn't seem to open my mouth without pissing her off. Donny's comment about Rolly Lee bringing her up a lot came back to me as she sauntered over to the table, her eyes fixed and dull on my face as if she could read my thoughts and didn't like what she was seeing.

We had a couple of beers and listened to the singer, Melissa tapping her foot off time and looking around the bar, for familiar faces, I guessed. For whatever reason, I hoped she didn't find any. The Painted Frog wasn't the kind of place you'd expect an attractive woman in her early twenties to know the regulars. And if you'd just slept with her, you'd hope deep in your heart that it wasn't the case.

When the singer announced he was taking a short break, there was a smattering of applause and he shuffled off the stage, a fresh cigarette hanging from his bottom lip. The jukebox kicked into some early Van Halen and I looked at Melissa across the table.

"So," she said, the smile she'd walked in with long gone.

"So."

"What you been up to?" she said.

"You mean since this morning?" It had been twelve short hours since Aunt Val had picked us up on Sanibel. "This and that," I said.

"You never told me which motel y'all were at," she said, looking around the room. "I thought maybe you'd call me."

I shrugged. "Sorry," I said, "I was out."

She rolled her eyes. "Out," she said. "Listen to Mr. Mysterious here." Her lips curled into a smirk that split the difference between playful and pissed off. "Out doing his special business, whatever that is."

I looked up to see if the guitar player was getting ready to play again. He wasn't.

Then Melissa smiled as though her mind had lit elsewhere and she grabbed my knee under the table. "You going to take me back with you? See how I like it up there? Buy me a snowsuit and one of them tocks?"

"Toques," I said.

"You know what I mean," she said.

I grinned. "Sure. You'd last about two days in an Ontario winter and you'd be on the first Greyhound back."

Melissa scowled and I felt her hand move off my knee. "I'm serious, you know," she said.

She was serious. "You need another drink? I do." I got up and went to the bar, feeling her glare across my back.

The bartender slid a Budweiser across the wet bar top and nodded toward the bottle of Jack Daniel's. "Why not," I said. "I'm on vacation." He held up two fingers and looked toward the table and Melissa. "She's trouble enough without the booze," I said. He grinned expansively and handed the shot to me.

"Let me tell you something," he said, in a low, chuckling drawl. "This girl is trouble the same way hurricanes are trouble. And the way she moves around this room some nights, she has about the same effect." He shrugged. "But she sure improves the scenery, what with being female and having all her teeth and all that jazz."

I knocked the shot back. "I'll take another," I said.

When I turned back toward the table, Melissa wasn't there anymore. I looked around the room and spotted her at the pay phone near the door, pressing the receiver between her shoulder and her blonde head and using one hand to block out the noise in the Painted Frog. Her eyes darted toward me as I walked back to the table, and I could see that she was wrapping the conversation up. In the small, open space near the front windows that had been painted over and had probably ceased to function as portals of light since the Depression, the guitar player wedged his cigarette between the tuning pegs on his National Steel and kicked into another song. This one was slow and mean, about a woman who slept all the time.

"I hate this stuff," Melissa shouted in my ear.

"You said." I was beginning to recognize that Melissa Wheeler disliked anything that took attention away from her.

We sat and watched the set. I was transfixed by the slight, intense guitarist with the thousand-yard stare. I could feel Melissa's eyes on my face throughout the set. Against all odds, the guitarist had grabbed hold of the collective attention in the Painted Frog, and when the last notes faded into silence, there was great applause. The singer blushed visibly and waved. A heavy-set older man with a white beard that hung halfway down his tight wifebeater rushed up shaking his head, a shot of bourbon in his free hand for the guitarist.

"You all must have corn cobs in your ears," Melissa said

loudly. She looked at me. "You done listening now? Don't know why you're hanging out at this place anyway."

"It's close to the motel," I said dumbly.

"It's close to the motel," she repeated. "I got a car, you know. There's more to Fort Myers than the motel and this old dive. And Denny's." The room seemed to get very quiet. "So," she said, "you been looking for your brother today?"

I suddenly felt even more uneasy about the path things had taken, the way we'd just happened to end up together on the beach the night before. Was she gathering information for Rolly Lee and having some fun while she was at it? Then there was Donny's comment about Rolly Lee being so interested in Melissa. It was all I could do to not stand up and bolt out of the Painted Frog right away.

"Listen, Melissa," I said, leaning closer. "What happened last night was probably a really bad idea." It was like trying to back slowly out of a leg-hold trap.

She smirked at me and leaned back in her chair. Thankfully, another record clattered onto the jukebox, a current country hit all about the Red, White and Blue and what you could do if it wasn't for you (love it or leave it).

"The thing about boys," she said, "is that they always realize these things after they come." I felt my face redden and she giggled. "Look at you," she said, "got a blush on."

"You're Hoyt's girl," I said. "I feel like an asshole."

"Hoyt's being an asshole," she said, "and I ain't his girl. Not no more, anyway." She giggled again. "But don't tell Hoyt that, because he won't be too happy. Not with some of the other prospects I got."

I drained my beer. "Need another?" she asked, smiling. I nodded and watched her strut to the bar, her hind end wagging with every step. That and the booze created a stir in my lap. I sank my nails into my thigh with the hope of forcing my brain into a hard right.

Melissa plonked two foaming mugs of beer onto the table. "No," she said, "there ain't much for old Jasper to do now but go along with the program." She leaned across the table at me and narrowed her eyes. "My program." I felt her hand searching for me under the table and instinctively my leg kicked out, hitting her in the bare shin.

"Fuck," she shouted. "The hell's the matter with you?" Heads turned and I could feel a low, menacing murmur pass over the Frog like a wave.

"Relax," I said.

She rolled her eyes. "You relax," she said. "Jumping like you're some goddamned queer who's afraid of girls."

"Melissa," I said. "I'm sorry about last night. I made a mistake. You're very beautiful and I think you're great. But you're Hoyt's girl." I swigged from my beer and looked at her. "I fucked up."

Her face softened and she laid her hand across mine, cold from holding her pint. "It doesn't matter," she said. "A lot of stuff has happened around here, stuff with Hoyt, stuff with his family. If you let me come back to Canada with you, it won't matter."

I looked at the beautiful Southern girl across the table from me. At the bar, a couple of grim-faced men were watching her with rapt attention. I thought about her plea and wondered when would be the next time someone so beautiful would beg me to take her home. Problem was, home was a long way away.

"I'm sorry, Melissa," I said, "I can't."

Her eyes narrowed and she leaned across the table. "Then go fuck yourself," she said, "and go on back to Canada." I tried my hardest not to watch her as she went across the Painted Frog and out the front door.

I was on my second Budweiser after Melissa's departure, watching the mosquitoes bat and weave in the lights over the pool table, when a figure crossed my line of vision and sat down.

"Jasper," Rolly Lee said. "Imagine meeting you here."

I wasn't surprised. "Rolly Lee," I said. "This one of your hangouts?"

He nodded toward the makeshift stage where a hairy tribe of pickers were setting up a drum kit and moving amplifiers around. "Doing a number with these boys. I used to play with Billy—the drummer—way back when you were still just a little squirt. Your momma and aunt came out to see us a couple of times."

I glared at Rolly Lee across the top of my glass and nodded.

"Haven't seen you around much," he said. "I thought you was down here on a vacation, visiting friends and family and whatnot." His droopy moustache stretched out over a grin. "Or you been making some new friends. At least that's what your aunt told me."

"Been busy," I said, motioning to the waitress who was now on duty for another beer.

"Busy." Rolly Lee nodded seriously and pushed away from the table, crossing his legs. I noticed his eyes, how dilated the pupils were, and I wondered if he'd been tweaking. "I'll say you've been busy. What you been so busy doing?"

An obese man with a plumed cowboy hat waddled down off the stage and over to our table, where he came up behind Rolly Lee and put his hand on his shoulder. "Rolly Lee, hope you still good for a song or two," he started, and was cut off by a raised palm. He shrugged and walked off. Rolly Lee hadn't even turned around. The grin was gone.

"What you been so busy doing?" he repeated.

I shrugged.

"You know something, Jasper," he said. "Fort Myers ain't that big a town. In fact, most people who've lived here a little while—like myself—know one another. So when somebody shows up from out of town and doesn't make a beeline for the beach or the bar, but goes out poking around hither there and yon, well, people get excited."

The waitress brought two beers and two shots to the table. I thought of Coleman and banged one down. Before Rolly Lee could blink, I grabbed the second shot, noticed a fruit fly skimming the top of the auburn liquor, and then drained that too, still thinking of my brother and how life might have been different if we'd never met Rolly Lee. I felt the shots hit my stomach and course through my bloodstream like a warm current.

Rolly Lee scratched at his cheek. "Thirsty?"

"Thirsty." I nodded.

"A last drink to cap off the trip, something like that?" His eyes flitted around the room before landing on the band setting up. He grinned at the drummer and gave him the thumbs-up.

"Maybe."

"No maybe about it," Rolly Lee said, still grinning at the drummer. "Your cousin Hoyt's good and pissed with you. Don't blame him. You come into town and fuck my woman, you'd be gator bait. Course that'd be your aunt, and I don't think you're quite that stupid."

My hands balled up under the table and my jaw clenched.

"Don't bother," Rolly Lee said. "Don't bother at all. Unless you came down here to take a long, nice dirt nap. Because honestly"—he pulled on one end of his moustache—"that's how it seems to me. Seems to a few people actually. Come down here, making friends with the local police, having a game of stinky finger with Melissa just for the fuck of it, looking around, asking crazy questions about your crazy brother—"

"Leave it," I said.

"That subway car knocked some sense out of you," he said. "Whatever sense you had."

"Yeah, Rolly," I said, "what with your head full of drug pudding, I'll take that to heart."

He grinned. "Get fucked, boy. You were a dumb-ass pussy of a kid and only difference now is you're bigger. But not quite big enough."

"Well," I said, "you've always been a big man. Big enough to leave a twelve-year-old out in the swamps to die."

Something flashed in his eyes and he drew his chair closer to the table. "Listen here," he said, "know when to leave well enough alone. That's finished. That was an accident."

"An accident." Now it was my turn to grin. "An accident." I nodded.

"Go home," he said. "Trust me." He tapped a long, stained finger on the table. "Now's the time for you to head home. And when you get there, stay there."

The obese man with the black baseball cap shouted from the stage. "You just about ready, Rolly Lee?"

"Yeah," Rolly Lee said, without turning around, his mind lost somewhere else in things that happened long ago. "I'm ready."

I looked at him, watched his skinny face twitch, the sunken, wide eyes dancing in sockets that ran as deep as sinkholes in the swamp, wondered how even as a child I was able to look up to Rolly Lee.

He drew his chair closer still, until I could smell the foulness of his breath and see the riot of broken capillaries in his eyes. "You're all alone down here, Jasper, and you're a long fucking stretch from home," he said, then pushed his chair away from the table and went to the stage.

As I left the bar, I heard the band kick into Molly Hatchet's "Flirtin' with Disaster," Rolly Lee singing the first lines with such gusto that you'd think raising trouble was the happiest thing a man could do.

It was so hard to believe that sixteen years had passed, that Coleman was gone, my father was dead, my mother stricken and bewildered, and that Rolly Lee was still living out his notion of the Southern man's utopia in Fort Myers, Florida. But he was right about one thing: it was time for me to go home.

On my way across the lot, I noticed his truck, the mud dried and caked above the wheel wells. Hunched down in the passenger seat, watching the front door of the Painted Frog, was Melissa Wheeler. I pretended not to see her and went back to the room.

Something caught my eye on the dresser top as I hunkered down into bed that night. A small white tube glinting amidst spare change and empty beer cans. I swung my legs out of bed and went to get it. I'd squeezed a liberal amount of "Vera's Volitive" out into my palm before I realized I had no idea where to put it. So I just rubbed it across my chest, went back to bed and tried to close my eyes across a lifetime of thwarted wishes.

37.

THERE WAS ONE THING that kept me going, one experience that had taught me that Coleman was not an ordinary person and that if anyone could disappear for ten years and still be alive, it was him.

"It was an accident," Coleman said. "I got lost."

After Coleman arrived home with the state trooper, my mother ushered me out of the cottage. "Say hello to your brother, Jasper," she said, "then why don't you head outside for ten minutes. We'll come find you. Go on down to the beach."

I looked at Coleman. A small smile quivered across his lips. "Hey," he said.

"Hey," I said, and held my hand out. Coleman delivered a weak high-five and I went past him, through the screen door and into the yard. I went under the tall pine, past the fire ant hill, through the sea oats and onto the beach. When I was sure no one was watching, I sat down in the sand, looked out across the cloudless horizon at the endless stretch of ocean, and began to sob.

I wondered what had happened to Coleman. When I turned and looked back at the cottage, I noticed another police car pulling up, and the policeman we'd met the day after the disappearance walking around to the screen door. I dried the tears with the back of my arm and stood up. I needed to know what was being said. I needed to know where he'd been, and what had happened to him.

I wasn't missing anything. The story Coleman told the police while I was sitting on the beach, getting over the shock of finding out that he was really alive, was the story he would stick to all through that vacation and through the next year until there was no story to tell anymore, and it became one of those rare, dark things that families keep hidden away in the collective memory with the hope that not speaking of it will someday lead to striking it forever from the record.

We had pizza that night. Coleman picked the toppings: ham, pineapple and anchovies. For once, I ate it and pretended to like it. I recall my mother bathing Coleman like he was a baby and my father calling, hardly able to hold back the tears when I answered the phone. Coleman was exhausted, shaken, but still Coleman.

I had to wait for the story.

That night, under the whir of the ceiling fan, my brother's familiar, comforting presence was back beside me on the pullout couch. When my mother turned the light out in the kitchen and went off to bed, I noticed that she didn't close her door all the way. I lay there in the darkness, listening to the waves on the beach, the click and drip of the dishwasher, and my brother's heavy, tired breathing.

"Coleman?"

There was a pause. "Jasper."

"Are you okay?"

He laughed a little. "I think so," he said.

I heard my mother roll over in bed and I lowered my voice. "Were you really out in the Everglades?"

"Yeah."

"For two whole days?"

"Yeah."

"Were you scared?"

"No."

"Bullshit," I said, even quieter, a whisper now.

"I wasn't."

"Honest? I won't care, Coleman."

He rolled over onto his side, his back facing me. I could see the outline of his spine in the moonlight that beamed over the top of the blinds. Thin, random scratches covered the back of his neck where the skin darkened to a deep brown. Coleman was shaking.

"Coleman," I said, putting my hand on his shoulder. I sat up in bed. "Coleman."

He turned over again, heavy sobs rolling a tremor through him. I pulled him up by the shoulders and wrapped my arms around him. His sobs were soundless, but he continued to shake and hot tears and snot dripped onto my shoulder.

I got out of bed and poured a glass of milk from the fridge. I opened the blinds so we could see the white foam of the Gulf down in the distance. Coleman had always loved the ocean, so much so that my father had a running joke that he'd been found washed up on the shoreline as a baby, born to a mermaid way out at sea.

I could see Coleman smiling, the white of his teeth flashing in the dark. "Pretty wussy, eh?" he said, sniffling.

I looked at him. "No," I said, not even trying to stifle my own tears.

I waited until he'd finished the milk, the two of us—brothers—sitting side by side on the hide-a-bed staring out at the ocean through the window, then I asked the question.

"Coleman," I said, "what happened?"

"I don't really remember."

"Come on," I said. "For real?"

Coleman pushed the hair up off his forehead and lay back down on the bed. "I'm tired, Jasper."

"I know," I said. "But please?"

"Why do you need to know? Why does it matter? I made it home."

I shrugged and, feeling cold, lay down in the bed next to him and pulled the coarse yellow blanket up around my neck.

"Don't be scared," he said.

"I'm not. Will you please tell me?" I said.

257

Coleman sighed, and for a minute I thought he'd drifted off to sleep. Then he spoke. "We went out into the swamps to look for gators," he said. "It was my idea. Then the weather got really bad. We spotted a gator, then stuff started happening really quickly. We lost track of him, then we saw him again near the boat. The next thing I knew, I was waking up in the water."

"What do you mean?" I said. "You went to sleep in the water?"

Coleman glared at me. "No, dummy," he said, rubbing at the back of his head. "I must have smacked my head on something. Feel." He held his hair up at the back of his neck. I ran my fingers over the back of his head and gasped when I felt the knot.

"Wow," I said. "That's bigger than when Russell Hill went up over the swing set and landed on his head."

Coleman smiled. "It's bigger than Barney Rubble's after the bowling ball landed on it."

"Yeah, right," I said. "Tell me what happened after."

This is what happened after:

Coleman woke up gasping for air, spewing hot, brackish swamp water from his nose and mouth. All around him, it was dark but for an open patch of starred sky above him. He was in the middle of a wide area of deeper water, the shoreline twenty feet away on either side.

He was exactly where the boat had been. Rolly Lee's skiff.

Coleman turned slowly in the water, surveying the expanse of swamp, tree and black sky. The boat was gone, and with it, Rolly Lee.

His head throbbed. Whatever he'd hit his head on was hard enough that, waking up in the water, his vision kept whiting out as he struggled to stay afloat. His first thought was of the big bull gator. As he thought of it, a heavy, long shape went past his kicking legs under the water, like in a dream. Coleman was not scared. It drifted by again, this time from the other side, and then it surfaced.

Coleman was treading water at eye level with the big bull gator. The bull gator's eyes were jewelled in the darkness. Behind the eyes, the full length of the gator stretched out in the water, row upon row of ridged spine disappearing under the water where his massive, thick tail would be shifting slowly like a rudder.

The distance between them diminished. With the slow, imperceptible bob of the water and his own disorientation, he couldn't tell if he was getting closer to the gator or if the gator was moving closer to him.

Coleman wasn't scared. I would not have believed this about anyone else, but I believed it about my brother.

Then there was no distance at all. They were so close that Coleman's hands brushed the end of the alligator's snout as he stayed afloat. The gator submerged, brushing past Coleman's legs, and then re-emerged on the other side of him. He drifted in a circle around my brother. For what seemed like hours to him, my brother bobbed in the water while the biggest bull gator in the swamps floated sentry around him.

Then he woke up on the bank, the sawgrass rough and itchy on his cheek. First light was approaching, and the sky was ablaze with deep reds and oranges, the world on fire at dawn.

The gator was gone. The temperature had dropped and even the mosquitoes had relented. The only sign of life was a pair of large white birds high up in a dead tree, their wings spread to full span, waiting for the sun to appear and dry their feathers.

Coleman started walking. Left to my own devices, I was the brother who could get lost in a grocery store, but Coleman had a finely tuned sense of direction. So with another infernal day dawning in the Everglades, he started to walk in the direction they'd paddled in, trying to find his way along the thickly vegetated periphery of the river of grass. When the heat and exhaustion became too much to bear, he lay down under the thick canopy of trees and rested. Then he got up and continued walking, the heat and fatigue twisting the world before him into a waking fever dream. He slept a little that night on a bed of brown pine needles at the base of a tree. The next day, he continued on. It was late that afternoon when Coleman, his feet throbbing through a pulp of mud and blood, finally heard the cars whizzing along I-41.

There was one thing he hadn't mentioned: the missing National Parks worker who disappeared into the swamps on the same day that Coleman and Rolly Lee had set out on their ill-fated gator-watching expedition. During the long, empty hours waiting for Coleman to come home, I'd elaborated a finely detailed private saga of Coleman and the missing National Parks worker, whose stoic nature and unflappable character I garnered from the small black-and-white picture that accompanied the news story. Dudley Hargrove was thirty-three years old, married with a young son. In the picture, his black hair was razed to a stubbled quarter inch and he stared the camera down with equally dark eyes as though he were facing a raised cotton-mouth. Dudley Hargrove had worked with the Parks Service for seven years, and had earned the Ranger of the Year award three times. I imagined Dudley injured in the swamps too, his boat crashed up on a knot of mangrove root, gas leaking into the swamps with an iridescent swirl, the young ranger pressing an oily handkerchief to the gash in his forehead. Somehow Coleman would find Dudley Hargrove, and together, they would find their way out of the swamp, trading one-liners and turning a bad situation into a bit of a lark.

Dudley Hargrove would be our surrogate Southern dad, what Rolly Lee could have been if he'd only get a haircut and lay off the beer.

The only problem was that Coleman *had* escaped. On his own.

"A park ranger?" he said, shaking his head, and then wincing at his bandaged feet. "Jasper, I was all alone out there."

Two days later, after Coleman had got his strength back and the three of us had spent hours lying on the beach and swimming in the ocean, recuperating from the two days of terror and panic, we packed up the car and left Sanibel Island at first light. We didn't see Rolly Lee before our departure, although I heard my mother speaking on the phone with Aunt Val. As the car hit the causeway that morning with dawn breaking and paradise spreading out for miles in every direction, I watched out the back window until Sanibel Island blurred into the distance. Somehow I knew it would be the last time. I lay down on the back seat of the car and buried my face in my pillow so my mother couldn't hear my sobs over the soft rock playing on the AM station.

I wasn't worried about Coleman hearing me: I could see his head lolling in the front seat, asleep as the most beautiful place we had ever been disappeared into the sea behind us.

38.

THE DAY DAWNED HOT and cloudless. I could feel the sun burning down on the motel roof as though it were an approaching planet. The pillow under my head was a damp cluster of feather and stuffing, misshapen from an endless procession of sweaty heads. I rolled over in bed and the sheet stuck to my flank. So began another day in Florida.

The motel room was quiet. I watched a fly circle the overhead fan that hung lazily from a mess of wires that suggested one more spin might bring the whole mess to the floor.

I sat up in bed. It was quiet.

Then I realized the source of the quietude: sometime in the night, the rattling, clattering air conditioner had given up the ghost. I wrapped the sheet around me and cracked the door to let some air in. It poured in like pea soup. I closed the door again.

Donny and Duane had taken off sometime before dawn. Their derby was on Lake Okeechobee, where Rolly Lee had taken my brother and me years before. I'd heard them gathering their stuff early in the morning with all the methodical intent of two warriors going into battle. I heard the tell-tale woosh of a beer can being opened and Donny's murmured admonishments to Duane, who sounded like he still had a slur in his voice from the night before.

I admired Duane and Donny for their passion. It had been a long time since anything had inspired me to get out of bed in the middle of the night. When I got back to Ontario, I planned to find that thing. For too long I'd only been able to see the reasons not to do things; my world view had been poisoned by disappointment and disappearance, and slowly I had come to feel that, in the grand scheme of things, there wasn't much point in anything. It had gone on for too long.

Lying there in the infernal confines of that motel room, I gave my brother up for dead. But the looking for him, while it might have made Sherlock Holmes eat his hat, had made me realize something: I was ready to go home and start anew. I supposed I owed Ronnie Orsulak a postcard and Duane and Donny a six-pack or three. It was time to find my own thing.

One thing I could be certain of: whatever I found, it wouldn't be fishing.

The phone rang while I was in the shower. I could hear it bleating miserably from the other room while I stood under a blast of cold water, trying in vain to lower my core temperature. I ignored it and concentrated on trying to coax a lather from the shale-like wedge of soap the motel had provided, so ancient that the paper wrapping wouldn't come off and I had to rub it until it dissolved.

It rang again while I was looking at the scars on my arm and leg in front of the mirror. This time I rushed out of the bathroom, kicking Duane's bedroll on my way to the phone. Three empty, crushed beer cans fell out of the stained blue quilt and onto the carpet.

"Hello," I said.

There was nothing but heavy breathing and highway noise.

"Hello," I repeated, this time with a singsong lilt.

Still nothing. Drops of water and sweat ran down my neck and back, hung off my balls then tumbled onto the burn-pocked carpet. "I'm not wearing anything and I'm all wet," I said.

The line went dead. As I towelled off, I imagined Melissa Wheeler slamming the phone down at the other end, wondering what the hell she'd been thinking in the first place.

Denny's was dead. I'd hit the midway point between breakfast and lunch on a weekday and had the place to myself, but for an elderly couple sipping coffee, resplendent in their matching pastel walking outfits. The same waitress who had served me the day I'd run into Melissa and Skeeter approached the table and nodded.

"How you doing today," she said. "The usual?"

"The usual," I said, impressed.

When the half-congealed plate of eggs and ham arrived, looking like it had been sitting under the heat lamp since early that morning, I grinned.

"Here's your Moons over My-Hammy," she said.

It was a good omen. I ate my breakfast and tipped generously.

I found the veterinary clinic Val was working at without too much trouble. She'd mentioned the name in passing and it was a tough one to forget—Wags-A-Lot Veterinary Hospital. I spotted it from the bus and got off at the next stop. There was a Dunkin' Donuts on the way back and I stopped in to grab a couple of coffees.

Aunt Val was sitting in the waiting room with an elderly man dressed in yellow and a bulldog. The bulldog could barely sit up.

"Don't he look like he lost his best friend," the old man said, "don't he just?"

Aunt Val glanced up at me and smiled briefly. "Well, I guess he would," she said. "You have to keep him out of the ocean."

The old man looked up at me. "You the vet?" he asked. "Anderson been eating shells again. Poor fellow looking for some seafood." He let out a crackling smoker's laugh and then huffed on an inhaler. "Pair of us getting ready for the boneyard."

"Don't say that," Aunt Val said. "You're still a spring chicken."

"That being the case then, can I take you to the movies tonight?"

She grinned. "Nice try. The vet'll be out in a minute." She stooped so that she was eye level with the dog. "Anderson," she said, "your food comes out of a can, not a shell." She patted his head and the dog's black and pink lips spread into a slobbery grin. "There's a boy," she said.

"Got time for a coffee?" I held out the cups.

"Sure," she said. "Let me just tell them I'm taking my break."

We went around the side of the clinic and sat down next to each other at a picnic table. Aunt Val fired up a cigarette and looked out at the road. I wondered if she was embarrassed about the day before, or maybe still pissed off.

"Taking off in the morning," I said. "Wanted to make sure you were okay."

She looked at me with sad eyes. "It's been good to see you, Jasper. Really. Yesterday was just a bad day. Rolly Lee'd hit the hay by the time I got back. That helped." She huffed out a blast of blue-grey smoke. "My God, that man can be infuriating. But Rolly Lee does try. He's been to rehab a couple of times. Stays clean for a stretch then drifts back into it. You know, Jasper, we all have our cross to bear. He's been a bastard, but Rolly Lee tries." Aunt Val looked at me, a hint of amusement in her dark eyes. "I don't know," she said, "maybe a shrink would tell me I just like being in charge." She was going to say something else and then stopped. We sipped at our coffees and watched the cars streaking past toward the interstate.

It was just more silence.

There'd been so much of it through the years between all of us and Val. My mother's little sister. The cool aunt we'd grown up loving. The silence felt sudden and eternal, like air trapped in a room after the door is slammed shut. Even though there were letters and phone calls and Christmas cards, it still felt like silence and it was shot through with all the questions I'd always wanted to ask her. About Rolly Lee and Coleman and that night in the swamps.

I'd left Sanibel as a kid. Sixteen years on, I'd run the narrative of those days through my mind so many times that surely it was printed on my brain, as tangible as Braille. Coleman and

Rolly Lee, out in the Glades, the swamp rat and the kid from
Canada. Rolly Lee rolling home, all alone.

I had questions, and I wasn't going home without a good
shot at asking them.

"What'd you think when you heard that Coleman left?" I said.

If Aunt Val was surprised, she didn't show it. She drew on
her cigarette and her eyelids fluttered. Then she looked at me.
"I was devastated, Jasper." We watched more cars pass on the
road and she smoked her cigarette down to the filter. "You and
your brother," she said, "your mother." Aunt Val laid her hand
over her heart. "You're my blood. And I recognized the strain
that ran through Coleman." She shook her head and ran the heel
of one hand over her brow. "Your mom had been calling me a
little more often. I was getting updates on the spaceship." She
took a deep breath and tried to suppress a smile. "Coleman," she
said, and now she laughed.

"It's okay," I said. "If I hadn't laughed over the years I'd
probably have built my own spaceship."

"You know," she said, "I can laugh because I had a lot of
crazy-ass ideas too. Hell, I got married to a manic-depressive in
North Bay when I was nineteen. Never considered if that was,
you know, a smart thing to do or not. I just did it." Aunt Val
grinned, looked at me with soft eyes. "I did whatever I wanted
and always felt this belief that what I was doing was the right
thing." Now she nodded gently. "Coleman was the same way."
Her eyes darted up at me, and I thought of what she'd said the
day before: *Gone is gone.* "Is," she said, as if thinking of the same
thing. She touched my arm. "I hope."

More silence.

"It nearly drove me nuts," I finally said. "Wondering where
he might be, who he was with, all the things he might be doing.

If there were people who maybe loved him or laughed at him like I did." I scuffed the dirt under the table with my shoe. "Or if he was just gone. Ceased to exist. And I had no way of knowing."

Aunt Val linked her arm through mine. "I don't think you ever thought that," she said.

"How do you know?"

"I didn't either. Coleman seemed so resilient."

I drew a breath thick with humidity. The air suddenly held the promise of a thundershower. "Especially after what happened down here," I said, "that summer."

She swallowed hard and ran her fingertips across her forehead. When she pulled them away, tears were in her eyes. Aunt Val looked off at the horizon, as if searching for clouds. After a moment, she took another cigarette from her purse and put a match to it.

"That morning," she said, "was the most scared I've ever been. That morning and that night. Thinking of Coleman out there, somewhere in the dark." She looked at me and I could see she was struggling to keep her lip from quivering. "A nightmare," she said, "and me, with your mom." Now her voice staggered along a tremor. "My sister. And the last person with her son was Rolly Lee. My husband."

A pickup truck pulled up into the lot. A yowling black dog paced around in back, looking for a way out. We watched as the owner dropped the tailgate and then struggled to lift the dog out.

"Yeah," she said, her eyes wandering across my face. "I knew how it looked." She paused. "How it sounded."

"I was just a kid," I said.

Her eyes flashed on me. "You're no kid anymore, Jasper. And I know," she said, "how much you all wondered. How much you must have wondered."

I shrugged, searching for the words.

"That day you left," she said, and then her hand went back across her eyes. "Your mother said goodbye over the telephone." She took a deep breath and continued. "It broke my heart. And then, to be real honest, it made me angry. Coleman had come back. And Rolly Lee"—now she was shaking her head—"it was like they hated him. Like there would never be even a chance for forgiveness."

I didn't say anything.

"Rolly Lee is an odd duck," she said. "Barely worked an honest day in his life, always got a beer in one hand and a patter of bullshit rolling around in his cheek. His troubles are like the rest of him: larger than life. He's run around on me some." She smiled a half smile that read guilt. "And truth be told, I've done a little running around myself over the years." Aunt Val tapped the table with one fingernail and the smile vanished. "But Rolly Lee," she said, "no matter how he seems, well," she said, "his heart is in the right place. He knew how much your brother loved gators and the Glades. Rolly wanted to make a little adventure, to show Coleman the swamps before you all went home."

A look of determined ferocity had replaced the sadness in her eyes. "I've had fun most of my life down here. Rolly Lee's taken care of me in his own way. He makes me smile."

It was tough to picture, particularly after gentle old Rolly Lee had threatened me with the eternal sleep the night before, but I let her go on.

"Point is," she said, "after you all went home that summer, I was the one down here with Rolly Lee. I saw the way this ate him up, the sorrow he felt even though Coleman had found his way back. That things had cooled so much with your parents. He knew it was his fault, that it was stupid and careless to go out in a storm."

"It was just that . . ." I looked down at my feet. "Coleman never much wanted to talk about Rolly Lee after that," I said.

"I guess he wouldn't have," she said. "He looked up to Rolly Lee, and any way you slice it, Rolly Lee failed him out there. In his eyes . . ."

"Val," I said, quietly. "You know how it sounded."

We both stared ahead. "I know," she finally said. "Of course I know. But Jasper," she said, "Rolly Lee swore. He swore that the way he told it was the truth. Even if I'd had a doubt in my head, there'd be no good reason for it. Why would it be any way but how he told it? And for what?" She picked up a shard of bleached white shell and side-armed it across the grass. "What happened out there, that night, was an accident. But I knew how you all felt."

"We never really talked about it."

"That's the kind of thing you wouldn't have to."

"I'm sorry, Aunt Val," I said.

"Sorry for what?"

"Leaving you back here," I said. "Not staying in closer touch. I missed you. Coleman did too."

"I missed you too," she said. "I still do. But don't be sorry about leaving me here." She shook her head. "Don't be sorry, because this is my home. My home and my family."

She reached over and squeezed my wrist. Another car pulled into the lot. This time an elderly woman got out, went round to the passenger side and pulled out a cage. She tottered toward the doors. "I better get back," Aunt Val said. "That waiting room seems to be filling up."

We stood up and I wrapped my arms around her. She buried her face into my shirt, right over my heart, and I could feel the deep breaths she was taking. When she pulled away, she was smiling. "If Coleman is out there," she said, "he'll find you."

"Either way," I said, "I have to get back home and figure out what I'm going to do next."

"You take care of yourself, Jasper. And you stay in touch. You and me, we're a vanishing breed."

"What about that seat?" I said. "You still want it saving?"

She smiled and shook her head. "Not this time," she said. "Me and Rolly Lee, we've stuck it out this long, I expect we'll keep sticking it out. Maybe next time," she said.

I looked into her proud, dark eyes. If only I could see what was behind them: whether she was putting on a brave face or if she really had been happily weathering the ups and downs that came with a life out of the ordinary. Either way, I hoped that she hadn't seen a whole lot of the Rolly Lee I'd seen last night.

There was one more thing I wanted to say. "Aunt Val," I said, "I'm sorry. About Melissa. It was a stupid thing to do."

She waved her hand dismissively and started taking the first small steps toward the clinic. "All men got one blind spot when it comes to common sense," she said. "But that girl . . ." She pursed her lips as if she'd bitten down on a lemon. "Well, I got my suspicions that she's got a hook into more than just my son and my nephew."

My mouth dropped open.

"Uh-huh," was all she said.

Manuel Sherrill was sitting in his office, feet up on the desk, when I went in. A radio was blaring from the windowsill, some kind of sports phone-in show that had Sherrill furrowing his brow. He looked at me and nodded toward the radio, shaking his head. A caller was finishing up by threatening to arrive at the next Marlins game drunk and naked if they dared trade Cliff Floyd to the Yankees. They went to a commercial and Sherrill grinned at me.

"Eh!" he shouted. "The Canadian has returned."

I held my hand out and he pumped it. "How are things?"

"Good," he said. "Better if they don't deal Floyd. All this fuss to bring baseball to Florida and now no one's going out to the games. Don't blame them really. Boring as hell. Saw the Marlins first year they were here and the chili I got at the park gave me the green apple quick step. Missed half the game." He took his feet off the desk. "Didn't miss jack," he said. "It's like watching paint dry. But they ought to hold on to Floyd. He's a good one."

"Listen," I said, "I just wanted to come by and say thanks. I'm heading out tomorrow."

Sherrill sighed. "No luck then."

I shook my head and shrugged. "It was a long shot to begin with."

"No such thing as a long shot," he said. "Something is or it isn't."

"Well, I guess this isn't then."

Sherrill leaned back in his chair and linked his hands behind his head. The chair gave a squeak and he smiled. "I'm sorry to hear that," he said. "Sometimes, this world'll kick your ass for you." He turned and looked out the window. "I wish you could have come up with something. Must be hard not knowing."

"Maybe not knowing is all for the better."

A grin spread across Sherrill's face and he leaned across the desk at me. "You know what?" he said. "We sound like a couple of half-baked philosophy majors."

I laughed. "Break out the black light, man."

Sherrill's phone rang and he glared at it suspiciously. "Shit," he said. "I got to get this." He stood up. His pants were undone and the front tails of his shirt barely covered his red boxer shorts.

"Jesus," he said, sitting down again. "Jasper. Nice to meet you. Anything else you need before you take off . . . just let me know."

I nodded. "Appreciate it." The phone continued to ring. "If you're ever in Canada . . ." I started.

He picked the phone up and cupped a tanned hand over the mouthpiece. "I'll look you up," he said.

I got out the door and was halfway down the hallway when I heard Sherrill shout after me. "Hoser!" he said, then, to the caller, "That's okay. We just got a Canadian in the house."

There was one more thing I needed to do.

I walked a few blocks from Manuel Sherrill's office to a bus stop. An elderly black woman with pewter glasses and a look that straddled the middle ground between ornery and anguished was waiting as well, a heavy suitcase resting unevenly on the bleached-out pavement next to her. When the bus pulled up with an exhausted squeal, she shot a look at me then toward her suitcase, as if to say, "Well?" By the time I'd got the suitcase onto the bus and found a seat by an open window, I'd sweated clear through my T-shirt. A pair of lanky teenaged boys smirked in the seat across the aisle. They probably had me pegged for an imminent heart attack. My back stuck to the hot vinyl seat and came away with a sickly peeling sound when I leaned forward. I heard the boys snickering, and I did a casual half turn in my seat.

"Hear they're going to trade Floyd," I said.

"Who the fuck's Floyd?"

The number 50 bus had emptied by the time it reached its most westerly point at McGregor. The thick, sweating driver nodded brusquely at me and I got off. I stood at the corner of the two roads and watched him loop the bus around, the stink of diesel fuel merging with the humidity and swamp like three sister scents bonding into an overwhelming whole.

McGregor Boulevard was almost enough to induce a Pavlovian response in me: anxiety. From the shoulder heading west, I could see the water opening up, the toll booths ahead, the suggestion of islands off in the distance. When my family had driven down, the last stop before hitting the cottage had always been the Winn-Dixie in Fort Myers. This final pit-stop on the road to the beach was more than I could bear. After three days sitting in the back of a car with Coleman, the last thing I wanted to do was spend a long, confused hour wandering around a crowded grocery store.

Looking back I could see that it only made the end point all the sweeter.

The woman at the booth was surprised to see someone on foot. "Where's your water, hon?" she smiled. "You're liable to dry up out there today." I shrugged, paid my money to cross and went on.

Coleman and I had a running dialogue about the causeway, that it would take hours to cross on foot and that no one ever did it because it was just too hot. Your sneakers could melt. Every year as we left, we made Dad promise that, next year, he would stop the car and let us walk across when we arrived at Sanibel. Every year, as we got past the toll booths, the automatic locks would click, and once Coleman and I realized the nature of the ruse, there would be impassioned protestations from the back seat.

Now the only protestations were coming from my leg. I'd long since abandoned my cane as well as the physio exercises I'd been given. Sure, I felt pain in the leg from time to time, but I figured good old-fashioned exercise would do the trick. As the land fell away on my left and the Gulf opened up beside me, slopping lazily against the concrete pillars of the causeway, I quickly forgot about the pain.

Halfway toward the first island of land that divided the trip across in half, I took my shirt off and stuffed it into the back pocket of my shorts. The sky was a deep, pure blue without even a fluff of cloud, and somewhere far up, miles maybe, two seabirds hung aloft, the slow breeze ruffling their feathers as they rose and fell. I breathed deeply and felt the sea air across my bare chest.

When I got to the small patch of land, I stopped. A few trucks and cars were parked and I noticed a young couple splashing in the water with a toddler. Off beyond a stand of pines a few men were standing ankle deep in the water casting their lines out. Further on was the Sanibel lighthouse. It seemed like once every vacation, my father would insist on an early dinner out followed by watching the sun set at the lighthouse. The bugs were murder and the beauty was lost on Coleman and me. More family traditions.

Now, staring northward, I wondered which traditions I had left in the absence of anyone to share them with. I lowered myself onto the sand, kicked my shoes off and stuck my feet into the water. If I was looking for relief from the heat, I'd have to find it elsewhere. The water in the shallows was like tea.

I knew that I would never come back to Sanibel, or Florida for that matter. Once I left, I'd close the door on a chapter of my family's history that would forever be deep at my core. But it was over. To try and relive the past, to try and revel in happiness decades gone was futile. And, despite the unchanging beauty of Sanibel, no matter how hard I looked all I could see was my family: my father, my mother and, most of all, Coleman.

And Coleman was gone. While I might never know this for sure, I would have to find the certainty needed to move on with things. Otherwise, I was bound to get lost as well.

It was time to find new traditions. New pastimes, new friends, fresh ideas and, most of all, a purpose.

Overhead, I could still see the seabirds, blurred points hanging between sand and sun. In the water, the young father held his toddler by the chest and the child kicked and emitted a gleeful screech. I decided to take a walk along the small stretch of beach then head back to Fort Myers and prepare for the trip home.

Three men were fishing as I went past: an elderly, stooped white man with a red baseball cap, a middle-aged black man and a boy who looked to be his son. A frayed lawn chair was positioned just behind the elderly man as though he expected to collapse at any moment. I stepped softly as I went past, not wanting to disturb their fishing.

There was some murmuring between the two older men as I went past, a tangle of drawls that disappeared into the waves rolling up on the shoreline and the slow stream of cars crossing back and forth to the mainland. When I'd stood long enough looking out at the Gulf and Fort Myers across the water, I turned to go back. The black man nodded at me as I approached.

"Light?" he said.

"Sorry?"

He pulled a cigarette out from behind his ear and wagged it at me. "Do you have a match?"

"Sorry," I said. "I don't think I do." I rooted in my pocket, knowing that I didn't have a lighter or a match for that matter, but grateful for the human contact all the same. The stooped man in the red ball cap lowered himself into the chair with a groan and set his rod on the sand beside him. The chair was so old and battered that his hind end nearly touched the wet sand. He glanced over his shoulder at me and mumbled something that both the black man and his son ignored. I held my hands out and shrugged. "Sorry," I said.

"Cool," the black man said. "I've been carrying this thing behind my ear all day. Probably better off cramming it up my butt at this point."

I laughed. "See you later," I said. I noticed the red ball cap twisting as the elderly man tried to get a look at what was going down behind him. He mumbled something else and the black man rolled his eyes at me.

"No goddamn teeth," he said under his breath, nodding at the red ball cap. "Can't make out a single word the man says sometimes."

I set off for the causeway, the ocean sound dwindling as the cars got closer. When I'd reached the small parking area flanking the road, I heard a shout behind me. It was the black man beckoning me back.

"Come on," the man said as I got closer. I must have had a surprised look on my face, because he felt the need to assure me that he was not going to hurt me. When I got back to where they were fishing, the boy I took to be his son was still casting out, but the elderly man had propped himself up on a cane that appeared to be sinking into the wet sand and was grinning at me, his lips nearly touching the bottom of his nose.

"Man says he knows you," the black man said.

I grinned. "Probably not," I said. "I'm not from around here."

The older man's eyes widened and a torrent of garbled invective issued forth from his wobbling mouth accompanied by some frantic, one-handed gesticulating.

"Where's your teeth?" the other man said, then, to his son, "Larry, where's his goddamn teeth?"

The boy didn't turn. "In the bucket with the bait," he said.

The old man stepped closer to me so that when he started his high-octane mumbling again I could see the three-day growth on his chin and the urgency in his eyes.

"Bring the teeth, Larry."

Larry sighed and put his rod down gently. He looked out again at the water, as if he were scared that the first lapse in focus might mean losing a big grouper or marlin. He strode over with a small red bucket and held it out for the old man. Sure enough, resting peacefully in the slush of half-melted ice, nestled amidst tendrils of fresh squid, was a set of yellowed false teeth.

I felt connections being made in my brain, lights going on and off, the internal struggle through the dusty corridors of the past. It happened as he got his teeth in, swished them around in his mouth for lubrication and then spoke one word to me, one word that was as crystal clear as the sky above:

"Canada."

It was Rook Bannister.

"Rook," I said, grinning, and held my hand out. He wiped his hand on the back of his jeans before shaking. Then he took his teeth out again.

The black man shook his head at me. "Says they're uncomfortable." He patted Rook on the shoulder. "A man gets to be his age, ought to be able to do whatever the fuck he pleases. Ain't that right?"

Rook grinned.

"You know this man?"

"I do," I said. "He used to babysit me way back when. My family used to come down from Ontario to stay on Sanibel."

"More Canadians than crackers in these parts," the man said, then looked at Rook and took a step back, cocking his head. "Having a hard time picturing the babysitting part though," he said.

"He did a good job," I said.

Rook grinned and then crammed his teeth back in. "You remember my dog?" He looked at the black man and then back at me. "Liked the dog," he said, "liked the dog." The teeth came out again.

"Reynolds," I said.

Rook Bannister nearly jumped up and down in the sand. "Renul," he said, teeth still in his hand. "Renul!" He grinned and took his baseball cap off. "Renul." He looked me up and down and said something that I couldn't catch. His friend sighed.

"Fuck's sake," he said, "put those teeth back in."

Rook glowered at him. "Bruvver," he said, dipping his teeth back into the bucket then wiping them on the back of his jeans. The teeth went back in. I was enjoying this. I had nearly forgotten about Rook Bannister, had relegated him in my head to the realm of the passed on. He'd seemed positively ancient the summer I'd met him, yet here he was, in the flesh. Even the teeth looked to be the same set.

He looked me square in the face and adjusted his teeth with his tongue, forcing a bulge in one cheek and then the other. Finally, he swallowed and looked at me. "Look just like your brother," he said.

The breath caught in my chest. "Sorry?" I said. But I'd heard him. "You remember Coleman? My brother?"

Rook scratched at the back of his head. "Remember?" he said. "Remember?"

The black man sighed. "I'm going to get back to the fishing, guys," he said, "leave y'all to it." I didn't acknowledge him. "Small world," I heard him mumble as he went off to where his son was casting into the azure water.

"You remember my brother, Rook?"

Rook kicked at the sand and shook his head.

"Remember him?" he said. "Seen him two weeks back."

My knees hit the wet sand, my eyes still fixed on Rook Bannister.

39.

MANUEL SHERRILL WAS NOT in his office. His secretary was on the phone when I arrived back at the station, whispering conspiratorially into the receiver, eyebrows raised. As I stood there at the desk, another cop went past carrying a folder. His eyes widened when he saw me. Once I'd arrived back in Fort Myers on the 50 bus, I'd started into a half-limping jog. I'd had to put my shirt on when I got on the bus, and now I was drenched. My hair was as wet as though I'd just stepped out of the shower. I could feel my heart bucking in the shallow pit of my chest, unaccustomed to the sudden burst of exercise.

"You okay?" the cop said. I recognized him as Grant, the cop I'd met earlier in the week.

I nodded, then caught my breath. "Sure," I said. "Fine."

"Waiting for this lady, are you?" He clapped the folder on the desk a few times. The woman looked up and scowled. She muttered an excuse into the receiver and then hung up. The cop walked off shaking his head and grumbling.

"Sherrill around?" I asked.

She shrugged. "Did you check his office?"

"No," I said, "didn't think that was protocol."

"Protocol," she repeated with a giggle. She picked up the phone and punched four numbers into the keypad. "Think he's at lunch," she said. "You know where the burrito place is?"

I thanked her and went out the door. Once I hit the pavement, I broke into a full lurch.

Rook Bannister never forgot a face but was not the most articulate man you might encounter. He'd never had to be. Rook had lived his life fishing, hunting, prowling around swamps in a skiff or an airboat, all the while with a beer in one hand, his teeth in a bucket and an equally monosyllabic companion along for the ride with him. When Rook dropped his bombshell and I collapsed in the sand, he hadn't even been fazed. Just a little confused.

What I managed to get from him, after I'd recovered from the shock, was in short, grunted bursts that required all my powers of decryption and extrapolation.

Rook moved from Clewiston in the mid-1980s, to a trailer park in the Fort Myers area. When I mentioned Rolly Lee, he'd spit in the sand and rubbed at his eyes. There had been a final falling-out over Rook's airboat. Rolly Lee had run it up on a hammock in the Glades and left it out there. Then he'd driven back to Rook's, drunk on bourbon, and claimed it had been stolen. Rook Bannister had no time for Rolly Lee. No sir.

I had to work him back to Coleman. Not five minutes after mentioning "your brother," his brow furrowed when I brought it up. Rook Bannister was an old man and there were connections not being completed inside his head. I persisted and, like the sky after a fierce Florida thunderstorm, his eyes widened and brightened and he began to nod.

Rook had a daughter who lived out of state. Once a year, she brought Rook's young grandson down for a visit. In fact, they had just left Florida to drive back. Long drive, Rook mentioned. I knew that all right.

The grandson was obsessed with alligators and was something of a computer whiz. By the time they rolled into Fort
Myers for their visit, he had a printed list of all the places he
wanted to visit. There was Disney World, the Epcot Center, and
a gator farm in St. Augustine. But St. Augustine was too long a
trek. Rook knew of a gator farm down in Everglades City, the
last point southward before Highway 41 snakes eastward toward
Miami and the Keys.

The place was located on the edge of Big Cypress, just off 29.
Like all reticent outdoorsmen, Rook could talk driving directions until the sun came up.

"My brother," I had to remind him.

"Your brother?" he said. "He works there."

I found Sherrill mid-bite, salsa trickling down his wrist.

"Hey," he said, standing up. "Back for one last burrito, are
you?"

I wiped the sweat from my eyebrows and nodded.

"Shit," he said, "you don't look so good. Sit down."

I sat down, breathing heavily. The air-conditioned burrito
shack was a shock to the system and I felt a chill pass through
me. "I need a favour," I said.

Sherrill put his burrito down and raised an eyebrow at me.
"Shoot," he said.

"I think I might have found my brother," I said. He nodded
at me, face expressionless. I knew that he wouldn't want to betray
either excitement or doubt. I gave him the brief version of my
encounter with Rook Bannister. "I need a drive down to Everglades
City," I said, "and it'd also be nice to have a local with me."

Sherrill grinned. "Folks down in Everglade likely to think
I'm from Cuba." He glanced furtively at his burrito then clamped

down on it. "Let me finish up here," he said. "I'm off duty and I got to get changed. Then we'll take a run down to Everglades City."

Sherrill lived in a small low-rise apartment a stone's chuck from I-75 and the Caloosahatchee. "Bachelor pad," he said, flicking the lights on. The shades were drawn and every surface was a conglomeration of clutter. "Got divorced last year, used to have a nice place north of here. The wife got it." He chuckled softly. "Deserved it too, truth be told."

The walls were festooned with posters of the Miami Dolphins, as well as one of Roger Clemens in full windup. Sherrill shrugged. "I let my sons decorate the place. Cheaper than when the wife did it, anyway."

Sherrill went off into a small bedroom that seemed to be floored with discarded clothing. When he re-emerged, he was wearing a Dolphins cap, white T-shirt and tight camouflage shorts.

"Wouldn't have recognized you," I said.

"That's the point," he said. "Fitting in."

On the way out of his building, a stooped, grey-haired woman stopped us. "Manuel," she said, pronouncing it Man-YOU-ell, "I heard the mouse again last night. He was rustling through my garbage."

"Okay, Mrs. Hamilton," he said, "I've got some business to attend to, but I'll come by later if it's not too late. You still got that trap set up?"

She nodded.

"That should do it then." He placed a hand on her shoulder. "See you later."

On the way out of the parking lot in his pickup, Sherrill turned to me. "Got to get out of here," he said. "All these old biddies know I'm a cop and they're knocking on my door every time the drain clogs or a telemarketer calls."

We rode in silence. My mind was elsewhere, busy trying to impose realism and calm over the ocean of possibilities that had opened up after my conversation with Rook Bannister. I'd been ready to go home, having made my peace with Florida and the loss of my brother. Now I was close to either a final, crushing disappointment or a miracle. Rook appeared to be gaining on addled. It was possible he was just mistaken. I tried to focus on the haze of highway ahead, relatively quiet in the mid-afternoon lull between lunch and rush hour.

"All right," Sherrill finally said. "Tell me exactly what you found out this morning. We've got a good hour to Everglades City."

I started from the beginning, with my family and our vacations down to Sanibel. I told him about Coleman's obsession with alligators and my father's busy job that, one year, pulled him back to Ontario mid-vacation. Sherrill listened intently, never moving his eyes from the road but nodding softly as I spoke. I told him about Aunt Val, and her troubles up north, and how she'd come to Florida with us and met a man. That man had served as our Florida babysitter, I said, and my brother and I had looked up to him. At first.

Sherrill interrupted me. "They still down here?"

I nodded. "I've seen them a few times over the last week," I said. I decided to not be more specific, thinking the Melissa Wheeler story might not paint me in the best light. "Yes," I said. "Old Rolly Lee is still here, making a mess, doing his thing, whatever that may be."

I felt the truck jerk in the road. Sherrill turned to me. "Rolly Lee," he said.

"Yeah," I said, "Rolly Lee. You know him?"

He ignored the question. "Rolly Lee is your uncle?"

I nodded. "By marriage, anyhow."

"Jesus," he said, rubbing at his brow. He sighed and I felt the truck accelerate. "Listen," he said, holding his right hand up.

I cut him off. "Manuel," I said, "I know what Rolly Lee's all about and what he gets up to, and that a lot of it isn't within the bounds of the law."

He pulled the Dolphins cap off and smoothed his hair back. "Do you?" he said.

"You're not going to offend me."

"Rolly Lee," he said, then glanced over at me. "We've met a couple of times. Fort Myers ain't that big a place."

We passed Naples and 75 began to hook east. "Rolly Lee," he said, "is just your garden-variety good old boy dirtbag. Got a list of priors two burritos long."

I grinned in spite of myself.

Sherrill continued. "Used to deal a little weed back in the day, until we popped him on that. Tried to sell a dime bag to an officer in civvies at the Painted Frog. Nope," he said, "your uncle ain't the sharpest knife in the drawer."

"I know it. My father used to say the exact same thing."

"There's more." He sighed. "A few years back, we caught Rolly Lee speeding up I-75 in his pickup. More booze than blood in his system. Jacked to the nines on meth. By the looks of it, he'd been up for days. When we had a look-see through his truck, we found half a dozen dead gators on ice in the box. Big ones, too. Got him on a poaching charge. Him and his son."

"Hoyt?"

Sherrill nodded. "Like poppa, like son," he said.

I thought of Aunt Val. "Shit," I said.

There were few cars out on the sun-bleached highway, and Sherrill was making good time. "All right," he said. "Tell me again about this guy you saw today. How do you know him and how does he know your brother?"

We blew past a silver-pink Cadillac with overhanging wheel-wells and ducked back into the right lane. "We got some road to go," he said, "so entertain me."

I began to tell the story of what happened on our last Florida vacation. How Rolly Lee left me with Rook Bannister while he and Coleman went off into the swamps not far from where we were headed now. How Rolly Lee had emerged the following morning—alone—armed only with a vaguely believable story about a rogue alligator that seemed to have been superimposed onto the dramatic arc of *Jaws*.

To tell it after all these years was to realize how ridiculous it sounded.

I watched Sherrill's eyes narrowing as I told the story. He nodded silently as I recounted Coleman's return and the story he'd spun that night as we lay in bed listening to the ocean. The story he would stick to until there was no longer any story he was willing to tell.

"And that was it?"

"We were happy to have him back," I said. "I think there was an element of not wanting to tempt fate, to not question the how or the why. It all just seemed so fucking crazy. I was a little kid. If my parents were happy, then so was I."

"Your brother never elaborated on his story?"

"No," I said.

"Never?"

"Never," I said. "Coleman was a funny guy. Easygoing with me, but a little odd—at least to others. I knew him better than anyone, and he had borders you didn't cross. Rolly Lee wasn't a name that came up very often after we stopped going to Florida.

My aunt kept loosely in touch with my mother, but that was about it."

"Tell me something," he said. "When did this happen? Which summer?"

"1982," I said.

"My first year on the job, 1982," he said, vaguely. "Worked up in Winter Haven. Real plum duties—working parades, directing traffic, that kind of thing. Grew up thinking I was maybe going to be a cop, then next thing I knew, there I was." He sighed and pulled his sunglasses off, glancing over at me. "Time flies, Jasper."

I looked out the window at the highway and thought of all the summers past, Florida rolling by from the back seat of a car, my brother beside me, needling me in the side while my mother told us to behave. "No shit," I said.

We took the exit off 75 onto 29, a two-lane highway that seemed to lead into utter nothingness, an overgrown prairie of sawgrass on either side. If you got on a highway in Southwest Florida needing to pee or eat, chances were you'd be dining out on a chocolate bar from a rest-area vending machine, and having a leak in a ditch behind an open car door. And if you were riding at night and happened to blow a tire, good luck. I could remember a trip back to Sanibel from the Keys and how dark the road had been that night. When a car approached from the opposite direction, it had the relative luminosity of fireworks going off in a broom closet.

"Pretty desolate," I said, but Sherrill didn't respond. He'd started drumming on the steering wheel again and I could see his eyes narrowing, the crow's feet spreading out from the corners of his dark brown eyes. I started to ask him how far we were from the alligator farm and he stopped me with a raised palm.

"1982," he finally said.

Two full highway mile markers passed before he spoke again.

"1982," he repeated. "I remember." He smacked the steering wheel and the horn gave a miserable bleat. I jumped in my seat.

"What?" I said.

"The weekend your brother disappeared," he said. "I remember it."

I started to speak and he cut me off. "The weekend your brother disappeared," he said, "a ranger went missing in the swamps too. National Park guy. I remember because a guy I worked with up in Winter Haven had gone to ranger school before deciding to be a cop. He knew the dude. Was pretty broken up over it and a couple of us actually went down there to help search for the guy."

"I remember that too," I said, thinking of the story on the news that weekend and my fantasy that the ranger would emerge from the Glades with Coleman in tow. "They never found him?"

He shook his head. "Nope," he said. "It was a big deal because people don't disappear in the swamps every day. Two in one weekend was a big deal. Hell of a coincidence. Your brother's story was all over the news." Sherrill slowed the truck down and turned onto a dirt road that jutted off from 29. Here the delineation between road and brush was less defined and the encroaching vegetation brushed up against the side of the truck as we went past.

"Young guy, too," he said. "It's a shame." Sherrill shook his head. "Man, all that time between then and now. Where the hell does it go?" A cleared lot opened up on our right, a clapboard shack standing at the far end of it, a vintage pickup rusted to a deep red in the rough dirt drive. "Welcome to wild country,"

Sherrill said. He'd stopped drumming on the wheel and was holding it firmly with both hands.

40.

"Wow," Sherrill said, after we'd parked at the Rivergrass Recreation Park and got out of the truck. "This is what we call slow motion weather, Jasper. So hot you'd be a fool to move any other way."

The sun had ducked in behind thick storm clouds and the smell of rain was in the air. I was soaked with sweat, the moisture beading on my legs from the raw heat boiling up off the tarmac. Part of it was nerves. This was where Rook Bannister claimed to have seen Coleman. A healthy sense of skepticism, honed over the years and sharpened to a razor edge during the last week of dead ends, stopped me from sharing my excitement with Sherrill. At any rate, he probably knew the mixed bag of emotions I was busy rummaging through.

A few cars were scattered in the small parking lot, most with out-of-state plates.

"Slow season," Sherrill said. "Come down to a place like this in the middle of March, it's like the United Nations. Lucky to hear a lick of English." Out on the water, an airboat roared to life.

We approached a small wooden building at the gateway to the park. A small sign was posted on the door. "Amission $8. Pay inside."

"There's a bad omen," Sherrill said.

"What, they can't spell?"

"Yeah," he said, "that and no one's been tough enough to get them to correct it."

A long-legged white bird wandered into view from around the corner, stepping lightly on the hot concrete, eyeing us sideways.

"Quite a bird," I said.

"That's a great egret," Sherrill said, stooping down and holding his hand out. "Hey, buddy," he said.

The bird moved elegantly toward his outstretched hand, and when he got within a foot, his head shot out and pecked Sherrill on the wrist. He withdrew his hand quickly and shook it.

"That thing's a menace," he said, faking a lunge toward it.

The bird skulked off toward the water, a look of self-satisfaction writ large in every delicate step.

Inside, a sporadically toothed woman sitting bored and smoking behind a Formica counter took our money and handed us each a ticket. All around us was the clash of two Floridas: the world of the swamps and the glitter of Miami Beach. A ceramic alligator wearing sunglasses and a white disco suit on display next to the counter neatly encapsulated this struggle.

"We close at four," she said. "Last airboat ride goes at three-thirty, but y'all need to buy a separate ticket for that."

"What's this get us then?" Sherrill asked. There was an edge to his voice that I guessed stemmed from the bird attack.

"Admission to the wildlife exhibits and the Indian village," she said. "The panther ain't here today though. He's up in Naples getting his shots."

Sherrill raised his eyebrows at me. "Too bad the bird couldn't get his shots. A lethal injection, maybe."

The woman coughed out a foul cloud of Marlboro Red and grinned through her crumbling teeth. "You met Carl, did ya? He's a little ornery but his heart's in the right place."

Sherrill smiled and nodded. On our way out, he looked at

me. "Heart's in the right place? Does he do charity work when he's not attacking tourists?"

As we got beyond the entrance, Sherrill nudged me. "Check it out," he said, "truly owner-occupied."

Off to the left, near the entrance to the wildlife exhibits, was a shantytown of battered RVs, pickup trucks, tie-dyed T-shirts hanging on washing lines strung between vehicles, and frayed lawn chairs. A sallow-faced teenage girl poked her head out of one of the trailers then disappeared back inside. On a picnic table almost entirely covered in empty Milwaukee's Best cans, a hibachi barbecue with a gaping hole in one side smouldered away, belching smoke through the breach. A series of small, simple shacks stood behind the congregation of campers.

Hanging lank from one of the trailers was Old Dixie: the Confederate flag. Unlike everything else in the makeshift campground, its vibrant red and blue had not been washed away by the unrelenting sun and rain. As we went past, it flapped lightly against the camper.

"Don't let that flag hit the ground, boy," Sherrill said in a thick redneck accent.

"Retirement community?" I asked.

"Something like that," he said. "Retirement for people who never worked an honest day in their life. Social Security won't cover 'em."

"How many people do you think work here?"

Sherrill shrugged. "Can't be that many. That's likely some good ol' boy's girl working the front desk. Probably pay her in cigarettes and cheap compliments."

I shook my head. "I thought police were supposed to have a fair and balanced view of humanity?"

"Who told you that?" He grinned. The smile disappeared and his brown eyes scanned the horizon. "Let's have a look around and see what we can see."

A thick, tattooed guy with a buzz cut and a serious look took our tickets. "Gators to your right," he said, "Indian village off to the left." A scrawny, limping man who could have been Duaner's Floridian twin stumbled into view and handed him a large can of beer. As Sherrill and I wandered off toward the alligators, I could hear them chuckling.

To call it a recreation park was misleading in both regards. The only recreation I observed beyond sitting in an airboat listening to the deafening roar of an engine was the two guys drinking beer at the front gate. While the park sat sandwiched between the outer western fringes of the Glades and the intricate, dense Ten Thousand Islands, access to the green space was cordoned off with a heavy chain. No park. They intended to get you in, let you have a look around, take your eight bucks and send you on your way without you getting your shoes dirty.

A crocodile lay motionless in a ten-by-ten-foot enclosure, the bottom a hastily painted green covered with an inch of fetid water.

"That's a big one," Sherrill said.

"I assume you're not talking about the enclosure."

Sherrill raised his eyebrow. "Hey," he said softly, to the crocodile. "Not many of these left in the wild. Hey," he said again.

"I hope that works better than it did with the egret."

The crocodile didn't move. An alligator next door was in the same boat, cramped into a small space filled with filmy-looking water. His mouth hung agape and flies buzzed in and out of it. One of his front feet was missing just below the knee, a sign that he'd been in the wild at some point—according to Sherrill—and tussled with another gator or a foe of the human kind. An alligator is a thick, expressionless beast that to most transmits only the most primal emotion: menace. Yet looking at Bruno, as the placard on his pen read, I saw an alligator that was merely fed up. It was a sad sight. Outside the pen, the alligator's natural habitat sprawled in every direction, yet here he was on display for pale tourists to stand and inspect at a safe distance. The few basic things Bruno had been born to do were now out of reach. But only just. As I watched him, the alligator opened one eye and scanned the periphery, then slid into the mottled water where he found a spot at the bottom and parked himself.

Sherrill sighed. "Sad."

I'd been keeping an eye out for anyone who might remotely resemble Coleman. Other than the men at the front, we hadn't seen anyone until the gravel path meandered around a corner and there were two men standing in a pen filled with small alligators. A man and two young boys were watching, the boys transfixed, holding tightly to the chain link, mouths agape.

Sherrill nudged me. "Anyone familiar?"

I shook my head. One man had a shock of jet-black hair tied into a ponytail, and the other was much taller than Coleman would have grown to be. Like the men working the front, both were drinking beers and smoking. They seemed oblivious to the spectators who had gathered.

"When they gonna get big?" one of the boys asked.

The tall man grinned. "Real soon," he drawled. "Real soon he's going to be bigger than you." He thrust a wriggling reptile toward the boys and they jumped back shrieking. I noticed their dad smiling uneasily.

"You want to hold one?" the other man said.

"Uh-uh," one of the boys said.

"Sure," said the other.

The tall man pointed at a sign taped to the pen. "Hold a baby gator for $5."

"Forget it, son," the father said. "That's too much."

"Too much?" the thick man said. "Hell, that's just to cover the insurance if someone gets an arm tore off." The men chortled.

"You ever get bit?" one of the boys said.

The tall man held his hand out. A scimitar-shaped scar stretched across the back of it. "Plenty of times," he said. "This one's the worst. Learned me not to tease an alligator when you're all full of beer."

"Whoa."

Sherrill and I moved closer to the pen. The stockier man had picked up on our presence and stiffened. I figured it was Sherrill. Some men had a built-in cop-detector, Sherrill's leisure-time disguise notwithstanding.

"And how many of y'all are there working here?" Sherrill said in a high-pitched, theatrical Southern whine. The ponytailed man swigged from his beer and busied himself with moving a water dish from one end of the pen to the other.

"How many *gators* we got in here?" the tall man said, ignoring the question. It was obviously a tactic he employed on bored kids.

Sherrill stepped closer to the pen. "You hard of hearing?" he said. Instinctively, the man corralled the two boys and headed away, back toward the entrance.

"Sheeeeeet," the man said.

"I'm just wondering how many men it takes to run an outfit like this," Sherrill said, dropping the phony accent.

The tall man put the baby gator down and walked over. Only the fence separated him from us.

"You the new parole officer?"

Sherrill shook his head and smiled at me. "Always a good sign when a place this far out in the middle of nowhere has its own PO." I kept my mouth shut and nodded.

"Luther," the tall man said. The man with the ponytail looked up from his busywork at the other end of the pen. "Go on and take a break.

"What do you want?" he said when Luther had disappeared.

"Looking for someone," Sherrill said.

"You a cop?"

Sherrill nodded. "Off duty. Doing my friend here a favour. He's come a long way to find someone."

The tall man swigged from his beer and glanced at me with tired, red eyes. "And who would that be?"

"Friend of mine," I said. I didn't want to give up exactly whom I was looking for. It made no difference anyway. "About my height, my colouring, a couple of years older than me."

"Kin?"

I nodded. Lying had never come easy.

"Well," he said, "there's me and Luther, Grimsby and old Carl, who you probably saw at the front. We got two girls—one works the front, the other at the Indian village. Other than an old boy who brings the panther down from Naples a couple times a week, that's the operation."

I felt my heart sink.

"That's it?" Sherrill said.

"That's it," he said. "Who told you any different?"

I told him what I'd heard from Rook Bannister. "My brother was always really good with alligators," I said.

"I hate to tell you, mister," the man said, "a lot of people had to get good with gators down here, just to make a living. They're a natural resource. *The* natural resource actually."

Sherrill sighed. I noticed Carl the egret come around the corner on his long elegant legs. Somewhere off in the distance an alligator grunted.

"Let's go," I said, then to the man, "Thanks. I appreciate it." Sherrill clapped me on the shoulder and we started walking toward the parking lot. Neither of us spoke a word.

We'd got within spitting distance of the front gates when the man called us back. "Hold up," he said. "I just thought of something." He was panting from the short run up the path and he took a minute to catch his breath. "I thought of something," he said.

My heart began to race. A bead of sweat materialized at the nape of my neck and rushed the length of my spine to my underwear.

"When'd your friend say he was down here?"

"Two weeks ago," I said.

The man nodded emphatically. "Every few weeks we got a couple of boys who come and clean the gator ponds out. Job don't pay worth a shit and most people wouldn't do it for all the whiskey in Tennessee. These fellers look like they've been down on their luck."

I could hear the blood pumping in my temples.

"One of them definitely ain't your kin, unless you got black blood up your family tree." He grinned at us. "This boy's black as the ace of spades."

"All right," Sherrill said. "I think we get the picture."

The man ignored him. "Other feller though," he said, looking at me through squinted eyes, "yeah, he's about your size. Got a big beard on him so it's hard to tell about the face though." He shrugged. "Probably in his early thirties. Difficult to say. People live hard down here." He waved his hand through the air.

"My mama used to say this goddamned heat aged you in dog years. Dry you up like a fuckin' raisin."

"When are these guys coming to work again?" I asked.

"Hold up," he said. He went up the path a little ways. "Grimsby!" he shouted toward the gate where we'd entered the park. "Grimsby! When's them boys coming back to clean out the gators?" Sherrill looked at me and smiled. I grinned back.

"You're in luck," the man said. "They're coming back tomorrow."

Sherrill and I walked in silence. We went past the alligators and the enormous crocodile that hadn't budged an inch since our first encounter. He grinned malevolently, one cold black eye following us like a slowly shifting planet. There was a low rumble of thunder and I felt the first hot drops of rain.

"Let's make a run for it," Sherrill said. "Don't want to get my disguise all crinkly."

By the time we got to the main entrance, we were caught in a torrential downpour. The ground seemed to grow instantly muddy under our feet.

"Let's take cover over there," Sherrill said, nodding toward the main building where we'd bought our tickets. "This'll pass within five minutes." We ran for it. An airboat pulled up at the dock, half full of tourists holding soggy park brochures over their heads for cover. They disembarked and made a run for the parking lot.

Carl the egret sidled up to us under the awning. He was trying to stay out of the rain too.

"Hey, buddy," Sherrill said, slicking the water back off his forehead. "How'd you like to become stew?" He stepped toward the bird. Carl the egret slunk off into the rain, glancing dolefully at Sherrill as he moved across the grass.

"That'll fix his wagon." Sherrill looked at me. "Hey," he said. "You all right?"

I nodded. "Good news, I guess."

"Yeah," he said. "I know I don't have to tell you not to get your hopes up too much. You've learned that the tough way."

"I woke up this morning happy to have given up on the whole thing," I said. "Ready to move on. You know, haircut, real job, that whole business."

"Well," he said, sticking a hand out from under the awning and catching a few drops in his palm. The rain was slowing. "Isn't that just the way things seem to go."

My leg was aching, so I lowered myself to the concrete, sweeping a cigarette butt away before I sat down. I stretched out and rubbed at my leg, feeling the pain blossom, burn and then dissipate. "I guess," I said. "I can always move on tomorrow."

But Sherrill wasn't listening. "Hold up," he said. "Check this out."

A pickup came clattering up to the entrance, went through the parking lot and then onto the grass behind the main building. The blurred outlines of two men in the cab were visible through the streaming windshield. The truck slowed and then swung into the space between the rough trailer encampment and the two small clapboard buildings we'd noticed off in the short distance.

Two men jumped out and went around to the back of the truck. They hoisted something heavy wrapped in a thick blanket and walked unsteadily with it to one of the shacks. I noticed a smear of something dark soaking through the blanket.

"Three guesses," Sherrill said.

I didn't say anything. Even at a distance, there was something familiar about the driver. A red baseball cap was pressed down onto a thatch of long blond hair. They lifted another similar-looking package from the back of the truck.

"Check it out," Sherrill said, motioning toward the entrance to the Indian village and alligator displays. The tall man we'd talked with emerged from the gates and crossed the grass at a deliberate pace. He shouted something across the trailer shantytown to the men and the truck. The two men stopped what they were doing and scanned the periphery. Even from my vantage, I could see one of them shrug.

"I'd say these old boys are doing a lot more than just keeping gators on display," Sherrill said. "Now that tall drink of water who was so helpful to us about ten minutes back is losing his mind. He ain't sure whether the off-duty cop went home or not."

The tall man had reached the pickup and was in serious discussion with the two others. In unison, the trio looked toward the parking lot. Sherrill's truck sat alone, like the last of a doomed species. He chuckled. "Didn't he hear me say I was off duty? I might not be tomorrow when I come back though."

One of the men slammed the tailgate shut and the group started walking toward the main building. Toward us.

"Sherrill," I said.

"I know," he said. "Just hold up, relax. This could be good for a laugh."

My leg began to throb. It bore the weight of what fun could come out of the blue. I kept my eyes on the blond guy.

The men had bridged the distance and were looking back at us as they crossed the lawn. "Oh, shit," I said. "That's Hoyt Lee."

"Well, I'll be," Sherrill said, squinting at the approaching trio. "It is."

"How many people are there in the state of Florida?"

Sherrill, distracted, replied: "Don't know. A bunch."

"Just that I seem to keep running into the same people everywhere I go. Coincidence, I guess."

"No such thing," he said. "You just haven't connected the dots yet."

Hoyt Lee had spotted me as well. His face looked briefly incredulous then dissolved into pure, tight-lipped hatred as they got within spitting distance. The tall man nodded and smiled. "Staying dry, I see, fellas. Good call."

Sherrill grinned at him.

Hoyt Lee didn't say anything as they went past and into the building, but his eyes, as cold and black and filled with threat as the crocodile's, watched me until he disappeared through the open door.

"Tomorrow," I said.

"Tomorrow," he said, "we're going back. First thing."

Off to our left, the sun had disappeared into the Gulf, leaving a violent sky swept through with fiery oranges and reds in its wake.

"Red sky at night," Sherrill said.

"Sailor's delight," I said softly.

We'd ridden all the way to I-75 in silence. But it wasn't a relaxed quietude. My mind was rushing along like a transport in the Appalachians with brake loss. I could barely keep up with the torrent of scenarios that were playing out in my head. It had all started with a phone call. Now, one way or another, it would end here, in the swamps, in the oppressive heat where mosquitoes lit on anything that walked and pumped blood. It would end right where it started and I would go home, with or without my brother.

I still had a feeling it would be without.

We pulled up outside the motel in the darkness. Only a few cars were scattered through the parking lot and a small number of windows along the row of rooms were lit up.

"Your friends around?"

I shook my head. "Gone fishing. They did another derby today and are coming home in the morning. I'm going to have to tell them we're not leaving tomorrow. Or at least, I'm not."

"Let's just see, Jasper." I could see him searching for the right thing to say.

"It's all right, Manuel," I said. "Listen, I can't thank you enough for your help—today and all along."

He shrugged. "It beats protecting pensioners from telemarketers," he said. "You going to be all right? Want to grab a beer or a bite to eat?"

"No," I said. "I'm done."

"Well, listen," he said, as I got out of the truck. "Take care of yourself. I wouldn't bother with a nightcap at the Painted Frog or anything like that," he said. "Got the feeling you might not like to run into any of your local friends and family right now."

"I'm going to shower then see if I can catch a ball game on TV," I said. "Get into bed."

"With the pyjamas with the feet in them, right?" He grinned.

"In Canada we normally sleep in a snowsuit," I said. "So I'll probably crank the air conditioning up just to feel like home."

Sherrill laughed. "Bright and early tomorrow," he said, "say eight o'clock. I'll come pick you up."

On my way up to the room, I passed a blonde girl of about eighteen on the stairs. She smiled at me. "Hi," she said, sweetly.

"Hi," I said, then went past her down the corridor to my room. I stepped inside and threw the deadbolt. Blondes had gotten me in enough trouble in Florida already.

The room was like a sauna. Someone had been to look at the air conditioner, but the extent of their repair was a red bucket strategically placed to catch the leaking water. I emptied it into the bathroom sink and then lay down on the bed.

The Braves were playing a spring training game against the Pirates on TBS. When I turned the game on, a Braves batter had just walloped the ball high and long, out toward the left-field bleachers. By the time it bounced off the concrete stairs between seating sections and into the hands of some jubilant fan, I was already asleep.

41.

I WOKE UP SOMETIME deep in the night. A sharp\clicking had stirred me. If the air conditioner had still been functional, I might have attributed it to that. But, lying there in a cotton trough of my own cold sweat, I could vouch for the air conditioner's dormancy without having to sit up. I reached for the glass of water on the bedside table and sipped at it, still lying down. A mouthful of tepid, bathroom tap water spilled onto my chest. It was a sweet relief. The rest went down my throat. It tasted like a dog had been soaking his paws in it.

The clicking had stopped and I wasn't sure if I'd dreamt it. I scanned the stucco ceiling in the dark, trying to focus on a spot. This had been my trick for getting back to sleep since I'd been a teenager. Coleman found it hilarious. "I'm looking at the stars, you're looking at the ceiling," he said. "That's about all you need to know about us." I'd thought about it a lot over the years and he was right. Whereas I'd once taken it as a mortal insult, a crack at my lack of intellectual curiosity, I now knew it was the reason

I was in a motel room in Florida trying to find Coleman, who'd wandered out into the vast cosmos of the world one morning, never to return.

A noise snapped my eyes from the ceiling. A creak rippled up from the floor. The sound of something moving across the carpet. My heart took off as though a flame had been put to it.

I waited.

Silence. I wanted to bolt upright, jump from the bed and be ready. I found I couldn't move.

A tremor kicked up in my bad leg.

The bathroom tap dripped into the chipped and stained basin.

Out on the overpass, a truck roared past, heading toward I-75.

Then, somewhere in the darkness of my motel room, a digital watch beeped, marking the changing of the hour.

A figure loomed over me in the blackness before I could leap out of bed. I thrashed out and caught him under the chin with the edge of my hand. There was a grunt, then he drove a fist into my stomach. It felt like a ten-pound sledge dropping onto my guts. Then he had me, pressing my arms down by my sides into the sodden mattress. I could hear him breathing. It was the sound of raw, violent intent.

A second figure appeared. A hand came down onto my face, holding a rag soaked in a bright-stinking chemical that rushed into my nostrils like liquid winter. I fought to catch a clean breath. Twinkling stars spread across the backs of my eyelids. There you go, Coleman, I thought. Well, there you are.

I went out staring at the cracks in the white stucco ceiling, the beeping watch echoing in my ears and out into the darkness.

I was turning in a deep black void, sounds distorting and elongating around me like a tape coming unspun on a reel-to-reel.

My arms and legs were anchors, my brain a dollop of rice pudding in a skull-shaped bowl.

I'm dead, I thought.

And then, *If this isn't hell, I can see it from here.*

There was a mechanical click and I felt a light hit my face. It was like a hot coal being dropped into the open basin of my head. A flash of white-hot agony ripped behind my eyes, and somewhere off in the distance I heard myself groan.

"He's not out."

"Told you."

"Told you."

"Should've used more of that shit. Gimme that rag."

The voices were familiar. Trying to find the names was like searching for a penny at the bottom of the ocean.

The blackness gathered itself around me. The universe without stars.

The stink brought me to. It was the smell of something dead, a living thing that had passed on and was now making the transition from solid to liquid. My head throbbed from the inside out, and every breath I drew singed my nostrils and left the chemical taste on my tongue.

I opened my eyes. I was in a burlap sack, still wearing the boxers and T-shirt I'd gone to bed in. My back ached from being cinched up in the bag. Somewhere outside, I could hear the drone of mosquitoes. I instinctively knew that it was the middle of the night. Another wave of stink hit me and I clenched my teeth hard against the gag reflex.

Dull, quiet laughter drifted through the burlap. Low voices murmured back and forth, the easiness of the exchange belying the fact that they'd just drugged a man and shoved him into a burlap sack.

I wondered where the hell I was.

The ground shifted underneath me and I heard water lap up against the side of whatever I was on.

A boat.

In an instant, I realized what the stink was. I could picture the five-gallon lard can in Rolly Lee's garage, Duaner having a laugh and asking me to close my eyes and smell it.

Mudfish and mullet in a closed can, out in the sun.

Bake for three or four days.

Gator bait.

Fear cracked a whip across my senses.

My first instinct was to lash out with my good leg and hope to hit someone through the confines of the bag. Even in my dazed state I knew it'd be a stupid move. If they planned to kill me, they'd probably just do it then. I couldn't see them, and they could see me. It would be suicidal.

The stink hit me again and I could imagine the same smell drifting out across the water, reaching the gators and drawing them toward the boat. They'd drift in the wake, languid, waiting for the bait. A wave of dread passed over me and I shivered, despite the heat. Perhaps suicide was a better option.

A paddle hit the water. "Here they come."

I could feel the vessel turning underneath my back. The motion sent a blinding bolt of pain up my leg. I clamped my teeth down so hard that I felt one of my back molars groan.

"Hold up."

Hold up. This was not happening. It couldn't be happening. I could feel the soft cloud of whatever had been used to knock me out drifting off. I was left with the electric pulse of panic and terror.

"Shit."

"Just a small one, huh?"

The boat turned again. "No rush."

I still couldn't make out the voices through the bag. The low, whispered tones rendered the two voices identical. Identical to one another and to nearly every male voice I'd heard south of the Mason-Dixon Line. It was a sound, sweet and low, that made me regret ever coming back to Florida. No matter how often you visit a place, you never really belong. Being a visitor makes you more foreign than if you'd never showed up in the first place. But it doesn't necessarily make you enemies. I'd made a few in Florida, and I could count them on one hand. I was superstitious enough to think that if I didn't identify them in my head, perhaps I could walk away from this. Be let out of the bag with my eyes closed and wander out onto the interstate. Like Coleman had. The boat swayed in the water and my stomach lurched.

We continued on. Time spun out and I lost track of how long it had been. I could feel us moving across water, the mosquitoes buzzing around the bag, the smell of the swamps thick in my nostrils. Now and then I'd catch small fragments of hushed conversation and the hazy, rusty smell of cigarettes. There was another smell too, something sweeter and possibly familiar if I could only manage to think straight. I wondered if it was all a ploy to scare the shit out of me and nothing more. If so, it was working.

There were other sounds, stranger still. The sound of something else confined on that boat, something struggling to get free, much as I was. My brain reeled from the pounding in my head and the bag seemed to draw tighter around me until it was like a second skin. I imagined the sounds I was hearing were only the sounds I was making trying desperately to find some way out.

I thought about Coleman. How he'd been lost in the swamps and walked out with a grin on his face. I knew I'd never find him now. Maybe he'd end up looking for me and that'd teach him all the things that I'd learned about loss over the last decade. I thought of my mother in the rest home—she might not even realize that I was gone. And my father in the ground. Then the worst thought of all hit me: I'd wasted my time. I'd stacked my grievances high under blue skies and ignored those things I should have been thankful for. I'd wasted my time. Wasted it on jobs I hated, women I couldn't be bothered with and a view of the world that asked little of me and brought little in return. I'd wasted my time waiting for Coleman to come home; for life to pick up where it had left off. Wherever Coleman was, dead or alive, he'd lived. He'd followed his own strange dreams. I wished I'd even had the guts to dream some for myself.

There was splashing in the water and the boat tilted uneasily. One of them gave out a small whoop. Then I could hear the heavy breathing close to the bag.

"Still out," I heard. "Help me out here. This one first."

This, I thought. I'm this.

Then I was being lofted up, my captors grunting in the dark Florida night like the alligators in the water below, while all around me mosquitoes batted against the sack like wayward, heat-sick angels.

There was a brief feeling of weightlessness. Then I hit the water.

42.

DEATH HAD ALWAYS BEEN on standby. A fallback position that I'd kept tucked away, deep in the crevasses of my mind, should things ever get to be too much to bear. It was never an active line of thought, but a backup plan. Now I realized it was the notion of a coward who'd never known what the stakes were to begin with.

There had been no great happiness in my life over the last ten years. I was just a regular guy doing regular things: working a job I could care less about, drinking too much on the weekend, drifting through a relationship on autopilot, dwelling on the things I'd lost and those things I'd never had, wishing for anybody else's life but my own. One among many. Ronnie Orsulak was like a get-out-of-jail-free card. Regular guys didn't wake up in a hospital bed after being pushed onto the subway line. Ronnie Orsulak made me realize that while there had been no great joy, there had been an abundance of small, subtle blessings.

Now, as the tepid, sulphuric swamp water began to seep into the bag like liquid death, it hit me strong and plain. I didn't want to die.

The bag had been tied at the top. There was a small hole where it hadn't been pulled tightly enough. But, at the same time, I knew my captors would still be watching me from the boat, waiting to see what happened. I knew my best bet would be to go under and wait for as long as I could.

There was another heavy splash in the water and the wake of it bobbed me up and then under. Foul, warm water shot up my nose and into my mouth.

Something long and wooden poked at me through the sack. There was more murmured conversation from above. I kept still.

I wanted them to think I was already dead. I heard something splash in the water nearby, and pieces of whatever it was landed on the top of the bag.

Gator bait.

As if on cue, something rushed past me in the water, a strong vector of pure intent. There was some splashing and I heard laughter from above. My bladder gave way. There was now little room left to breathe inside the bag. I'd rotated so that I was underwater up to my chest and the rest of me was sinking quickly. I felt the dull prod of a paddle against the back of my neck and I resisted the urge to shout. Panic was giving way to rage.

Another shape moved past me in the water. Then another. More gator bait was doled out in a spray across the swamp. I could feel the water froth as the bag filled up. I reached up and loosened the ties as one of the gators nosed into me. My heart raced into the red. This is it, I thought. The dull chatter from the boat had become louder. It was the sound of cowards working themselves up. Then the paddle came down flat and heavy across the top of my head and once again the blackness swallowed me and I sank into the swamp like a million living things before me, while all around a sea of reptiles twisted and roiled.

People talk about a white light; of walking down a narrowing corridor toward an ethereal glow. At the end of it friends and family, long since gone, await your arrival. I saw none of that. What I saw was blackness, like looking at the backs of your eyelids in a dark room as you drift off to sleep. My brain willed my limbs to move, to get out of the bag before it was too late. But it was no use. I might as well have been encased in cement.

Then I was moving through the water.

I remember Coleman yammering on about alligators and

their habits. In typical big-brother fashion he would bring this stuff up as we lay in bed at night. How gators got hold of their prey and spiralled down to the bottom of the swamp in a death roll, choking off what life remained as they went. But alligators didn't eat you fresh. They'd sock you away in a swamp hole and let the sun and the humidity and the bugs do their work. Then, when you'd aged to a delicate ripeness, you were ready for dinner.

I could hear myself laughing inside my own head. The echoes of a lunatic in a large, empty space. Then the blackness got deeper and deeper until I couldn't hear or feel anything. This is it, I thought, not a bad way to go.

And then there was nothing.

43.

BIRDSONG PULLED ME from the blackness. A high-pitched, electronically precise keening unlike any bird I'd heard before. I'm in heaven, I thought. My eyes wouldn't open. When I tried to rub at them, I found I couldn't move my arms. But oddly, I could hear myself breathing.

Dizzied moments passed, and gradually I could feel the sensation returning to my arms and legs. I immediately wondered whether I'd found my way to heaven or hell. Either way, I was surprised to find you wound up in the same state you left in. In my case, drenched to the skin and plagued by swarms of mosquitoes and other insect denizens of the swamp. I touched my eyes and found the lids covered in a baked layer of mud.

When I got them open, daylight was breaking and I was at the edge of the water. From my side I scanned across the top of the water for beady reptile eyes and ridged spines. But for the mosquitoes flickering against the tea-coloured water, I saw nothing. The boat had gone, and with it my captors. I struggled to sit up. The blood rushed to my head with an agonizing throb. My bad leg felt like a hinge that had rusted open. There was no way I was dead. I hurt too much.

I'd washed up into a small cove. One foot was still tangled in the burlap sack. I noticed a second bag nearby. They double-bagged me, I thought, and it made me grin. A vague recollection of being dragged through the water returned to me. It was all too much to consider, so I laid myself back down into the soft, warm mud.

Then I heard the faint crackle of branches breaking underfoot, further up from the water where the pines and scrub that bordered the swamp began to grow. I clenched my fists and began to slowly raise myself up. I'd been drugged, thrown in a bag, spattered with gator bait, whacked over the head with a paddle, and left for dead. If further torment was on the agenda, I wasn't going to go without a fight.

I got myself to my knees and turned toward the sound. The sun was streaming between the tall, sparsely branched trees, making the blanket of sawgrass glow as if nestled on embers. A burning, apocalyptic land. Perspiration beaded across my forehead and a wave of nausea hit me. My vision blurred and the sunlight shifted through the trees. My eyes filled with a white light. I felt my breathing slow.

Out of the trees, a shadow of a man appeared with the sky blazing at his back. He moved with deliberate economy through the sawgrass, like a spirit that had risen up from the loam, as weightless as a strand of Spanish moss borne to the air. I'd been lucky to hear anything. It had to be Hoyt or Rolly Lee, returning to finish me off. But as the man got closer, the light falling away behind him, I knew that it wasn't.

I got to my feet and readied myself. Adrenalin had taken over and banished the pain from my head and legs. I could no longer taste the residue of whatever chemical I'd been knocked out with. If this was it—the end of the line—blood would be spilled before I lay back down in the mud again.

All sound and sensation fell away as the man approached. Twenty feet. Long, dark hair hung against his face and down over his collarbone where it met up with a thick black beard. Even with the sun at his back, I could make out his eyes. They were bright and filled with intent.

Fifteen feet. Ten feet.

Then we were close enough to shake hands. I looked at him and he looked at me but not a word was spoken. It was as though the morning heat had slowed the drift of time. Two men, standing in the middle of the Everglades in silence. Two men, staring at one another, across the void of years and loss and hope. I watched the bearded man's eyes well up, hot tears streaking across a face burnished to a deep brown by mud and sun.

Now I wondered if I really was dead.

Two men.

Brothers.

Coleman and me.

Coleman and I didn't speak. We sat down in the mud at the edge of the swamp with the rising sun bearing down on us. If I had been able to gather my thoughts into anything resembling co-herency, I wouldn't have known where to start. It was all completely unreal.

Finally, Coleman spoke. "You all right?" His voice was rough and deep and not how I remembered it. I nodded. His eyes were bright but changed, like he was seeing things from a great distance and struggling to bring them into focus. It was all I could do before the tears came; silent sobs that racked my spine and pushed me close to hyperventilation. Coleman patted my shoulder and sighed, nodding his head. And that was how we stayed for what seemed like hours, sitting in silence, watching the sun dapple the water, Coleman nodding. Off across the swamp, an alligator emerged from the mangroves and slid down the muddy bank and into the water. We watched him drift and then disappear, both of us wondering where to start.

"Stand up." His voice was gruff and tired. "We need to walk."

We started walking. Morning had come to the Everglades and in the trees, birds chattered and spiders worked across branches at dew-stricken webs. Though I was no longer tied up and drowning, I was no more at ease for it. Coleman moved quickly through the swampland, and I struggled to keep up, stumbling along the path, branches whipping across my face, bugs landing on every patch of exposed skin. I watched him go, the bones standing out in stark relief all down his bare, browned back. A skeleton wrapped and rattling in thin skin. He wore only a tattered pair of jean shorts and some ruined tennis shoes. His matted hair fell down across his shoulders. He smelled like he had slept outside every night since he'd left home. I didn't doubt that he had.

"Hold up," I said. His pace only seemed to quicken. I was at the end of my tether. My head ached and my bad leg felt locked up at the knee. In trying to keep up with him, I was doing a combination stagger/lurch. My throat ached with thirst and the heat was making me nauseous.

And I still had no idea how I'd ended up here. Part of me still believed I was dead.

"Hey," I said. "Can we slow down for a minute?"

He didn't turn around but shook his head. I noticed a blur of colour off the trail and watched a snake disappear into the thick vegetation. We had been walking for hours with not a word spoken. The swamp was closing around us, the water disappearing and the canopy swallowing the sky. Everywhere I looked there were mosquitoes, and their buzzing filled my head. The path narrowed and as I watched it, trying to keep one foot in front of the other, it seemed to throb with the heat. I stopped, steadied myself against a tree and then threw up. Coleman kept going.

"Hey," I said. "Coleman."

He went faster still, now almost in a jog.

"Hey!" I shouted. I wiped the sick from my chin and took off after him.

Pine needles swept across my face, palmettos nagged at my ankles. He was pulling out of sight. I gritted my teeth and began to run. I jumped a log and landed in a puddle of fetid water. "Coleman," I shouted. Now I could only see flashes of skin through the trees.

I made it out into a yellowed grassland and ran harder. I was gaining on him now. He might have known the swamps, but I could see every breath heaving up his frame as he struggled on and knew that there was nothing left to keep him going.

When I got within reach I dove, catching him across the waist. He went down in a sweaty, writhing heap. I blocked one hand as he struck upward at my face. I grabbed his wrists and looked down at him, his eyes wild and filled with terror and the weight of years, distance, loneliness and loss.

"Why are you chasing me?" he said.

I let go of his wrists and pushed myself off him.

"Coleman," I said, "where the hell have you been?"

"We have to keep going."

"Why?"

He was still on his back, trying to get his breath. "We have to keep going."

I slammed my fist into the ground. "Tell me where you've been."

He started to speak and I cut him off.

"Why did you leave? Where the fuck have you been?" I stood up and kicked at his foot. "Tell me why, Coleman."

He sighed and sat up. He was shaking his head over and over, his eyes glazing toward the horizon.

"Why, Coleman?"

He stood up. "We have to keep going."

"Why?"

The sun blazed down on the prairie, cruel and oppressive, willing the world to burn. But now a chill twinkled across my neck and down my spine.

Coleman's eyes seemed to sharpen and focus. "I was in that boat too."

44.

WE CONTINUED WALKING, now more slowly. It was the hottest part of the day and I knew I was badly dehydrated. At least the heat had driven the mosquitoes off, particularly as we crossed the dried-out, open stretches that cropped up in and amongst the pinelands. I had to get back to the highway and let Duane and Donny know that I was okay. The shock of being snatched up in the middle of the night had given way to the shock of finding Coleman.

It wasn't easy getting a handle on anything as far as Coleman went. He'd always been odd, progressing to the point just prior to his departure when my parents had looked into hospitalization. But now he even looked ill. We were about the same height, but I had at least fifty pounds on Coleman. He was so skinny and slouched that he took on a concave look around the gut. The man had been living outside and I wasn't about to judge him on his hygiene. I did, however, plan to offer up the shower in our motel room when we got back.

His brown skin was riddled with scars. There was a thin pale line that ran like a river from the small of his back and disappeared under the waistband of his shorts. Raised pocks on the backs of his arms and his hands. Most striking of all was a thick blotch that looked like a supernova exploding from the topography of his upper shoulder. I watched it bob as we went down the path, following it like a beacon.

And I wondered how many other scars there were, the visible and those I would never see.

It was Coleman's mental state that worried me more. After ten years, I had come to accept that death was the most likely conclusion to his story. When I allowed myself the indulgence of dreaming that he was alive somewhere, I'd always end up worrying myself into sleepless nights that he'd been institutionalized. Now I could see that he wasn't well. His eyes twitched and darted and he mumbled under his breath. Most troubling of all, it seemed like just another day for Coleman. He acted like I was anyone he might have met in his travels, and he dodged my questions about where he'd been and why he'd never been in touch with a shrug and a vague, humourless smile. I was just happy to have found him. But I knew that inside Coleman, whatever had led him to leave home had probably only grown in magnitude, like a black cavity blossoming inside him.

—

"They were going to send me to the hospital," he said. His eyes creased at the corners and I watched the muscles ripple up his jawline. His face seemed to get even more hollowed as he thought of it. "No way. I had a mission." He shook his head and I put my hand on his arm.

"It's all right, Coleman," I said.

His eyes darted toward the ground, and he picked up a stick and began turning it in his hands.

"Dad's dead, Coleman. Mum's alive but in a home."

He sighed and stabbed at the ground with the stick. "I had to come back," he said.

I took a long look at him. It was as though I was still trying to goad my conscious mind into believing that here I was, sitting with Coleman. I noticed another scar that made me wince, this one on his upper chest, below his shoulder. It took me a second to register that it corresponded with the one I'd seen on his back.

"Jesus, Coleman," I said, reaching out to touch it.

He jerked back and an uneasy smile set into his face, as if he'd remembered who I was. "My souvenir from North Carolina," he said, glancing down at the scar almost fondly. "Two hunters, up in the mountains."

"An accident?" I said.

"Nope. I got hunted." He paused to scribble at the dirt with his stick. "They got sick of me scaring the deer off. On purpose." He gave me a gentle smile and for a second we were in the woods again behind my parents' house, lying on a rock and spotting clouds through the canopy. "Gave me a ten count then one of them shot me on four with a crossbow." He ran a finger over the scar, as if it were Braille and might call forth the small details within this memory. "It was sticking straight through me. It'd been the other side, might have pierced my heart."

"That was kind of them," I said.

"I had to saw the tip of it off with a shard of scrap metal I found."

"Jesus."

"He wasn't no help. Took me two hours before I could pull it through. Stung some. I filled the hole with shoplifted whiskey and, well, that was that time." He looked down at the scar again, almost admiringly, as if a top surgeon had done the job.

"That time?" I said, and to my surprise my voice was failing, choked with tears.

"Devils," he said, "the world is full of them. So I moved on."

Florida had always been the destination. It had taken him time to get there; time spent moving through Vermont and Pennsylvania, Virginia and the Carolinas. It was a slow, south-ward drift. The path of a meandering migratory bird hard-wired to the endpoint.

Coleman had been hospitalized after arriving in Florida. "I was walking and I was hungry and I couldn't remember where I was. Who I was." Coleman scratched his head. "Did you ever lose track of yourself?" He looked at me, batted a mosquito away from his face. "Jasper," he said, as if reminding himself of where he was at this moment.

"Sure," I said, knowing my disconnections had all been on the figurative level.

"There was a girl there," he said, "a bright-eyed girl. A girl with eyes like new pennies. And she'd been living out for a while, and she fed me something." He winced as if the effort of recollection was causing him pain. Then he broke into a grin and clapped one hand down on my shoulder. "A hamburger," he said. "A hamburger with cheese and a slice of tomato and the bun wasn't green in any spots and man . . . well, it was some hamburger." The grin faded and his eyes narrowed. "I just wish I could remember her name. But she was turning tricks. You know what that means?"

"Yeah, Coleman," I said, "I know what that means." The bugs were landing all over me and I wanted to get moving again, wanted to stop hearing this stuff, wanted to think that everything had somehow been okay through all these lost years. In that way, I was as lost as he was.

"And not long after all this she turned up with her throat torn up. Some man got angry, I guess." He jolted and turned to me wide-eyed. "That's how she paid for the hamburger, you think? Having sex for money?"

"I don't know, Coleman," I said. "Probably." I put a hand on his arm. "I'm sorry though. I'm sorry about your friend. About everything."

He nodded as if I'd just given him the time. "I woke up in a clean white bed and they told me I was in Ocala. And lunch that day . . ." A bird let out a livid, ascending call and Coleman gave me a knowing look like we were about to share a joke.

"Lunch that day," I repeated.

"Was a hamburger. With cheese, and a slice of tomato."

I couldn't take much more of this. The unreality of it all was going to land me in my own clean white bed. "Coleman," I said, "we should keep walking."

"Right," he said, "let's get going." But when I went to stand up, he put a hand on my shoulder. "Just give me one second."

He wanted to finish his story.

After Ocala, he continued south. He found work in the carnivals outside Tampa, lived under bridges with men like Rodney and Devron Jacobs.

At some point, one of his co-workers took notice of Coleman's kinship with alligators. I could only imagine how this'd become plain: a dip in a gator-swarmed canal where the saurians swam to him like puppies treading water. I'd seen it before.

"Why?" I said, finally. "Why, Coleman? Why did you ever leave?"

After all the talk, the blankness drifted in again, like thin white clouds blotting out the moon on a dark night. I could feel my stomach churning with anxiety and anger and I swallowed hard. "What the fuck, Coleman? Why?"

I saw his jaw set, watched his eyelids flutter and then close as if he was drifting back through the years to the morning he'd walked through the back gate. "Something," he said, eyes still shut, "something was disappearing."

"What, Coleman? What was disappearing?"

He pressed the heels of his hands against his forehead and opened his eyes. "Everything," he said. "The world around me. The shape of things. It was like there was no difference between being asleep and awake, dreaming and thinking . . . feeling. Everything all around me, starting to disappear." He nodded emphatically. "So I disappeared first."

"Coleman," I said, "you were sick." The past tense felt like a sham, as did what I said next. "We were going to help you."

He laughed, cracked lips stretching over ruined teeth. "There was no helping," he said. "And I couldn't let you see me like that. Bugged out in some room with some other head cases, you all bringing me cupcakes and sad smiles. Nobody was going to see that. Not you, not Mum, not Dad."

The swamplands blurred to a green wash in front of me. "But Coleman," I said, the words sounding weak and ruined, "why did you come back here?"

Coleman looked at me. He blinked and scratched at his beard, shaking his head as though I'd asked a stupid question. "Rolly Lee," he said. "I came to get Rolly Lee."

But Rolly Lee had got him first. All thanks to me.

45.

THE SUN WAS GLOWING like a downed star through the swamps to the west when we finally heard the highway. By the time we reached Everglades City, two miles up the road, a blue-black night sky had settled in and the bugs were out in force. Frogs chirped from puddles as we crossed a small footbridge heading toward what passed for town in Everglades City. We drew not a glance as we staggered along, mud-covered, bug-eaten, arms and legs scratched and torn from our passage through the swamps, me in my boxers and T-shirt and Coleman looking like Crusoe twenty years into his tropical vacation. Everglades City had grown up from the swamp and seen far worse than us. We found a lone phone booth out in front of a restaurant at land's end.

"I don't suppose you have a quarter."

Coleman gave a brief smile. "Flat busted."

"Well," I said, looking at the restaurant, "I guess there's only one thing for it. You'll wait out here?"

Coleman nodded, but his eyes were cast downward.

The restaurant was styled like a hunting lodge, all dark wood panelling and dim lighting. Three rifles were hung on one wall next to a mounted deer head that watched me with glassy indifference. They were doing good business and the place seemed to hum with chatter when I swung the door open. Then I could just about hear the lettuce wilting in the salad bar as a roomful of diners took in a mud-caked, wild-eyed Canadian in his underwear.

The hostess was an older woman with perfectly permed silver hair and pressed blue pants. Her bottom lip trembled under the weight of her saucer-sized eyes. "Can I . . . help you?" she finally managed.

"The phone, please," I said, smoothing down the front of my once white shirt.

"It's for customers," she said, regaining a little of her composure. She moved toward the door. "Let me help you outside, sir."

"Ma'am," I said, "I hate to do this to you, but if you don't let me use the phone right away, I'm going to sprint right across your beautiful restaurant and dive straight into that salad bar."

"Everglades City," I told Donny. Around the room, people were returning to their steaks and chicken. The hostess was keeping an eye on me from a safe distance. "I'll be out front of a hotel called the Captain's Table. Can't miss it."

"Jesus, Jasper," Donny said. "A lot of people have been going crazy trying to find you. I even called Kim."

Donny had gasped when he answered the phone and heard my voice. They'd returned from the fishing derby and found the room overturned and then called the cops. When I told him what happened—getting thrown in a bag and then into the swamp—there was silence at the other end of the line. Finally, I spoke up: "I'm all right, Donny," I said. I could hear Duane talking off in the background. Donny cupped his hand over the phone and told him to shut up. When he came back on the line, there was pure silence except for his voice.

"We're not going to leave without you," he said. "Duane and I are going to call in sick for the next couple of days." There was a whoop in the background and I could almost imagine Duaner opening another beer off the edge of the vanity.

"Donny," I said, "I have to tell you something. I found Coleman. Coleman found me."

"My God," he said.

"Yeah," I said, and could think of nothing else.

After I hung up the phone, I turned to the hostess. "Ma'am," I said, "thank you so very much. And folks," I called out to the restaurant, "enjoy your meals."

The sky was full black when I stepped back outside. I looked from the road to the water and back again. Coleman was gone. The sun-bleached stretch of road leading out of town dissolved into absolute darkness without a soul wandering into it. I listened and all I could hear were the frogs.

I didn't even bother to call his name.

46.

HALF AN HOUR LATER, Donny's truck pulled up out front of the Captain's Table.

"Wow," Donny said, his big face grinning in the driver's side window. "Is that the swamp thing?" He looked me up and down. "All things considered, you look okay. Nothing a long shower and a fresh set of clothes wouldn't fix."

I got in, slammed the door. Donny handed me a bottle of water and I drank greedily from it, water running down the sides of my mouth and onto my shirt.

"You found your brother."

I looked straight ahead out the window into the darkness. "And then he ran off."

A motorboat cut a slow white wake across the black water toward the docks behind the hotel and Donny watched it, slowly shaking his head. "Well," he said, with a sigh. "I guess that's the way things go sometimes."

"Donny," I said, "if you told me that these last twenty-four hours had been a dream, I'd believe you. But I swear he was right here with me. Coleman." Now that I was sitting down I began to realize just how exhausted I was. My entire body seemed to hum with an electric current.

Donny gave me a small smile and I managed to return it. "Any ideas where he might have gone?"

"One," I said. "The same place he came from. Nowhere."

"Well," he said, "let's head that way then and see what we can see."

We trawled our way out of Everglades City and then went back the way Coleman and I had come down the highway. Donny drove slowly and we watched the narrow shoulders dissolve out into swampland.

"This is the darkest stretch of highway I've ever seen," I said. And it was true. No lampposts, not a gas station or a rest area in sight, or even another car materializing from the blackness. Not one tin shack with a candle burning for light.

"Stop and turn around," I said. "Let's go back."

"You sure?"

"I'm sure."

Donny eased the truck around and we started back toward the highway.

"So," he said, after we'd picked up 75 going north, bound for Fort Myers, "you ready to go home yet?"

I smiled and looked out the window at the blackness. It'd be dark at home too.

Donny caught the look on my face. "Hey," he said, "on the way down here I told you to have faith. You saw your brother today." Just hearing those words sent a chill skittering down my back. "Don't fold on me now, Jasper." I straightened up in my seat and took a deep breath. "So," he said, "you got any other ideas where your brother might have headed?"

"Yeah," I said. "Same way we're going. Fort Myers."

I felt Donny put the hammer down. Mosquitoes pattered the windshield and rushed past the open windows.

The highway was quiet and we made good time. The exhaustion had burned off and I'd caught a wide-eyed, heart-pounding second wind. I didn't know what was waiting for us at the other end of the trip, only that I had to be there.

"I had to let your cop friend know you were okay," Donny said. "He said he'd be round to talk to you but that they were looking into the matter, whatever that means."

"It means Rolly Lee," I said.

Donny motioned toward my swamp-stained shirt. "Tell me what happened."

I started where we had left off the night before, with Sherrill dropping me off in front of the motel. When I finished, there was a shocked silence.

"Well," he said. "Any chance this *wasn't* Rolly Lee?"

"Whoever it was grabbed both of us. I don't see how it could be anyone else."

"What now?"

I watched out the window, thinking on it for a second. Off beyond the storm ditches I could see the wreckage from the hurricane that'd been through the previous year. A stand of trees bent and splintered, a high-mast light pole that had been folded in two. A dark land sown with wreckage.

"Now," I said, "we go see Rolly Lee."

"Jasper . . ." Donny started, but I cut him off.

"I need to look in his eyes," I said. "And there's going to be no changing that, Donny."

Donny sighed. "Well, then, time's a-wasting."

47.

THE SIGN SAID "LEE," and as the headlights lit upon it Donny slowed the truck up.

"Last chance to head back," Donny said, "and leave this to the law."

"Drive," I said.

It was a dark, moonless night, and as we turned down the dirt road toward Rolly Lee's, it got even darker. The trees flanking the trail were ink-blot shadows, bleeding out above us, blackening the sky. The Christmas lights that had lit our way in on the first visit had been turned off. They were strewn across branches overhead like strange tropical fruit. The only light came from our headlights dappling the metallic detritus that lay all over the property.

"I still can't get over this place," Donny said. "It's like Sanford and Son with acreage."

We crawled along, crickets and cicadas calling out through the trees.

Off in the distance, something else caught my ear. It began to get closer and I realized what I was hearing was music. Donny eased the truck forward a little faster and the volume continued to swell, cut through with a sharp crackling. Then I remembered our first trip in and Rolly Lee calling us Snow Mexicans.

"It's those speakers he's got wired up out here," I said.

We pulled up next to one and a deafening blast of guitar-duelling Southern rock filled the car.

As we sat there, the song ended. Then there was another sound from somewhere far off, closer to the house. A gunshot.

"Go!" I shouted.

Donny put his foot down and I felt the tires scrabbling at loose dirt. Gravel ping-pinged against the underside of the truck. We hurtled down the trail, branches catching the side mirrors, the truck banging over potholes. Then the road changed course and we were swinging sideways. I felt the wheels lose traction, then we were up on one side and I was falling toward Donny. Something large and immobile rose up in front of us and we were thrown forward into a cacophony of erupting lights and yawning metal. The engine whined high in protest then sputtered out. There came the sound of a spinning wheel and then silence. The sound of my breathing filled my ears.

"Jasper," Donny said. "You okay?"

I ran my fingers through my hair and then inspected my outstretched palms, looking for the glisten of blood. There was a nag of pain in my neck, but that was about it. I unbuckled the seat belt and got out. Something hissed under the buckled hood. Donny got out and looked the truck up and down. "Not good," he said.

"Unless you're Rolly Lee," I said. "Lots of usable parts left on this thing."

He went into the back seat and came out with a flashlight. He handed it over and then looked at me, the whites of his eyes glowing in the darkness.

"Let's go," I said. There was a crackle through the speakers and then another song kicked off. We took off running toward the house, our feet crunching through the brush in time with the music.

There were no signs of life in the clearing. Rolly Lee's truck was parked off near the barn where I'd watched Hoyt Lee's band play. There was a mud-caked ATV, a dirt bike, and another car in an advanced state of ruination that I didn't recognize. The big doors on the garage were up, portals to more darkness.

We were just inside the woods, watching the house. The lights were out but other signs pointed to people being home. A thin wisp of smoke rising from a dying campfire somewhere off behind the house. Two lawn chairs set up out front. And, most obviously, the front door wide open.

Donny nodded toward the barn. "Hang back for a second," he whispered. There was the sound of something small and four-legged wandering past behind us and I felt my skin crawl. The absolute wash of darkness was leavened only by the music still drifting through the trees.

As Donny moved out and into the open, a blur of movement drew my eyes back to the barn. Donny was stepping lightly in a half crouch. Neither one of us had forgotten the gunshot.

He was steps from the old car when I saw something again. The toe of a boot just inside the barn. A shard of light from the clearing falling across it. The music skipped and stuttered for a minute and there was silence. Then there was an explosion of light from the barn and a sharp metallic clang off the car. I took a step back into the woods. Donny had sprawled out in the dirt, trying to get behind one of the oversized back wheels for cover. He hadn't been hit. There was another detonation and the wind-shield went out, needles of glass shimmering across the hood and into the dirt.

I had to think quickly. I stooped down and searched in the brush and came up with a rock about the size of a golf ball. I stepped out of the clearing in time to see the figure emerge from the barn, a rifle held high obscuring his face.

Somewhere back in the wilderness of failed engines I heard the first, tentative notes on a piano and the cheers of a large crowd, stirred by the recognition of this song, the anthem of the South, the path of true righteousness for men like Rolly Lee.

"Free Bird."

"Hey," I shouted, taking a running step toward the barn. I reared back and threw the rock. The figure hit the dirt as it banged into the metal sheeting of the garage close beside him.

Donny, the ex-pro football player, saw the opportunity. He got to his feet and threw his own rock. But the man was already disappearing around the back of the barn, where Donny, Duane and I had watched Rolly Lee's cronies take target practice on our first day in town.

I made it to the car and there was another shot, this one from the trees at the other side of the property. Now I could hear sirens in the distance.

"Man," Donny said. "He's got a whole militia up here."

"And look at us," I said, "showing up to the gunfight with rocks. Something very biblical about that, Donny."

I found another rock and hefted it up. Adrenalin was surging through me and I felt like if I stopped to think, I might collapse.

"Let's go back to the truck," Donny said. The sirens were getting closer. "Wait for the cops there."

"No," I said, shaking my head.

There was another musket clap and a bullet skidded across the dirt five feet away. Donny gritted his teeth and stood up, launching a shard of rock toward the shooter. This time there was the thud of impact and then an agonized shout. The music seemed to get even louder, the crowd of fifty thousand strong transplanted to the swamps, screaming out through the pines.

"Boy, do I ever hate this song," Donny said. Then: "Look."

I glanced behind us and saw the faint, strobing wash of red and blue lights drifting through the trees.

"I'm going," I said, jutting my chin toward the house.

"That's ridiculous," Donny said in a hoarse whisper. "Just wait."

There hadn't been any movement near the house and I wondered if the sirens had put them on the retreat. I looked up over the car again, gauging the distance across the yard. Not so long ago, I'd been prone on a subway track while a car weighing seventy thousand pounds had nearly ruined my leg. Now I was expecting that same leg to help deliver me through this darkness to the house on the other side of the yard.

"No," Donny said. "Forget it, Jasper."

He grabbed at the back of my shirt but I was already gone. I took off sprinting from behind the car as the song reached its crescendo and the first police car reached the clearing. There came no shots. But I could hear a voice coming from inside the house. It was Aunt Val. Screaming for all this to end.

I went along the side of the house in a jog, trying to get a look in to see Aunt Val. There was nothing but darkness. As I approached the back lot, I realized that the pain had completely gone from my leg. I ran harder, feeling stronger than I had in years. Once upon a time I had run along a beach only miles from where I ran now, before the accident that nearly destroyed me, before my brother disappeared, before I realized that not only can bad things happen, but that they're nearly inevitable. For a moment I was that boy, the sound of my breathing and my pounding heart filling my ears, running under a dark Florida sky with only the elation of motion filling my mind.

I was looking up at that sky, that endless sweep of jewelled blackness, when I hit Rolly Lee. There was no time to feel any surprise; just the bone-jarring impact of two grown men meeting in a full sprint when both are looking elsewhere. There was a strobing light behind my eyelids and then I was crawling, the last notes of "Free Bird" dissolving into the trees like an effigy.

Two hands closed around my neck. I reached for them and a boot came down on my wrist. I kicked out into empty space with my legs as the hands crushed down onto my windpipe. I could hear him breathing, smell the whiskey on his breath as he bore down on me.

Very slowly, the grip loosened and I was managing to breathe again.

Manuel Sherrill was standing over Rolly Lee, his pistol resting against his blond head. We were at the edge of the yard. I had kicked out over the drop into swamp water. He had tried to kill me three paces from where I'd sat with Aunt Val just a few nights earlier.

Hoyt Lee was sitting on the back porch, a bloody swath across his right shoulder where a jagged shard of rock had caught him. My aunt rushed out the back door and fell on him, sobbing.

"Stand up," Sherrill said. "Unless you want to keep up with the choking." He tapped the blue-grey tip of his revolver against the back of Rolly Lee's head. Rolly Lee stood up and spat into the dirt beside me.

"It'd be worth it," he said. "Fully." He struggled to his feet.

"Turn around," Sherrill said. Rolly Lee did as he was told, turning toward the house. I could hear more sirens in the distance. He looked across his yard with cold, dark eyes.

Rolly Lee looked down at his feet where I was sprawled. Even if I'd wanted to, I doubted I could get up. Fatigue had swung back hard on me and I'd reached the end of my rope. So when I heard something in the water and then saw something rising up in my periphery, my first thought was that I was hallucinating.

I watched two hands close around Rolly Lee's right ankle and pull hard. Then there was a splash.

It was Coleman.

In an instant, they had wrestled under the dark water, legs and arms lashing out as they fought. "I remember," Coleman shouted as he went under. Sherrill rushed to the edge of the bank, gun poised, but they had twined together in combat like some rare, infuriated creature of the swamps.

They weren't alone.

Rolly Lee had supposedly poached even his own property until alligators were extinct from it. But alligators are masters of survival and repopulation, particularly where an open spot of water is available. So they had come back. Like Coleman.

Rolly Lee had my brother in a headlock and was struggling to keep his mouth above the waterline when the bull gator's jaws first opened. There was a flash of pink from inside the beast's mouth and then it clamped furiously down into the water. There was a shriek and they went under again, Coleman's wide eyes looking up from below the surface. Further off in the water, other gator prowled, waiting for the first taste of blood.

The gator thrashed his tail and disappeared under the water again. Screaming filled my ears. When I looked again, Coleman was coming toward the bank, rising up out of the water, his arm torn and trailing blood. Rolly Lee loomed up behind him, a length of thick swamp wood raised aloft with one shaking hand.

Sherrill pulled the hammer back as Rolly Lee brought it down across Coleman's back. I heard Aunt Val scream, and the raw anguish of it filled my head. Then the water erupted and the gator sank his teeth into Rolly Lee's leg, a mist of water spraying from his nostrils, the ancient, fearsome stink of him heavy on the air.

The alligator began to roll over, the leg still in his mouth. Rolly Lee looked at us through eyes that already seemed to see a world fading from view. His lips spread in a full grin, and then he was pulled under.

Coleman struggled up the bank from the water. His arm seemed to be hanging by something tenuous and failing. Aunt Val was on her knees at the water's edge. The gator had disappeared and with it, Rolly Lee. Her mouth hung open and she looked up at Coleman. Any shock she might have felt at seeing him, if she even recognized him, was lost in the wake of all that had happened.

He dropped something in the dirt at his feet. It was a small bone. A bone just about the size of a grown man's pinky finger.

48.

THE BONE WAS THE KEY: the explanation for everything, from the day I watched Coleman latch the back gate and wander off into the great blue beyond to the moment it was dropped in the dust at his feet.

The bone was the reason Coleman had spent ten years wandering. It was the reason he'd returned to Florida.

He was searching. Searching for proof.

For atonement. For a reprieve from the guilt that had been eating away at him every minute since he'd walked out of the swamps.

In the end, the bone didn't belong to Dudley Hargrove, the young park ranger whom Rolly Lee shot in the Everglades that night he and Coleman had gone out looking for big alligators to poach. Hargrove wasn't the first man to meet evil in the swamps and then be swallowed up by the ancient murk, never to reappear.

Dudley Hargrove had confronted them late that night, after I'd been left with Rook Bannister and his peanut-butter-coloured dog. Rolly Lee had insisted on bringing Coleman because he was convinced that my brother had a supernatural quality when it came to dealing with alligators. My brother was something akin to the horse whisperer: he was the boy who swam with alligators. And alligators were money.

Hargrove knew what Rolly Lee was up to. He'd seen enough of his kind to know that he wasn't out paddling through the swamps on some kind of nature jaunt. He was doing what men had done in the Everglades since the turn of the century when the first settlers had staked their claim to the boiling, mosquito-plagued tip of the continent: trying to make a living off the beasts that swam in the waters, from the birds that roosted in the trees. Hides and feathers, skin and teeth, handbags and boots, necklaces and earrings, internal organs that would be dried and chewed by men in exotic countries wishing to restore their flagging sex drive.

There was an argument, and then there was a shot.

Rolly Lee filled Hargrove's state-issue browns full of rocks, bound him and dumped him into the deepest, most remote corner of the swamps he could find.

Then he'd gone to work on Coleman. I could imagine the argument echoing through the trees as the night faded and the sky began to brighten on a day where everything had changed. The pathetic sounds of a grown man pleading with a child, begging for a vow of secrecy. The pleading gave way to threats, to dire promises of harm to body and soul, to his family, to the rest of his life.

And then, when all else failed, the boy was struck over the head and pushed into the water, where he bobbed, the whites of his eyes diamonds in the rusty water, watching as the boat drifted away through the trees and into the blackness.

My brother, Coleman.

But in the end, it would take years for Rolly Lee's luck to run out. Because somewhere between walking out of the swamps and finding his way home, Coleman decided that he wouldn't say a thing. He would keep the secret and keep all of us safe from whatever evil lurked out in the world, waiting. But the guilt never dissipated. Instead, it crowded out an already fragile hold on reality, made him seek solace and comfort in dreams of things far away, above the skies, the clouds, in the upper realms of an uncharted universe.

Only every morning when he woke up, the guilt was the sun that rose in the sky, shining down on him.

The spaceship, crazy as it seemed, had a very simple purpose: it would take Coleman far away from the earth and the memories of the terrible night in the swamps. When that failed, there was only one option left in Coleman's mind. If he couldn't leave the earth, he would return to Florida instead.

He'd watched Rolly Lee from afar. Coleman was the man in the shadows, the embodiment of Rolly Lee's paranoia that he was being followed. And along with my birthday, there was one other anniversary that Coleman marked with a mysterious message.

For five years running, near the end of August, Rolly Lee received a letter. It was a simple letter with two words and a date: *I remember,* it said. But it was enough to keep Rolly Lee thinking. Wondering.

The date coincided with a night a long time ago, when Rolly Lee had gone into the swamps with a young boy and come out all on his own.

49.

THE BOY WHO SWAM with gators had taken a nasty bite from one. Sherrill patched it up with a first aid kit from his trunk. "Another couple inches and you'd be left-handed," he said.

Coleman shrugged and looked at his arm. "He got me a good one," he said with a hint of admiration.

"What now?" I said to Sherrill.

He sighed and looked at Rolly Lee's house. Aunt Val and Hoyt Lee were huddled on the front step, her arm around him, his face buried in the crook of her arm. I could hear him sobbing and apologizing to his mother over and over again.

"This was an accident," Sherrill said. "I'm sure Hoyt Lee over there is going to agree."

The old car in Rolly Lee's lot belonged to Coleman. He had little beyond the filthy shirt on his back, but he'd saved a little and bought a car. The state of it suggested that it wouldn't have taken long to save for. It had drawn the first shot Donny and I heard as we were on our way in.

335

As we were getting in, Aunt Val came across the yard to us. Her eyes were crackled with red and she looked like a gentle breeze would knock her over.

She looked at Coleman and the breath caught audibly in her throat.

"My God," she said, tears welling in her eyes.

Coleman's lip trembled and he looked down at the pavement.

Aunt Val looked at me. "Is it really . . ."

"Yes," I said, smiling.

"Coleman," she said, moving toward him, her arms stretching outward, "I'm so sorry."

We left Florida late the next morning. Donny's truck had needed a new tire, headlights and a little work under the hood, but otherwise the damage was all cosmetic. No one was keen to spend another moment in the Sunshine State, save for Duane, who was enjoying beer for breakfast and long, sunny days without demands.

I left Aunt Val at the motel, having paid for the room for another week. She was going to make sure Hoyt was okay then head up to Ontario to see my mother and get away from all that had happened, if only for a while. I couldn't imagine what she was going through. Rolly Lee was gone. Hoyt had lost his father. The pair of them had tried to kill Coleman and me.

Gone was the ferocity in her eyes, the brightness that conveyed the strong person she was. Aunt Val looked like she'd aged ten years in a day.

We stood out on the balcony overlooking the motel parking lot, my arm around her. Duane and Donny had gone out to get supplies for the trip back home. Coleman was in the room sleeping. A cleaner pushed past us with her cart, the relaxed look on her face showing that it was just another mundane day in the life. I felt a flare of envy in the pit of my stomach.

"You know," Aunt Val said, "I left once. Not long after that summer."

We'd been standing there in silence long enough for Aunt Val to smoke two cigarettes. She'd been given something strong at the hospital for the shock and her voice was weak and stuttering.

"I got a little north of Atlanta. Commerce, Georgia. And then I turned back." She looked over the railing then dropped the butt end of her cigarette. "I needed to see your mom, to look her in the eyes and ask her what she believed happened. Because," she said, her hand trembling toward her pocket where her cigarettes were, "I couldn't stop thinking about it. About Rolly and Coleman. But I turned back."

"Why?"

"I was pregnant," she said. "I got pregnant right after that summer. But I didn't tell anyone. Then," she said, "I wasn't." She closed her eyes. "Not long after, Hoyt came to live with us." She started to draw off her cigarette, but her hand was shaking too much to keep it at her lips. "He's still my son," she said, "still my son after all this." Aunt Val dropped the cigarette to the pavement and started to cry.

"This is on me," she said. "This is all on me. My husband, my son."

"No," I said, wrapping my arms around her. "Coleman came back." I looked over my shoulder toward the room and then smiled at her. "He's in that room, sleeping. That's what counts."

"He came back," she said, nodding. "Just like he came back before. And when I thought about it, that's where I always ended up. Coleman came back. And he and Rolly had the same story."

She winced as she said Rolly's name. "He was my husband, Jasper," she said. "I thought it was concern for me that was eating him up. But it was guilt. And now he's gone." She closed her eyes and took a deep breath. "Jasper," she said, opening them again. "What was I to do?" Her red eyes widened and filled with tears as if she was realizing that the wreckage in the past stretched far out on the road ahead. "What am I going to do?"

"Look after your son," I said, "and then why don't you come north for a vacation. Give it a couple of months and you'll catch the snow."

She fell into my arms, sobbing.

I didn't blame Aunt Val and I hoped that Coleman didn't either. She'd been caught between two families and chose to stand by her husband. I hoped in my heart that she would be okay and planned to do everything I could to help. We all have choices we must make and sometimes it takes decades for the gravity of those choices to become clear.

Now Coleman and I were making ours: to leave Florida for what, once again, felt like it would be forever.

As we pulled out of the parking lot that morning, a red car with one grey door at the far side of the lot caught my eye. When we got closer, I saw who was slumped down behind the wheel: Melissa. A prickle ran down my neck. Had she come to say good-bye or to get a crack at finishing me off? Her eyes met mine as we rolled past. Then something hit me, something that set my head pounding and made me feel like I was going to be ill.

That night in the swamp, amidst the stink of gator bait and rotten vegetation, I'd smelled something else. Something sweet. Now, watching the blonde girl who'd appeared in the parking lot like something terrifying and beautiful conjured from my own nightmares, I realized what that smell was. It was Melissa Wheeler's perfume, the perfume I'd first smelled during our night together in the gazebo. She'd done more than gather intelligence for Rolly Lee. She'd come along for the ride.

I held the stare as Donny pulled the truck around and then she was all in the rear-view.

We made one stop on the way out.

Manuel Sherrill gripped my hand and smiled.

"I'm sorry for the mess, Manuel."

"Hey," he said, gesturing across his desk. "You've given me enough paperwork to stay air-conditioned for the summer." He grinned at me. "Now get out of here. Eh!"

The real work was only just beginning. The matter of trying to find the way forward. To figure out how to go on now that I'd found Coleman. I'd never expected to find him in one piece, and in a sense I hadn't—he'd managed to find some relief from the guilt he'd been carrying for so long, but in the process had only retreated further into his personal wilderness. It would take some doing to even move Coleman toward any kind of normal life. And I knew that it would take much more than me. It would take doctors, medication, support and purpose.

Then again, I knew that "purpose" had been on my list of things to find.

I realize now that my life had been in stasis; never wanting to settle on anything because there was a piece missing, an integral piece to me that might one day be restored and throw everything into disarray.

It had started with a phone call, placed from a phone box beside the interstate on a night like many others. But it was all

I needed to start the trudge back into the past and do what I had wanted to do for so long.

Coleman had been missing, but in my own way, so had I.

50.

LAKE CITY, FLORIDA, is the last major city on I-75, heading north out of Florida. My family had often spent the first night on the road home in a hotel there. Today we'd only be stopping for gas and a sandwich. We were set on getting back to Ontario— and out of Florida—as quickly as possible. Duane and Donny got their lunch and sat down to eat it inside the air-conditioned travel plaza. Coleman and I took ours to a picnic table outside, close to where cars rushed along the interstate.

"So," I said, looking at him. "What do you think?"

Coleman looked up at me, his teeth locked around a bacon-cheeseburger. "This is good," he said.

I hadn't meant the burger.

"Are you sure about this?" I said. It was a question I'd been afraid to ask. His reaction justified my fears.

"I don't know," was all he said.

I pushed my burger off to the side. Two seagulls landed on the pavement nearby and watched it with fierce eyes. "We can figure it out, Coleman. I can help you find work someplace."

He nodded. I watched his eyes drift toward the highway.

"What else are you going to do?"

Coleman shrugged. "I'll be okay," he said. "Hey," he said, looking at me, noticing the look on my face. "I've been out here a long time." He smiled. "You see me working in an office somewhere?"

I shrugged. Truth was, I was having a hard time seeing myself ever working in an office again. "It'd be good to hang out."

He smiled, his ruined teeth reminding me of all the years that had passed since we had been together. "Don't look now," he said, "but I think we're doing it."

I grinned back. "Asshole." One of the seagulls hopped up onto the table and we watched it peck furtively at the burger. "So what are you going to do? Do you even have somewhere to live?"

"I've got a tent," he said. "You don't need to worry about me." The same tent he had been pulled out of by Rolly and Hoyt, just a mile from the Rivergrass Recreation Park.

Quiet moments crawled past. I watched a family walk toward the building, a mother and father and their young son. The kid broke free of his mother's clutch and sprinted ahead, grinning over his shoulder at their calls to watch out and be careful.

"All those years we came down here," I said, "it seems like another lifetime."

"May as well have been," Coleman said. "We were just kids."

"You ever think back on those times?" I caught myself. "The other years, I mean, before the last one."

"Some things," Coleman said, looking away from the young boy and his parents, "some things you don't forget. You can't forget. The good shit and the bad." He shook his head. "There's no use trying to separate them after a while. Before . . ." He paused, breathing deeply, and I wondered if he'd continue. "Before I left," he said, "I used to try and retrace all the tiny steps, all the small decisions that put me where I was, where I ended up having to go. Ways that I might not have ended up out in that swamp that night."

It was little wonder that Coleman's mental balance had ended up in such a precarious state.

"What I always came to was that I was born to walk into those swamps. I was headed toward that night from the time I was small. There was nothing I could do, same reason there was nothing I could do but come back."

"You're wrong," I said. "You had choices. You could have told someone any time after. You never had to leave the way you did."

"Fated," Coleman said, scuffing at the asphalt.

"Forget fate," I said. The cars on the highway blurred through a shimmer of tears. "All that time, Coleman, it's all gone. You have no idea what it was like. Life had to continue but you just weren't there anymore. Walking through the woods by the train tracks, waking up every morning in our house . . ." I took a deep breath and put one hand on his shoulder. "Seeing Mum and Dad, how this tore them up. Coleman," I said, "it was the world as it always was with one huge thing missing. And they couldn't bear to talk about it, about where you might have gone. Where you might be."

Coleman was perfectly still, his eyes on the road. I watched his lips move slightly as if he was about to speak but kept thinking better of it. So we just sat there at the picnic table watching cars arrive and leave. I could have sat like this for the rest of time.

When Coleman finally spoke, his voice was little more than a whisper and I could see the pain in his eyes. "I was there, Jasper." He nodded and took a deep breath. "All these years, I was always there. With you."

I saw the family emerge from the travel plaza, the father carrying a bag of food, the son holding a stuffed alligator and walking arm in arm with his mother. Coleman chuckled, then I laughed too and I knew he was as relieved as I was for it. But silence quickly gathered around us again. I knew we were a long way from real levity, from a beer on a porch somewhere, from the kind of easy times brothers could have without a second thought if they'd shared a lifetime together.

"Why did you call me, Coleman?"

Coleman was still watching the family. They got in their minivan, slammed the doors, then the dad backed slowly out of the parking spot and eased his way toward the on-ramp.

"Well," Coleman said, still watching the road, "it was your birthday."

I got slowly to my feet and pulled my half-eaten lunch toward me, sending the gulls into the air with an irritated cackle. The pain in my leg had returned with a vengeance and I knew that physio was something I'd need to embrace when I got home. I limped across the lawn and found an overflowing garbage bin swarming with wasps and threw out the remnants of my burger and drink.

When I got back to where we had been sitting, Coleman was gone. I sat down at the picnic table. Chips in the surface blurred through an array of colours, revealing how many times it had been painted and repainted over the years. Even still, the initials and names that had been carved into the wood had not disappeared. People had been here, stopping on their way to somewhere else if only for a moment, and left their mark.

When I finally looked up, I saw a solitary figure dissolving in the shimmer of heat, way down the road, heading south. I watched him, shielding my eyes from the sun, until the grade swept over him.

Until once again, I saw him disappear from sight.

ACKNOWLEDGEMENTS

Sometimes you really do meet the right person at just the right time. Meeting Lesley Grant changed my world and I can never thank her enough for her encouragement, story smarts, her dead-on gut instinct, her skills in navigating the business of publishing, and most importantly, her friendship.

A million thanks to Michael Schellenberg for taking a chance on a new writer and for his passion, support and unparalleled editorial chops.

To my late friend Dennis Richard Murphy whose mentorship and love of story made all the difference. Wish I could have told you about this one, Murph.

Thanks to my Mum and Dad, my brother Jonathan and his family, my sister Katharine and her family.

Thanks to Jeff Alpern, Michael Kot, the Fabrizio family, Rachel Fulford, Brad Smith, Marion Garner and all at Knopf Canada.

To all friends and family, too many to mention, for their love and support.

And most of all, thanks to my wife, Jennifer, for her love, encouragement and infinite patience. For being my first reader and for never questioning just what the hell I'm doing down in the basement all the time. It's really not possible without you.

And of course to Benjamin. I love you, little buddy.

NICK CROWE was born in Montreal and raised in Kingston, Ontario. He worked as a paperboy, dishwasher, psychiatric hospital janitor, laundry worker and guitar player before starting a career in television. He has been writing fiction since childhood, but *A Cold Night for Alligators* is his first novel. Nick lives in Toronto with his wife and young son.